MIDDLE AGE SPREAD
Lucinda Roberts

Middle Age Spread
© Lucinda Roberts 2013

Cover artwork by Celia Lewis

CONTENTS

~ LUCINDA ROBERTS ~

BOMBSHELL

Caught by a gust of summer wind, the back door flew open with a bang, knocking yet another chunk out of the already chunked plaster where the handle met the wall. Staggering across the threshold, a plastic carrier bag hanging from each finger, Fiona McLeod returned from her Friday morning prepare-for-the-weekend shop.

One environmentally friendly culprit expired, cascading its contents all over the small boiler room. Pesto, peanuts, peppercorns and cat food rolled and mingled happily together on the fake terracotta tile floor, the laying of which had been a hard-won concession from Hamish, who considered it to be an unnecessary extravagance. Hamish was Scottish, to the last bone.

"Damn," breathed Fiona, kicking a stray tin of *Whiskas* out of her path as she hurried through to dump the rest of the shopping on the kitchen table. Putting it all away was almost more boring than battling round the supermarket with an unsteerable trolley before standing in a disgruntled queue whilst Brenda, proudly sporting her name badge, sat at the till discussing her bunions with anyone interested enough to listen. Fiona remembered when the children were small, and they used to play what they called The ID Game while they were waiting; trying to decide from the purchases in front of theirs on the conveyor belt, the lifestyle of the buyer.

At least today the checkout machine had not run out of paper just when Fiona had unloaded her mountain of shopping behind the Next Customer notice, and the previously closed till next door had suddenly acquired its own 'Brenda', opening up with a cheery shout and bunion-free smile. No, one had to be thankful for small mercies, and Fiona considered one split bag a small price to pay for her domestic security.

Flicking down the switch on the electric kettle, she decided a cup of instant coffee was essential before tackling the task of opening, sorting and putting away everything she had bought. Being a methodical sort of person, she liked to get this chore finished before considering shopping time over and done, but today she felt in need of a break before modern packaging temporarily turned her into a plastic assassin as kitchen scissors and a sharp pointed knife became essential weapons in the fight to release her purchases from their constrictive wrapping.

As a child of the fifties, Fiona had grown up with paper bags, MacFisheries and nice men in khaki coloured coats who weighed out her mother's groceries, and gave her a boiled sweet or perhaps a fat red cherry as she stood on tiptoe to peer over the counter. They always said things like 'My, haven't you grown then!', even though Fiona knew she could not possibly have grown since last Friday. She had loved the mixture of smells in the shop and looked forward eagerly to the time when she would be in charge of her own household shopping. The reality of marriage and the rise of the supermarket had soon extinguished that ambition.

Bubbling and belching out steam, the kettle clicked off and Fiona brewed up in her favourite Isle of Mull mug, a souvenir of their final family holiday together before the children grew too old and superior for such things. Hamish's now dead mother, a terrifyingly tweedy beanpole of a woman, had owned a holiday house near Tobermoray, where they had spent their annual fortnight's summer holidays. The children and Hamish had loved the place but Fiona had worried endlessly about the treatment of the property, as her mother-in-law was inclined to write cryptic little notes referring to small chips and scuff marks which 'she was sure would not happen again'. When she died, six months after that last holiday, Fiona had suffered an uncomfortable little twinge of guilt that somehow, as the unsatisfactory house-wrecking Sassenach daughter-in-law, she had unwittingly contributed to the old girl's death.

Sipping the hot coffee, her thoughts were interrupted by a demanding 'miaow' as Mactavish the cat strolled into the kitchen. A relic of the days of the children's animal phase, unlike the guinea pigs and the goldfish, Mactavish had lived on. And on. His arrival reminded Fiona that the boiler room floor was still playing host to some of the shopping, but as she gave the old ginger monster an affectionate stroke, she thought 'What the hell – let it wait!' Thoughts seemed the order of the day today, and a worrying one that had been lurking around the edge of her consciousness finally came out into the open.

"Do you know something, Mactavish?" she said aloud. "The horrible truth is that I am bored." The cat's response was predictable and unhelpful, as he looked at her with his round citrine eyes, and stalked off. "I shall ring Dodo and have a good grumble – that's the answer."

Feeling better already, Fiona reached for the telephone and punched out her old friend's number. After six rings the answer-phone clicked in, and she slammed the handset down in irritation. It was no good leaving a message, she needed to talk, now, this minute, and Dodo was the only person who would do.

Feeling let down and gloomy, Fiona wandered through into the boiler room to pick up the scattered shopping. Mactavish had helped himself to the 'reduced for quick sale' smoked haddock so that was the end of the kedgeree she had planned to make for supper. There was nothing for it but to 'brace up' as her mother would say, concoct a substitute and get on with the household tasks that needed doing before Hamish returned on the 5.30 commuter sardine tin from Waterloo. He would be late, tired and grumpy, as he had been on every Friday evening since before Fiona could remember and somehow, without meaning to, he would make her feel responsible for his having to sweat his life away in the dreary rooms of Webster, Chattle & Peabody, accountants to nobody in particular.

Suddenly the sound of the front door knocker broke into Fiona's thoughts and she made her way through to the hall with little sense of anticipation. None of their friends ever used it, only Jehovah's Witnesses, travelling salesmen or the water board.

"You Mrs McLeod?" demanded an ugly youth as she opened the door, noticing with surprise that he was clutching a bouquet of flowers.

"That's me," she smiled.

"'Ere you are then." He thrust the flowers at her, sniffed loudly and slouched away through the front gate.

Impatient to discover the identity of the sender, Fiona dumped the flowers on the hall table and ripped open the little white envelope that was stuck on the front.

'Look in my sock drawer – H' was all it said.

'My God,' she thought, 'What's this in aid of? Has Hamish gone mad and bought me a huge diamond?' Laughing aloud at the very idea, Fiona raced upstairs to raid the sock drawer.

Placed on top of a neat row of navy blue socks lay a brown envelope bearing her name. She stared at it for an instant, a strange knot beginning to form in the pit of her stomach, before tearing it open and taking it to the window to read, her glasses being downstairs and Hamish's writing small and squiggly. She was so stunned by the contents that for a moment, she could not breathe and her brain froze.

Eventually, it thawed, and ripping the letter to shreds, she threw them all over the marital bed and ran downstairs to the drink cupboard. Pouring herself a large slug of sherry she made for the telephone, praying that Dodo had only been in the loo when she had rung earlier. For once her prayers were answered, and as she choked on a gulp of sherry, her friend came on the line.

"Dodo," she spluttered desperately, "it's me – Fi."

"I know it's you, you idiot, I've got one of those phones that shows who's calling – you know that. I hope it's important anyway as I've just started on a new design for a cockerel. Are you all right? You sound a bit odd."

"No, I am *not* all right and fuck your bloody cockerel! *Hamish has left me.*"

There was a short pause.

"Fiona McLeod," gasped Dodo, "I've never heard that word pass your innocent lips before!"

"Well you have now – and didn't you hear what I said?" bellowed Fiona hysterically.

"I don't believe it! That dull old husband of yours! I say Fi, I didn't know he had it in him – is it a bloke or a bimbo?"

"Neither – it's that terrible old trout of a secretary – Margaret 'pearls & twinset boot face' Crutchley. *Me* turned over for *her*." Fiona screamed before bursting into tears.

"I say Fi, hold on, I'll be right round as fast as I can. I won't fuck the cockerel, it's kind of the wrong way round – but I know a crisis when I hear one."

"Oh Dodo, please hurry," Fiona sobbed and the two phones went dead in unison.

***

Dodo stopped only to wash the clay off her hands and grab a bottle of wine before jumping into her ancient, battered Polo to speed to Fiona's relief. The Surrey roads, verdant with high summer growth, were heaving with traffic and every light turned red at her approach. Beating the steering wheel in frustration, she drew curious glances from her neighbouring queue victims which worried her not one bit. Shaking her short blonde hair and giving the thumbs-up to a boot-faced old couple beside her, she put her foot down on amber and shot off. Twenty-three minutes later another chunk of plaster bit the dust as she rushed through into the kitchen.

"I'm here," she shouted unnecessarily, plonking the wine down on the table and embracing the distraught Fiona. "Tell all Fi – the absolute *rat* – I can't believe it!"

"Neither can I," gulped Fiona, empty sherry glass and small pile of soggy kitchen roll surrounding her slumped figure. "Whatever shall I tell my mother and the children – whatever am I going to do?" she wailed.

"First things first. Stop blubbering and get some glasses and we shall have a rational discussion. Where's the corkscrew?"

5

"In the top drawer, over there." Fiona trumpeted into the last bit of kitchen roll and throwing the debris of her crisis into the bin, put two wine glasses on the table.

"That's better," announced Dodo briskly, filling the glasses before pulling a squashed packet of Silk Cut from the pocket of her clay-covered jeans. "Here's to you kid!" she smiled, raising her glass to Fiona. "Now, to business."

Dodo's manner had always been forthright and when, aged 10, the two girls had first met at school, the then apprehensive Fiona had greatly admired her new friend's confident and devil-may-care attitude. Her character somehow seemed at odds with her passion for creative art at which she excelled, greatly exciting the Art Master, most of whose pupils merely daubed paint or flung clay whilst sniggering at his manhood.

"As I see it," Dodo continued, "the salient point is whether or not you want the brute back. If I were you, I would send him to old Crutch with a bow round his neck and open a bottle of champagne – but I do understand you might feel differently. But how did he tell you? D'you know – it's the most exciting thing that's happened in years!"

"Oh shut up, Dodo! Just because you never liked Hamish doesn't mean that to me he's like one of your failed sculptures – a wet, grey lump to be squashed into another shape or binned."

"Sorry Fi, and you know perfectly well that when, encased in my rose-pink watered silk bridesmaid's gown I caught your bouquet, I really believed you would be the happiest person alive. Of course I'm shattered for you – completely gob-smacked in fact – but I still want to know how he told you."

Fiona recounted the story of the flowers, the sock drawer and the ripped up letter, watching Dodo's wide grey eyes grow even wider with amazement.

"But what did it actually *say*?"

"I shall never forget." replied Fiona dramatically, refilling her glass. "It was pretty typical of Hamish I suppose. What you might call short, to the point and pompous."

And taking a swig, she shut her eyes and recited the words that had ended her thirty-two years of marriage.

'My dear Fiona,

Margaret Crutchley and I have formed a relationship. I know this will come as a great shock to you, but she and I have found happiness together. As the children are now grown up and gone, I know you will understand that I wish to make a new life with Margaret. I am grateful for all you have given me and will be in touch about arrangements. Sorry.

H.'

"That was it, just like that and even the flowers were the cheapest bunch you can get from Interflora! I threw them out and stamped on them – poor innocent things. And to answer your question, a big **No**, I do **not** want him back. I never want to see him again and I hope Margaret effing Crutchley gives him chlamydia."

"Don't be ridiculous, Fi," giggled Dodo. "I'm sure the Crutch has never even been invaded as it were! But what a cowardly way to tell you. Had you any idea at all that things between you were dodgy?"

"No, none whatsoever, I mean life just went plodding on as usual and Hamish didn't behave in a strange way or anything or start buying designer underpants and expensive aftershave. That's why I'm so shocked I suppose – not to mention the total devastation of my whole life," Fiona ended gloomily.

"What about sex, was the old Scottish ram performing properly?"

"Oh Dodo, you know our sex-life was virtually non-existent. Apparently it's quite normal after 32 years of marriage, and I can hardly remember when we last did it."

"Hmm," mused Dodo, "maybe you should have buffed yourself up a bit. I mean you have rather let yourself go you know, and at our age the odd bits start dropping off and more effort is needed. Grey hairs, wrinkles, sagging bum, everything sagging actually, age spots, whiskers – God! You name it."

"Don't tell me, I looked at my face in the Aga top when I cleaned it the other day and nearly died. If Hamish had gone off with a bimbo I could understand it but that old bag of a secretary, that's what pisses me off almost more than his going. I mean, it's so humiliating."

"Hmm, but I bet she panders to his menopausal male ego like mad – and how do you know she's not a raging sex maniac under that prim efficient exterior?"

"Gosh, d'you really think so?" Fiona's rising hysteria was channelled into laughter as they both collapsed at the thought.

"I say," spluttered Dodo, re-filling their glasses, "we've drunk nearly all the wine – got any more?"

"You must be joking, you know Hamish's views on booze. One small sherry for me and a wee dram for him plus a third of a bottle of plonk each for our unfortunate dinner guests. But hang on a minute..." – a crafty smile spread over Fiona's tear-blotched face – "Somewhere he's got some amazing bottle stored away, the last one from his father's cellar. I'll go and look."

Fiona returned a few minutes later carrying a Bordeaux-shaped bottle of red wine which she placed with a flourish in front of Dodo. "Found it – this will really annoy him!" she said gleefully.

"Wow!" breathed Dodo, who knew a bit about wine. "A 1979 Chateau Petrus. You can't get much better than that. We should let it settle and warm a bit you know, it's not exactly a normal afternoon quaffing wine!"

"Bugger it, this isn't exactly a normal afternoon, and anyway I don't want Hamish getting his grimy paws on it if it's that special."

"I tell you what, I've got a much better idea, and we mustn't drink any more anyway – I don't want to loose my licence and neither do you. Why don't you fling a few basics into the car, feed that wretched old cat and come to me for the weekend. I'll take the Petrus, buy some steak on the way home and we can get stuck in tonight. You don't want to sit here by yourself brooding on what's happened – that's the worst possible thing – and we can sort out your future while we're at it."

"Yes Ma'am." Fiona bobbed a little mock curtsey. "Good thinking, but should I abandon ship do you think?" – a worried look crept over her face – "Supposing Hamish rings or one of the children, and oh my God!" she gasped, biting her lip, "the Bucknells and Mayhews are coming to supper tomorrow."

"Stop worrying and throw your cares aside! Hamish is the last person you want to speak to until you've formed a plan of attack; Roddy and Grania can live without you for 48 hours, and just tell the others you've got smallpox or something. I'm off now, so hurry up and don't waver!"

"OK. I promise I'll be with you a.s.a.p. In fact I can't wait to get out of this house." And as Dodo breezed out shouting 'A bientot', Fiona was left to contemplate her upturned life.

Deep down inside, she found it impossible to take in what had happened and felt as if she were playing the lead role in some hideous kitchen sink drama. As she had said to Mactavish, truthfully she was bored and had recently begun to question the point and direction of her life. She had not, however, anticipated the boredom ending quite like this. She could not even analyse her real feelings, but as the uplifting effects of the wine wore off and turned instead to depression, a spasm of panic overtook her as she contemplated her future.

Fiona had met and married Hamish at the age of 22 and he had been the only man she had ever slept with. The free moral spirit of the Swinging Sixties had not penetrated her middle-class suburban upbringing and marriage. Homemaking, children and submission had been her subconscious mantra.

As she had made her vows in front of the altar on her wedding day, complete with mini-blobs of fidgeting candyfloss, dewy-eyed old grannies and a paste tiara, Fiona had never even dreamt that it would not be until death did them part. Stability and her two children had been the reward but now she had to face up to the fact that the rug had been well and truly pulled from under her feet. She and Hamish had nothing left; their relationship was empty, and she realised that the seeds of dissent that had never germinated in her youth had been moving in the earth of her being since the children had grown up and gone.

Fiona wandered about the empty house, trying to unravel her tangled emotions, memories of happier days coming back as she picked up photographs here and there: Roddy and Grania aged four and seven, laughing with their father on the beach in Mull; herself in front of Ivy Cottage, their tiny first home together; and Hamish, the young smiling Hamish of their engagement photograph. He had been rather handsome then, before the sandy hair thinned and the sculptured cheeks turned plump and suety. She put the photograph face down in his sock drawer, a sort of tit-for-tat and a symbolic token of acceptance that their marriage was over.

As Fiona began to pack a small bag to take to Dodo's, the telephone rang and without thinking, she ran downstairs to answer it. She hadn't meant to but too late, her mother's voice came on the line. "Fiona? Is that you dear?"

"Oh hello Mummy, yes it's me, who else could it be?"

"No need to be sharp, dear. Is anything wrong? You do sound a little off."

Fiona took a deep breath – it had to come sometime and the sooner the better. "Yes Mummy," she said firmly, feeling her resolve weakening, "Everything's wrong. You had better prepare yourself for a shock. Hamish has run off with his secretary."

There was a deathly silence from the other end, then a strange little squeak as her mother started to speak. "I'm absolutely dumbfounded. For once in my life I really don't know what to say. Nevertheless Fiona, for one terrible moment I thought you were going to say you had cancer or something ghastly had happened to one of the children. I do wish you wouldn't give me these shocks, you know at my age my heart might go at any minute."

"Mummy, for heaven's sake be reasonable! I have never given you a shock before that I can remember and since when has there been anything wrong with your heart?"

"Well, you never can tell. Anyway, what is all this nonsense about my son-in-law? Men really are the limit, you know! I remember when your father cast an eye at Mavis Drinkwater, that dreadful woman at the golf club. I soon put a stop to that I can tell you and I would advise you to do the same. Buff yourself up a bit, I've noticed you've let yourself go rather recently."

"Mummy!" Fiona broke into the flow, furious that her mother had echoed Dodo's harsh words. "I don't want Hamish back. I'm sorry to shame you in front of your cronies but our marriage is over and my appearance has got nothing to do with it."

"Hmm! Don't you be so sure my girl, and as for saying you don't want him back, that is just a reaction – you're far too young to know what's best for you and my grandchildren."

"I'm 55, Mummy, and your grandchildren are 30 and 27 and living their own lives. There is no question of my changing my mind and I'm sure Hamish feels the same way. He's not exactly a man of impulse, is he? And please let me finish – I'm going to Dodo's in a minute for the weekend, and I shall be back on Monday to face the music and try to sort my life out. You don't seem to realise that just because I don't want him back I'm not very upset."

"I'm sorry dear, of course you are. I'm a silly old woman but this has been a terrible shock to me too you know – but I'm your Mother and I shall always be here when you need me. Mind you, I never quite trust that friend of yours, a flighty sort of girl who might easily lead you astray; and Hamish of all people, so steady and well – I have to say it – almost dull. Dear oh dear!" – and a tinkly little laugh reached

Fiona's burning right ear.

"Look Mummy, I must go but I'll ring you on Monday when I get back and perhaps you'd like to come over for a night or two. It would be very nice for me," she added as an afterthought.

"Of course I will dear, I'm always on hand in a crisis! I shall cancel my Tuesday bridge evening immediately – oh, and the hairdresser on Wednesday."

"'Bye Mummy, speak Monday," broke in Fiona resolutely, before a further catalogue of her mother's social events poured forth. She put the phone down feeling drained but relieved that the biggest hurdle had been jumped. Roddy and Grania would be flabbergasted, but they were young and forward-looking; their lives lay ahead, not in the past with their parents. Besides, their generation had very different views on the sanctity of marriage, and many of their peers came from homes that had broken up in childhood. She would contact them on Monday and hoped that Hamish, as the guilty party, would already have had the decency to tell them himself.

Now all Fiona wanted to do was get away and drop out with Dodo. She finished packing, stocked up Mactavish's automatic feeder and checked his cat flap was operational before locking up the house. As she started up the car she remembered she had not telephoned Saturday's dinner guests to cancel them.

'Bother!' she thought. 'Never mind, I'll ring from Dodo's. I can't go back now.' And she drove away.

DODO

The drive to Dodo's was even worse for Fiona than it had been in reverse for her friend earlier in the day. By now the Friday evening traffic had built up to horrendous proportions, and as she was carried along in its alternatively whirling jamming honking mass, Fiona was able to reflect on her conversation with her mother. It had gone better than she had expected, and she would genuinely be glad of her mother's company for a night or two when she returned home after her weekend with Dodo.

Angela Bateson had been a bad widow and after Fiona's father died she, as the only child, had borne the brunt of her mother's misery and slow readjustment to life on her own. It had taken two years for her mother to come to terms with her new situation but gradually her old spirit had won through and in her own words, the time had come to pull her socks up. To those who didn't know her well, Angie appeared frivolous and superficial but like her good friends, her daughter knew this facade was her panacea for the loss of a much-loved husband. After much muttering about memories and money, to Fiona's relief she had stayed in the house at East Horsley where Fiona had been brought up and still thought of as home. It was an ordinary sort of a house but Fiona loved it and when her children had been small, she had enjoyed reliving her own happy childhood there with them when they went to stay with Granny. It was just the right distance away – not too near and not too far.

Her mind far away, Fiona nearly overshot Dodo's lane and earned an angry hoot from behind as she braked sharply before indicating. Luckily there was no bump but she raised a hand in apology before turning off the main road, just catching sight in her rear mirror of a V-sign from the white van man behind.

Dodo lived in what had once been the stable block of a large Victorian house which was now split into flats.

Although most of the land had been sold off for building, a generous acre of what once must have been lovely old gardens remained for the use of the tenants. The unimaginatively named Stable Flat was set well away from the main house, and a delightful air of peaceful dereliction hung over it that somehow suited Dodo's character perfectly. Apart from her quarters, the old yard was on its way to falling down and Mother Nature and her weeds had taken over, but tucked away in one corner, an oasis of geraniums and blue lobelia proclaimed habitation.

As she drove in, Fiona pooped her horn a couple of times and before she had time to switch the engine off, Dodo appeared in the doorway.

"Where on Earth have you been?" she shouted as Fiona got her bag out of the car. "I feared there might have been a drama!"

"Well there was, in a way – my mother rang just after you left and the traffic was terrible."

"How was Mama – did you tell her the news?"

"Of course. No time like the present and all that. Not too bad actually – after some of her typically bizarre remarks she took it pretty well. She did rather think your evil influence might somehow have had something to do with it though."

"Bollocks!" shrieked Dodo, bursting out laughing. "Come on in – dear Hamish's precious bottle awaits our pleasure though I thought we might start with something a little lighter in the garden – it's such a beautiful evening."

"Suits me, but I'll just dump my things and have a wash. It was a sweaty drive and I nearly had a white van man up my bum."

"Wow, you should be so lucky! Hurry up – I'll put the spuds on then we can settle down."

Fiona loved the natural brightness and organised chaos of Dodo's dwelling; a style she would never have dreamt of creating in her own home. Hamish would have considered it wholly unsuitable and dangerously 'arty'. Bright throws enhanced the cheap sofa and chairs and the old polished floorboards were made cosy with rugs. Examples of Dodo's sculptures stood about as well as those of her fellow artists, and modern paintings rubbed shoulders happily with the small collection of Victorian watercolours she had inherited from her mother.

As Fiona ran up the steep open stairs she felt the tension begin to drain out of her body, and she took in a deep breath of revitalising oxygen. The tiny bathroom, nestling between the two equally tiny bedrooms, was surprisingly neat and sparkling, and Fiona noticed that Dodo had even put out a brand new piece of Fiona's favourite lemon-scented soap. She sniffed it appreciatively and smiled as she washed her hands and thought, not for the first time, how very much she valued their friendship. There was no-one else in the whole world to whom she could bare her innermost soul and upon whom she could rely on to rescue her in times of crisis.

Finished with her brief ablutions, Fiona poked her nose into Dodo's bedroom which was, as usual, a heap of denim, trendy boots, multi-coloured pashminas and paperback books. Peering through the clutter were the faces of her dead parents and Australian emigree brother with his buxom Aussie wife and brood of sturdy Aussie children. Poor Dodo, Fiona knew she had been distraught when Peter announced he was off to the other end of the world for they had been very close, and he was her only remaining near relation after their parents had been killed in a plane crash whilst on holiday in Africa. That was the time when Fiona had been on hand to help pick up the pieces – now it was Dodo's turn.

Clattering back down the stairs, she found Dodo waiting at the bottom with a glass of white wine. "You're not an ABC are you?" Dodo asked.

"A what?"

"Anything but Chardonnay." She laughed.

"Good heavens no – it's such a treat to be allowed anything to drink at all!"

"Come on, let's go and inspect my amazing vegetable garden – home-grown beans, spuds and tomatoes with the steak tonight."

They wandered out together into the old yard where Dodo's collection of pots and Gro-Bags burgeoned with a rich harvest.

"Looks really good," said Fiona, genuinely impressed with her friend's efforts. "But before we collapse, let's have a look at your studio and the famous cockerel."

"Actually, I scrumpled him up. I know it sounds silly but your phone call about Hamish rather capsized me. My Muse vanished and I just couldn't get him right."

"Sorry about that."

"Doesn't matter – let's relax now and maybe tomorrow I'll show you some of the other ideas I'm working on and see what you think."

"I'd like that. You're right, let's sit down and 'chill out', as my daughter would say."

"Talking of Grania, how is my god-daughter and have you told her yet that her father has run off with his secretary?"

"No," replied Fiona slowly, "I've been a bit of a coward about that. I just wanted to escape from everything until I'd had a chance to convalesce with you and mend my wounded vanity before facing the world. Anyway, as far as I know she's still in Namibia helping dig a well or something. Your god-daughter usually only communicates when she's run out of money. Roddy's in Singapore for another year and loving it. I wish they would come home though, I do miss them and having them both away leaves a big hole in my futile existence."

"Don't be like that, Fi. Your life is only futile if you let it be and of course you must miss them but you can't live through your children for the rest of time." Dodo paused for a drink. "I know I'm not in a position to talk but I'm sure I'm right. Look on the bright side – they'll probably both reappear with armfuls of sweet little multi-coloured grandchildren!"

"Heaven forbid!" Fiona laughed, and they sat for a moment in companionable silence, enjoying the peace of the evening and the cold Chardonnay.

"Help!" Fiona jumped up. "I've forgotten to ring the dinner people – can I borrow your phone, I can't relax till that's done."

"'Course, help yourself and I'll check the cooking."

Fiona appeared in the kitchen a few minutes later, to find Dodo draining the potatoes and putting the steaks under the grill. "Supper's nearly ready. What excuse did you make?"

"My poor old mother's got flu and I'm Florence Nightingale! I'll lay the table if you like and I must say, I'm starving."

"Good, I'm glad to hear the great shock hasn't taken away your appetite."

Five minutes later they were seated at the scrubbed pine with two delicious plates of food and the sacred bottle of Petrus in front of them. Twilight had come and Dodo lit the phalanx of candles that lived permanently on the table.

"Now for the great moment." She breathed reverently, picking up the bottle and carefully pouring the deep ruby wine into their glasses. "Don't swig – swill gently then inhale the wonderful bouquet and savour each mouthful – you may never sample the like again."

"Hmm," Fiona obeyed orders. "I've never tasted anything like it – it's delicious."

"E-x-q-u-i-s-i-t-e," sighed Dodo. "Well done Hamish!"

At that moment the telephone rang. "Blast! I had better answer that. You never know, it might be a commission."

But it was not a commission, it was Hamish.

"I have no idea where she is, Hamish." Fiona heard Dodo say in her most crushing tone of voice. "Yes, I have spoken to her and I think you are a complete shit... I shall say what I like in my own home." After obviously listening to something Hamish had to say, Dodo slammed down the phone. "Sorry Fi," she said as she sat back down, "wish I hadn't answered it."

"What did he say?" asked poor Fiona, her temporary island of calm blown apart.

"Not much really. Just wondered if you were here and said if I spoke to you to tell you he will be calling in on Monday evening to 'discuss the situation'. I think he guessed you were here but I imagine you didn't want to speak to him?"

"Absolutely not."

"Have you had any thoughts yet about the future or don't you want to talk about it tonight?"

"Not really, on both counts. I'm having a great time forgetting it all at the moment and there's two whole days before I have to get serious. Update me with your love life instead. Is the bearded monster still around?"

"Alas no! He got too clingy so he had to go – wanted to be part of my life and all that, which is not what I wanted at any price. He was good in bed though, once I got used to feeling my body was being swept by a besom two or three times a week! No, I'm in between at the moment though I have my eye on a new recruit to my Tuesday sculpture class – useless at modelling but may have talent in another direction!"

"I don't know how you do it!" laughed Fiona.

"Well, it's time I gave you a few lessons now you're footloose and fancy-free. You cannot possibly go to your grave having only slept with one man and that man Hamish, of all men."

"I think I'm too tired to be a good pupil tonight but I shall bear your offer in mind," replied Fiona, yawning. "Thank you for this evening, it was just what I needed but if you'll forgive my drabness, I think I'll head for bed – I feel knackered."

"You carry on, the water's hot if you want a bath. I shall potter about for a bit, see you in the morning. Sleep well."

"And you – 'night."

Dodo sat on for a while, half listening to the sounds of Fiona going to bed and half listening to the sounds of the dark. As silence fell upstairs, she wandered out into the garden to breathe in the summer night air and let the mantle of the day slide from her shoulders. She seldom went to bed before midnight and often worked in her studio until the small hours, too absorbed in her art to notice the passing of time. Not tonight though; tonight all her thoughts were for Fiona, and stubbing out her last cigarette of the day, she went back into the kitchen to clear up supper before creeping quietly upstairs to bed.

***

They both slept late in the morning and when a chipper Dodo arrived beside Fiona's tumbled bed bearing a cup of tea, the baggy eyes and tousled appearance of its intended recipient shrieked 'hangover'.

"The trouble with you is you don't drink enough," announced Dodo. "Your alcohol-starved system can't take the shock and I blame The Hamish Regime for that. Now behold thy friend, a shining example of an old soak."

"Oh God!" groaned Fiona, struggling to sit up. "Give me that steaming cup, I feel terrible. I thought good wine wasn't supposed to give you a hangover."

"Don't blame the Petrus, it was all that awful Chardonnay we drank before supper. Or, on second thoughts, perhaps the wily Hamish injected the bottle with some tasteless but noxious substance lest his scheming wife should make off with it!"

"Go away," wailed Fiona, making a feeble attempt to throw a pillow. "And don't mention that man again!"

Dodo gave an irritatingly chirpy little wave and disappeared downstairs to get her breakfast, relieved that Fiona had not burst into tears at the mention of her husband's name. The aggressive approach was much more to her liking than the maudlin recriminations she feared might have set the scene for Fiona's second day of abandonment. Never having been married herself, Dodo could not begin to imagine what it must feel like to have been dumped after thirty-two years of conjugal stability, if not bliss. Her own parents had been devoted to each other but Dodo had never found a man with whom she wished to share her life.

The underlying ethos of the men she had dated in her

twenties had still belonged to the pre-Sixties era when women subjugated themselves to the greater good of their men, and her feminist hackles had been sufficiently raised by this attitude to quash any desire to join this merry band of martyrs. Her mother had repeatedly told her of the joys of marriage and children, and she had watched her best friend with a mixture of envy and relief as Fiona had tramped the traditional road of womanhood. Now Dodo knew without question that for her, she had made the right decision.

Fiona's arrival at the breakfast table coincided with that of the newspapers and as she aided her recovery with the teapot, they buried their heads in the mountains of print that comprised the Saturday publications. The sun shone in through the small window of what had once been the tack room, and as the muffled sound of the main road increased to the steady hum of Home Counties world coming to life, Dodo banged the table.

"Come on Fi, we can't sit here all day, it's too beautiful outside. I've had an idea. Let's take a picnic and a couple of trashy books and go on the river. You used to be able to hire boats on the Wey, d'you remember?"

"Oh yes," agreed Fiona enthusiastically, "that's a great idea. We'd better get moving before it gets too crowded. I fear things will have changed a bit since our youth. Honestly, we were a pair of romantic idiots then, weren't we? Dreaming of knights in shining armour and wondering what sex would be like!" – and laughing at the thought, they rattled round the kitchen buttering baguettes and loading up a basket full of picnic essentials.

"Let's take my car," Fiona suggested as they headed out into the yard. "I can fill up on Hamish's account on Monday morning."

"I'm shocked Mrs Macleod, that whilst grieving for your errant husband you can even think about such a vulgar thing as money."

"Actually, I've thought about it quite a lot since the bombshell," countered Fiona, lapsing back into gloom.

20

"Come on – no cloud shall darken our day, I'm banning any mention of you-know-who for twelve hours. You must cast aside THR and let your spirit soar into the summer sky."

"Do stop talking drivel – and I'm not on HRT anyway."

"Not HRT, THR – *The Hamish Regime* – you should take HRT though, it helps keep the juices flowing!"

"And gives you breast cancer."

"Not proven."

"Oh, let's go," Fiona sighed.

"Damn!" exclaimed Dodo as they rattled along the lane towards the main road.

"What now?"

"I've forgotten the string."

"What on Earth do we want string for?"

"To hang the wine over the side of the boat to keep cool of course."

"Can't go back now and anyway, I don't drink in the middle of the day."

"Well it's time you started."

The journey took less time than expected but as they approached their destination the car jinked and an ominous 'flumping' sound proclaimed a puncture.

"Can you beat it," moaned Fiona, pulling in to the side of the road, "I'm hopeless at changing wheels. I don't even know where the spare is."

"Fret not, I can do it in a jiffy. Always had to, you see."

Dodo went into action with jack and tools while Fiona, under her direction, located and released the spare wheel. Unfortunately the wheel nuts were jammed tight and as Dodo jumped on the wheel brace in her efforts to free them, her foot slipped off and she hit her ankle bone. Swearing and hopping around, she nearly fell into the path of an oncoming car which pulled into the side of the road in front of them.

"You ladies look as if you could use some help," said a male voice.

"Oh, yes please," replied Fiona quickly, spotting the cross stubborn look coming over Dodo's face. "These nut things seem impossible to shift."

"No problem. Stand aside and I shall have you back on the road in a minute."

Fiona inspected their rescuer as he effortlessly whirled the offending nuts off and zipped the spare on as if it were a Formula One pit stop. He was the sort of man her mother would approve of: clean-shaven, fifty-something, no paunch and uniform dress of polo shirt, jeans and light-weight desert boots. The job done, he stood up smiling and wiping one well-manicured hand against the other. "Sorry about your ankle," he turned to Dodo, blue eyes crinkling as he smiled at her.

"It's nothing, but thanks anyway," she replied grudgingly.

"Yes," endorsed Fiona effusively, to make up for Dodo's manner. "Thank you very much indeed – we could have been stuck for ages."

"My pleasure. 'Bye then." He returned to his car and drove off.

"Condescending prig!" sniffed Dodo. "Going on as if we were little old ladies – and you didn't have to add that bit about being stuck, one more go and I would have done it."

"That's rather unfair, and let's face it, we're not exactly teenagers. Come on, time for messing about on the river."

And the incident was forgotten as anticipation of the outing took over. They took it in turns to row and pulled for over an hour until the river was clear of the main crowd of boats, most of which were full of noisy, splashing children. Blisters were forming as they decided it was time to find a mooring, get out the picnic and cool the wine in the shallows. Some cattle watched lazily as their drinking place was invaded and a couple of moorhens scooted into the reeds as Fiona and Dodo disembarked.

"This is perfect," cried Fiona. "I'm glad we pressed on even though my shoulders are screaming. It's just as I remember it now we've got away from the mob."

"Shit!" yelped Dodo, first out of the boat. "Watch out!"

"What's wrong?"

"Cow pats and I've just trodden in one."

"You would – for heaven's sake keep your feet away from my lunch."

"Don't worry, these old trainers can have a dunk in the river – hand me the basket, I've forgotten the glasses so we'll have to swig."

"I expect we'll manage!"

Food and wine disappeared rapidly and Fiona lay back on her elbows, turning her face up to the sun to drink in its heat. One other boat slid past, its occupants waving in river camaraderie; otherwise all was peace and quiet.

"Hmm," Fiona sighed. "Why is it that food always tastes so much better eaten on a river bank than in a house?"

"Don't know, but it does," murmured Dodo, already deep in her book.

"I think I might have a zizz," yawned Fiona. "Wake me up if anything exciting happens."

A grunt was all she got in reply, and she soon drifted into sleep until...

"Wake up Fi! I think we ought to move."

"What's the time?"

"Nearly six. I've finished my book and I don't know how you can sleep so long."

"Goodness, I can't believe it, I've been asleep for nearly two hours."

"All part of the healing process I suppose. I'm off to find a bush."

"Don't upset the cattle, we don't want a stampede on our hands!"

Fiona packed up the remains of the picnic and had loaded everything into the boat by the time Dodo returned.

"Sorry, had to go miles to find the right spot. Shall I row first to give you a chance to wake up?"

"If you like. I must say my hands are rather sore."

In the end Dodo rowed the whole way back and as they were rounding the final bend, the river all but empty now, another boat came into view moving towards them.

"There's another boat approaching, you'd better pull over a bit," Fiona alerted the oarswoman from her position in the stern.

Dodo glanced over her shoulder and steered their boat over as instructed as the other one drew near.

"Ooh look!" exclaimed Fiona. "Can you believe it, it's the man who changed the wheel and he's got a bird with him!"

"Probably his ancient mother on the way to death by drowning," replied Dodo sarcastically. "And let's hope he doesn't try and give us a lesson on changing the rollocks."

"Hardly an ancient mother – looks more like a bimbo to me."

"Hello again!" his voice called out as they came abreast. "Fancy seeing you here. Had a good day?"

"Wonderful thanks," called back Fiona as Dodo increased her stroke rate, "there's a great place for a picnic a mile or two on on the left."

"Thanks for the info – we'll look out for it. 'Bye," and they shot past, the pretty blonde girl smiling and waving as they disappeared round the bend.

"Cradle snatcher!" commented a red-faced Dodo, immediately slackening her pace and heaving a sigh of relief as the boat station came into sight at last.

"She certainly made me feel old," laughed Fiona as they unloaded their gear, "but then with a son of 30 and a daughter of 27, I'm not surprised. After all, plenty of my generation are grandmothers."

"That's quite a sobering thought," agreed Dodo as she climbed wearily into the car. "I mean, remember how incredibly ancient and stuffy grandparents seemed and how we vowed never to be like them."

"Yes – it's all very peculiar when one starts to think about old age and the generation gap. I mean, every decade ahead of you seems so old but when you get there yourself you still believe you're young, if you understand me."

"I suppose everyone thinks that, but let's wait till we make 60 and then take a view – it's not that far away."

The drive back to Stable Flat passed without incident and the great orange ball of the sun was sinking into the western horizon by the time Fiona and Dodo had cleared up the picnic debris and settled down for the remainder of the evening.

"I always think that the world has got it all wrong." Dodo sounded pensive.

"What do you mean?"

"Well, the longest days should be in late July and August which is supposed to be high summer, yet here we are in August and the days are already drawing in. It's no good having all that light in early spring when it's too cold to sit out. The summer solstice should be later."

"Hmm, I see your point but must admit I've never thought about it. I'm not much into nature I suppose but I enjoy my bit of gardening."

"My dear Fiona, your garden is about as anally retentive as your house, your wardrobe and your vocabulary!"

"Dodo!" cried Fiona plaintively. "That's jolly mean of you. I happen to like my style."

"Hamish's style, you mean."

"I thought there was a twelve hour embargo on mentioning his name."

"Quite right. Sorry – I didn't mean to be a bitch, it was supposed to be a joke. Forgiven?"

"Of course," Fiona smiled. "I could forgive you almost anything after a day like today, it was one of the best I've had in ages."

"It was fun, wasn't it? I'm never sure about trying to turn the clock back – so often it turns out to be a disappointment but today really worked. Let's have something to eat and an early night, all that rowing has left me quite whacked."

"Old age, I'm afraid." Fiona replied, earning a V-sign from Dodo as she disappeared into the kitchen to rustle up supper.

BITING THE BULLET

Fiona slept the sleep of the dead, and couldn't believe it when Dodo appeared and woke her with the news that it was 8.30, breakfast was ready and the day had begun. It seemed years since she had passed such a night without waking in the early hours when, after visiting the loo, she would toss and turn, screaming inwardly at Hamish's relentless snores, before eventually drifting back into uneasy sleep. It annoyed her that she always felt alert and active at this time, yet when the alarm shrilled out at 6.45 on weekdays, getting up was an effort and she felt leaden and unrefreshed.

Today was different. The sun shone in and the smell of frying bacon wafted up her nostrils as she sprung out of bed. Taking a quick shower, she was relieved that Dodo's bathroom mirror was rather small and well misted up from the hot water, as she had no desire to dampen her spirits with a reflection of what the passage of time was doing to her body.

"You look rather perky this morning," commented Dodo as Fiona arrived in the kitchen. "Better than yesterday!"

"I feel rather good actually – and jolly hungry."

"How many eggs?"

"Oh, one please and quite well done but I'll do it, you get on with yours."

"It's OK, I've finished. Tell you what though, I have to fetch the Sunday papers so I'll go and do that while you carry on – you know where everything is, and I'll only be ten minutes."

"No problem and can you get a *Telegraph* please – we always have it and I like knowing my way round a newspaper, if you know what I mean."

"Sure – won't be long and if the phone rings, leave it, I've got the answer machine on."

The telephone remained silent and Dodo was soon back, weighed down under armfuls of newsprint which she dumped on the table.

"What's on then today?" asked Fiona, as she started clearing away the breakfast things.

"I'm all for a lazy day here if that suits you – it's going to be roasting again and I've got a bit of paperwork for my Autumn exhibition I ought to do at some stage. Don't bother to wash the frying pan, I use it every morning – it's not due its monthly scrub for a week or two."

"Really Dodo! I'm surprised you don't get food poisoning, neither do I know how you stay so slim the way you eat. I would explode if I stuffed my face with all that fried food."

"You should take more exercise and worry less about kitchen hygiene, anyway a bit of dirt's good for the immune system. So what about today?"

"I'm very happy to laze around here too – it'll take most of the morning to read these papers and most of the afternoon to recover from lunch!"

By early evening the air had become heavy and sultry with not a breath of wind to stir a leaf. Dark clouds gathered on the horizon and as Dodo returned from watering her pots and Gro-bags, the first distant rumble of thunder foretold the coming storm.

"That was a waste of time!" she said. "I think Mother Nature is about to do the job for me."

"Hmm," mumbled Fiona, deep in her book.

"I'm going to unplug the computer in case we get struck, then let's take a drink outside and watch the storm brew – I love doing that and I think we're in for a cracker."

Fiona shut the book and came back to life, the oppressive air and thought of Monday morning settling on her like the black clouds above.

"What am I going to do, Dodo?" she said woefully as they sat outside in the gathering gloom.

"I was wondering when you would want to talk, and of course my ear is all yours. I haven't got the answer though, because at the end of the day it's your life and you must decide."

"I know, but at the moment my mind is just one big muddle, and I don't know where to start trying to sort it all out. The only thing I do know is that I don't want Hamish back at any price."

"I'm glad to hear you say that as that's the most important starting-off point. I feared that when your initial anger had died down you might change your mind on that one."

"No, I've been thinking about it this afternoon when you were in the studio and I know I could never feel the same way about him. In fact I'm beginning to realise I haven't loved him properly for ages. He's just sort of been there, like the furniture I suppose, and he probably feels the same way about me. I assumed it was a normal condition after years of marriage and I never dreamt of upsetting the apple cart, or that he would. What you would call my bourgeois attitude I expect," Fiona ended, on a lighter note.

"You could say that! Seriously though, when you've seen the brute tomorrow and heard what he has to say, it might make it easier to plan the way forward. Whatever you do, don't let him steam-roll you into making life-threatening decisions before you want to, or do you out of your cut of the loot. I know a good divorce lawyer, rather well as a matter of fact, when you need one."

"Really Dodo! Yet another of your conquests – still, they do seem to have their uses."

"Oh, I fear it was all a long time ago but he was pretty good in the sack and pretty good at settlements."

"I shall only be interested in the latter, thanks."

"Not for ever I hope – blast, there's the phone." As Dodo went to answer it, the thunder rolled nearer and the first heavy drops of storm rain followed close behind.
And as Fiona gathered up the glasses and bottle, Dodo shouted through the open door:
"It's for you, hurry up."

"Who is it?" Fiona arrived in the sitting room. "Nobody knows I'm here except Mummy."

"It's your wonderful Uncle Greg," replied Dodo, handing her the phone.

"Uncle Greg!" cried Fiona, surprise and genuine pleasure in her tone. "How did you know I was here?"

"Your mother of course, who else! My dear sister has been burning my ear the entire weekend. Now what's all this nonsense about Hamish ditching my favourite niece in favour of that dried-up old prune of a secretary of his?" Uncle Greg spoke with a staccato intensity.

"I'm your only niece you may remember and yes, I'm afraid that's exactly what he has done."

"Frightful fellow – always thought he was a bounder – never trust a man with ginger hair."

"Oh, Uncle Greg!" Fiona couldn't help laughing. "I seem to remember you saying what a 'decent chap' he was and how you 'liked the cut of his jib' when we got married."

"Rubbish!" snorted Uncle Greg. "Couldn't stand that old snob of a mother either. I say, Fiona, I hope you're not too cut up about all this?"

"Oh no, Uncle Greg, why should I let such a trivial and everyday occurrence as my husband of 32 years bolting with his secretary get me down."

"That's my gel!" he guffawed, heedless of the loaded sarcasm. "Now the point is, that barmy mother of yours has come up with one of her crackpot schemes that you should go and live with her at The Larches – back in your old room with the teddy bears and all that. Thought you ought to know – forewarned is forearmed."

Fiona was struck dumb with horror.

"You there Fiona – Fiona?" he shouted as if she were on the other end of a First World War trench telephone.

"Yes Uncle Greg, and please don't shout. I was just digesting what you said and thanks for the warning. It's not that I don't love Mummy, but..."

He cut in before she could finish. "Say no more, darling, say no more. We all love your mother but loving and living with are two totally different things. I should know," he chortled. "I have loved many women but thank God always managed to avoid living with any of 'em! Now look, I have a plan. Pop up to town on Tuesday and I'll stand you lunch at my club. We can have a jolly good old chinwag and sort you out. Love telling those silly old buffers I'm lunching with my niece – never believe me you know – so don't look drab."

"I'll do my best," sighed Fiona, "and yes, I'd like that very much. Mummy's coming over in the evening so am sure I shall be well and truly sorted by Wednesday morning!"

"Wilco and don't be late. Chin up." The phone clicked off.

"All OK?" asked Dodo, reappearing from the kitchen where she had had an ear to the conversation.

"Yes, fine thanks. I'm having lunch with him on Tuesday which will be entertaining if nothing else."

"I love your silly old uncle and if he were a bit younger I might fancy him myself. How old is he by the way?"

"Pushing 80 I think and still behaving like a 20-year old. He's older than Mummy and she's 77 this year."

"I wonder why he never got married – can't be gay by all accounts!"

"Quite the opposite I should say but I suppose he just never found Mrs Right. Pity really, he would have been a brilliant husband and father. He's terribly kind you know, under all that gung-ho nonsense."

"Lucky you having a nice uncle – and you must be his heir I suppose."

"I fear that won't do me much good," laughed Fiona. "By the time he's wrecked another sports car or two and squired a few more blue-rinsed widows around town there won't be much left. I'd rather have him alive anyway."

At that moment the storm broke overhead and they both jumped as a shattering crash of thunder shook the house and the room was illuminated by lightning.

"Quick, all the windows are wide open everywhere – I'll do the cars, you do the house," cried Dodo as the rain beat down and another great clap of thunder drowned out her voice.

The storm passed as quickly as it had arrived, but the evening sky remained overcast and dull, and a light drizzle continued to fall in the wake of the torrential thunder rain. 'Just like my feelings,' thought Fiona, as she went upstairs to pack her things ready for an early start in the morning.

They had walked out after lunch over the fields that bordered the edge of the old garden and had been excited to find a patch of early mushrooms had popped up. Dodo said the farmer had given her permission to walk there and wouldn't mind if they picked a few as she had asked him once before. She was interested in cooking, and an avid watcher of the endless programmes on the subject that appeared on television. Certainly the mushroom omelette and home-grown radicchio salad Dodo produced for supper were delicious, and Fiona complimented her on her skills as she herself cleaned up every last bit with a piece of bread before attacking a wedge of Brie that had every intention of running away over the table. Beautiful ripe white-fleshed peaches followed, and as the accompanying wine started to take effect, Fiona's spirits began to rise.

"Where on Earth did you find these peaches? I can never find decent soft fruit, it's never ripe and either goes rotten or crinkly before it's worth eating. These peaches have still got down on them."

"Hmm, rather like your chin!" said Dodo, staring thoughtfully at Fiona.

"You bitch, I'm no hairier than anyone of our age, so speak for yourself!"

"I pinch the peaches from the old greenhouse in the back garden, I always do, every year. Nobody cares a jot about them and the whole thing is falling down but the tree goes on growing despite broken glass and brambles, and I think it deserves to have its fruit-producing efforts rewarded by someone appreciating them. Imagine sweating away giving birth and all your babies being left to rot on the ground or be eaten by wasps. As for your chin," Dodo continued artlessly,

"I've seen worse but you must keep a monthly whisker watch – they have a habit of creeping up on you, you know, and there's nothing worse."

"Well thanks for the tip, I'll bear it in mind when next I scrutinise my disintegrating visage and if needs be, I can always buy a packet of razor blades."

"O-o-o-h-h-h," shuddered Dodo. "*Never* shave, always wax – d'you want to end up looking like Hamish on a Sunday morning? You won't pull a new man that way."

"Oh shut up – my chin's fine and the last thing I want is a new man – I haven't got rid of the old one yet."

"That's the spirit," laughed Dodo, splashing the last of the wine into her glass. "Now look, I think it's time for bed, but first you must promise me you'll ring tomorrow evening and tell me how the great meeting with the shit of the year went, and you jolly well stick up for your rights."

"Of course I will, and on both counts. I'm for bed too and I shall sneak out early tomorrow to beat the traffic. I've just remembered it's Monday and that means Mrs P at 8.30. Once she knows about Hamish the whole world will know, which will save me the business of telling them."

"Yes, I'd forgotten about your redoubtable charlady. Does she actually do anything useful or does she sit there drinking tea and gossiping all morning?"

"Bit of both I suppose, but she's been around longer than Mactavish and she likes to escape from old Pinker for an hour or two I think – he's a terrible old bore and moans the whole time about his 'screwmatics' – what normal people would call rheumatism. Of course, she runs around him like a slave and by the time she gets to me the poor old thing's exhausted. And I shall be too if I don't go to bed so I'm off, but thanks a million Dodo, I don't know what I'd have done without this weekend – I really don't."

"That's what friends are for, you clot. Hope you sleep well and speak tomorrow evening."

***

In spite of Dodo's hopes Fiona slept badly, and when her

alarm went off at 6.30 the clock was already packed in her case and in the car as she sped back towards reality. Not bothering to stop and deal with it, she turned up the volume on the radio to drown out its insistent beeping and by the time she swished into her drive, it had given up the ghost. Nerves knotted in the pit of her stomach as she drew to a halt, fearful that Hamish might be there, but to her relief the garage was empty and Mactavish alone was waiting on the doorstep to greet her, back arched and tail up as he rubbed round her legs in delight at her return.

"Sorry old man." Fiona bent down to stroke him before unlocking the back door, treading on a half-eaten mouse carcass in the process.

"No need to worry about you, you fat old killer." She smiled as he zipped in through the door in front of her, pleading hunger and neglect.

Dumping her luggage in the kitchen, Fiona flicked on the kettle and dropped a couple of slices of bread into the toaster before having a look-round to see if all was as she had left it. It occurred to her that Hamish would probably have turned up over the weekend to pick up some clothes and personal belongings, knowing full well that she would have been staying either with Dodo or her mother. Sure enough there was evidence that he had been there and this was confirmed by the presence of an envelope addressed to her which she found propped up on the hall table.

Taking it back into the kitchen, she decided to postpone reading it until she had fed Mactavish and organised her own breakfast. The cat received his food gratefully, but the milk was on the turn and nasty little gobbets of white curd flecked the surface of her tea as Fiona fished out the bag and settled down at the table to bite the bullet and learn what Hamish had in store for her. Now that the initial shock had begun to wear off, Fiona was beginning to feel that her emotional recovery could actually become a reality, but her thoughts were still in turmoil, and the practical side of her future was a different matter. She had never been independent and had always toed the line, of first her parents and then Hamish, believing – as she had been brought up to believe – that was the way life worked. Hamish had run the show and the thought of coping with money, insurance, cars and electricity bills alarmed Fiona considerably.

Unfolding the A4 sheet, Fiona plunged in. Hamish, it seemed, preferred not to meet her at this early stage of their separation as he didn't consider it necessary. The situation could easily be sorted out, he felt, by telephonic or written communication which both he and Margaret would prefer. 'I'll bet the old cow would,' thought Fiona. Besides, a meeting could have an upsetting effect on Fiona as the deserted party. 'Ha! Dream on, big-head!' He and Margaret wanted to get married as soon as possible and he felt sure that Fiona would agree to the terms he proposed for her settlement as he knew them to be fair and generous after consultation with his lawyer. Basically she would have half of everything he had which, after the house was sold, should be ample for her relatively modest needs provided she exercised prudence. He very much hoped that the whole affair could be resolved without animosity and as quickly as possible as there was no point in prolonging the unfortunate situation. 'Suits me.' Would Fiona please contact him either by ringing the office or writing to him there. 'God! it's all so typically Hamish.' He was, however, extremely distressed to find an item of importance missing from the house. Could she possibly throw any light on the disappearance of a bottle of wine called Chateau Petrus?

Fiona burst out laughing and clapped her hands with glee, knocking over her mug as she jumped up and danced round the astonished Mactavish who, having eaten his food, was sitting on the floor cleaning his undercarriage. The tea spread over Hamish's letter, blurring the words as the ink ran under the force of the liquid and she blotted it quickly with a drying up cloth to preserve the epistle for Dodo's delectation. Her reply could wait until she had had time to think it through properly and take advice but for now, a clatter in the boiler room announced the arrival of Mrs Pinker.

"Mornin' Mrs Mac," she screeched over the clatter before bustling into the kitchen and dumping a pint of milk on the table. "God give me strength but I could die for a cuppa, Pinker's screwmatics 'ave been playing 'im up something shocking!" As she darted towards the kettle, her black beady eyes scrutinised Fiona's face. "Me oh my, dearie, but you look a mite peaky – not got something have we?"

"Yes and no Mrs P. Not the 'something' that you mean but a something that's news – big news actually. Make the tea and come and sit down – I'll find some biscuits."

An instant look of anxiety crossed Mrs Pinker's kindly wrinkled face and even her tightly crimped grey hair managed a slight wobble as her head bobbed with the scent of drama.

"Not the children nor Mr 'amish I 'opes?" she queried, grasping a ginger nut in her work-worn little claw.

Fiona swallowed a mouthful of tea, took a deep breath and poured out the whole story.

There was a brief silence as Mrs Pinker tried to digest the news, along with several large gulps of tea and dunked ginger nut. Finally, tea finished, judgement was pronounced: "Well strike me dead Mrs Mac – you could an' all. If you was to tell me the Queen 'ad worn a bininki at the Derby I'd 'ave believed you more!"

"Bikini Mrs P, not bininki." Fiona's automatic correction was ignored.

"Mr 'amish of all people," she tut-tutted, "gorblimey!"

"Well, I must say it was rather a shock, as you can imagine."

"Fancy! Pinker won't 'arf think I'm off me nut when I tell him. But poor you dearie, I'm ever so sorry, ever so. I've 'ad quite a turn 'earing that I can tell you. More tea?" – and without waiting for an answer, she brewed afresh. "Mind you, I always said them men was never to be trusted – 'ere today, gone tomorrow. Dear oh dearie me, this is a pretty kettle of fish if ever there was one."

"Now the thing is Mrs P," Fiona broke in to stem the flow of Pinkerisms which seemed in danger of getting out of hand. "I'm trying to be very positive about all this and sort my life out as quickly as possible. There is no question of Mr Hamish and I getting back together and I'm afraid this means we shall have to sell the house and I really don't know yet where I shall go." Fiona paused for a sip of tea before finishing lamely, "so I'm terribly sorry to say, that means no job." She had been dreading having to make Mrs Pinker redundant, yet like so many big dreads, the deed turned out to be easier than the thought.

"Bless you dearie, don't you be worrying about me. I been thinking lately what with Pinker and me age and one thing and another praps it's time I packed in work. We've a bit put away you know and you being me only lady nowadays, it's just well, like I'm one of the family and 'sides, I like to see you right if I can."

"You're a star Mrs P and I don't know what I would have done without you. I would be very grateful if you could stay for as long as it takes to get things sorted but I quite understand if you prefer to go before all the dreadful clearing out and packing has to be done – that's not something I'm looking forward to," she added pointedly.

Mrs Pinker rose to the bait. "*Course not!*" she practically screamed. "Now would I leave a sinking ship, Mrs Mac? That's not to say as I mayn't give that Mr 'amish a piece of my mind if I sees 'im but don't you worry dearie, you've no legs in the grave yet and you never know what's around the next corner. Now me, I don't want no change at me time of life but me old Ma used to say 'Edie me girl, don't you ever think the sun rises and sets on marriage and men. When the kids 'ave gone, pastures green can beckon.' Clever woman, me old Ma." Well satisfied with her profound words of wisdom, Mrs P sat back in her chair, hands folded on her lap, and drew in a deep breath that pinched her small nostrils tight into her nose.

Fiona wondered if Mrs P had been reading too many

stories in women's magazines, and fearing that her next speech might contain romantic notions of knights in shining armour, decided that practicalities were the best antidote to starry-eyed fantasies.

"Now Mrs P, I think it's time we made a move. My mother is coming to stay tomorrow so could you start with the guest room and then flick a duster round the downstairs – you know how fussy she is about things like that. I've been away all weekend, staying with Dodo, so haven't done anything in the house at all I'm afraid."

"Ooh, that was nice for you then – bit of a rackety one though, that friend of yours. Mind you, just what the doctor ordered, I shouldn't wonder."

"It was actually, we had a lovely time and I think I would have gone mad sitting here all alone."

"Hmm. Well, I'd best be getting on – idle 'ands for the Devil's work – and remember me to Mrs Bateson – nice lady, your mother." Mrs P scuttled off to the boiler room to gather up her cleaning equipment.

Fiona stuffed a load in the washing machine before sitting down with pencil and paper to write a menu plan and shopping list for her mother's forthcoming visit. The weekend with Dodo had been a wonderful and necessary visit to cloud-cuckoo-land, but that was over and the real world was back with a bang and in need of urgent attention. The thought depressed her and she wondered for the hundredth time how on Earth she was going to manage, and what on Earth she was going to do. Clutching at the straws of domestic normality, Fiona made her lists and then fiddled about in the kitchen, sorting out the fridge and wiping down the already clean work tops.

"This won't do," she said aloud, throwing the cloth into the sink. "I must contact a solicitor."

The trouble was, who to contact? Fiona herself had never had any dealings with a lawyer and obviously Hamish's solicitor would be the enemy. Knowing Dodo, her ex-lover was probably a complete charlatan who might well demand payment in kind – Dodo had commented gleefully on his voracious sexual appetite – and that left her parents' old family firm. She supposed they would be as good a bet as any to start the ball rolling and remembered that, somewhere in Hamish's desk, there should be some correspondence from them relating to her father's will.

Feeling like a guilty child, Fiona rootled through the forbidden drawers, rather hoping she might come across something illicit or exciting like love letters from La Crutchley. Alas no, it was all typically Hamish. Underneath two files labelled Roderick and Grania, she came upon her own – 'Fiona' neatly printed in the top corner. It was a very thin file but it did contain the information she was seeking and she hurried back to the telephone to make the call before Mrs Pinker reappeared for her next cup of tea and chat session.

The letters had been signed by Arthur Peabody, whose name also appeared amongst the short list of partners at the top of the expensively embossed writing paper. He had written in a friendly and informal way, and Fiona hoped he would be available to speak to her as she punched out the number.

"Napper, Napper & Cruickshank – Julie speaking, how can I help you?" sang out a saucy young female voice.

"I'd like to speak to Mr Peabody, please," Fiona answered.

"'Fraid that might be difficult," there was a hint of a giggle, "Mr Peabody passed away last year."

As Fiona's heart sank, her irritation with Julie mounted and she took a more demanding stance. "I'm sorry to hear that, but put me through to one of the other partners, please. My family has been dealing with your firm for many years and I would like to speak to someone in authority."

"Mr Napper senior is available. Who shall I say is calling?" The voice a little sulky now.

"Mrs McLeod."

There was a click and Fiona waited, fervently praying

that the pervasive Allegro from *Eine Kleine Nachtmusik* would not assail her ear. Her prayers were answered – no Mozart, just a short silence and then "Mrs McLeod? Henry Napper speaking," said a polite voice that clearly belonged to an educated and senior man. "Am I correct in thinking that you are Hugh Bateson's daughter?"

"Yes, that's right," replied Fiona, enthusiastic with relief that she had been identified.

"I knew your father quite well you know, we used to play golf together occasionally, although poor Arthur dealt with his affairs."

"Yes I know, and I'm sorry to hear that Mr Peabody is dead. Your receptionist told me."

"Ah yes. That would be Julie." His tone of voice implied an ambiguity of feeling towards the company telephonist that endeared him to Fiona. "As a matter of fact, he expired on the 18th green while playing in the local Law Society Veterans Foursome. Nice way for him to go but rather ruined our chance – missed the vital putt you see – poor old chap."

"Oh dear." Fiona tried to sound interested but wished they could get on with the business. Pinker's tuneless trilling was getting nearer and time was running out.

"Anyway, enough of that," at last Henry Napper was back on track."How can we be of assistance, nothing untoward I hope?"

"Yes, as a matter of fact, I suppose you could call it that," Fiona recounted the story of her abandonment. Henry Napper was a good listener and allowed her uninterrupted air time, and if it hadn't been for the occasional little murmur of distress she might have thought the awful Julie had cut them off.

"I am extremely sorry to hear of your predicament, Mrs McLeod," he said as Fiona finished her story. "We shall of course be only too happy to handle your divorce, although I myself am not a specialist in that field so I shall hand you over to Reginald Cruickshank, our man in matrimonial malfunction." He laughed at his own words as no doubt he had done a hundred times over the years, and Fiona tittered dutifully whilst privately considering her plight to be no laughing matter. "Unfortunately he is out of the office today," Henry Napper continued ('playing golf no doubt' thought Fiona) "but I'll transfer you to his secretary so that you can arrange an appointment to see him. In the meantime I suggest you have no contact with your husband at all unless absolutely necessary, in which case say no more than that the matter is in the hands of your lawyers."

Fiona thanked him and a click and a buzz later an appointment had been made for her with the said Reginald for Thursday afternoon.

Things were moving and a new sense of identity filled her as she realised it was the first time she had actually been the prime mover in a grown-up affair; no more Hamish to dominate the little woman and surprisingly no wracked nerves either. She decided to ignore Henry Napper's advice and telephone Hamish to inform him of her progress – that would let him know which way the wind was blowing.

"There we are Mrs Mac, all done and dusted," Mrs Pinker arrived in the kitchen. "Just time for a quick cuppa then I'd best be on me way – there's Pinker's dinner to see to and the Lord knows what else but 'e won't split – one for you dearie?"

"No thanks Mrs P, I'm OK but you carry on. I must try and contact the children today but I can never remember the time difference in Singapore and Namibia – I think it says somewhere in the phone book now I come to think of it."

"Hmm, that'll be a nasty one right enough. Fancy 'aving to tell your kids their Dad's run off with a floozie. Our Eric and Pearl would 'ave 'ad something to say about that I can tell you – knocked the old sod's block off I wouldn't wonder."

"Miss Crutchley is not exactly a floozie and I'm sure Roddy and Grania will be very upset to hear about what's happened though I doubt they will be catching the first available flight back to assault their father," Fiona replied, laughing.

But Mrs Pinker was not to be denied her moment of glory. "Any woman what pinches another woman's 'usband 's a floosie. You mark my words Mrs Mac, no good will come of it."

"We shall have to wait and see, Mrs P. I don't want Mr Hamish back you know, and I'm angry, and hurt I suppose by what's happened, but I don't wish him any harm. Life is going to be very strange until I've adjusted, but right now I just want to get through this difficult time and start again."

"Poor dearie!" Mrs Pinker reached over the table and gave Fiona's hand a little pat. "You keep your pecker up now and I'll be 'ere next week, but if you get in a pickle you just give me a tinkle."

"Oh, you are kind, Mrs P," said Fiona, touched by the old girl's loyalty, "and I'm sure I can rely on you to spread the bad tidings and save me the job!"

"Oohh," she cackled, "that you can – you know me when it comes to a bit of gossip! Ta-ra then." She bustled out, muttering and chuckling with relish at the thought of her forthcoming gossip-spreading orgy.

Fiona was left alone to contemplate the next move, and seeing that it was now approaching 12.30, decided to put a call through to Hamish's office. Obviously she knew the number of his direct line and thus hoped to circumnavigate the ever-watchful Crutchley, who the children had nicknamed The Doberman, so fiercely did she guard her boss. It had never occurred to Fiona that this behaviour had any significance beyond the purely professional desire of a typical spinster secretary to devote herself to her lord and master in the office. She had in fact never given the woman a thought and had had very little to do with Hamish's work life beyond enquiring how his day had gone. She secretly thought that accounting must be dreadfully boring, and he clearly thought she was much too stupid to understand anything about it. The 'don't you trouble your little head, stick to the sink' attitude had left her feeling there was little point in trying to 'express interest in her husband's business' as her mother had instructed her on numerous occasions, and Fiona had been quite happy to leave it at that.

But now a knot of apprehension gathered in her stomach; supposing Hamish was out or in a meeting and The Doberman rushed into his office to answer his direct line, what on Earth could she say? She would put the phone down, that was the answer. Nevertheless, Fiona felt nervous and decided to visit the drink cupboard for a bit of Dutch courage. 'I must not make a habit of this' she thought as she poured out a small measure of sherry – but as an afterthought, she took the bottle back with her to the kitchen. Heart pounding, she dialled the number; her fears were unfounded for it was Hamish who picked up the phone.

"Hello, Hamish McLeod speaking."

"Er Hamish, it's me – Fiona."

"Ah Fiona, yes."

She was pleased to note he sounded embarrassed and took another quick swig of sherry before cutting in, determined to gain the upper hand. "I'm only ringing to tell you that I shall be using Napper Napper & Cruickshank for the divorce and I'm seeing Mr Cruickshank on Thursday afternoon. I presume you'll be using old Wilkins so you can tell him who to contact. Oh, one more thing, have you been in touch with the children?"

"No, I haven't yet. I rather thought you might have done that."

"Well, as the guilty party I consider it to be your responsibility. Never mind, I'm going to contact them both today anyway. It's ages since we spoke and I like to keep in touch as you know."

"You seem to be taking rather a high-handed view, most untypical of you, Fiona. I don't much like being referred to as the guilty party you know."

"I don't care whether you do or you don't, Hamish. You broke up our marriage and that makes you the guilty party – and as to my tone, what did you expect, that I would grovel at your feet and beg you to come back?"

"Really Fiona, I do hope you are going to be reasonable about all this – if I didn't know you so well I might think you had been drinking – Oh, and talking of drink, I think I mentioned a bottle of wine in my letter?"

"Indeed you did Hamish and I am delighted to tell you that Dodo and I enjoyed it immensely!" As the laughter bubbled up into her voice, she slammed the phone down. "Wow!" she said aloud, sitting back and puffing out her chest, "now I really am Fiona McLeod – no more Mrs. Hamish for me!" She returned the bottle to the cupboard. 'No more need for that either' she decided. Now for the children.

Fiona checked the time difference in Singapore, having remembered that Namibia was the same as England, and put a call through to Roddy. With any luck she would catch him at home as it would be nearly 8 o'clock in the evening and he should be between office and night life. Six rings later and he was on the line.

"Roddy, it's me – Mum."

"Hello Mum, great to hear you. How's things at home?"

"Well darling, that's what I'm ringing about – are you sitting down with a whisky?"

"Yes I am actually," Roddy sounded worried, "but what's all this about?"

"Your father – don't worry," she added quickly, "he's fine – but I'm afraid he's left me."

There was silence. "You're joking. I can't believe it – dear old Dad and you – the Rocks of Gibraltar, Grania and I used to call you."

"Did you Roddy? I never knew that."

"Seriously though Mum, I'm absolutely gob-smacked, tell me what's happened. I mean, did you have a row or something? I'm sure it's only a blip, lots of people have them you know – particularly at your time of life."

"No darling, it's not a blip. He's fallen in love with The Doberman."

"Oh no no!" Roddy hooted with laughter. "Come on Mum, it's not April Fool's Day you know – have you been out in the sun or something!"

"Roddy!" Fiona almost shouted. "Will you please listen to me, I have never been more serious in my life. *Your father has left me for Margaret Crutchley.* Now will you believe me?"

"God Mum, I don't know what to say except the old man must have gone off his rocker. I'm terribly sorry Mum – poor old you. I'll come home if you like – I've got a spare week's holiday saved up and maybe I could talk some sense into him."

"It's sweet of you darling but the truth is that I don't want him back, not after this. I hope you don't blame me in any way though I suppose it must partly be my fault for not realising he was fed up with me."

"Nonsense Mum, of course I don't blame you in any way and I don't blame you either for not wanting him back. If I ever get married and my wife is as good a wife as you've been I shall count myself lucky."

"Oh Roddy, that's the nicest thing anyone's said to me for years, and I couldn't wish for a better son. But listen darling, I'm fine, really I am. There's no need to waste your precious holiday now though it would be lovely if you could come home for a few days at Christmas – it's such ages since we've seen you. I'd better stop now as I haven't spoken to Grania and she's so difficult to get hold of. I'll keep you posted but I don't want you to fall out with your father over all this – it's just one of those unfortunate things."

"OK Mum, I can't promise but I'll try. How's everything else?"

"Just the same – Granny's coming tomorrow, Mactavish sends love and Mrs Pinker's in her element as you can imagine!"

"I'll bet!" Roddy laughed before getting serious. "But you really are OK are you, Mum?"

"Yes honestly Roddy, so don't worry. Everything going all right with you?"

"Couldn't be better – I'm having a great time and work's

good too."

"I'm so glad darling. Speak soon and lots of love."

"'Bye Mum."

Only Grania left now. Fiona was beginning to feel drained with the effort of so much talking but she was determined to off-load the unpleasant task of telling her nearest and dearest about Hamish. Hopefully her haywire daughter would have her mobile switched on and in working order. It was.

"Hi Mum," the sing-song voice was music to Fiona's ears.

"Darling, how did you know it was me?"

"Oh Mum, you are so dim – there's a thingy on the phone that tells me!"

"I need to talk, are you busy?"

"Yup but carry on, it can wait – good to hear you by the way."

Fiona went through the whole saga again, and her daughter's reaction was predictably different from that of her brother.

"Man that's c-o-o-l!"

"What on Earth do you mean, Grania? I tell you your parents' marriage has bust up and you come up with this ridiculous language you should have grown out of years ago," Fiona snapped.

"Sorry Mum – what I mean is... well I don't really know what I mean. Think I'm in shock. I can't imagine Dad – you know – doing it with The Doberman! But look on the bright side Mum, a whole new avenue of opportunity has opened up in your amazingly uneventful and boring life."

"Thank you for those words of wisdom, you sound just like your godmother."

"Look Mum, I've gotta go but give my love to everyone."

"Of course darling, and all well with you?"

"Yup, great. Be in touch soon and hang loose."

"Bye darling," but the line was already dead.

Could Grania truthfully be so insouciant about the break-up of her parent's marriage, Fiona wondered, or was her reaction her way of protecting herself from hurt and distress? She hoped and suspected it was the former, as her daughter had always been an extrovert who took life as it came, and consequently had seldom suffered from the inner turmoil and stress that could assail an introvert.

A small black cloud settled on Fiona's head as she ate a cheese sandwich and a banana before setting out on her shopping trip. She missed the children badly and wished that at least one of them would return to England permanently. Surely Grania would soon get fed up with gallivanting around the world and settle down to marriage with a nice, secure Englishman and produce some nice ordinary babies. At least Roddy's time in Singapore was due to end next year when hopefully, he would be recalled to London.

'It's no good moping' she thought, kick-starting herself into action. There was a lot to be done before her mother's arrival tomorrow and, with her lunch date in London, not much time to do it in. Besides, Dodo would want an update on the situation and that would be a lengthy call. Fiona couldn't wait to tell her about Hamish and the Petrus. The black cloud lifted by the thought, she drove off to the shops with a smile on her face.

RENAISSANCE

Dodo had been gratifyingly delighted by Fiona's update phone call, the highlight of which had been Hamish's reaction to the missing bottle. Apart from that, the evening had been uneventful and dull, and after cooking a chicken casserole ready for her mother's visit, Fiona decided on an early night. Bath, bed and book seemed to be as good a solution as any to the what to do next problem and as she settled comfortably into the middle of the bed, she breathed a sigh of relief that Hamish's plump Vyella-striped body was elsewhere and she could stretch and shift about as she pleased and enjoy the silence of a snore-free night.

Despite the improved conditions, Fiona slept badly and woke early feeling tired and grumpy. Mactavish 'miiaaowed' loudly under her bedroom window, demanding access to the comforts of a warm bed, but she was not in the mood and shouted crossly at him to find something else to do. Ignoring her words, he persisted with his demands and eventually she abandoned the unequal contest and went downstairs to let him in.

"You are a pest Mactavish," Fiona told him as he nipped in through the front door and wound himself round her legs, purring loudly as she made a cup of tea. "Now I suppose you will insist on joining me in bed," she continued, as she made her way back upstairs with the tea. The cat's agreement was expressed by his swift ascent up to the bedroom and by the time Fiona arrived he was already settled on her bed.

"Lucky for you your master isn't here," she smiled, giving his head a rub.

'Lucky for me too,' she thought as she settled back with her tea and book, amazed that she could think like that when less than four days ago her whole life had been turned upside down after 32 years of unquestioned normality which she had expected to last for ever.

The world outside suddenly started to come alive and as

the sound of speeding cars began to drown out the bird song, Fiona decided it was time to get up and select a suitable outfit for her lunch with Uncle Greg.

'Silly old thing' she thought affectionately, 'he would love me to turn up in something outrageous!'

Unfortunately for Uncle Greg, there were no outrageous clothes hanging in Fiona's small and conservative wardrobe and after disconsolately discarding every hanger as old and boring, she started again before finally deciding on a poppy print cotton dress she had owned for at least five years. There was nothing stunning about the dress but Fiona knew it suited her and was less frumpy than the alternatives.

She pottered about through the first half of the morning and was relieved when the kitchen clock showed it was time to change and leave for London. Mindful of Uncle Greg's words, she took extra care with her hair and make up, anxious not to let the old boy down, and was quite pleased with the result. 'Hmm, some hope for me yet' she thought, twirling in front of the ornate cheval mirror, a rather ugly legacy from Hamish's disapproving mother. Realising suddenly that time had passed and that she was running late for the train, Fiona grabbed a navy linen jacket and, stuffing all the essentials into a matching handbag, locked the house and rushed off to the station.

There was only one elderly woman in front of Fiona when she hurried up to the ticket office, rummaging in her bag for her purse. She heard the woman ask for a First Class ticket and as the old girl moved away towards the platform, to Fiona's astonishment she heard herself asking for the same thing. A hot wave flushed over her and she felt her cheeks redden as she handed over the money, shocked at her own extravagance. Hamish would have died.

"Um, perhaps I... I mean..." she stuttered, aware that the man was staring at her oddly.

"Make up your mind Madam," he said in a bored voice, obviously thinking she was a bit mad. "One First Class return to Waterloo if you want it. Train due in three minutes,

Platform Two, but it's running late."

'Damn it, why shouldn't I go First Class?' Fiona thought, annoyed by his attitude and the fact that the train was late after she had rushed. "Yes please, that's what I said."

He grunted something unintelligible and handed over the ticket and change.

'Gosh,' Fiona thought, as she headed off to buy a magazine, 'my first real breakout!'

The train was only a few minutes late in spite of Jonah of the ticket booth's grim prediction, and by the time Fiona had bought her magazine and arrived on Platform Two, the silhouette of its front could be seen in the distance as it made its way towards the station. As she made her own way towards a blue First Class label, Fiona peered into the carriages that she would normally have squashed herself into and her receding guilt disappeared altogether as she saw the crammed seats, complete with yelling toddlers and crisp-eating headphone-encrusted youths. She found herself a nice window seat and settled down to enjoy the journey in peace and quiet. She had just selected a supplement about country properties when the door opened and the woman who had bought a ticket in front of her came in.

"Mind if I join you?" she smiled.

"Of course not," Fiona smiled politely, whilst secretly hoping that the woman was not looking for an amateur agony aunt.

"Thank you dear," she said in a soft rural accent Fiona could not place. "You see I never like to be quite alone on public transport – you never know these days what might happen."

'Chance would be a fine thing' thought Fiona, but she nodded and smiled again before returning to the paper.

The train pulled out and silence reigned for a while, enabling Fiona to reach page four, which contained an article on the desirability of the West Country as a place to 'get away from it all and live the rural idyll for unbeatable value,' when rustling and munching proclaimed the arrival of a packet of biscuits.

"Would you care for a biscuit? I always like a little something at elevenses." A packet of digestives arrived under Fiona's nose.

"Oh, that's very kind of you but I had a late breakfast and am expecting a big lunch so I won't, thanks."

"Going somewhere nice then?"

Fiona knew defeat when she saw it and surrendered. "Yes as a matter of fact. I'm meeting my uncle at his Club. Nowadays they allow females into the dining room and the food's very good, I've been before."

"Oh that *is* nice, dear, I'm going to visit my son. He's ever so kind to his old mother and told me to buy a First Class fare and he would pay. I've been staying with my daughter, that's why I got on the train at Milford – but my home's in Devon."

"Oh really? I was just reading about property in the West Country and Devon gets a good write-up."

"Ah," the woman sighed, "and so it should. Born and bred there I was, and my parents and grand-parents before me. Lived there all my life and wouldn't have it any other way. Farmers we've been for generation after generation but my Martin won't have none of it. 'That's not the life for me, Ma' he said, and I can't say I blame him."

"Oh dear," replied Fiona, not quite sure how she was supposed to react. "It must have been a bitter blow for you and your husband after such a long family tradition."

"Yes, it was. And then the Foot and Mouth came and we lost the herd. I always say it broke Dad's heart and then he went too, not long after."

"He must have been awfully old," said Fiona, getting confused.

"Oh bless you no!" the old girl laughed, "Dad was my husband but well, I always called him Dad you see. Silly really but there it was."

"Oh, I'm terribly sorry – how silly of me," Fiona kicked herself and hoped her gaff had not upset the kind old Devonian. "So what's happened to your farm now?"

"Well, old Alfie, our hand and I struggled on together for a bit but we were both too old and tired and the children wanted their share, so I sold all the land except for two acres round the house, just so's I could keep a few ewes and my fowl, and there I am."

"At least you didn't have to sell the house too."

"Oh no, I shall never sell Middlecot. I was born there and I shall die there. When I'm gone, the children will do as they please and maybe without the land to worry about, one day Martin might go back there."

"You never know," smiled Fiona encouragingly, "back to his roots and all that. I must say, Devon does sound lovely but then I suppose it would do in the newspapers. I imagine these sort of articles are really sales pitches for house agents."

"Yes, they would be," her companion agreed. "But the trouble is the incomers don't always understand our ways and they push up the house prices so that our young people can't afford to buy even a tiny cottage. It's what they call progress but most of us old timers would just as soon Devon stayed the way she's always been."

"I'm afraid that seldom happens though," replied Fiona. "Surrey was once a lovely county but now it's too full of people because of being accessible to London and eventually the population will have to spread out west – there's nowhere else for it to go."

"I suppose so, but I expect I shall be long gone before that happens and I hope so too."

"Oh look," said Fiona, "we're nearly there. Goodness, the journey went quickly!"

"It has been nice to have your company and we don't even know each other's names. I'm Mary Poole."

"Fiona McLeod – and good luck with everything."

"And you." Mary smiled and pulled her case off the rack with surprising ease, born no doubt of a lifetime of sack-hefting around the farm, as the train pulled in to the station.

Fiona left her paper on the seat and was on her way to the

door when something made her go back for the supplement. She folded it into her handbag before making her way onto the platform and out into the hot, bustling London air and the queue at the taxi rank. Lunch with Uncle Greg beckoned, and Fiona looked forward to it with genuine enthusiasm.

***

Uncle Greg was waiting to meet Fiona in the hall of his Club and after kissing her fondly, suggested they have a drink before going into lunch. He was looking his customary debonair self, dressed in a sharply-tailored chalk-striped suit, pale yellow shirt and bright yellow-and-grey checked tie. He smelt mildly of expensive male hair tonic and Fiona guessed correctly that he had visited his barber that morning. An ageing Lothario with a kind heart, Fiona hoped that Uncle Greg would never have to suffer the indignity of a decrepit and infirm old age for she knew how much he would hate it.

"Usual for me and a Tio Pepe for my niece please, Tom." He ordered their drinks from the waiter, who gave Fiona a curious glance.

"I don't think he believes I'm your niece," said Fiona, smiling.

"Hope not! Like the boys to think I can still pull a young 'un, and I may say my dear, you look most charming today."

"Thank you Uncle Greg. I didn't want to let you down in front of your cronies." She enjoyed pulling his leg.

"That's the spirit – what a lucky chap I am to have a charming niece like you. Luck of the draw you know, you could have been quite ghastly! Cigarette?" he asked, whipping a gold case out of his pocket and offering her a Sobranie Black Russian.

"You know I don't smoke, Uncle Greg!"

"Good girl, filthy habit but can't give up all life's little pleasures you know. Damn difficult to smoke anywhere these days but at least this place sticks to the old traditions – won't be long before they ban it everywhere though." He lit up with pleasure before taking a long pull at his double gin and tonic.

"So what's the news in your life since we last spoke?"

asked Fiona, shifting slightly to avoid a cloud of tobacco smoke.

"Rather exciting actually," enthused Uncle Greg, swallowing another large mouthful of gin. "I've bought a share in a racehorse."

"Good heavens!" exclaimed Fiona, "I thought racehorses were the quickest way to ruin. Isn't there some old saying about slow horses and fast women?"

"I say, you're not turning into a prude like that dull dog of a husband of yours I hope," blustered Uncle Greg, failing to answer her question. "Anyway, I've got both – a fast horse and a deliciously fast woman. Actually, I only own a tiny part of several hooves, if that. Time I had a new interest for my old age though – frightfully important you know – and I've always fancied a little flutter on the nags. Diana's a bit shabby about it all but a couple of days at Glorious Goodwood and a new hat perked the old thing up a bit."

"Sounds great Uncle Greg, but how does it work?"

"Simple, I've joined a syndicate called Multiple Matriarchs. About fifty of us involved so we're not talking big bucks, but we get all the benefits of ownership and terrific involvement. You must look out for our runners in the paper."

"I shall, and perhaps you could give me a tip when they're going to win," replied Fiona, a hint of irony in her tone. "But what a queer name for a syndicate," she continued, "I know nothing about horses, but what does it mean?"

"Ah well, here's the clever bit. Fillies are usually cheaper to buy than colts, but if they do well, their stud value increases and the syndicate policy is to sell the horses at the end of their careers, hopefully for a profit, and then reinvest in more yearlings. We've several two-year-olds in training and a couple of three-year-olds to go hurdling, and guess what – one little beauty is entered for next year's One Thousand Guineas, and if she gets black type in her pedigree she'll be worth a fortune!"

Uncle Gregory nearly choked with excitement, but as

Fiona had no idea what he was talking about she was rather relieved when Tom appeared to summon them to their table in the dining room.

Fiona loved the splendid dining room with its atmosphere of outdated opulence and masculine mahogany pomposity. Peppery old dignitaries from past times glared down out of their massive rococo frames, vying for space on the dark panelled walls with fearsome chargers and dead pheasants. An extensive array of cutlery dominated the tables, nicely topped up with heavily starched white damask napkins and a daunting number of sparkling glasses.

Uncle Greg led the way to their table – which was pretty obvious as it was the only one that remained vacant. The hum of conversation quietened momentarily as they made their way across the room and several old buffers nodded and greeted him as they passed by.

"My niece you know," he muttered, and to Fiona's amusement she noticed the winks and smiles that passed between the old boys. 'Let him have his bit of fun' thought Fiona as she smiled her most dazzling smile, making the most of one of her better features, a row of even white teeth.

A white-coated waiter pulled out her chair and as she sat down, Fiona noticed a bottle of Premier Cru Chablis ready and waiting in its ice bucket. Choosing from the menu was never a problem as Uncle Greg always ate the same thing and Fiona was happy to go along with his habitual selection of prawn cocktail, Dover sole and apple pie, topped up with a piece of Stilton to accompany a glass of 15 year-old Tawny Port. The waiter hovered expectantly, ready for Uncle Greg to taste the Chablis.

"Pour it out Walter, pour it out. Can't be bothered with all that fuss and falderal. Never had a corked bottle yet and I'll soon tell you if I do!"

"I thought you might say that, Sir," grinned Walter, as swiftly and with style he poured the wine.

"Ahh, that's better," sighed Uncle Greg contentedly, settling back in his chair. "Here's to you m'dear." They clinked glasses. "Now tell me what's to do in this life of yours; having any trouble with that bugger of a husband?"

"Not really I suppose, but then it's early days. I mean, nothing's happened yet though he seems to want to get on with the divorce as quickly as possible, which suits me fine. I'm going to see the solicitor on Thursday to start the ball rolling – thank you." Fiona acknowledged the arrival of her prawn cocktail.

"Hmm, bad show. Never had a divorce in the family you know."

"Never had a racehorse owner either!" Fiona countered with a smile.

"Ha-ha!" chortled her uncle, "*Touché* – but quite different thing you know – sport of kings and all that."

"That's as may be, but your precious Royal Family have more success in the divorce courts than on the turf!" Fiona laughed as she said it, knowing her uncle's staunch royalist views and unable to resist a tease.

"I say, steady old girl – have me blackballed from the Club," protested Uncle Greg as he almost choked on a prawn, "but has the fellow got any money? That's what divorce boils down to in the end, you realise; sometimes think you're rather naïve about life, Fiona, and I shouldn't like to think of my niece on the streets."

"I don't think your niece would do too well on the streets I'm afraid, even equipped with a black suspender belt and crotchless knickers!"

"How d'you know about things like that?" Uncle Greg snapped. "That husband of yours a weirdo? Can't believe it, the bastard!"

"No no! Of course not," Fiona giggled at the very thought, "I may not be worldly wise, but I'm not quite as naïve as you seem to think and to try and answer your original question, I've no idea about Hamish's money as it was not a subject he ever discussed with me. I think he thought it unfitting for the female ear."

"Silly arse! Hmm, this Dover's top-hole. That old dragon

of a mother must have left some boodle – you get your solicitor chap to look into it. Don't want you done out of your rights and I know a Scotsman when I see one – lives like a church mouse and dies as rich as Croesus."

"I think most of her money was in trust for Angus, Hamish's elder brother who inherited the place in Scotland, but they never got on and Hamish never spoke about it. I'm sure he'll be fair and honourable about it all, and if push comes to shove I shall get a job. I can't imagine what though as I doubt I'm even capable of working a supermarket checkout machine."

"I should certainly hope not," Uncle Greg expostulated, "never heard of anything so ridiculous. Perhaps a couple of days a week in one of those exclusive little dress shops you females inhabit might be more the thing – I shall ask Diana, very chic filly you know." He twirled the ends of his mustachios, as if checking that they were up to scratch for the elegant and immaculate Diana.

Whisking the Dover sole bones away, Walter re-appeared bearing appetising- looking plates of apple pie and custard, and Fiona thanked her lucky stars that she had declined the offer of Mary Poole's biscuits. Uncle Greg attacked his pudding with relish but Fiona paused, spoon in hand, before making a self-staggering statement: "Actually Uncle Greg, I've decided to try a complete change of scene – I'm going to investigate living in Devon – so don't bother to ask Diana as I don't suppose there are any chic little boutiques down there."

Stunned by her own words, which seemed to come out of a mouth disconnected to her brain, Fiona popped a spoonful of pie into the offending orifice and awaited her uncle's reaction. He stared at her across the table, chomping jaws stilled in mid-mouthful; there was a momentary silence before he spoke.

"Stone the crows!" he spluttered, a small gobbet of half-chewed pastry landing on Fiona's arm, "Have you gone completely mad? The country's a ghastly place – only fit for fox hunting and fornication – not for *living* in. It's all your mother's fault – she's barmy and you've inherited it."

"Calm down, Uncle Greg," hissed Fiona, cheeks reddening as she glanced round at the neighbouring tables and noticing cheese-laden biscuits halting in mid-travel from plate to mouth. "My mother has nothing to do with my decision and doesn't even know yet, so please don't tell her and let me finish what I have to say."

"Hear hear!" shouted a clipped military voice from behind Fiona's chair. "Let the gel have her say Grego, country's a fine place y'know – least till that idiot of a PM ruins it!"

"Shut up Washy, and mind yer own business. Family affair this."

"Ah-ha!" sniggered Washy, "So she really is your niece – bad luck old chap!"

"Sorry Fiona, sorry about that. Don't take any notice of old Washy, silly arse never could mind his own business. He's got nothing to smirk about anyway – that old trout's his wife, they lunch here every Tuesday."

The arrival of the port, which Fiona declined, seemed to mollify her uncle and to her relief, their conversation returned to as near normal as any conversation with Uncle Greg could be.

"Now tell me what this Devon business is all about and where you got such a crackpot idea? Nothing to do with that friend Didi is it? Lovely girl but flighty."

"Her name is *Dodo*, like the extinct and flightless bird, and no, it's nothing to do with her. In fact, I have only just thought of it myself! I was reading about Devon on the train and then this old woman came in and started on about how wonderful it was and then, when you asked me what I was going to do, this kind of thunderbolt zapped into my brain and said 'Devon'!"

"Now if that isn't the most typically illogical example of female illogicality, then I'm the Queen of Sheba," guffawed Uncle Greg, relief spreading over his face. "Thought you were serious for a minute. Shouldn't have been quite so stiff with poor old Washy – bit of a joke eh?"

"Well no actually, Uncle Greg." Fiona watched his expression change as he beckoned to Walter to refill his port glass. "I am serious, but my plan is to rent somewhere for six months and see how I like it. As fox hunting and that other thing you mentioned are not top of my list, no doubt I shall soon come running back to my suburban homeland."

"Should think so too – your mother won't like it y'know – losing her only child."

"For goodness' sake Uncle Greg, I'm not going to Outer Mongolia. I believe Devon has moved on from horse transport and carrier pigeons, you know. In fact I intend having a push button telephone and rather hoped my family might enjoy coming to stay – there is a railway line and a thing called the M5!" she finished tartly. If this was her uncle's reaction, Fiona shuddered to think what her mother would say when she told her of her plans that evening.

Uncle Greg put down his precious glass of port and reached out his hand to clasp Fiona's wrist. He gave it a little squeeze and leant forward towards her, the expression in his brown eyes for once serious and concerned. "My darling girl," he said, still holding the trapped wrist, "I'm just a silly old fool who will miss having my cherished niece within lunching distance, but if your mind is made up, then to Devon you must go – and with my blessing."

"Oh Uncle Greg," Fiona relented, "I'm sorry I snapped and of course I shall miss our impromptu lunches but Devon really isn't that far away and who knows, there might even be a racecourse or two nearby."

"I say, that's a thought!" The mustachios twitched again in anticipation as Uncle Greg's hand relinquished Fiona's wrist and moved back to the port glass. Drained once more, he pushed it aside and what Fiona called his 'pronouncement mien' came over his face. She waited expectantly.

"Matter of fact, been giving er... the old status quo a bit of thought. Don't like to think of my niece pinching the pennies – nasty cheap little frocks – that sort of thing, so propose to make you a little allowance. Not much – pin money really." He blew his cheeks out with relief that his speech was over.

"Oh Uncle Greg!" Fiona gasped in amazement, "How very sweet of you to think of it and how kind. But honestly, I'm sure I shall be OK under my own steam."

"No no – no. Mind's made up, no point leaving the pot for the Chancellor's greasy paws and I don't want you arriving in the Club looking like a drab – that wouldn't do at all. Not a word to that rat of a husband of yours though, I shall hold on till the legal eagles have had their way then fix a monthly direct debit to your account."

Never a touchy-feely type, Fiona was surprised to find herself reaching out for her Uncle's well-manicured, age-spotted hand which rested on the table. Giving it a bashful little pat, she smiled into his dear crinkly face. "That's so kind of you Uncle Greg, I really can't thank you enough. Just wait and see how stunning I look for my first lunch date with you when I come up to town. Pity we've let the cat out of the bag with your friend Washy!"

"Don't you worry about old Washy, my dear. So senile he's probably forgotten you really are my niece already!" He laughed loudly, winking and rubbing the side of his nose.

Then shooting back his left cuff, he glanced at his watch and banged both hands down on the edge of the table. "Ought to go I fear – rendezvous with Diana later. Need to have a bit of a foots-up you know – plenty of zest left but the old stamina's not quite what it was."

"Me too. Don't forget Mummy's arriving this evening to sort out my life, and I 'd like to get an early train before the rush hour starts."

"Hmm yes – well give the old mater a suitably fraternal greeting and don't stand any nonsense."

Fiona stood up, rescuing her dropped table napkin on the way. "Don't worry, I won't – and thanks a million for everything."

"My pleasure Fi, as always, and keep the old man

posted."

They were the last to leave the dining room, and having thanked the ever-patient Walter, who was clearly relieved to see them go, niece and uncle kissed goodbye on the steps of the Club and went their separate ways.

＊

Fiona hurried back to Waterloo and as luck would have it, arrived in the nick of time to catch a train back home. To her relief, the carriage was empty and with no Mary Poole to disturb her, she was able to scrutinise undisturbed the supplement on Devon, most of which contained adverts for properties for sale or rent. Why had she ever told Uncle Greg that she was going to live there? She had absolutely no inkling. The idea really had been a sort of thunderbolt but now, the more Fiona thought about it, the more she liked it. A complete change was what she needed, and the realisation hit her that she desperately wanted the chance to escape from the confines of what now seemed a futile existence. She had never questioned the narrow pattern of her life, yet suddenly the urge to break out was strong, and she identified at last the little worm that had been gnawing quietly away in her guts since the children had ceased to be dependent on her, and the essence of her life had disappeared.

The train rattled and clattered its way back to Surrey with such speed that she had only earmarked three possible letting agents by the time it drew into the familiar station. The falling drizzle was light and warm and did nothing to dampen Fiona's excitement as she swung the car out of the station car park and put her foot on the accelerator. *Dancing Queen* thumped out of the car stereo as she sped along, windows wide open, hair blowing in the damp breeze. *'Young and sweet only seventeen'* she sang at the top of her voice, zipping past a 30-mph speed limit sign. 'I really do feel 17 – if only Hamish could see me now!' she thought, laughing aloud at the thought.

The lurking police car, anxious to up its tally of convictions, was soon on her tail and the dreaded flashing light and whining siren bought Fiona back down to earth with a nasty thump as she remembered the Chablis at lunch.

"Oh noo!" She turned off the tape and pulled dutifully to a halt as the car cut in in front of her, nearly removing the off-side bumper, and two men in blue jumped out. Trying quickly, and failing, to think up what she ought to say, she smiled weakly at the round red face that presented itself at the open window.

"Do you realise Madam, that you have just entered a 30-mile an hour speed limit travelling at 41 miles per hour?"

"I'm terribly sorry officer, I really am." Fiona jumped out of the car, having read somewhere that it was a good thing to do.

"That is not a satisfactory explanation for your reckless speed in a built-up area."

Sweat broke out on the back of Fiona's neck as she anticipated his next question. "Have you been drinking?"

"Oh no!" she lied, sounding shocked and crossing her fingers behind her back as she watched the big chief's young side-kick keenly fingering the breathalyser bag. For once perhaps, her age might be an advantage. Looking PC Important appealingly in the eye, she tried to squeeze out a tear, but failing, did the best she could. "I've never had a conviction before, you can check my record. And I know this sounds bizarre but my husband's just left me for another woman and well, I'm just so devastated I suppose I momentarily lost control of my senses. I can only reiterate how sorry I am and assure you it won't happen again."

"Hmm, I see." He shuffled uncomfortably, scratching the back of his neck while pondering the next move. Fiona bit her lip in genuine anguish and thanked God that he was not some young smart-arse or worse still, a bossy female, and felt she stood a small chance of reprieve.

"Well Madam," at last he pronounced judgement, "given the circumstances and no harm done, I think we shall go on our way, but let this be a warning to you that future misdemeanours will not be tolerated."

"Oh thank you, Officer," Fiona could have hugged him, and noticed with glee the irritation on the face of hovering breathalyser-bag-man.

"And if I may say so Madam, your husband must be a very foolish gentleman."

Fiona practically fell into the car with relief and vowing to be more careful in future, waited for the police car to pull away before continuing her journey at a careful 29 miles an hour.

***

Mactavish was waiting to greet her as usual, and a glance at the kitchen clock showed there was barely an hour to go before her mother was due to arrive. The sky was clearing and a fine evening promised so she wiped the garden furniture and put cushions on the chairs, noticing as she did so that the lawn looked rather shaggy, having missed its traditional Saturday morning mow by Hamish.

'Too bad' she thought, rushing in to grab a cup of tea and prepare the vegetables for supper. A sudden idea popped into her head and she abandoned the potato peeler and reached for the telephone. "Dodo – hi, it's me."

"Hi me, how's things?"

"OK, but look, bit last minute but can you come over for supper this evening? Mummy's coming and I might need some moral support. In fact I've got something rather important to tell you too."

"Let me guess – Hamish and La Crutch have shagged themselves to death? And yes, I'd love to come tho' I doubt your mother will be too thrilled!"

"Great!" Fiona ignored Dodo's comments, "Come in time for a private yak, Mummy always baths around seven o'clock."

"I'll be there."

"See you later. 'Bye."

Feeling a lot better, Fiona returned to her domestic tasks, just finishing in the nick of time as she heard the scrunch of tyres on gravel and the double toot of the horn with which her mother always announced her arrival. The car door slammed and the tap-tap of her mother's heels sounded on the paving outside the front door.

"I'm heeaar!" shrilled Angela Bateson – who never used the back door.

"How lovely to see you, Mummy!" Fiona shot through to the hall and kissed her mother in greeting as she crossed the threshold. "Would you like to get your things in now or after a cup of tea?"

"Oooh" (pause) "I think tea now, settling in later, don't you?" (interrogative question). "But first let me look at my poor, poor abandoned daughter." Angela Bateson rattled on, holding Fiona at arms length and scrutinising her, head on one side, as if expecting her only child to have undergone some strange metamorphosis and turned into an unrecognisable apparition. Fiona held her tongue and awaited the maternal verdict.

"Well dear, I'm sure I am most surprised," she seemed almost annoyed, "I have seldom seen you look better and even quite pretty!"

"Sorry to disappoint you Mummy, but actually I feel absolutely fine and I've had lunch today with Uncle Greg in London so I made a bit of an effort – he likes that sort of thing. Shall we go and have tea?"

"Oh!" The inflexion in her voice indicated disapproval. "And how is my irresponsible brother?"

"As gorgeous as ever as far as I am concerned and he sent his love. We had a slap-up lunch in his club and he's got a new lady friend called Diana." Fiona felt it prudent not to mention Multiple Matriarchs.

"He really is incorrigible," sniffed her mother, "I cannot imagine how we can possibly share the same genes."

"Come on Mummy," laughed Fiona, "let's go and have tea. Maybe Granny did a naughty with the milkman!"

"Gracious Fiona, what a thing to say, I'm sure I don't know what's come over you – you don't seem yourself at all."

"Maybe I've become a middle-aged free spirit." Fiona

laughed as she plopped a couple of tea bags into the pot and unearthed a 'reduced for quick sale' slab of ginger cake from the cupboard. "Shall we sit outside? It's lovely now and I've got the cushions out."

"Yes dear, that would be nice and then we can have a good old chat. Naturally I have been very worried about you, I mean I am your Mother after all and it's not everyday that one's daughter rings up and announces that her husband has walked out after 32 years of marriage. I even stopped and bought a box of extra soft Kleenex tissues," she finished plaintively.

"Grab the cake could you and I'll bring the tray." Ignoring her mother's last statement, Fiona headed resolutely towards the patio, followed by her cake-bearing mother, and finally settled down to tea.

Angie Bateson took a sip of tea and toyed with a small crumb of ginger cake as she contemplated the garden. "The lawn could do with a cut," she remarked.

"I know, but that was one of Hamish's weekend jobs. No doubt old Pinker might bestir himself and show me how to work the mower, I'm sure it can't be very difficult."

"Oh my dear," Fiona's mother intoned, "men do have their uses you know, and I'm afraid you may live to regret your cavalier attitude towards Hamish's departure."

"Mummy, I would rather live in a hay field than have him back so don't let's waste talk-time on that. I'm off to see the solicitor on Thursday and that's the end of it."

"Well Fiona," her mother tossed her expensively styled short grey curls, "as long as you know what you are doing, that's up to you. I've had a teeny-weeny little idea though, that perhaps you might like to come home – your old room is looking v-e-r-r-y pretty now I've had it redecorated." Her bright blue eyes sparkled with hope at the thought, making Fiona feel the rat of the year, but she knew prevarication would only lead to more disappointment.

"It's a very kind thought Mummy, and I do appreciate it, I really do but I don't think it would be for the best – anyway, at the moment," she added, to try and soften the blow, "you are far too busy and independent to want a middle-aged daughter under your feet, and I feel I need some time to myself to try and decide how I really want to spend the rest of my life."

"Well dear, it was just a thought – it would have been lovely for me but I do understand. We might have rather cramped each other's styles." To Fiona's relief, her mother summoned up a tinkly little laugh and the subject was dropped. "Oh look, here comes Mactavish! Coming to greet Granny are we?" Fiona's mother smiled at the old cat and stroked his fat orange back. "Time to get unpacked I think," she said, returning to her usual brisk, bright self.

"I'll get your case in and anything else that needs to go upstairs," Fiona offered.

"Just the case thank you, I'm perfectly capable of carrying the rest, not dead yet you know," she answered crisply and set off towards the car.

Angie Bateson seldom travelled light and her paraphernalia filled a large portion of the spare bedroom floor. "I see Mrs. Pinker's been missing the cobwebs again," she commented, putting her smart leather beauty box down on the dressing table.

Fiona laughed and defended her loyal cleaner. "She's getting on, the poor old thing, and I expect her eyesight's not what it was. I think she was quite pleased in a funny sort of way, when I told her the news because now she can retire. I shall make Hamish give her a decent golden handshake – she's been with us since the children were tiny."

"I know dear, and good cleaners are i-m-p-o-s-s-i-b-l-e to find nowadays." Angie Bateson raised her eyes to heaven at the thought and began energetically to unpack her belongings.

Fiona hovered by the door, watching her mother and wondering at the older generation's obsession with order. She never bothered to unpack for two nights. Hamish liked order too, even at his age, and she wondered what on Earth he would be like when he grew old. Thank God that would not be her problem.

"It's great to have you Mummy – I do appreciate your making the time to come, you know."

"Of course I wanted to come," she flung a lacy negligee onto the bed, "if I can't miss a rubber of bridge and a hairdo for my daughter it would be a poor state of affairs. I must be off early on Thursday morning though as I'm playing in the Evergreen Ladies' foursome with Betty Anstruther and we're hoping to win the Sackwell Salver for the over 75's. Of course all my friends at the Golf Club were horrified to hear about Hamish, as you can imagine." She clattered the coat hangers in the wardrobe.

"Sorry about that – I'm glad to hear the golf's going well – let me know how you get on. Oh and by the way, Dodo's coming over for supper – hope you don't mind but we shall have tomorrow night alone together." Fiona added quickly, anticipating her mother's disapproval.

"Not at all Fiona dear, not at all. Even though I don't entirely approve of your friend Dorothy, at least she is never dull and I can't abide dull people as you know."

"I'll be off then and fiddle about in the kitchen for a bit." Fiona left her mother to it, thankful that at least the first hurdle had been jumped without undue fuss. The Devon announcement might yet prove to be Becher's Brook.

***

Dodo breezed into the kitchen as Fiona was mashing the potatoes. Her long, slim legs were encased in a pair of faded designer jeans, topped by a fabulous Christian Lacroix jacket over a skin-tight white T-shirt, a rope of gold chain masking the incipient creases on her neck. Her blonde hair gleamed and bounced and her artfully made-up face belied her age without appearing to have come out of a tube.

"Hi Fi!" Dodo rhymed the two words like the musical equipment, an old joke from school days. "Your local representative of HOMM has arrived."

"What on Earth is HOMM?" asked Fiona, laughing,

forgetting instantly how dowdy Dodo made her feel.

"Help Overcome Mad Mothers – fancy not knowing! How is the MM by the way?"

"Amazingly OK actually. A bit dodgy to start with as she obviously expected me to be prostrate with grief and constantly blubbing – she even bought a box of tissues, can you believe it! But she's taking it all on the chin and even admitted that she found Hamish rather dull."

"Your Ma's a good egg you know – spirited old bird and never boring, I'll say that for her."

"Funny you should say that – it's exactly what she said about you."

"Good God, I thought she disapproved of me – any chance of a drink, by the way?"

"Yes she does and yes, there's a bottle in the fridge so help yourself and me while you're at it. She'll be down in a minute for a chat before disappearing up again to bath and change for dinner, ready for her first G&T. Then I must talk to you." Fiona hissed quickly as she heard her mother's approaching footsteps.

"Hello Mrs B," Dodo greeted her, putting down the bottle and stepping forward. "How nice to see you."

"My dear Dorothy, come to support my poor abandoned little girl," came the dramatic reply, a peck landing in the air somewhere in the region of Dodo's right ear. "Drinking already I see, not the garden path you should be leading Fiona up at a time like this." She sniffed disapprovingly, neat nose raised in the air.

Dodo turned away and drawing the cork with consummate skill, produced a satisfying 'pop' before filling the two glasses Fiona had put ready. "I think, Mrs B," she said firmly, "that a little letting down of the hair is exactly what your daughter needs at the moment, and I don't think you need worry about the garden path as I can assure you, she is most unlikely ever to arrive at the end – or trip over the nasturtiums on the way."

Fiona suppressed a giggle and dropped a large lump of

mashed potato on the kitchen floor as she reached out for her glass of wine. Luckily Mactavish chose that moment to join the party and swiftly demolished the offending blob, wiping his face with a paw before stalking out of the room.

"Don't worry Mummy," Fiona pulled her face straight, "I'm not about to become a wino and *please* don't call her Dorothy – you know she hates it."

"I tell you what Mrs B," Dodo chipped in, "as we are now all grown ups, let's have a pact. I'll call you Angie and you call me Dodo. How about that?"

There was a moment's silence as the three players in the tableau froze, awaiting the verdict. Mrs Bateson sat down at the kitchen table, nostrils pinched from in-drawn breath – decision made.

"A very good idea," she said at last, "I can't think why I didn't suggest it before."

Dodo was about to point out that the suggestion had been hers, but catching Fiona's pointed look, kept quiet.

"The water should be nice and hot by now Mummy, if you want to have a bath," said Fiona hopefully, finishing the supper preparations and the attendant clearing up. "Just the table to lay then we can all relax – everything's ready."

"I do hope, Fiona dear, we are not having too heavy a meal," said her mother, showing no sign of moving towards the bath, "my digestion is a little delicate you know and I shouldn't like it upset."

"That's the first I've heard of it," answered Fiona ungraciously, slapping the cutlery on the table, "you usually eat like a horse! Don't worry, it's only chicken casserole followed by apricot souffle and minced mouse on toast!"

"I can see you've become rather silly since Hamish left. Still, I suppose living with him all those years must have been rather repressive." She sighed on her daughter's behalf before continuing. "And as to my digestion, old people eat less you know, and prefer a light meal in the evening."

"I shall only give you a small portion in that case," replied Fiona, smiling, "I don't want to be kept awake all night by your groans and snores!"

Angie jumped up, laughter trilling and embraced Fiona. "Give your old mother a kiss – I'm off to my bath and don't forget I like two lumps of ice and no lemon."

"Quick Dodo, grab the bottle and let's sit outside – I've *got* to talk to you before Mummy reappears." Fiona set off towards the garden.

"God Fi, your mother is priceless!" exclaimed Dodo, obeying orders and following Fiona out into the warm August evening. "What's the big drama anyway?" she asked, lighting a cigarette as they sat down together at the round teak table, a 50th birthday present from the children to their mother.

"I'm going to live in Devon," announced Fiona without preamble, downing a large swig of wine.

"Fi!" Dodo practically screamed. "I don't believe you – you can't leave me – I shall never see you again!" She clutched her head in horror at the thought, dropping her cigarette onto the stone patio in the process.

"Dodo *please*," Fiona hissed, "keep your voice down and listen to me – I want your back-up when I tell Mummy and you're sounding just like her!"

"Well what do you expect? My oldest and best friend tells me she is buggering off to God knows where and I'm supposed to dance with joy and say 'jolly good show' – get real!"

"*Will you listen!* I'm going to rent somewhere for six months because I need a complete change of scene and a chance to sort out my life. I've been having a problem with what I call 'the point of it all' since before Hamish left, actually. With the children grown and gone, what am I doing? I never achieve anything worthwhile – basically I just get up in the morning, fiddle around running a small house and one cat, do a bit of this and a bit of that and go to bed at night. There's something in me that wants to get out before I die but I don't know what it is and I feel it's now or never, a sort of watershed I suppose. It's different for you, you've got your work, you're creating something."

"I can understand that, but why Devon, why not try a mental renaissance in good old Surrey? Anyway, what *is* this great fulfilment that is suddenly going to spring into your life – I mean have you had a mind-blowing epiphany or something?"

"Yes – no – I don't know and I can't explain but I just know staying here wouldn't work – I'll never get out of my rut, and as I told Uncle Greg at lunch today, Devon isn't Outer Mongolia. You'll come down and stay of course," Fiona continued desperately, beginning to get serious cold feet herself. "Think of all the new inspiration you could get for your sculptures, birds and animals and ancient rustic faces and that sort of thing."

"Oh Fi!" laughed Dodo, "You're as batty as your mother – have you never noticed that Surrey is full of birds and animals? But..." she paused, "drop the ancient bit and think about rustic faces and then you might be talking business. Hard riding bucolic squires, breeches bursting with lust tally-ho'ing across hill and dale, wow!" She gave a mock shiver of excitement.

"So my plan has your approval does it?" asked Fiona, smiling but serious too.

"No, certainly not. I shall never approve of you deserting me but I will support you because it's what you've decided to do. Anyway, you'll be back after six months, bet you anything you like, and besides, I shall enjoy coming to stay and saying 'I told you so' when you fall weeping with misery into my arms!"

"We shall see about that," Fiona retorted. "Look out, Mummy's coming – I'm going to get an extra strong gin – you will back me up, won't you?"

"'Course I will – and bring some crisps or nibbles while you're at it."

Fiona returned to find the two chatting amiably about the wonderful weather and the joys of an English summer garden. Her mother looked immaculate in ivory trousers, primrose silk shirt and a discreet quantity of gold. Not a hair was out of place and she smelt faintly of Floris.

"Thank you dear, that does look good," Angie acknowledged receipt of her drink, ice cubes cracking and sparkling in the fizzing tonic. She took a sip. "Goodness me, have a little tonic with your gin!"

Dodo winked at Fiona as they watched Angie digest the strength of the drink.

"It'll do you good Angie – put some strength into your legs."

"There's nothing wrong with my legs thank you very much, Doro... Dodo. It's just a little stronger than I'm used to, that's all. Now, you two girls, what have you been chattering about so busily?"

"Well actually Mummy, I was just telling Dodo about my plans."

"Oh! I didn't know you had any yet – I mean it's early days." Angie jerked her head back and forward, reminding Fiona of a vexed hen.

A small flock of house sparrows twittered and chirped above them as Fiona crossed her fingers and plunged in. "I've decided to rent a cottage in the country for six months. I think a complete change of scene would do me good and help me sort life out a bit."

"Gracious me, what an extraordinary idea! Still, I suppose a nice little place in West Sussex might be quite fun and not too far away."

"No Mummy, I've chosen Devon."

"*Devon*!" The squeal of disbelief drowned out the sparrows and frightened Mactavish, who was happily squashing a clump of Nepita in the flower bed. Dodo choked on a swallow of wine and spluttered with laughter at the expression of horror on Angie's face as she stared at her daughter as if she had gone completely round the bend. "If this is a cruel joke, then I am not amused." She announced, sipping frantically at the fast-diminishing gin and tonic.

"Mummy, you know I'm not the joking type – I'm

absolutely serious."

"But Fiona, apart from abandoning your poor ageing mother without so much as a thought, think how *ghastly* it will be. All those *dreadful* yokels with red faces sucking bits of straw and the mud and the smell and the you-know-what that cows do – oh my God, get me another drink, I think I'm going to faint!"

Dodo and Fiona could contain themselves no longer and collapsed with shrieks of laughter as Angie slumped back in her chair, fanning her face with an imaginary fan.

"Sorry Angie," said Dodo, pulling her face straight and lighting a cigarette, "I was a little shocked too to begin with when Fi told me but having thought about it, I think it's not such a bad idea. After all," she finished, her tone placatory, "it's only for six months and it will be fun to visit and I'm sure there are lots of golf courses in Devon."

"I can just imagine what they would be like," shuddered Angie. "Ploughed fields for fairways and sheep grazing the greens – no thank you. And I wish you wouldn't smoke Dorothy, it's a revolting habit."

Luckily at that moment Fiona reappeared with her mother's drink and took charge of the proceedings, nipping in the bud the row brewing between the two of them.

"Here you are Mummy, rather weaker this time." Fiona put the glass firmly on the table, giving her mother's shoulder an awkward little pat before sitting down. "Now will you please listen to me for a moment. I know my decision has come as a shock and I'm sorry its upset you but it's my life and it's what I want to do. Devon is not that far away, neither is it full of ridiculous people going round with straw in their mouths. And if you read your newspaper properly, you would realise that the West Country is the IN place to go and is full of people just like me. In fact I think your yokels are now an endangered species and frankly, I'd rather have a bit of cow muck around the place than some of the things you find in our village bus shelter."

"I bet there's plenty of them around too!" Dodo rolled her

eyes in mock horror, "Lots of rumpy-pumpy in the country!"

Ignoring her unhelpful comment, Fiona turned to her friend, and kicking her on the ankle, innocently asked her opinion. "What do you think of my plan Dodo – have you ever been to Devon?"

"Um... no, I haven't," (pause) "but I've read lots about it. Like you say, it's forever in the colour supplements and sounds great. You know," she carried on eagerly, "lots of upwardly-mobile townies seeking good-lifey stress-free living; chutney bubbling on the colour co-ordinated Aga, gleaming copper pans festooned with dried hops, chubby children playing with the pet pig – gosh, it sounds absolute heaven!"

"I sense a conspiracy," pronounced Angie, twirling a chunky gold bracelet round her wrist in agitation. "You, Dodo, have no idea what you are talking about, and you Fiona..." and here she seemed momentarily lost for words, "*You* – well – what can I say?"

"If I were you Angie, I should say 'jolly good luck and can't wait to come and visit,'" said Dodo helpfully.

"What would you know about a mother's feelings?" snapped Angie, "I'm not aware of you having any daughters."

"Oh Mummy, come on," Fiona interjected, "I'm sure Grania will be thrilled. After all, it's en route for Cornwall where all the young go, you know."

"I'm not talking about Grania and anyway, it may have escaped your notice Fiona, that my grand-daughter is living in a foreign country and appears to have as little desire to be with her nearest and dearest as you do. Maternal feelings seem to be a thing of the past in this family."

"Of course, at the moment, but she'll come home sooner or later, you know that. Please try and see my point of view," Fiona was getting desperate, "perhaps if I'd sown a few wild oats when I was her age I wouldn't want to go to Devon now."

"Wild oats are a man's thing, dear." Fiona knew her mother's ironic smile well and kicked herself for giving her the opportunity to wrong-foot her, but all was not lost as she noticed that the look of dismay had passed from her mother's eyes and been replaced by one of her old wicked humour. "However," Angie continued, "my daughter is a chip of the old maternal block, and I know that if her mind is made up then God help the rest of us. Who knows," and she gave her hair a coquettish little touch, "I might fall for a delicious, straw-sucking yokel!"

"Oh Mummy!" Overwhelmed with relief, Fiona jumped up and embraced her. "I knew you would understand, and when I've found somewhere you shall be the first to see it."

"I've got an idea," chipped in Dodo, "let's all spend Christmas with you and really go to town on the old tradition bit – you know, ye olde yule log and tongue sandwiches under the mistletoe!"

"Really Dodo!" Angie spoke as if to a tiresome child, "Nevertheless, it does sound rather fun."

"Devon, here we come!" Dodo drained her glass.

"Let's eat," suggested Fiona,"I'm starving."

Harmony restored, they made their way into the house.

AND SO TO DEVON

The rest of the week spun by at a speed Fiona never dreamt possible, and when she awoke on Sunday morning she lay in a state of exhausted oblivion, incapable of thought or movement. The sun shone in through the half-drawn curtains and its insistent rays eventually penetrated her consciousness, forcing her back into the land of the living.

What a week it had been, and as she dragged herself out of bed, yawning and stretching, it seemed as if more had happened in those last few days than in the whole of her adult life put together. Pulling on the pile of yesterday's clothes that lay abandoned on the bedroom floor, she made her way downstairs to start another day.

Her mother had left, whirling away in a cloud of optimistic vitality, eager to slot back into her own busy life; Reginald Cruickshank had hummed, hah'd and scribbled and told Fiona he foresaw little problem with the divorce provided Hamish continued to play the game; Roddy had rung to check his mother was all right; Dodo to say she would be away teaching for a few days, and Hamish to inform her that Gribble & Parks would be contacting her on Monday to arrange a visit to measure up the house and prepare sales particulars. Mrs Pinker made the extraordinary gesture of arriving for work on Friday bearing an ancient bottle of Babycham which she considered Fiona might enjoy that evening when she commemorated, alone and bereft, the week ago departure of Hamish. Much touched by the thought, Fiona binned it as soon as the old girl left.

Thoughts of Mrs Pinker put her in mind of housework, and as she chewed on her toast and marmalade, she realised that some would have to be done before the impending visit of the estate agent; and what about the rapidly growing lawn? She would have to ring up the Pinkers and see if Mr P could be persuaded to crawl out of his chair and show her how to work the mower. The thought of it all depressed her, and she decided to abandon the problem for now and spend the day hunting through the property sections of the weekend papers to begin compiling a list of West Country agents to contact in the morning. Fiona's future seemed to her to be a much more exciting prospect than the remains of what would soon be her past. As a small sop to her conscience though, and as it was such a beautiful day, she agreed with herself that a couple of hours spent tidying up the flower beds would do her no harm.

The morning passed pleasantly enough and as she straightened up to ease her back and admire the weed-free flower bed, the telephone rang – it was Uncle Gregory.

"Been doing a spot of reconnaissance for you, my dear," he announced, coming straight to the point. "Chap at the Club knows Devon well, grew up there or something. He recommends you head for what they call mid-Devon – easy reach of Exeter and civilisation apparently."

"That's useful to know, thank you." replied Fiona. "Funnily enough I've planned to scour the papers after lunch to try and find some agents' names and numbers."

"No need Fi, no need. My wonderful Diana's got one of those computer machines – frightfully clever at all that sort of stuff you know – she's done something with a net – God knows I don't understand it! Result is a printed list of letting agents and properties to let advertised privately. Marvellous don't you think? She should have been at Bletchley Park!"

"I must say that's extremely kind of her and fantastically helpful. Will you thank her very much for me please?" Fiona, being IT illiterate herself, was genuinely impressed that someone of Diana's age had got to grips with the modern world, and she decided that a PC would be top of her shopping list when she finally got settled.

"Good show eh? Anyway, lists on their way first class so should be with you by Tuesday, then you can crack on. Oh, apparently there are a couple of racecourses near Exeter – National Hunt only – but got the *Multiple Matriarch's Newsletter* last week and it appears two of the nags failed on the Flat but will try their hands or hooves – ha, ha – over hurdles this season, so let's hope they run at Exeter or Newton Abbot! I should enjoy taking my niece to the races."

"And I shall enjoy coming." laughed Fiona, visualising her inheritance going down the drain.

"One thing though, Fi," continued her uncle in a more serious tone of voice, "Have you thought about missing your friends? I mean it's one thing to hike off into the blue yonder imagining some kind of folksy Utopian existence, but friends are friends you know."

"I have thought about it actually Uncle Greg, and I have come to the conclusion that our local friends will fade away remarkably quickly. Since Hamish left, I haven't been overwhelmed with offers of support and comfort, and the only one I bumped into in Waitrose made me feel like a social pariah."

"I say, who on Earth was that?" Uncle Greg sounded most offended.

"Oh, just someone called Jane Dartnall – a sort of dinner party friend if you know what I mean. Our children went to the same little school and I rather liked her as a matter of fact, but I got the distinct impression that bolting husbands weren't the thing at all!"

"Hmm, serve her right if hers bolted!" he snapped. "Just thought I'd mention it – wouldn't like to think of you being lonely."

"Don't worry Uncle Greg, I'm sure I shall soon make new friends when I get there. Country people are supposed to be very neighbourly, I believe."

"Let's hope so. Keep me posted."

"I will and thanks again for your help. 'Bye now."

Fiona wandered back out into the garden to finish clearing up the debris from her weeding efforts, the rattle and roar of next door's lawn mower reminding her that Pinker needed ringing sometime soon. She wondered about asking the lawn conscious neighbour for help but decided against it as they had only recently moved in and so far, the only contact had been a complaint about Mactavish's interest in their plastic goldfish pond. 'Poor Mactavish,' Fiona thought, 'what on Earth will he think of Devon?'

There was no need to bother now with the newspapers as the efficient Diana's list should arrive on Tuesday at the latest, and possibly even tomorrow if the Royal Mail chose to pull its finger out. Rather relieved, Fiona awarded herself a thoroughly lazy day; the coming week would be busy enough.

***

"Would 4.30 this afternoon suit, Mrs McLeod? I've a window in my schedule and I know your – er Mr McLeod – is anxious to expedite the sale." Peregrine Sinclair, junior executive of Gribble & Parks was on the line at 9.05 on Monday morning and obviously knew the scenario.

"Um..." Fiona hesitated, kicking herself for spending all Sunday afternoon lying around with a book and for not tidying the house. "I suppose so – will you be taking photographs?"

"We would like to, yes – get it all done in one hit. No need for you to go mad though, just not too much clutter and perhaps a few glossy magazines and some flowers dotted around, that sort of thing. Oh, and make sure the lawn is mown, it's amazing how nice straight stripes can enhance a photograph." he finished earnestly.

Fiona groaned inwardly and agreed to be ready for inspection by 4.30.

After much muttering and grumbling about his 'screwmatics', Mr Pinker agreed to come and cut the lawn, and better still Mrs P, not to be left out, said she would come with him and give Fiona a 'lift' with the cleaning whilst he was working. Considerably cheered by the news, Fiona decided the first move was to acquire a bunch or two of flowers and a pile of suitably glossy magazines to strew casually around the sitting room – maybe the odd copy of Playboy might excite some potential purchasers! A pity they didn't have a coffee table, perhaps she ought to buy one of those as well!

Fiona returned home about an hour later, armed with flowers, glossies and a litre of milk – a necessary addition to the Pinkers' essential lubricant of countless cups of tea. She was astounded at the price of the magazines and hoped they were sufficiently up-market to win the approval of the eager Peregrine.

'Clutter' removal was easily dealt with, Fiona simply dumped everything that she considered fell into that category in the boiler room. She hoped that her definition of clutter was the same as Peregrine's, and assumed that the boiler room would not feature in the brochure, as it was now nearly impossible to swing the proverbial cat in it.

Lunch consisted of a cheese and tomato sandwich, and Fiona had just put the kettle on when the slamming of car doors proclaimed the arrival of the Pinkers. Mrs P swished in, complete with overall and carton of milk.

"Just in case you'd forgot, dearie." she chirruped, pushing past Pinker and flopping into one of the kitchen chairs. "Ooh, but me legs is killing me!" she exclaimed. "Got the kettle on 'ave we?"

"Won't be long, Mrs P." Fiona replied breezily, purposefully declining to enquire about the offending legs and fervently hoping that maybe one cup for each leg would restore their vitality.

"Stanley Pinker," barked his wife, "them that lets the grass grow under their feet gets no tea, so get yourself on with Mrs Mac's mowing!"

"I'm very grateful for your help Mr Pinker," babbled Fiona, unused to their normal method of communication. "Would you like your tea now or later?"

"'E'll get on now like 'e's told an I'll fetch 'is cha when 'e's done."

Smiling weakly at the taciturn Pinker, Fiona led the way to the mower shed where, hobbling and grunting, he assured her he could manage. It occurred to her on the way back to the kitchen that the Pinkers' strange interaction denoted a deep and vital need that the one had for the other, and that the relatively polite relationship that she and Hamish had enjoyed was as chaff in the wind compared to these good people.

Tea drinking over and Mrs P's legs sufficiently restored for her engine to burst into life, she armed herself with every known cleaning aid and whirl-winded through the house, arriving back in the kitchen just as Pinker was finishing his well-earned reward. The lawn was striped to perfection and, profuse with her thanks, Fiona handed over a generous amount of cash and waved them on their way.

She had about half an hour left before the dreaded Peregrine was due to arrive, and realising that she looked rather scruffy, made her way upstairs to tidy up. Hamish had liked to see her in a skirt, preferably made of McLeod tartan. Consequently, her limited wardrobe contained several incredibly frumpy examples of his taste. Overcome by a momentary sense of remorse at the failure of their marriage, she selected one and swapped it for the pair of jeans she had been wearing. As she inspected herself in her mother-in-law's Cheval mirror, Fiona noticed properly for the first time the grey hairs flecking the mouse brown, the lines radiating out from the unremarkable grey/blue eyes fringed with short non-event lashes and, horror of horrors – a small whisker on her chin! Grabbing a pair of tweezers, she plucked it out.

'My God,' she thought. 'Dodo and Mummy are right – I have let myself go!' Middle-age required more effort than youth, but what was the point if there was no one to appreciate it?

A loud knocking on the front door jerked her out of her disconsolate reverie and, dragging a brush through her hair, she raced downstairs to answer it. Peregrine – plus photographer, a skinny bearded wonder of indeterminate age – stood on the doorstep. Peregrine was everything Fiona was sure he aspired to be: the archetypal young potential partner, complete with immaculate tweed jacket, expensive silk tie, fresh face, Hugh Grant hair and dazzling smile. Weirdy Beardy, whose name was Donald, gazed gloomily round the garden before loping off to the other end of the lawn to work his photographic magic and turn Wood End Cottage into a mini stately home.

"Peregrine Sinclair from Gribble and Parks." He extended a smooth pale hand, "Mrs McLeod I presume? I'm sorry we are a few minutes early."

"That's quite all right." Fiona shook the proffered hand. "Where would you like to start?"

"I think I'll have a look round outside and then do the house. I'm quite happy to do my own thing if you're busy; shouldn't be too long anyway."

"No, it's not very big is it?" Fiona couldn't resist a dig at his implication, hoping to fluster the composure of this urbane young man. She failed.

"Big is not always best you know, Mrs McLeod. This is a charming property and from what I have seen so far, very saleable." The white teeth dazzled again and a glossy brown lock fell forward over the smooth young brow.

"Well that's a relief," Fiona smiled. "So you don't want me to hold the end of the tape measure then?"

For a split second, he looked nonplussed. "Oh no – no thank you, we've moved on from tape measures. We use this little gadget now which does it all for you. It's called a Distolite – absolutely brilliant," he finished seriously, producing a small, grey, proboscis-tipped brick for Fiona's inspection. Clearly a sense of humour was one attribute that had fallen off the silver spoon when Peregrine was born.

Leaving him to it, Fiona went and sat in the kitchen. Suddenly her house was no longer her home, and a yearning to see her children overcame her. Dear, kind, funny Roddy, the complete antithesis of young master Peregrine, with his wispy sandy hair and rugby-broken teeth; and her beloved zany daughter, dreadlocked, irresponsible and up to heaven knew what. And why did Dodo have to be away when she badly needed her friend to talk to? A telltale prickle behind Fiona's eyes heralded the arrival of tears, but this was definitely not the moment for a wallow in self-pity. Action was the antidote, so she set course towards the sound of voices coming from the sitting room.

"I think the flowers on that table and perhaps the button-backed chair by the alcove – pity there isn't a coffee table. Any silver photo frames? – No, never mind. Just do the best you can Donald, and I'll have a look at the kitchen."

Fiona and Peregrine met in the hall.

"Ah there you are, Mrs McLeod! Just on my way to look at the kitchen and boiler room. Kitchens sell houses, you know."

Fiona's heart sank. "Would you and your photographer like a cup of tea?"

"That would be very nice. Actually I prefer coffee if possible, strong and black, and Donald only drinks water."

'God, how boring!' thought Fiona, flicking on the kettle.

"Hmm." The forelock flopped again as Peregrine's eyes roamed round the kitchen, searching eagerly for signs of granite worktops and Belfast sink with arched mixer tap. "Yes, well perhaps we could describe the kitchen as 'country cottage'."

"I'm sure you know best how to market the house, Mr Sinclair." Fiona fought to keep the irritation out of her voice as she dolloped an especially small spoonful of Nescafé into a mug. "It is and will remain as you see it today, and all I require is a reasonable amount of notice before showing people round."

"I understand, Mrs McLeod, and I can assure you that we have every reason to hope for a quick and satisfactory sale. As I said, properties of this type are much in demand at the moment."

"Good." Fiona handed the mug to Peregrine, rather pleased to notice it was chipped. "Do you think Donald is thirsty after all his efforts?"

"Oh no, I shouldn't think so – and thank you for the coffee."

Fiona muttered the usual rejoinder and silence fell as Peregrine sipped away whilst scribbling notes on a pad.

Donald appeared to announce that he had 'done snapping' and was there any chance of a glass of water? Downing the proffered liquid in one swallow, he drifted away towards the garden and to Fiona's relief, that seemed to be the end of the inspection.

Peregrine jumped up, leaving most of the coffee, and after the customary words of estate agent's parting and one last smile, he gathered Donald up and climbing into his shinier-than-new BMW, gave a little salute to the waiting Fiona and roared away.

'So, it really has begun,' she thought, 'and I had imagined ending my days here.' An acute yearning to be up and away to her new life overcame Fiona. Anything that contributed to that end became instantly attractive, and she spent the rest of the day enthusiastically attacking the years of clobber that had accumulated in the attic. A leading member of the 'it might come in useful one day' club, Fiona's inability to throw anything away had not only driven Hamish mad, but resulted in a jam-packed attic; but now a new and ruthless spirit entered her bruised soul as old magazines, moth-eaten blankets, broken badminton rackets, empty boxes and dismembered dolls hurtled through the hatch down onto the landing floor. Clearly a visit – or several – to the Council Tip would be the next move.

By 8.30, Fiona had had enough and retired to the kitchen armed with pencil and paper. Lists were the thing; making lists made you feel more positive and efficient, and gave a structure to an otherwise hollow existence. Roddy and Grania's belongings, to be boxed up and taken to her mother; her own, that she wanted to keep but not take to Devon, to be boxed up and taken to her mother. Luckily mother had plenty of space! Most of the valuable furniture belonged to Hamish, and Fiona was quite happy for him to have it provided he ensured that it would ultimately pass to the children. She was much more interested in their practical possessions and was damned if La Crutchley was going to get her hands on Fiona's Sabatier knives, Port Merion china and duck-down duvets. Tomorrow should see the arrival of Diana's list of letting agents, and with that exciting thought, Fiona and Mactavish made their way upstairs to bed.

"If only Hamish could see us now!" said Fiona as she stroked the old cat's fat back. "You on the bed, me well-oiled and the house upside down!" And with a deep sigh, she turned out the light and went straight to sleep.

***

Diana's communication arrived on cue, and Fiona dived in headfirst at one minute past nine. After a mentally exhausting morning, bolstered by endless mugs of coffee, she established that few properties were available to rent before the beginning of October because holiday lets were still good news in September, and those whose properties were eligible for both types of let naturally wanted to make the most of the available profit. There was, however, one cottage that 'had been on the books for a while and would be available at any time'. Fiona was now desperate to shake the dust of her old life from her feet – and why should she have to deal with the problems of showing people round and selling the marital home? After all, Hamish had walked out, not her. She was enthusiastic.

"I might be interested, but why has it been difficult to let?" Fiona asked, trying to sound switched-on and ask the sort of questions she knew Hamish would ask.

"Well, Mrs McLeod," the male voice on the other end paused, "you could say the property is in need of some modernisation; but it enjoys a most charming secluded situation yet is within a short distance of the nearest village which has both a shop and a primary school."

"Yes, well I'm not interested in the school but no doubt a shop could come in handy. When you say a short distance, what exactly do you mean and what is the name of the village?"

"A short distance in rural terms you must understand is not quite the same as the Home Counties, about three miles I would say; and the village itself..." (deep breath) "is called

Longbottom-in-the-Mire, but is generally referred to by the locals as Longbottom."

"I'm not surprised!" Fiona stifled a giggle. "But is it constantly under water? I don't think I should like to live in a bog."

"Oh no, not at all! The name is extremely misleading. I believe many hundreds of years ago the land was marsh but it has long since been drained and anyway, Stone Lea stands on higher ground up behind the village with beautiful views over Dartmoor."

"I would definitely like to come down and see it – perhaps Thursday or Friday – and I shall probably stay in Devon for a night or two and look at anything else suitable while I'm at it."

"Excellent Mrs McLeod, and if you let me know which day, I will make arrangements for you to view the cottage."

"I shall love it Mactavish – I know I shall!" Fiona whirled the cat round the kitchen in a dance of joy. "Who could resist Longbottom-in-the-Mire?" Dropping the protesting animal with a thump, she rushed to the phone to ring Dodo on her mobile.

Dodo would be home on Wednesday and wouldn't miss the trip to Devon for the world. Why not spend a couple of nights in a nice pub and check out the area properly while they were at it? Or they could take pot luck with a B&B. Too risky in August they decided, and Dodo said she would surf the net and fix something up.

***

Thursday couldn't come soon enough for Fiona, but the time passed quickly as she busied herself with junk clearance and a trip to the tip. She also bought an Ordnance Survey map that covered Longbottom and the surrounding area, and spent a considerable amount of time studying it and plotting the route she and Dodo would take the next day. The excitement she felt was reminiscent of long ago Christmas Eves, when as a small child, Fiona had driven her parents mad rushing about the house, searching for presents and refusing to go to sleep so as not to miss the arrival of Father Christmas. She remembered her own children doing the same thing, and wondered what they would think of their mother's plan to relocate to the middle of the Devon. She would sit down this evening and write them both a proper letter about the whole aspect of their parents' divorce as well as her own immediate future. They were both entitled to more than a couple of telephone calls.

Fiona was tired by the time she went to bed, and for once slept like a log. Refreshed and energised, she sprung up at 6.30, not bothering to wait for the alarm to go off, and packing a few things for the trip, ran downstairs to breakfast.

Anticipating a slow journey, she and Dodo had decided to leave at 8.30 to allow plenty of time to have a bite of lunch before the appointment to view Stone Lea at two o'clock. Dodo arrived as planned, and armed with maps, cassettes, gumboots and a thermos of coffee, they hit the road for Devon.

"Longbottom here we come!" Dodo sang out, giggling. "Honestly Fi, only you could unearth somewhere called that! D'you think the original inhabitants all had long droopy bottoms?"

"More likely be to do with the name of a field or something I should think, though your guess is as good as mine."

"Let's hope it's that and not a genetic failing – I do like a tight bum on a man!"

"I'm not going there to find a man and don't care how droopy their bums are but the 'in-the-Mire' bit worries me."

"Didn't your agent bloke say that was all old hat and anyway, the cottage isn't in the village, is it?"

"No, that's true, but I wonder why it's been so difficult to let."

"Perhaps it's haunted," Dodo said with relish. "Gosh, that would be fun – clanking chains and headless horsemen! D'you know how old it is?"

"Not really, no. But the man did mutter something about

a late medieval doorway, so I suppose parts of it must be quite old. I'm not really sure when medieval was – you know how useless I was at history."

"As I recall, you were pretty useless at most things except English!"

Ignoring the jibe, Fiona put her foot down to overtake a lorry and when they had settled back into the middle lane, continued the conversation. "OK brain box, when was late medieval? It sounds hideously old to me!"

"Well, strictly speaking the Renaissance marked the end of the Middle Ages, but I consider they ended in England with the arrival of the upstart Henry Tudor in 1485. I guess your old doorway is probably late 15th century or thereabouts."

"God, I hope the rest of the house is younger – he did say something about it being in need of some modernisation! Help, Dodo! D'you think there's any plumbing?"

"Didn't you ask?"

"Er no, I just assumed…"

"You are an idiot, I expect you'll have to crap in a *garderobe* but who cares – I think the whole thing's thrilling and I can't tell you how much I'm going to enjoy our little jaunt! By the way, aren't we supposed to be going on the A303?"

"Yes of course – and you are supposed to be the navigator!"

"Well we're in the wrong lane, so you'd better get over!"

The traffic was whirling and heavy but oblivious to angry flashing lights and hooting, Fiona managed to squeeze in, in the nick of time, and leave the M3 for the relative calm of the road to the West Country. The dual carriageway on the A303 was fine, but where it became single, the traffic quickly built up as the inevitable caravans made overtaking virtually impossible.

"Ooh look, there's Stonehenge!" exclaimed Dodo.

"Bit boring, I think." Fiona replied, glancing to her right as their speed dropped to 35 mph.

"Oh no, I think it's fascinating and terribly mysterious. Imagine, lugging all those bloody great stones there – they must have had a pretty good reason for doing it."

"Yes, I suppose so. Rather gloomy though; it reminds me of poor *Tess of the D'Urbervilles*."

"Hmm, I'd forgotten you're a Hardy fan – bit pessimistic for me, I like a good helping of juice and a happy ending. When d'you want to change by the way?"

"Let's get to Wincanton and try and find somewhere to stop. I wouldn't mind a cup of coffee and then we could swap – I think we've got time for a break."

Dodo studied the map for a moment before agreeing with Fiona's suggestion, and as they picked up speed with the arrival of more dual carriageway, they made good time and found a pub just off the main road that catered for their needs.

The remainder of the journey passed without incident, and as Exeter started to appear on the signs, they caught their first view of Dartmoor rising up into the distant skyline.

"Oh do stop a minute when you can – I must have a look!" Fiona had her head buried in the map for the route was becoming tortuous and the navigation difficult. Dodo pulled into a gateway and they both jumped out, eager for a leg-stretch and some fresh air.

"Gosh Fi, this is fantastic country – unbelievable!" Dodo enthused. "Hardly a house to be seen and not a car in sight and just look at Dartmoor on the horizon – I'd no idea it was so high."

"Wonderful air too." Fiona breathed in deeply. "It's not really that high though, according to the map the highest point is about 2,000 ft and it's called High Willhays – rather a nice quaint name don't you think?"

"I think the whole thing's brilliant, I may have to move down here myself!" laughed Dodo. "Tell you what though – I'm dying for a pee. D'you think it's OK to nip over the gate and avail myself of the hedge?"

"I don't see why not, I'll keep a lookout for the *Hound of the Baskervilles!*"

"Bugger the Hound, what about Farmer Giles sizing up my rump for his Sunday roast? Or a rampant bull, mistaking me for one of his harem!"

"Oh hurry up, Dodo, time's ticking away!"

Nerves were beginning to knot in Fiona's stomach as the impending property inspection drew near and the reality of her crazy idea began to hit her. It was all very well for Dodo to eulogise about the beautiful country and the lack of people and habitation, but used to her suburban life as she was, the prospect of settling in this alien environment suddenly filled Fiona with alarm. She would go through with it though, come hell or high water, for no way was she going to admit to her nearest and dearest that they had been right and she had been wrong. A filthy tractor roared past and the driver raised a hand in friendly greeting. He looked quite normal and instead of a straw in his mouth, he had a roll-up. Things were looking up!

Dodo hopped back over the gate, unmolested by human or animal, and they continued on their way.

"Tally ho!" she shouted triumphantly as, half an hour and several wrong turns later, a bent and muddy sign proclaimed Longbottom-in-the-Mire.

"Phew!" Fiona exclaimed, drawing to a halt in the tiny car park of The Black Dog Inn. "I thought we'd never find it. These roads are a nightmare – there's hardly room for a vehicle and the banks are so steep it's like being trapped in a sort of open air hose pipe! God knows what happens if you meet a huge lorry!"

"You practice reversing, I should imagine!" laughed Dodo. "Come on, I'm thirsty, let's case the joint – it looks rather dead to me. D'you think they speak English or some strange native tongue?"

"Probably come from Surrey!" Fiona snorted, trying the door, which reluctantly opened with a loud groan. The place was dark and fusty and smelt strongly of beer; it was also empty and there was no sign of life behind the bar.

"Anyone at home?" shouted Dodo, knocking impatiently on the top of the bar, and was rewarded by a voice from the depths telling her to 'Stay put and he would be right with her'.

She raised her eyebrows at Fiona who was hovering in the background, and, perching on a bar stool, lit up a cigarette. "Perhaps Mine Host is part man-part black dog – a canine centaur from the mire!"

"Shush!" whispered Fiona, joining Dodo at the bar, "He'll hear you!"

"Morning ladies, this is a welcome surprise I'm sure." The Landlord was a tiny little ageless man with red apple cheeks, bright beady eyes and strange tufts of grizzled hair that stuck up all over his head and out of his ears. He walked with a pronounced limp and his accent was definitely not Surrey. Fiona liked him on sight and could detect no sign of paws or a tail! "Don't get many strangers in these parts," he continued, smiling at Fiona and Dodo, "so what can I get you?"

"Do you have any dry white wine – preferably French?" asked Dodo. "Oh – and cold." she added as an afterthought.

"Cold dry white, yes; but French, no. You see m'dear, this is a farming community and those Frenchies not popular hereabouts."

"Why's that?" asked Fiona, ignorant of the British meat bans imposed by the French in the past.

"Trade, that's what. They don't buy our stuff, we don't buy theirs."

"Never mind," Dodo interrupted, "we'll have whatever you've got – and do you do any food?"

"I can do you a Ploughmans or sandwiches – beef, ham, cheese and tomato – lovely fresh brown bread." The landlord looked hopeful.

"That sounds great. I'd like a round of beef – Fi, what about you?"

"Um, I'll have a cheese and tomato please – and if you have any lettuce, a salad would be lovely."

"I'll enquire of the vegetable garden." He winked and

smiled before pouring out two glasses of wine and disappearing back from whence he had come.

"Life could be interesting with a local like this." Dodo giggled, downing half her glass in one gulp and wandering over towards a notice board. "Do look at all these amazing happenings! You'll be able to join the Longbottom Ladies Skittles Team; enter for the heaviest marrow and longest bean class at the Flower & Produce Show; Host a Roast in aid of the Countryside Alliance – wow, the sky's the limit!"

"Can you imagine me doing any of those things?" laughed Fiona, beginning to relax after the journey.

"I don't see why not! After all, when in Rome and all that, and if you're going to desert your only true friend and plant yourself in the middle of mud and shit land, then you might as well make the most of it!"

Before Fiona could think of a suitable riposte, the little man had reappeared to enquire about the state of their glasses and tell them that the sandwiches would be five minutes.

Dodo asked for the same again and sat down on the bar stool as he refilled her glass from a screw-topped bottle.

"On holiday then are you?" he asked, obviously wanting to talk.

"No, we've come down because my friend is looking for a cottage to rent for six months and she's found one near here. We're due there at 2 this afternoon."

"Ooh! Is that so? And which property is that then?" He turned to Fiona, who had joined them at the bar.

"It's called Stone Lea and is up the hill somewhere a few miles out of the village. Do you know it?"

"Oh yes, I know it well enough – belongs to old Abraham Croaker – queer old devil, he lives at Stone Barton further on up the lane with his son Adam and daughter-in-law Corah. They've got quite a chunk of land thereabouts. The old man likes his Devon Rubys and young Adam runs the milking herd – black and whites of course."

"What's the cottage like though?" enquired Fiona, who had no idea what Devon Rubys were and no interest in cattle either.

"Well now, that would be hard to say as it's been empty a while and I've never been inside. My missus would know I expect, women know everything, but she's away at the market today."

"Never mind," smiled Fiona, "we shall know soon enough. Do you think our sandwiches are ready?"

"Should be." He disappeared, returning a minute or two later with the food.

Fiona and Dodo removed themselves to a table in the window and set into the sandwiches and salad with gusto. Everything was delicious; fresh, generous and nicely presented, and their opinion of The Black Dog Inn rose.

"We ought to go in five minutes." said Fiona, emptying her glass. "Hmm, those sandwiches were really good. Not sure I like the sound of Abraham Croaker, what do you think he means by a 'queer old devil'?"

"Not gay I should imagine, in any sense of the word. Probably a voyeur with a special appetite for middle-aged women! Or maybe a knicker-nicker!" Dodo was enjoying herself now. "So don't hang your knickers on the washing line!"

"Don't be silly Dodo, you're frightening me. I'm going to pay, we're getting late. Here're the car keys, if you drive I can navigate."

"OK, I'll go and rev up."

Dodo walked out into the bright sunlight, blinding after the gloom of The Black Dog. She thought about Fiona as she waited, wondering whether she should try and dissuade her from her intended flight to Devon. Privately she was worried about how her old friend would cope with no one on hand to lean on.

'Ah well, wait and see' she sighed, watching Fiona approaching the car and wondering why she bothered so little with her appearance. Years of marriage to Hamish, Dodo supposed, giving Fiona an encouraging grin as she slipped into the passenger seat, brow furrowed with anxiety.

"Cheer up! If you don't like it we'll find somewhere else."

"I'm going to like it!" Fiona was emphatic. "I've got a feeling about it. We turn left here, through the village and up the hill, then first right and after about a mile right again, on for another mile or so then down a track with stone gateposts and an old milk churn stand."

"Right, sounds straightforward enough. Off we go!"

They drove slowly through the village, across an old stone bridge over a pretty stretch of river and begun to climb up the hill the other side.

"It's a lovely little village." Fiona remarked, spirits rising. "The shop-cum-post office doesn't look too bad either. This must be the turn – look – it even signs Stone."

"Another Devon lane," sang Dodo, swinging the car round a bend as the road closed in on them. "The wild flowers are gorgeous and look at the colour of the soil – it's almost *Basque Rouge*. Shit, look out!" Dodo slammed on the brakes as round the corner thundered a great yellow monster of a combine harvester which filled the road from bank to bank.

"Reverse gear I think – and quickly," squeaked Fiona, "there was a passing place not far back."

Dodo was already rushing backwards, praying that another vehicle was not coming up the road behind them. They reached the passing place and squashed the car as tight into the edge as possible as the combine bore down on them, assuming absolute right of passage.

From high above in his cab the driver glared down on them and no acknowledgement was forthcoming as he roared on past, narrowly missing the wing mirror.

"Rude bastard!" Dodo gave him a V-sign but his eyes had already swivelled back to the road ahead.

"Gosh, that was close!" said Fiona as they pulled out onto the road to try their luck again. This time all was well, and having bumped and bucketed over several hundred yards of potholes, they drew up outside Stone Lea at one minute past two o'clock.

Fiona was pleased that there seemed to be no sign of life. She wanted the chance to gain a first impression without the intrusion of introductions, chatter and a guided tour. Dodo instinctively understood her need and stayed in the car, fiddling with her hair and pretending to look at the map.

For the first time in her life, Fiona experienced love at first sight. Overgrown, scruffy, and forlorn, the long low thatched cottage caught her heart. The sand-coloured render, flaking and cracked under the mossy thatch, was covered with sprawling climbing roses and the little open-fronted porch a riot of tangled honeysuckle. The whole building was much bigger than she had expected and there was a sizeable area of unkempt grass in the front, split from the cobbled path round the house by an old flower bed where the massed poppies outshone the weeds.

"Dodo!" she called in delight. "What are you doing – hurry up and come and look!"

As Dodo got out of the car, the sound of an approaching vehicle broke the spell and an ancient, dirt encrusted Land Rover drove into the drive of Stone Lea. A thirty-something woman got out, followed by a small boy and a collie dog, both as encrusted as their vehicle. The woman should have been pretty, and probably still was when done up for a night out, if she ever had one. But today, she appeared as tired and lank as her shoulder-length fair hair. Relieved that it wasn't the strange Abraham Croaker himself, Fiona smiled at the woman, whom she assumed correctly to be the daughter-in-law.

"Hello, Mrs McLeod? I'm Corah Croaker, the daughter-in-law." The pleasant, educated voice ended with a touch of irony. "I'm sorry I'm a bit late."

"That's fine, we've only been here a few minutes." Fiona shook hands and introduced Dodo. "I've had a look round the outside, it looks lovely. Do you know how old the cottage is?"

"The oldest part is thought to be late 15th century and was tiny, but it has been added onto over the years, mostly late 1700s. My husband's family have been here for generations."

"Any ghosts?" asked Dodo hopefully.

"None that I know of," Corah laughed, "though my father-in-law's mother died here – peacefully in bed by the way! She was over 90 and smoked a clay pipe and never went out of the parish of Longbottom in her life."

"How amazing!" commented Dodo, watching distastefully as the dog dumped a large pile on the wannabe lawn. The boy had disappeared but his mother seemed unconcerned as she unlocked the medieval front door and led them into the cottage.

Sunlight filtered through the small dirty windows, illuminating the dancing motes of dust that their footsteps disturbed as they made their way round the ground floor. Dodo and Fiona were speechless in the presence of their guide, for neither of them had ever seen anything like it, and were in danger of being overcome by fits of giggles and sneezing that might offend the unfortunate Corah.

A loud crash from somewhere outside saved the day and excusing herself, Corah disappeared to go and track down her missing son.

"Holy shit!" gasped Dodo, bent double with laughter. "Fi, you cannot possibly contemplate living in this tip – I mean look, at it! D'you think the old crone with the pipe was the last inhabitant?"

"I must say, it looks like it!" Fiona wiped her eyes. "Can you imagine my mother staying here!" And they collapsed with laughter all over again.

"Seriously though," Fiona pulled herself together, "don't you think a coat of paint, a good clean and my things would make all the difference? I do rather love it, you know. Look at these beautiful old beams and stone floors and woodwork," she gabbled on.

"Bollocks Fi – you must be nuts to even consider it. Apart from the possibility of the whole structure collapsing, you'll die of cold! Don't forget it's high summer at the moment!"

"Where has your zany romantic streak gone, oh artist friend of my bosom?"

"Out through that broken window along with your wits!" retorted an incredulous Dodo.

"How are you getting on?" Corah's voice floated up the staircase. "I've found Sam, the door fell off the shed."

"Is he all right?" Fiona enquired, coming down the stairs, followed by Dodo.

"He's fine – I was more worried about the door! He's gone back to the farm with Sally – the dog." she added as an afterthought. "Looking at houses isn't much fun for a 9-year old. I suppose now you've seen the cottage you won't want it?" Resignation was in her voice and Fiona wondered how many other people she had had to show round her father-in-law's property.

"Not necessarily." Fiona replied briskly. "Shall we go outside to discuss? My friend suffers from dust fever!"

Dodo deliberately trod on Fiona's foot as she shot back out into the garden, inhaling fresh air and Silk Cut smoke as she narrowly avoided treading in Sally's dump.

"The thing is," began Fiona, "I appreciate that the rent is low, but as it stands the cottage really is almost uninhabitable. Apart from that, it's exactly what I want. If Mr Croaker is prepared to do some basic renovations like mending the broken windowpanes, converting the Rayburn to oil and installing a proper bathroom, then I am quite prepared to take the property at a slightly higher rent. You will never let it in its present condition, you must know that."

Fiona practically fell off the old garden seat with shock at her own words. What had happened to the shrinking, cautious creature – Hamish's spare rib – who had deferred to her lord and master and never taken the initiative? What a pity Dodo was out of earshot, enjoying her fag whilst inspecting the back garden!

A tiny spark of hope ignited in Corah's tired hazel eyes, quickly extinguished by disbelief, and for a moment she was silent. "That's what I've told him time and time again. The problem is you see, there's no money in farming but neither he nor my husband Adam will accept that diversification is the way forward. To have a property on the farm that stands empty but could be bringing in good money is ridiculous, but I cannot make them see that it would pay to spend a bit on it and get a good rent."

"Hmm, speculating to accumulate." Dodo had rejoined the party.

"Yes, that's it I suppose," smiled Corah, "trouble is, father-in-law is still living in the dark ages and thinks women should sit in the corner, cook and have children – his mother had 11 by the way – and what was good enough for her to live in is good enough for anybody. I'm a failure because I've only managed to produce Sam, but it's his future that I'm thinking of, and that's something I shall fight for."

Having no knowledge that such people as Abraham Croaker still existed, Fiona was astounded by what Corah said. She liked the woman and felt a certain sympathy for her, which she doubted that the independent and childless Dodo could really understand. Already Fiona's head was churning with ideas as she wanted, above all else, to become the tenant of Stone Lea.

"Look Mrs Croaker, we're staying down in Devon for a couple of nights, so do put my proposition to your father-in-law. I'm absolutely serious but I do want to get on with it and would like to move down at the beginning of October at the latest. I 'm prepared to clean and paint the place and have my own furniture, but would have to insist on the things I mentioned being done. I'm sure you will be able to persuade your father-in-law to see it would make sense financially."

They watched in silence as Corah Croaker's inner feelings crossed her pale, high-cheek boned face: hope, doubt, fear, all flashed by. Drawing in a deep breath, she tightened her lips and stuck out her chin. "I shall try. Yes," she repeated "I shall jolly well try, and this time, at least I can say we really do have a live possibility of a good tenant. To be honest, only two other people have been, and they only got out of the car to stretch their legs!" She smiled briefly before the black look flitted back across her face. "But you won't let me down, will you? I mean, you really do mean what you say?"

"I really do mean it," stated Fiona firmly, before turning to Dodo. "Can I give them your mobile number in case of need?"

"Of course," replied Dodo, who obviously still thought she was mad, but delved in her bag and scribbling the number on a scrap of paper, gave it to Corah.

"You don't know how nice it would be for me to have someone like yourself living in the Lea, Mrs McLeod, so don't worry, I shall do everything I can."

"We must be on our way, but thank you for showing us round. We're booked in at the Traveller's Joy at Dartbridge but given the roads round here and the odd combine harvester practically squashing us, it may take longer than we anticipated finding it."

"Yes," agreed Dodo, "and the locals aren't exactly free with their acknowledgements when they've run you off the road!"

"Oh dear!" Corah sounded genuinely concerned, "if it was a yellow one down the lane, it was probably Adam. I'm afraid he gets very tense during the harvest. We don't grow much corn but the combine's old and prone to breaking down. It's a difficult time, I suppose," she finished loyally.

Weak smiles all round and goodbyes said, Fiona and Dodo bolted to the car before Corah had a chance to enlarge on her husband's harvest stress factor. There would be more than enough opportunity for that, they suspected, if Fiona became the first tenant of Stone Lea, Longbottom-in-the-Mire. The mire, it seemed, might well be a mental rather than a physical one.

Dodo had done her homework well, and the Traveller's Joy Inn was as traditional and welcoming as its name implied. It was also extremely comfortable and the menu enticing. A stiff walk up over the fringes of Dartmoor had sharpened their appetite and after a long soak in the bath and a change of clothes, they were both ready for a drink and a good dinner.

A tacit agreement not to discuss Stone Lea had prevailed up until then; it had not been difficult with so much new and unusual to see and exclaim about, but as Fiona sat down at a small round table for two while Dodo visited the bar, an impatience to chew over the future engulfed her. Nervous of Dodo's adverse reaction to the cottage, she awaited her long-time mentor's return with some trepidation. Her friend's opinion was highly valued, and in spite of Fiona's own longing to live at Stone Lea, very likely to influence her ultimate decision.

The pub, which obviously enjoyed a good reputation, was filling up quickly with fellow diners and local drinkers, and Dodo was ages queuing at the bar. Fretting with anxiety, Fiona chewed at her thumbnail, illogically cursing Dodo for her enforced wait. Then, through the crowd she saw her pushing her way towards their table, carrying two glasses of champagne. Carefully putting them down on the rather unstable table, Dodo sat down herself and, raising a glass to her lips, said "Here's to you kid, and to Stone Lea!"

Fiona let out a long sigh, like a deflating air bag, and swallowing a mouthful of champagne, laughed with overwhelming relief. "Oh Dodo, this is brilliant! I thought you hated Stone Lea and the whole idea!"

"Well, I did," Dodo replied, before continuing with pseudo pomposity, "but I've been giving the matter my mature consideration and I've come to the conclusion that I think the whole crazy idea is a complete winner and I can't wait to hear it's yours – and I can come down and help grunge the medieval spiders out of their medieval webs."

"D'you think I'm mad?"

"Absolutely! But what the hell – go for it and I'm right behind you!"

FAIT ACCOMPLI

"Yes, she's right here, I'll hand you over." Dodo thrust the tiny phone at her across the table. "It's Corah," she hissed, crossing her fingers madly as Fiona took the phone.

There was silence from Fiona as Corah gabbled on, and then a broad smile broke over her anxious face.

"Oh that's marvellous news! And he's agreed to everything?" More silence. "Great – I can't believe it – don't worry about the sheds, I shan't be keeping any animals and they're fine as they are for logs and things." Pause. "Yes, absolutely. Thanks so much Corah, I'll be in touch with the agent, get everything sorted and give you a ring... OK... jolly good... see you then, bye."

Eyes shining, Fiona handed the phone back to Dodo. "I've got it! The old man's agreed to my demands and it'll all be ready for 1st October."

"Brilliant!" whooped Dodo, causing their fellow breakfasters to pause in mid-chomp and stare askance at their table. "I'm so pleased for you Fi, I really am. I shall raise my glass of concentrated orange juice and toast your joining the ranks of liberated women – God knows it's taken long enough!"

"I'm over the moon D, I really am – I never thought it would come off but I just loved the place the minute I saw it," babbled Fiona, whose pleasure was made all the greater by her friend's approval. "You will come down won't you?" The old demons of doubt came creeping back to tarnish her excitement.

"Try and keep me away – and I'm pretty handy with a paint brush you know. Don't forget your mother and I are coming for Christmas, so you'll have to get a move on with the DIY."

"D'you *really* think I'm doing the right thing?" Fiona asked pensively as she poured a second cup of tea. "Now it's a reality, I feel an attack of cold feet coming on."

"Rubbish!" Dodo retorted through a mouthful of sausage. "Act on impulse for a change and free your spirit – the trouble with you is you're so unused to making decisions beyond what to put in the washing machine that you don't know how to cope with taking a hand in your own destiny. I'm as certain as can be that it's the right thing to do and having got over my initial dislike of your scheme, I'm behind you all the way as you know. So wipe that glum look of your face and replace it with some decent make-up! It's only for six months anyway, not a life sentence."

"Yes that's true." Fiona brightened. "And who knows, I might stay longer."

"Who knows indeed!" Dodo cleaned her plate and moved onto toast and marmalade. "The only thing that worries me is what you're going to do all day before darkness falls and the lusty Longbottomers claim your virtue."

"Ha-ha to that," snorted Fiona, "but as to my occupation, I've got a plan. You might be surprised to learn that I've been thinking about it a lot – when I've had some clear brain time that is."

"No, don't tell me, let me guess – the Longbottom Ladies Crochet Circle, or perhaps the Morris Dancing in the Mire Society."

"Wrong again, but hold your breath, and don't laugh. I'm going to try and write a book."

"Now why should I laugh?" chuckled Dodo. "Seriously, I think that's a great idea. – any ideas yet for a plot? Plenty of lurid sex and violence I hope – always sells you know."

"In fact, I'd like to try my hand at writing for children – sort of 7-11 age group – so probably not too much S&V! I really do want to try and achieve something all off my own bat and just can't think of anything else I'd be capable of doing. I enjoy writing and am sure I can write as well as some of the authors my children read at that age."

"Hmm, jolly difficult market to break into – still, mustn't be defeatist and I seem to remember you were the awful Miss Upton's star pupil when it came to essays. D'you remember how her false teeth used to drop out when she got angry?"

"Oh heavens yes!" laughed Fiona, "and it was usually you who caused the trouble!"

"I'll put my thinking cap on when I get home and see if any of my ex's happen to be in publishing. It's a very nepotistic world you know, and any connections might help."

"I haven't even started yet." Fiona became very earnest. "But thanks anyway. Some ideas are beginning to circulate round my tiny brain though, and I've decided to have a few basic computer lessons when I get back and then get one installed in Stone Lea."

"I'm relieved to hear that," – Dodo's tone was equally earnest – "I'd visions of you scratching away with a home-plucked goose feather by flickering tallow candles, made from your own sheep!"

"Honestly Dodo," Fiona grumbled, "you never take me seriously."

"What d'you expect – apart from Roddy and Grania, you haven't produced anything yet worth taking seriously!"

Dodo was determined to spur her old friend into action and help build her lacking self-confidence, and she knew the best method of motivation was attack. Although apparently ignoring her jibe, Dodo suspected that her ploy would work, and the seeds of determination would start to germinate in Fiona's mind. The lack of response and deliberate change of subject did not fool her for one moment.

"After we've seen the agent, how about buying a picnic and doing some exploring? Looks like another beautiful day."

"Suits me. We might as well make the most of it while we're here, being back to the grindstone will come all too quickly tomorrow."

The meeting with the agent went to plan, and apart from expressing astonishment and disbelief at Fiona's decision and Abraham Croaker's acquiescence, he was clearly so delighted to get Stone Lea off his hands that he positively gushed with co-operation and assured Fiona he would have the paperwork ready for signature as soon as possible.

Dodo was dying to go back and have another look at Stone Lea but, frightened of getting caught by the mad male Croakers, Fiona vetoed the idea and suggested they drive right across the middle of Dartmoor and find a good place for their picnic lunch and a little of exercise.

The Moor was packed with August tripper traffic and it took them quite some time to find a quiet spot to park up for lunch. The picnic, purchased in a service station en route, also left something to be desired, but luckily two small bottles of lager provided by the Traveller's Joy saved the day; at least until Dodo fell into a bog during the work-up-the-appetite-for-dinner walk, ruining her smart jeans and totally unsuitable footwear. The walk had done its job though, and after another delicious dinner and rather too much wine, Dodo and Fiona crashed into their beds.

***

The drive home was slow but trouble free, but as they turned into the entrance to Wood End Cottage, to Fiona's horror she saw the back door was open and a horribly familiar car parked outside. "Oh no!" she exclaimed, "It's Hamish."

"Bugger, I'm dying for a cup of tea. Trust him to scupper my cuppa." Dodo was unsympathetic.

"Quick, let's bolt." And ramming the gear stick into reverse, she backed out in a shower of gravel, just catching sight of Mactavish's hopeful face as he rounded the corner of the house, having heard her car.

"Now what are we going to do?" demanded Dodo as Fiona roared off up the road, executed a hair-raising left turn and juddered to a halt in a pull-in on the edge of a wood.

"There's a footpath through this wood that comes out behind our garden – we can cut across and spy on Hamish through the hedge. Come on, let's hurry." Fiona was already over the style and on her way up the track as she spoke, leaving Dodo trailing in her wake.

Fiona was no athlete and Dodo soon caught up and they arrived, breathless, at the appointed spy-spot from where they could see the back yard.

"I don't want to meet him," Fiona gasped, "but I want to see him. Dodo, wouldn't it be awful if seeing him again made me want him back?"

"If that happens, all you've got to do is leap over the hedge, gallop across the lawn and hurl yourself into his arms crying 'Hamish I love you' in true Brontë style and then he says 'Frankly my dear I don't give a damn.'" Dodo giggled.

"Pig! *Gone with the Wind* to you! This is serious." Peering through the hedge, Fiona nearly choked on a beech leaf that popped into her open mouth as she spoke. "Quiet – look – he's coming out!"

"Let me see." Dodo insisted, elbowing Fiona aside for a quick peek before springing back.

"Ah-ha!" Dodo drew her breath in sharply. "You won't believe what I see – the *uber* shit!"

Fiona snapped her eyes back to the spy hole. "The bastard!" she exclaimed. "How dare he bring that creature into my home – I've a mind to break cover."

Sensing Fiona's intense anger and hurt, Dodo grabbed her arm and dragged her back. At that moment, Hamish looked towards their hiding place, his eye obviously caught by some slight movement. He was wearing his office suit and carrying a holdall in each hand; his thinning hair looked wispy and dull, his face pasty and tired. He was not a tall man and walked with an ungainly, pigeon-toed gait.

Towering above him and two paces behind came the gaunt frumpy figure of La Crutchley. She too carried a bag in each hand and putting her burden down, opened the hatchback for Hamish to stack in the luggage.

Bowing to Dodo's prudent restraint, Fiona froze and after a short stare, Hamish looked away and busied himself with loading the car. La Crutchley settled herself in the passenger seat and waited while Hamish went back to lock the door, but instead of getting into the car and driving away, to Fiona's dismay he wandered round towards the front of the house, apparently inspecting the flower beds. At the same moment,

Mactavish, with his sharp feline intuition, strode purposefully towards them across the lawn, 'miiaaoowing' loudly as he came.

"Hell Fi!" whispered Dodo urgently. "Let's get out of here!

The two of them turned and ran. Safely back in the car, they sat in silence for an instant while Fiona regained her breath and composure.

"Phew!" exclaimed Dodo, lighting a nerve-calming cigarette. "Trust that manky old moggy of yours to let the cat out of the bag!" She giggled, but Fiona's mind was elsewhere.

"How could I ever have married that man. To think that I loved him – or thought I did. Still, we did have some good times together, lots of them – and the children, and I believed all that 'till death us do part' stuff." Fiona's voice rose to a squeak as Dodo let her ramble on and get it all out of her system. "I mean, how was it that I never realised I wasn't in love with him and what would have happened if he hadn't done a bunk? I suppose in a way I should thank him. I've read about it you know, waiting in the dentist, 'trapped in a loveless marriage', but never thought of myself," she finished sadly.

"No racing across the benighted moor into his arms then?" smiled Dodo.

"No, no and no again." Fiona returned the smile. "Those two are welcome to each other, but I do hope for old time's sake that she makes him happy. Otherwise it would all be for nothing, if you see what I mean."

"Hmm, in a way. But I consider your liberation much more important. Bugger Hamish and the old crow! He must be off his rocker to swap you for that creature."

"I rather hoped you might say that! At least it's removed the last little seeds of doubt from my mind though, and I can really look forward now and not back. I've been having a lot of doubts you know." But before Dodo could answer, saying that was only to be expected, Fiona turned the key and fired the engine. "Come on, let's go home and have that cuppa."

Tea over, Dodo sped away back to her life, sad that their little jaunt was over but much happier about Fiona's state of mind. Fiona felt tired and a little lonely with only the old cat to keep her company, but was relieved to find that Hamish's unscheduled visit had resulted in the removal of all his clothes and personal possessions. Somewhat to her surprise, she noticed that the photograph of her as a blushing bride that he had kept in his dressing room had gone too; binned, she wondered, or to be kept as a souvenir of times past. She could almost feel sorry for the Crutchley woman if the latter applied, for now that Fiona was free of Hamish for ever and nothing he did could touch her anymore, evil thoughts seemed pointless.

As Fiona inspected the fridge, searching for something to have for supper, the telephone shrilled out. Wondering calmly if it might be Hamish and now having no qualms about speaking to him, she picked it up.

"Mum? Hi – it's me."

"Grania darling!" Fiona exclaimed in delight. "How lovely to hear you." Communication from her daughter was a rare event. "All well I hope?" she asked, suddenly anxious.

"Brilliant, and guess what – I'm coming home for Christmas. The project's nearly finished – building a proper well by the way – and we both reckoned Christmas in England would be great."

"That's the best news I've had for ages darling – but who's 'we'?"

"Oh! Jumbo of course – my man – didn't I tell you?"

"No, but never mind that now, I shall look forward to meeting him. Have you had my letter?"

"Not yet but that's no surprise out here."

"Oh well, never mind – but this may come as a bit of a shock, Wood End is being sold. Daddy and I thought it for the best and I'm renting a house down in Devon for six months, but I shall take as many of your things as possible to the cottage and leave the rest with Granny so you can sort it out when you come home." Fiona's palm grew damp round the handset as she awaited her daughter's reaction to the news that her beloved childhood home would be gone.

"C-o-o-l Mum!" came over the line from Namibia. "Hope Mactavish is coming too."

"Of course – he's part of the family."

"More than Dad!" There was anger beneath the levity. "Anyway Mum, this is costing a fortune but I'll be in touch nearer the time."

"I can't wait to see you darling; if only Roddy would come over too. Take care and I'll ring you soon. Lovely to hear you."

"Bye Mum." The line went dead.

Fiona's spirits shot up as she contemplated the return of her daughter. Hopefully this would mark the end of Grania's peripatetic life and she would settle down in the country of her birth and one day get married and have children.

Frowning as she scrambled some eggs, Fiona wondered about Jumbo. This was the first she had heard of him – who and what was he, would she like him? It was impossible to tell with Grania how serious she was about anything or anybody; so obviously she would have to wait and see when they arrived, there was nothing else she could do. Images of delicious little baby clothes and toys and the stories she would write for her grand-children floated across Fiona's eyes as the eggs burnt and stuck to the bottom of the once non-stick saucepan. Not caring a jot, she scraped the mess onto a piece of toast, and chucking on a tin of cold baked beans she shovelled up the food, her mind racing with plans for Grania's room at Stone Lea and how she would furnish it when the decorating was done.

Food finished and plans made, Fiona decided to ring Uncle Greg and tell him all her news. At this hour of the night he would probably be cavorting with the lovely Diana but what the hell, it was worth a try as a sudden burst of animation and a desire to talk seized her.

Uncle Greg obviously was cavorting as, to Fiona's

disappointment, there was no reply. There was no point ringing her mother, as Saturday night was bridge night with the Percival-Browns, when the local widows gathered and rubbers galore were hotly contested under the masterful eye of Teddy Percival-Brown, a jocular old 'winco' who referred to them as 'my harem', and whom Fiona privately considered a bit of an ass.

There was nothing for it, she would drop a line to Roddy telling him about Grania's plans and try and persuade him to come home for Christmas too. That done, a long hot bath and an early night. The coming weeks were going to be busy and she would need to be on her mettle to cope with the unfamiliar demands of her newfound independence. If only she could go to sleep and wake up on October 1st in Stone Lea, but that moment seemed a lifetime away.

***

In fact, those six weeks passed with startling speed and far from waking up each day wondering what she ought to be doing until Hamish came home, as she had become used to, Fiona hardly knew which way to turn. Documents for signature plagued her; potential house purchasers and rubber-neckers swamped her; packing cases overwhelmed her; and the telephone never stopped ringing. Reginald Cruickshank quibbled and queried every little detail of the divorce; the exquisite Peregrine bombarded her with fatuous questions, and her mother became tiresome about the number of boxes Fiona dumped in her empty-for-twenty-years shed.

On top of all the fluster, Mrs. P went down with a bout of 'fluenza – brought in by them furriners'; and Fiona completely forgot to book the removal men.

Needless to say, the final straw was provided by Uncle Greg who, whilst demonstrating his own spirited version of the Charleston at a Roaring 20's party given by an old crony, slipped and broke his leg. Diana was very tight-lipped about the affair and more than indicated that Gregory had taken a drop too much; but Fiona loved her old Uncle and rushed up to London to visit him in the private hospital where he languished in considerable comfort, heroically enjoying all the attention and the nurses' bottoms which he pinched at every available opportunity.

Struggling, but determined to fit in the computer evening class she had enrolled in, Fiona fell exhausted into bed each night, abandoning her life-long habits of teeth cleaning, hair brushing and face washing. Her mother would have died had she known of her daughter's slide into sloppiness and her abandonment of what Angie considered a vital routine – but Wood End Cottage was a depressing half-packed-up place, a house no longer a home, and Fiona's only desire when she climbed up the stairs each night was to sleep.

Like his sister would have been had she known, Uncle Greg was disapproving of her new life-style. He had just come out of hospital, confined to a wheelchair, and boredom was setting in after the initial excitement of his accident wore off and he was no longer today's news. His antidote was the telephone, and his niece fair game. "Must keep the old beauty routine going you know – won't catch a fish with a sagging line," he snuffled down the telephone. "Now Diana, she spends hours fiddling with her face and by Jove, she's a cracker for a gel of her age."

"Have you got a cold?" Fiona was definitely getting bored of the flawless Diana.

"Hmm, picked up a slight sniffle in that wretched hospital. Devilish places you know, lucky to come out alive."

"People don't usually die of a broken leg Uncle Greg – though I suppose you might have had a blood clot."

"I say Fi, bit sharp tonight. Dash it all, bloody painful a broken leg, and a nasty cold can damage the heart you know." He sounded aggrieved.

"I'm sorry," Fiona softened, "but I'm sure you'll be right back to your old self with a bit of R&R and I believe colds only damage your heart if you work hard while you have one." She nearly added 'No chance of that' but decided against it.

"R&R, what the devil's that?" Now it was his turn to be

sharp.

"Rest and Recuperation, that's all."

"Humph, sounded rather nasty – glad to hear it's actually what I'm getting. Diana's top hole at that sort of thing." Uncle Greg brightened up.

"I'm delighted to hear it Uncle Greg, and by the way, Grania's coming home for Christmas and I'm trying to persuade Roddy to come too. And guess what, Grania's bringing a boyfriend called Jumbo – that's all I know about him."

"Jolly good show, time the gel settled down. Any sign of my great-nephew taking the plunge?"

"Not that I know of but then he's always been rather secretive about affairs of the heart. Mummy and Dodo are coming too, it'll be a bit of a squash but..." (pausing for an instant, Fiona decided 'definitely no Diana') "it would be great if you came as well – a real family Christmas."

"Sweet of you my dear, to invite the old Uncle. Sounds very tempting I must say but leave it with me for a day or two – got a few knots to unravel first if you know what I mean."

"Of course, no rush, weeks to go yet."

"Better sign off now, supposed to be doing some idiotic exercises – I ask you! Rosa Kleb's due any moment – she's the physio, ghastly old battle-axe! Lots of love Fi."

Fiona swallowed with relief at Uncle Greg's apparent grasping of the 'no Diana nettle' before wondering briefly how on Earth they would all squeeze into Stone Lea if everyone decided to come. Sufficient unto the day she concluded, returning Uncle Greg's love and putting the phone down.

Fiona had been dreading having to deal with the unfamiliar and perplexing complications of divorce, house sale and tenancy agreements. Tangible tasks such as packing boxes and showing potential buyers round were straightforward and caused her no worry, but Hamish had always muttered darkly and become stressed and tetchy whenever he had had to deal with lawyers. She had neither wanted nor dared to become involved, and had never imagined that she would have to be. But now she was determined to stand on her own two feet, and cope for herself with the problems that had, from time to time, beset Hamish during his reign as king of the castle.

Much to Fiona's surprise and relief, the intricacies of the law proved to be minimal and well within her grasp, and her self-confidence grew as she dealt easily with the few small queries and problems that arose. She began to suspect that Hamish had made rather more fuss than was necessary as one by one, the various documents wound their weary way through the various necessary legal processes without a major hitch.

Wood End Cottage was under offer to a young couple with one small child and another well on the way, and Fiona was pleased that her old home would once more come alive with the sights and sounds of a growing family. She liked them and hoped that their time at Wood End would be happy, as hers had once been. That time was drawing to a close and, as she overheard them discussing the changes they would make, a twinge of sadness hit her as she realised that the house no longer welcomed her. The era of the McLeods had come to an end and had been but a passing chapter in the history of a building that would endure far beyond the lives of its inhabitants.

The divorce would run its course, but there were no problems there either. Both Fiona and Hamish were keen to get on with it and true to his word, Hamish was determined that Fiona should not suffer financially as a result of his departure. They agreed on everything, including the apportioning of their possessions, and there was not even a battle over the custody of Mactavish! 'Thank goodness the children are grown up' Fiona thought, as she read and signed yet more documents.

The Assured Shorthold Tenancy Agreement between Abraham Croaker and Fiona McLeod was signed and sealed, and a quick phone call to Corah revealed that work was going on apace and all would be in readiness for her arrival on 1st October.

Excited by the news, Fiona rushed out to the local printers and ordered sheets of stickers with her new address on them, only to realise that as yet there was no telephone and therefore no number. The printer, a nice man called Dave who had done work for the McLeods in the past, smiled sympathetically and advised her to contact BT without delay. He assured her he could produce the stickers within 24 hours when he had the relevant information but seemed amazed, when suggesting he print Fiona's mobile number to save delay, to learn she did not have one. Yet another IT purchase would have to be made along with the PC, Fiona decided, determined to hasten her belated entry into the world of 21st century technology – Dodo could teach her how to use it.

Fiona's computer classes were now going well after a sticky start when, flummoxed by the jargon and unable to control her mouse properly, Fiona had been on the verge of quitting. The rest of the class, mostly earnest and unattractive men, were years younger than Fiona and aspiring to much higher levels of computer manipulation than she dreamed of or desired. They clearly thought her a frightful nuisance and fit only for an old people's home, and their attitude towards her ranged from patronising to downright unfriendly.

Luckily their tutor, a large and humorous woman called Stella, took a liking to Fiona and patiently cajoled and encouraged her into mastering the basic skills required for her forthcoming career as a would-be author. At the end of her final lesson, Fiona gave Stella a large box of chocolates as a token of appreciation for all the extra effort she had made to help her. It seemed an appropriate present for one who obviously enjoyed life to the full and preferred a good munch to a good figure. Somewhat to Fiona's horror, Stella clasped her in a bosomy embrace before presenting her with a little home-produced booklet that she had entitled 'Basic Computer Skills for Middle-Aged Ladies', inscribed 'To

Fiona – a breath of fresh air! Good luck – Stella.' Much touched by this gesture, Fiona cocked a snoop at the supercilious young men and bore her new treasure home with pride, stowing it safely away in her brown leather attaché case.

Soon it would be her last night at Wood End Cottage, and some of the old nerves crept back in as Fiona contemplated the immediate future. Sitting alone at the kitchen table – even Mactavish had decided on a night out – she consulted the endless lists she had made to check that everything that should have been done had been done. All her goods and chattels that were to go to Devon were marked with a red sticker saying 'Stone Lea'; she personally would only take one suitcase, the cat's paraphernalia and of course Mactavish himself, confined in a smart new travelling cage that she had bought at the local pet shop – an item that would definitely be added onto the cost of moving bill that Hamish had volunteered to pay.

Fiona planned to go down the day before the removal lorry and stay overnight in the pub – another addition to Hamish's bill – so as to be on hand when the lorry arrived. Her mother was lined up to oversee the loading at Wood End, having nobly sacrificed a game of golf to help her daughter, though she was rather miffed at Fiona's refusal of a bed in her house for her last night 'in civilisation'. Fiona's excuse that it would only upset Mactavish even more than he was going to be upset anyway was greeted with a classic Angie sniff, registering her disapproval that a cat's feelings were more important than a mother's.

Fiona had, however, organised a strange little gathering for the final evening at Wood End; Dodo, her mother and Mrs Pinker would eat fish and chips round the kitchen table. Feeling obliged to include Mr Pinker in the invitation, Fiona's relief was great when, without hesitation, Mrs P declined on his behalf, insisting that he would prefer to stay home and watch 'some rubbish' on the television.

"Hi Fi!" The door burst open and Dodo minced in,

swaying idiotically in a mock dance, bottle of wine held high in each hand. "First as usual, I see," she sang, dumping the bottles on the table.

"And jolly pleased you are too!" Fiona returned the greeting, eyeing the bottles with relief as she realised she had forgotten all about drink, apart from her mother's customary gin and tonic.

"How you doing then old mate?" asked Dodo.

"Actually I'm fine D and thanks for the booze – we might need it and I have to admit I've slipped up a bit in that department."

"D'you think we could get old Mother P tight? God, I can't imagine what she might say, she's cuckoo enough when sober!"

"Might not be the greatest idea. Don't forget she's got to get home and the last thing I want on my hands at the moment is a plastered Mrs Pinker!"

"Hmm, maybe you're right, it could prove a bit of a problem. But I could use a glass – what about you?"

"Sure thing, can you deal?" And Fiona fetched some glasses as Dodo pulled the cork.

"Now, old thing," Dodo continued as they sat down together, "are you really OK? I mean in mind, body and spirit?"

"Hmm, yes." Fiona hesitated. "Yes, I really think I am. I've been through everything a million times and don't think I've forgotten anything vital, so mind and body are in order – and spirit..." she momentarily hesitated again, "yes – spirit's OK too."

"Great!" Dodo raised her glass, "Here's to you Fi!"

At this, the back door banged and a loud "Hellooee – I'm heere!" announced the arrival of Angie, who appeared looking immaculate as usual, and bearing a *tarte tatin*.

"Hello Mummy." Fiona stood up to greet her mother with a kiss. "That looks good, did you make it?"

"Good gracious no, there's a wonderful little man in the village – terribly expensive but who cares? I told him it was for my daughter's last night in the land of the living." She shuddered theatrically before turning to greet Dodo with her usual airborne peck.

"You're looking very chic tonight, Angie." Dodo backed away and sat down again. "Pity it's only us females. Couldn't you find an eligible man for your Mother, Fi?"

"I can assure you Dodo, that one husband is quite enough." Angie had no intention of allowing her daughter to reply. "Had you had one, you would know exactly what I mean and don't forget, I was lucky with mine. On the whole, Fiona's father was a most accommodating and admirable man and perhaps it is *you* who should be looking for one," she bristled, "though I suspect you've left it a bit late!"

"Thank you for those kind words Angie, but I have no intention of saddling myself with a husband and upsetting my very satisfactory way of life." Dodo was bristling now. "But it's not through lack of offers, I can assure you."

"Will you two stop winding each other up!" Fiona butted in quickly, handing her mother a gin and tonic, "Mrs P will be here in a minute so please can we change the subject."

"I'm glad you asked the old girl." Angie simmered down. "She's been a part of your life for so long, rather like that awful cat. Are you having him put away? I can't believe the poor creature would wish to move to Devon at his age."

"Certainly not Mummy!" Raised in indignation, Fiona's voice drowned out Dodo's splutters as she choked on a dry roasted peanut. "How could you suggest such a thing when dear Mactavish is the only friend I shall have... to begin with," she added hastily, but too late.

"And whose fault is that, I should like to know?" was Angie's predictable retort. "If you must go traipsing off to darkest Devon, what can you expect but the company of a decaying animal?"

"Oi oi, you two!" Dodo, role now switched to that of interceder, was loving every minute. "'Alas poor Mactavish, I knew him well; a fellow of infinite jest, of most excellent fancy.'"

"Please, Dodo!" begged Fiona, who was tired and edgy and not in the mood to cope with her mother and friend in full steam, tonight of all nights.

"Pax, Angie?" winked Dodo at her willing opponent.

"Pax," agreed Angie, returning the wink, a mutual understanding of Fiona's mental state bringing the realisation that for now, enough was enough.

"Honestly, you two are like a couple of children." grumbled Fiona, not quite grasping that the stimulating little skirmish was over.

But at that moment, a loud and imperious banging on the door announced the arrival of Mrs Pinker. Fiona made tracks to open the door, wondering as she did so if Mrs P considered she should be formally let in and welcomed over the threshold as she came as a guest, not a servant. Evidently this was not the case, as Fiona had barely reached the end of the kitchen table when the door banged shut and her treasured helper made her entrance.

There was a split second's silence as the assembled company gazed in wonder as a small, bobbing, out of season Christmas tree dashed into the room. No one had ever seen Mrs Pinker in her evening finery and she glittered from top to toe in a gold-threaded green woollen ensemble. Two red ping-pong balls hung dancing from each ear lobe, matched by a set of beads, and her shoes were decorated with elaborate golden bows.

"Evenin' ducks," shrilled Mrs P, her smile encompassing the whole room. "Lord luv us, but this is a treat an' all!"

Angie was the first to regain her composure and jumping up, pulled out the chair next to her and patted it invitingly. "My dear Mrs Pinker, come and sit down. You look wonderful and it's lovely to see you again."

"And you too Mrs Bateson, if I may say so – treating you well life is then, by the looks of things."

"Can't grumble Mrs P, can't grumble." Angie smiled her most dazzling smile.

"Now what about a drink, Mrs P?" Fiona offered.

"Ooh Mrs Mac, don't knows as I ought – whatever would Pinker say if I comes 'ome tipsy!"

"Come on Mrs P," urged Dodo, "just one teeny-weeny for old time's sake!"

"Ooh Miss Dodo, you're a terror you are – but maybe one little nip won't do no 'arm. The good Lord 'imself took the odd drop and 'er Majesty too." Having established the all-important holy and royal precedent, Mrs Pinker accepted her small glass of wine with aplomb.

"Well, dearie," she turned to Fiona. "The Lord bless us but I shall miss you an' that's a fact and I says to Pinker 'You mark my words, no good will come of this. A rolling stone gathers no moss an' never a truer word spoken'." The ping-pong balls bounced alarmingly as she shook her little grey head.

"Quite right Mrs P." agreed Angie vigorously, her own discreet gold earrings managing a refined tremble in sympathy with the ping-pong balls.

"I'm sure there's plenty of moss in Devon should Fi wish to gather it." Dodo came to the rescue. "In fact, being rather a wet county, I should imagine the place is covered in it!" She acknowledged Fiona's grateful look with a brief eyes-to-heaven face and a wry smile.

"I do wish you wouldn't be facetious, Dodo," Angie snapped, "you know perfectly well what Mrs Pinker and I mean."

"Let's have supper." suggested Fiona briskly, nipping further conflict in the bud. "It's fish and chips and they're getting soggy. Put the spanners round could you Dodo – anyone like ketchup?"

"I loves a drop of vinegar on me chips Mrs Mac – got any brown? – not that fancy frog stuff you 'ave for the salad." Mrs. Pinker did not approve of anything foreign.

"I'll have some ketchup Fi, it's in the larder isn't it?" Dodo went to find it.

"Yup and there should still be some vinegar there too, somewhere."

"Have you any *sauce tartare*, Fiona?" enquired Angie.

"Sorry Mummy, I'm afraid I threw the last bit out when I cleaned the fridge – it smelt rather odd."

"Never mind dear, I shall look forward to my *tarte tatin*."

The evening stumbled on until just before ten o'clock, when Angie was ready to leave. Mrs Pinker too felt she should be on her way, and to Fiona's chagrin clamped her in a gripping embrace, moistening eyes swiftly mopped with a lace handkerchief.

Fiona hated emotional scenes, and pecking her old henchwoman quickly on the cheek, unhanded her gently and ushered her out with assurances of continued contact and a reminder that the train service to Exeter had moved on from steam.

Angie followed straight away, her 'putting a brave face on it all' expression the best Fiona had ever seen. "Well, Fiona dear, this is it – goodbye to my daughter."

"I'll ring you tomorrow evening, Mummy." Fiona smiled, wondering why her mother had never gone on the stage.

"I shall be gone by 7.30, dinner with the Hetheringtons you know." she sniffed.

"That's OK, I'll try around 6 – before you have your bath." Fiona added, kissing her mother and trying not to giggle at the faces Dodo was making behind her. "As soon as I've got everything sorted, you must come down, you'll love it I know and we'll have a great time wurzle-spotting and then it'll be Christmas – I've asked Uncle Greg too by the way."

"Huh – my dreadful brother!" Angie's face brightened. "I hope you haven't invited that woman as well?"

"Certainly not. I'm sick to death of hearing about the wondrous Diana and we're going to be squashed enough as it is. Don't worry Mummy, it will all be brilliant."

"I know Fi dear, I know. But I shall miss not having you round the corner, you see. Perhaps you should take up golf – yes..." she paused thoughtfully, "now that *is* a good idea. One does meet such a nice class of person on a golf course."

"Oh Angie!" hooted Dodo, unable to contain herself anymore, "you are priceless – Fi's eye for a ball is non-existent – at least, the sort of balls you're talking about," she added inevitably, "and the other sort too!"

"Dodo!" cried mother and daughter with one accord, before all three fell about with laughter and Angie wisely headed towards the door, chin up and dramatic 'brave face' gone.

Fiona and Dodo waved her away and, accompanied by a comfort-seeking Mactavish, returned to the kitchen to clear up the remnants of their unorthodox dinner and brew a mug of instant coffee.

"D'you mind if I camp down for the night, Fi?" asked Dodo, eyeing her half-full glass. "I don't fancy risking driving home and I chucked in a duvet just in case, so I only need something to lie on."

"Course not, no problem. Better safe than sorry and I wouldn't say no to a night-cap with my coffee either. That was some evening!"

"You can say that again! I thought your Ma and old Mrs P were really going to get stuck in with the maudlin 'you silly girl' bit – and as for you taking up golf, all I can say is little white bollocks to that!"

"'Well, you never know!'" Fiona aped her mother's voice and posture.

"Tell you something Fi, you'll be a dead ringer for your mother in twenty years."

"I wouldn't be that sorry, actually. If I'm as active and up-together at her age as she is, I won't complain."

"Too right." replied Dodo thoughtfully. "You'll be OK, you've lived a clean life, unlike me with the booze and the fags, but I've thought about it sometimes and come to the conclusion that old age is ghastly and I don't think I want it. Starting to think about time running out is the worst downside of middle-age because up till now, it's not something one's ever considered. And unlike bodily deterioration, there's bugger all you can do about it."

"I know what you mean." Fiona replied, "It's only just dawned on me that I've lived well over half my life already. I mean I've just bought some new table napkins and the chilling thought occurred to me that if they last as long as the old wedding present ones did, I'll be dead before they are – frightening!"

"Oof!" Dodo shuddered. "The eternal table napkin!"

"And Mummy's forever going to funerals and talking about poor old so-and-so who's lost their marbles." Fiona went on, worrying the subject like a terrier.

"They're the lucky ones in a way though; at least they don't know what's happening – better than being aware that you're a pain in the arse to everyone and constantly ill with no future other than death to look forward to."

"Hmm, awful isn't it?" nodded Fiona. "You should hear the old things in the Post Office on a Monday morning. There's always a queue for pensions and they talk about nothing but their ailments and hospital visits and who has died over the weekend – not to mention night-time peeing, failing eyesight and arthritis – it certainly doesn't inspire one to live to a great age."

"Eat, drink and be merry before all your teeth fall out – that's what I say!" stated Dodo. "Who knows when the Grim Reaper may strike!"

"Hear hear!" yawned Fiona, finishing her coffee.

"Come on Fi, it's bed-time and I think we've said our goodbyes to Wood End Cottage. You've got a long day tomorrow and I must be away early to meet the plumber from hell who's supposed to be replacing the shower. Just think," Dodo sighed, "this time tomorrow you'll be in Devon."

"I can hardly believe it." Fiona rinsed out the dirty mugs and left them on the draining board. "You will come down the weekend after next, won't you?"

"You bet, and armed with my painting gear so make sure you've got plenty of paint for me to splash around."

Fiona's weary face broke into a smile and while Dodo went to the car to get her duvet, she told Mactavish that he could spend the night on her bed.

Purring his thanks, he followed them upstairs for his last night in Wood End Cottage.

NEW FACES

The October sun beamed down on Longbottom-in-the Mire, bathing its funny little thatched dwellings in a golden light of approval, and highlighting the beautiful early Autumn colours of the trees. Cattle and sheep grazed contentedly in the fields, uninterested in the sundry tractors that chugged up and down, busy ploughing and cultivating before drilling the winter corn.

Fiona breathed in the very essence of her new life and gave it the thumbs-up. Not so Mactavish, who was finding the joys of his new luxury travelling cage not at all to his liking, and who expressed his disapproval by indulging in an aria that would have put the finest diva out of business. Fiona's remonstrations fell on deaf ears, and fearing that hers would go the same way if the caterwauling continued much longer, she decided to administer a dose of the emergency tranquillisers that the vet had given her before they left Wood End.

The pre-arranged rendezvous with Corah at Stone Lea was at 4.30, and as Fiona drew up three minutes early, she saw the front door was open and guessed that Corah had beaten her to it. Thankfully there was no sign of Sally the dog, so both Mactavish and the newly-cut grass could rest untroubled by any assault from either end of her body. The cut grass was an encouraging portent, but Fiona still suffered a twinge of trepidation as she crossed the threshold and called out "Hello."

She need not have worried for, true to her word, Corah had ensured that the necessary reparations had been carried out, and that the cottage was now fit for habitation.

The transformation was unbelievable – and Fiona decided that Corah Croaker's fragile exterior must contain a core of steel for her to have achieved this revolution in so little time. Then she remembered Sam; Sam the door wrecker, the small boy whose mother would fight like a tiger to lift the outlook of her only child out of the slough of his Croaker inheritance.

"Come on up, Mrs McLeod," Corah's voice echoed round the empty, curtainless house. "I'm in the bathroom."

Fiona clattered up the twisted, narrow staircase, noting as she went that the dark surface of the ancient rises and treads, previously obscured by a thick coat of grime, were now waxed and shining; it was obvious who had been responsible for that.

"Do call me Fiona." She smiled, arriving in the bathroom doorway, where to her astonishment she saw Corah perched up a step-ladder, paint brush in hand, furiously slapping pale aquamarine paint on the wall above the loo.

"You've just beaten me to it, five minutes and I'll be done." Corah briefly returned the smile but kept on painting. "I do hope you don't mind my choosing a colour for you but I thought you'd like to kick off with a nice bathroom and it matches the border on the tiles."

Sea-green blobs and smears on her face and clothes indicated the speed with which she must have been working and Fiona was speechless for a moment, overcome with gratitude at the kindness of this woman, imprisoned in a hopeless misalliance by the existence of her child.

"It's exactly what I would have chosen myself – I love it and can't thank you enough for what you've done. You must have worked incredibly hard and I'm over the moon with it all."

"Sam cut the grass yesterday." There was pride in her voice.

"It's the first thing I noticed, it looks very smart. Will you thank him for me."

"Of course. He's good at that sort of thing. He's done a few logs up ready for you too – they're in the shed."

"Would he like to earn some pocket money and keep on doing odd jobs like that for me, do you think?" Fiona hoped her suggestion would not be taken as patronising.

"I'm sure he'd love to and I've no objection but I'd best mention it to Adam first. Sam has plenty of jobs to do on the farm you see, and then there's his homework. I don't like him to get too tired but his father expects quite a lot of him – he's only nine – and I do want him to do well at school."

"It was only a thought." Fiona played down her suggestion, sensing the tension in Corah when she mentioned her husband's name. "Don't worry about it, I often did the logs at home so I'm quite used to it."

"There!" Corah jumped off the steps and putting down paint and brush, stood back to admire her work. "All done."

"It looks great, and you and Sam shall be my first guests when there's something to sit on and a table to eat off!"

Corah smiled her wan, weary smile and pity stirred in Fiona's heart. Her good fairy looked even thinner and lanker than she remembered, and there were dark rings under the wide strained eyes. At least Hamish had never been a bully.

"Look Mrs McLeod, I must dash, but the keys and my phone number are on the window ledge in the kitchen. I could come down tomorrow after lunch for a while if you need help with anything."

"Yes please, and *do* call me Fiona. 'Mrs McLeod' is ridiculously formal for this day and age and makes me feel a hundred and one! I'm staying tonight at the Traveller's Joy but will be back here straight after breakfast ready for the removals men, so it will be chaos but great if you could pop in in the afternoon."

"I will, and..." Hesitating and looking embarrassed, Corah handed Fiona an envelope. "If you could give me a cheque for this I would be very grateful. It's the oil bill. My father-in-law thought you should order it yourself but I didn't like the idea of your spending your first few days without any hot water or cooking facility."

"Oh, Corah," there was compassion in Fiona's voice as she took the envelope, "I'll give you a cheque right now if it makes it easier for you. You've been so kind."

At that moment, the ancient blue Land Rover roared past up the lane, clanking and banging as it crashed over the potholes, Sally's panting face peering out of the back alongside a stack of fencing posts.

"No no, not now," panicked Corah, "tomorrow will be fine."

And without another word she flew off in pursuit, leaving Fiona to stare at her retreating figure until the cloud of dust thrown up by the Land Rover swallowed her up. It had been a very dry summer.

No husband was definitely better than a bad one, Fiona decided as she meandered peacefully round her new home. In fact, no husband was better than almost anything if one could feel as happy as she did. After its years of neglect, the old place seemed to welcome her into its fold and rejoice in the new life that she brought with her. Corah had done her work well and only the three spare bedrooms and the sitting room remained undecorated.

The kitchen was long and thin, and having started life as the dairy, was on the north side of the house, but Corah had had the imagination to knock out the old doorway that led through into what had once been the front parlour, thus creating an ideal eating-cum-general-purpose area, where there would also be room for Fiona's computer. The sitting room, off the other side of the cross-passage had originally been the kitchen, where for hundreds of years the inhabitants of Stone Lea had lived for most of the time, only using the parlour for the few high days and holidays that brightened up their life of toil on the land. The old range had been removed and in its place the builders had created a fantastic inglenook fireplace, complete with bread oven, black oak beam and massive wooden mantleshelf. In Fiona's imagination, she could visualise old Mother Croaker sitting in her rocking chair, clay pipe in mouth, warming her tired gnarled feet by the massive blackened range. Life must have been hard in those days she concluded, no doubt about it.

A plaintive 'miaow' from the car brought Fiona back into the present, and with enough ideas already in her head about the placement of the furniture when it arrived tomorrow, she decided it was time to lock up and make her way to the pub.

She couldn't wait to get on her new mobile and tell Dodo and her Mother how excited she was about it all and how marvellous Stone Lea was going to be when it was properly finished.

'I shall ring Uncle Greg too,' she thought as she drove along the winding lanes, buoyed up by a surge of energy and enthusiasm that she'd assumed had vanished for ever along with her youth.

The landlord of the Traveller's Joy welcomed Fiona back with a friendly smile and gave permission for Mactavish's cage to go up to her room. Dogs were welcome so why not a cat, he insisted, much to Fiona's relief, even offering to carry the cumbersome cage up for her.

"And how's your friend?" he asked, depositing Mactavish on the floor.

"She's fine thank you, and coming down to stay next weekend."

"Ooh! You coming to live here then?"

"Yes – I've rented a cottage near Longbottom and I'm moving in tomorrow."

"Ah! That's nice then." He paused, frowning slightly and rubbing his chin. "That wouldn't be old Abraham Croaker's place would it?"

'Obviously there are no secrets in Mid-Devon,' thought Fiona, beginning to wish he would leave her in peace. "As a matter of fact it is." she replied, poking a finger through the bars of the cage to tickle the top of Mactavish's head.

"Aarh! Met the old buzzard then have you?"

"Not yet, no. I've been dealing with his daughter-in-law Corah, who's been most helpful."

"Aarrh yes – young Corah." (The *r's* were beginning to roll as his curiosity deepened, and he forgot his 'smart landlord' speak). "She's from these parts you know – educated like, her father being a teacher, nice people. Why she took up with that Adam Croaker none of us know."

"Oh well," Fiona smiled brightly, making a pointed move towards her suitcase, "other peoples' lives are their own affairs!"

Pondering deeply on this extraordinary statement, the landlord took the hint and 'aarrh'd' his way out.

Fiona's heart sank when ten minutes later, a knock on the door proclaimed his return. She had given Mactavish his tranquilliser in a small lump of Whiskas and was about to run a bath and relax before hitting the mobile when the interruption occurred.

"Come in." she barked, determined not to allow him the chance to gossip.

The door opened and the landlord stood there holding a saucer on which was piled a small mound of chopped up white meat.

"Is this room service?" Fiona snapped, aghast at her unaccustomed temerity.

"Well, you could say that, but I thought your poor puss looked a bit down in the mouth and maybe a bit of chicken might cheer him up. Left over from lunch – no charge you understand."

"Oh, that's really kind!" Fiona relented, kicking herself for being such a cow, "He'll love it, chicken's his favourite and he is rather fed up, as you can imagine."

"No trouble, no trouble at all. You'll be wanting some dinner yourself I expect?"

"Definitely yes," Fiona smiled, keeping a hand on the door. "I'll be down in about half an hour and I might even try the chicken!"

"Aarrh!" And he turned and shuffled off down the stairs.

Fearing for the state of the mobile litter tray, Fiona withheld most of the proffered delicacy, but as Mactavish was already well on the way to a deep sleep, he was not too bothered and chewed the few presented morsels with dispassionate gratitude.

Without any further unwanted interruptions, Fiona enjoyed her bath, spoke briefly to her mother – who sounded very chirpy – failed to get Uncle Greg, and then got through to Dodo. The sound of her friend's voice immediately dispelled the tiny feeling of loneliness and isolation that had been creeping in as the evening wore on.

"Hi, it's Fi!" she almost shouted when Dodo answered.

"What are you shouting for, Fi?" Dodo was deliberately banal. "Anyone would think you were on the top of Mount Everest – I'm only about a hundred and fifty miles away you know and I'm not deaf yet! Actually, I'm amazed you've managed to work the mobile. How's it going anyway?"

"Brilliant D! I can't wait for you to see the cottage – Corah's done a fantastic job and it's really nice – you won't recognise it."

"That's just as well considering what a shit heap it was! How's the pub, any talent in tonight?"

"Don't know yet, I haven't been down since I arrived but the landlord's a bit of a pain. He wants to gossip all the time and appeared at my door with a saucer of food for Mactavish – asked after you by the way."

"Hmm! Probably fancied me but has to make do with you instead – better lock the door – can't see him being your type!"

"I haven't got a type and I'm not looking for one either, thanks."

"Thought you'd say that." Dodo's voice scrunched in her ear.

"Are you eating something? You sound most odd."

"A rather delicious packet of salt and vinegar crisps actually – sorry – just finished. Anyway, glad to hear you're OK and not in a strait-jacket yet. I shall be down next weekend as planned so let me know if you need any Red Cross parcels or a length of sackcloth to stitch a new gown for the Mangel-Wurzel Ball."

"I don't know what you're talking about Dodo and neither do you!" giggled Fiona, "Can't wait to see you, though next weekend seems ages away."

"Fret not – it'll soon be here – *tempus fugit* when you're in your fifties. And busy." she added as an afterthought.

"Don't tell me!" groaned Fiona, "But now I shall make

my way downstairs and inspect the non-existent talent in the bar before ordering myself a slap-up dinner. After all, it's definitely a 'moving expense' and Hamish is footing that bill."

"You're coming on Fi, definitely coming on. I see some hope for you yet – and you can have a few for me!"

"Will do and speak soon."

"Good luck with it all tomorrow and for God's sake don't fall in love with the dreaded Abraham!"

Fiona pressed the red button before any more verbal idiocies came over the air and, laughing to herself, made her way down to the bar.

She followed Dodo's instructions and had 'a few for her' to accompany her excellent game paté, fillet steak and Devon tart – a few too many she decided as she returned to her room, dragging the tranquillised Mactavish from his cage and plonking him on the bed before collapsing into it herself. Closing her eyes against the whirling ceiling, Fiona tried some mental furniture arranging but got no further than the kitchen table.

***

Much to her fury Fiona overslept, and hurtling her possessions back into case and cage, she swallowed a cup of tea, paid the bill and bade the landlord farewell. Considerably less loquacious than the previous evening, he expressed a hope that he would see her again and wished her good luck, his tone implying that she might need it.

'Bollocks to that,' she thought, employing one of Dodo's favourite words, and putting her foot down, sped back to Stone Lea.

As Fiona opened the front door, the first thing she almost fell over was a small pile of mail.

"Oh no!" she groaned out loud, "Don't say junk mail has hit Stone Lea already."

But closer scrutiny revealed that hidden amongst the immediately to be binned, irritating rubbish, were several enticing-looking hand-written envelopes addressed to herself.

A frisson of excitement cleared away the remnants of her hangover as she gathered them up and returned to the car to open them. Fiona liked to be seated when she opened her mail and as there was no chair in the house, and her glasses were in the car, it seemed the logical place to go.

Recognising her mother's handwriting, Fiona tore open the first envelope and was delightfully surprised when a cheque for £100 fell out of the 'Good Luck in Your New Home' card. Inside, Angie had written: 'A little help towards your first shopping basket!' Fiona smiled, wondering how she might manage to spend such a sum in the Longbottom village store – Hamish would have had a fit.

More cards followed; from Dodo, a predictably zany offering sporting several naked men doing strange things with milk bottles, on which she had written 'Now you're in dairy country!'; a card from Stella with a picture of an exploding computer on the front; and a glitter-encrusted beauty from dear Mrs Pinker wishing her:

'Every joy in your new life.
May all your days be free from strife
And filled with happiness and pleasure,
Honest work and honest leisure!'

Most of the glitter had come unstuck en route and fell onto Fiona's jeans but she was too touched by Mrs P's kindness to notice or care. 'Where on Earth could she have found such an amazing card?' she wondered, ripping open the last envelope. No card this time, just another cheque and a slip of paper.

'A little in advance with my love, Uncle Greg,' was all it said, but when Fiona looked at the cheque, she gasped – it was for £5,000.

"Wow!" she exclaimed, kissing the cheque, "Good old Uncle Greg." It was the first real money of her own she had ever had.

Stuffing the mail into the glove compartment, a glance at her watch told her it was time for 'feet back on the ground and some honest work', otherwise the furniture would arrive and her head would still be somewhere in the clouds. Hauling a cardboard box out of the back of the car, Fiona hurried into the house and putting it down on the floor, unpacked the contents. It contained the essential ingredients for making tea and coffee, and a mug of the latter was definitely 'a must' before she could get into serious action.

By the time the lorry rolled in, Fiona was back on track and well in control of the situation. The men moved with incredible speed, handling the furniture with an ease born of practice, and as she rushed from room to room instructing "Here," "There," "No, sorry – on that wall," her face flushed pink with the effort, the cottage became hers as her familiar possessions settled into their new surroundings.

Cups of tea all round, many thanks and a grateful tip later, Fiona waved the men on their way and drew a deep breath of satisfaction. Life in Mid-Devon would have to be exceedingly grim for her not to stay on beyond the original six months, and she had every intention of ensuring that this would not be the case.

Corah phoned to apologise for not coming over as planned, but 'something had come up' and she hoped Fiona was getting on all right. Secretly relieved that she would be able to spend the rest of the day on her own, Fiona thanked Corah for her concern and assured her that all was going well.

The next move was a visit to the Longbottom Village Store for some basic supplies, and that in itself could well be a novel experience.

It was.

An antiquated bell ding-donged as Fiona pushed open the brown painted shop door. The window was full of fly-blown curly-edged cards, advertising a variety of desirables from 'Good as new' horse hair mattresses; countless kittens; logs cut to size; hedging and stone walling, to 'Quiet bay gelding, suitable for novice rider'. Dodo must definitely be kept away from that one, Fiona decided.

"Afferrnoon Mrs McLeod." The female voice emanated

from behind a stack of lavatory paper.

"How on Earth do you know...?" Fiona began. ('Silly question' she thought, advancing towards the voice). "I'm afraid you've got the better of me on names!" she laughed, making out a titanic female shape standing behind the tiny counter.

"Jes call me Verrra – all doos in these parrts."

"Well, hello Vera and yes, I am Mrs McLeod but do please call me Fiona. I'm sure I shall be a regular visitor to your splendid emporium."

"E-m-p-o-r-r-i-u-m" Vera repeated slowly, a look of confusion crossing her kindly round face. "Folks round 'earrs calls this place a Shup – and that's what 'errs be, no emperorr what not."

"Sorry," laughed Fiona, "it's just another word for a shop that sells a wide range of things, and I can see yours does. It's a compliment really." she added brightly, fearful of getting off on the wrong foot with the Queen of Longbottom.

Vera's shop did indeed sell the most diverse collection of items ever gathered under one roof, and Fiona could see that virtually all her needs could be met once she had learnt her way round the extraordinary jumble where cabbages rubbed shoulders with light bulbs and firelighters with Fisherman's Friend cough lozenges; not to mention the unmentionables which nestled discreetly between paint stripper and shoe polish. But for now, all she needed were some basic stores and a few easy meals. These were readily provided and competently stacked away by Vera in an old Ajax box, which a minion called Perce was peremptorily summoned from the depths to carry out to the car.

"Thank you Vera." Fiona smiled, getting out her purse. "How much do I owe you?"

"Ooh, done 'e trouble yourrsel nowe – it's a slate you'll be wantin I spect – most doos."

"Well yes! That would be very handy but don't you want a reference or anything? I mean, you hardly know me." Fiona was amazed, particularly as she must have spent a considerable chunk of her Mother's shopping basket cheque already.

"I knows werre yu'm be to, and I knows a good un when I sees un. You ask me or that Corrah if you wants ought, 'errs knows but not that Adam – 'ims a funny one."

"Corah's been very helpful, in fact she's been marvellous, but I haven't met either of the Mr Croakers yet. Plenty of time though." Fiona grinned weakly, careful not to give the wrong impression in case Vera turned out to be Adam's great-aunt – you could never tell in these country villages, and 'funny one' or no, blood was thicker than water and without the shop, Fiona's life would definitely take a downward turn and an upward petrol bill.

Old Perce shuffled back into the shop, skinny and bent, and Fiona wondered if he was Mr Vera. She smiled and thanked him for carrying her box, but the only response was a strange grunt. No doubt she would soon learn who was who in Longbottom-in-the-Mire, but for now it was time to go back and get on with the task of organising Stone Lea.

When Fiona returned, she found a note from Corah pinned to the door saying she had managed to pop in briefly after all and was sorry to have missed Fiona. But she had got the Rayburn going and laid a fire ready in the sitting room and if she had any problems, to get in touch. On the strength of her new-found wealth, Fiona decided to treat Corah to some sort of outing when life had calmed down a bit. She didn't quite know what form it might take yet, maybe a hair-do or the cinema, she really had no idea. But the woman had been so kind and Fiona suspected that outings of any description were a rarity to Corah. For now however, there was work to be done, and a lot of it.

By eight o'clock, Fiona had had enough. Her bedroom and the kitchen were more or less organised, and her stomach was rumbling. She was pleased by what she had achieved and energised by the prospect of getting stuck into the next project the following day. She had not felt so alive for years and as the days passed since Hamish's departure, her pathetic fears about lone woman living had evaporated as quickly as her former dependance on her errant husband.

Ensuring that all the doors and windows were shut, Fiona let the now-awake and complaining Mactavish out of his cage. She felt so tired and content that she had no desire to speak to even her nearest and dearest, and alone together, she and the cat ate their dinner before inspecting their new home. Satisfied with what they saw, they retired happily to bed.

***

The morning brought low cloud, blotting out the view over Dartmoor, and it wasn't long before the staccato tap of large drops on the window panes announced that the high moorland rain had arrived over Stone Lea. As all her jobs were indoors, Fiona was not sorry about the bad weather, as it curbed her desire to be outside in the fresh air, such a precious commodity so close to the onset of winter.

By the end of the week, the house was sorted to her satisfaction except for the sitting room pictures, which were still stacked on the floor. Some of the old cob walls were so soft it was impossible to persuade the X-hooks to stay in and she didn't want to risk the bigger pictures crashing down. Vera had recommended a good handyman, but Fiona decided to wait till Dodo's forthcoming visit before selecting the right spot for each picture. Dodo was good at that sort of thing, unlike Fiona, whose hit-and-miss method usually resulted in several pin holes for each final placement as she chopped and changed her mind, gauging heights and levels by eye.

Mactavish loved his new home and settled in straightaway, rewarding his mistress with generous presents of dead mice and shrews, and even on one occasion a small rat.

'At least he should keep the place vermin free,' she thought, donning a glove before removing the corpse with some distaste.

Rolling out of bed on Sunday morning, Fiona made her way downstairs to make a cup of tea to accompany her book during her intended lie-in, a well-earned luxury she had been looking forward to for several days.

"Mactavish!" she called, wondering why he wasn't waiting for his breakfast in the kitchen. 'Better check the night's kill.' she thought, putting the kettle on before opening the back door.

"Oh my God!" Fiona cried, gazing in horror at the mound of bloody ginger fur that lay on the mat.

A pathetic 'mew' told her he was still alive, and she raced upstairs to fetch a bath towel to wrap him in. It was impossible to tell the extent of his wounds, and never having had to deal with an injured animal before, Fiona was struck by panic as to what to do. Corah would know – she would know the local vets.

"Please don't let him die." she prayed to no one in particular, frantically searching for the mobile.

"Hello, Mr Croaker?"

"Yerrs."

"It's Fiona McLeod speaking, from Stone Lea. I'm sorry to bother you but my cat..." the handset went clonk and Fiona heard him shout: "Corrah come 'erre. Tis wummen from t'Lea."

Fiona chewed her thumb with impatience.

"Fiona hi, what's up?"

"Oh Corah, it's my cat Mactavish, he needs a vet badly. I've just found him outside the back door all covered in blood and I think he's about to die – I don't know what's happened to him." Fiona's voice was shrill with distress.

"Sounds as if he's had a punch up with a badger or a fox. Don't worry, I'll ring Dan – he's brilliant with small animals. Be back to you in a min." The phone clicked.

Fiona rushed to the prostrate Mactavish, bundled up in a pale yellow towel on the floor in front of the Rayburn. He was definitely still alive as she could see his fur moving up and down as he breathed and one poor ripped ear twitched slightly when she touched him.

The mobile beeped. "Put him carefully in the car and go to the surgery behind the church in Longbottom. You can't miss it, there's a bridle path sign pointing down the lane and just on the right beyond a bungalow, you'll see a notice saying Acorn Vets. Dan will get there as soon as he can but it might take him 15 minutes or so."

"Thanks a million Corah, I don't know what I would have done without you."

"Let me know how you get on and don't worry, I'm sure he'll be OK. I've got to go now, bye."

Fiona was about to scoop Mactavish up and rush to the car when she realised she was still in her nightdress. Too frightened to find the situation funny, she rushed upstairs and flung on the dirty crumpled working clothes that lay on the floor from the night before, and without touching her face or hair or even cleaning her teeth, she loaded the cat gingerly into the car and sped off to Longbottom. Finding the surgery without any problem, she was disappointed to see that the small, scruffy car park was empty.

"For God's sake hurry up!" she said aloud, beating the steering wheel, and about two seconds later, a green Subaru estate pulled in and a tall, lean man jumped out. His long, forceful strides brought him to her car before she had time to do more than open the door and put one foot on the ground.

"Mrs McLeod I presume, with the cat. Daniel Cann." He shook hands briefly with a firm, dry grasp. "Wait there while I unlock the surgery, then I'll bring him in and have a look."

Obviously not a man of many words, Fiona watched in silence as he picked up the bloody bundle and, ignoring her completely, carried Mactavish into the surgery and laid him carefully on the examination table. Not quite knowing what she should do, she hesitated before following along behind.

"Come in, come in." His tone was abrupt. "Shut the door and stand over there. Hmm, nasty." Daniel Cann bent over the now-exposed Mactavish, who seemed to be coming to life again. "Pity about the bath towel." Quickly filling a syringe, he injected the cat, who shortly lapsed back into his limp state.

"Right. That should keep the old fool quiet while I sew

him back together again."

"He will be all right, won't he?" asked Fiona anxiously, not too sure about the vet's bedside manner, which seemed rather brutal.

"He's got a few of his nine lives left yet." And glancing at her white face he continued. "You're not going to faint or anything tiresome like that, I hope? I shall be some time if you want to sit in the car."

"No, no. I'm sure I shall be fine and I'd rather stay with him."

The vet's face said 'Bloody silly females and their pets' as he bent to his task, but he remained silent, brow furrowed in concentration as he dabbed and snipped and stitched, gradually returning Mactavish to something like his usual self.

"There." He stood up and stretched his back. "He'll have a few honourable scars but hopefully will have learnt not to poke his nose into other people's business." He filled another syringe and shot it into the sleeping body. "Antibiotic. Keep him quiet and watch he doesn't start worrying the stitches."

"Will they dissolve?" asked Fiona, thinking back to when she cut her finger badly.

"No. Best mono-filament nylon. Bring him back on Tuesday week, evening surgery, they should be ready to come out by then. He'll need a daily antibiotic for four days. I presume you would prefer oral to injection?" Fiona withered under the condescending tone.

"Yes please," she squeaked, "but I'm afraid I don't know about oral ones either. You see he's the only animal I've had, apart from guinea pigs and a goldfish, and he's never been ill."

The dark, arched eyebrows rose a fraction in disbelief and he turned away to rootle through one of the cupboards, pushing a lock of grey-streaked dark brown hair back from his face as he shut the door with a bang.

"Here." He handed her a packet. "Just take one each day, shove it in his mouth and squirt it in. If you've got any worries, ring the surgery. Sandra knows what she's doing."

'Lucky Sandra' thought Fiona, as the green eyes bored into her own, urging her to hurry up and get out so he could go home to his Sunday roast.

"Thank you Mr Cann, I'm sorry to have ruined your Sunday." Fiona's tone was sarcastic -'bugger you' – she decided as panic receded and resolve returned.

"All part of the job and slightly more interesting than a goldfish." Daniel Cann picked up the recumbent cat and strode out to Fiona's car.

By the time Fiona got home, Mactavish had more or less come round. He looked a terrible sight with his normally genial furry face swollen and shaved and sprouting plenty of best mono-filament nylon. One ear was drooping and torn and he had a long gash on his left shoulder. Luckily both eyes were intact, though somewhat blurry.

"Cage for you, my lad," Fiona announced, stuffing Mactavish in and chucking the gory towel into the washing basket, before raiding the fridge for a glass of wine to steady her nerves.

'What an odious man' she thought, annoyed with herself for appearing so feeble. 'And why did I have to look such a sight?'

She was even more annoyed with herself for contemplating the state of her appearance, considering the emergency of the situation. She wondered if she should ring Corah, but decided against it as the Croakers were probably in the middle of their Sunday lunch and were clearly the sort of people who considered telephone calls from tenants to be a serious imposition. Some bread and cheese, the Sunday papers and a walk seemed the best antidote to the drama of the morning.

A footpath, starting on the road at the end of the lane, crossed the fields not far from the back of the house, circled round above Stone Barton and joined the lane just below the farm house. Fiona had noticed the sign off the road, and having double-checked on her Ordnance Survey map, considered it looked an ideal length walk for a rather unfit, mature female.

Donning gumboots and jacket, she stuffed the map in her pocket and locking the house, set out on the trail, rather later than originally intended due to having fallen asleep reading the papers. Clambering over stiles and passing through hunting gates, she soaked up the beauty of the Devon countryside. Woodcock jinked away at her approach and a buzzard gazed majestically down on her as she tramped along; a fox slunk through a field of sheep and as the day began to fade into dusk, hundreds of rooks circled over a little wood, their gruff 'kaa' voices filling the late afternoon air as they started to muster for bed.

Suddenly a loud shout broke into Fiona's thoughts and, turning in the direction of the sound, she saw a man rushing towards her, waving his arms and shouting again, "Oi you, clear off, this is private property."

Fiona stood still, watching his approach, and as he came close she recognised him as the rude driver of the combine harvester and knew instinctively that she was about to meet Adam Croaker. He was wearing a filthy green boiler suit and a small woollen hat which left exposed two large ears and had the effect of making him look rather like a double-handled teapot. A long, bent nose made an ideal spout but there was nothing funny about the angry, pale blue eyes.

"I'm sorry," Fiona decided to take the initiative, "but I thought I was on a footpath." She pulled the map out of her pocket, ready to prove the point. She was beginning to get rather fed up with being trampled on by the Longbottom locals and treated with the scorn reserved for ignorant townees, even if she was one.

"That map's out of date." he snarled rudely, long arms beginning to wave again like a demented windmill.

"That's strange – I've only just bought it." Fiona stood her ground.

"Well I'm telling you and I own this land so bloody clear off."

Fiona was surprised that his voice was only lightly accented with the Devon burr and his command of English, if basic, was less rustic than she had imagined. At that moment, Sally snuffled up, wagging her tail in greeting.

"Hello Sally." Fiona stooped to stroke the sycophantic collie's head.

"How the hell d'you know that dog?" He kicked Sally away from Fiona, a puzzled expression crossing the teapot face.

Ignoring the question, Fiona fixed him with the steeliest glare she could manage and continued with her defence. "I was under the impression that this land belonged to Mr Abraham Croaker, a man of greater age than yourself."

"That's as may be but I'm his son which makes this land as much mine as his."

"Right. Well I'm as keen to get off your father's land as you are for me to go, and as I haven't any wings, I shall have to continue on foot. So if you would stand aside, I shall make my way to that gate over there and shake the dung of your field off my boots." And sticking her nose in the air, Fiona strode forward.

"Wait!" A sly look came into the mad eyes. "I know who you are – you're the woman from Stone Lea."

"Ten out of ten," snapped Fiona, "Sherlock Holmes would have been proud of you!"

Croaker muttered something rather obscene, and wholly inappropriate to Holmes's lifestyle, before turning and stomping off back towards the farm, the unfortunate Sally cringing at his heels.

"Tell Corah the cat's going to be OK." Fiona shouted as an afterthought, but he either didn't hear or chose to ignore her.

Back at Stone Lea, Fiona realised that she was quite shaky. The confrontation with Adam Croaker had alarmed her, and it was the first time in her life that she had really faced up to an unpleasant situation and given as good as she got.

'Dodo would be proud of me' she mused, mashing up some bread and milk for Mactavish, who was staring dolefully out of his cage and obviously taking his wounds very seriously. 'Poor Corah though, whatever was she doing with a man like that?'

Preparing for a quiet evening in front of the television, Fiona went to draw the sitting room curtains. It was pitch dark outside, but in an instant of light as the clouds raced past the moon, a movement caught her eye and she could have sworn she saw a figure dodge back into the trees on the edge of the lawn. She stared out, heart pounding, but the clouds came again and the garden went black. Snapping the curtains shut, she raced round the house, locking all the doors and closing the windows and wishing she had the *Hound of the Baskervilles* hidden in the shed – on second thoughts, she decided it would probably have made a tasty meal of Mactavish! Hearing no sinister noises, she calmed down and lit the fire before cooking some bacon and eggs for supper.

'Perhaps I'm getting fanciful, living alone' she wondered, 'Hamish would think me quite mad!' And she realised that was the first time she had thought of him since she had moved to Stone Lea.

By the time Fiona had eaten, cleared up and watched a suitably trashy, non-spooky film, it was time for bed. She had great plans for the forthcoming week, determined to be well ahead of the game before Dodo's arrival on Friday. Impressing her friend was definitely top priority and besides, Fiona had no desire for them to spend the whole of the precious visit wielding paint brushes. Friday could not come too soon.

THUNDERBOLT

Fiona was standing on a milk crate, paint brush in hand, trying to cut in wall to ceiling without leaving a wavy line of Antique Cream on Bright White, when she heard the front door knocker.

"Blast!" She put down the equipment, annoyed at the interruption, and went downstairs to see who it was.

"Hello Mrs McLeod, I was over this way and thought I would drop in to see how your cat's getting on. We like to keep our patients happy, you know."

"Oh, Mr Cann!" Fiona's hackles went up. "Mactavish seems perfectly OK to me thank you, but then who am I to say."

A nano-twitch of his mouth suggested registration of Fiona's sarcasm, but the rest of his face remained expressionless. Fiona supposed that for Mactavish's sake, she ought to let him in.

"Obviously I've come at a bad time – I can see you're busy with the paint brush but I would like to check him out. It was a nasty battering for an animal of his age."

"Yes of course, come in. I'll show you where he is." And she led him into the kitchen where Mactavish was snoozing in his cage by the Rayburn.

Watching as Daniel Cann inspected the cat, and grudgingly impressed by his concern, Fiona relented sufficiently to offer him a cup of tea.

"I wouldn't say no if you're having one."

"Milk, sugar?" She remained brusque.

"Both please – and two sugars." He stood up, watching her as she clattered about with mugs and spoons. "He's done well – I'm very pleased with his progress. Once the stitches are out, he can return to normal life and as I said, I shall be very surprised if he hasn't learnt a lesson from his encounter."

"Good." Fiona plonked the mug ungraciously down on the table, tea slopping onto the stripped pine surface.

"Thank you." Ignoring the drips, he sipped the hot tea thirstily before replacing the mug in its puddle and sitting back with a sigh. "Long day." He smiled as Fiona sat in silence. Then, "Look, I suppose I owe you an apology – I was rather rude on Sunday but it was my first day off for weeks and I was working on a bit of DIY that should have been finished ages ago when Corah rang. No excuse," he held up his hands in surrender, "am I forgiven?"

"I'll think about it!" Fiona pursed her lips before breaking into a rueful grin. "Of course! I'm being childish but you made me feel such a fool, and I was very upset about Mactavish."

"I know, and I don't blame you. He's obviously an old friend and it must have been horrid finding him like that."

"It was."

"I must go." He glanced at his watch. "Duty calls. Thank you for the tea and don't forget to bring him in on Tuesday."

"I won't, don't worry."

They stared at each other for a moment before his long, loping strides carried him swiftly back to the Subaru.

"Oh, my God!" Fiona sat down again with a thump, a strange heat spreading up through her body as the electric current that passed between them hit her like a thunderbolt. Beautiful young heroines in corny romantic novels were the *coup de foudre* specialists, not frumpy 50-plussers whose husbands had bolted.

'Must be a hot flush' she decided disconsolately, washing up the tea things before going back upstairs to continue with the painting.

An hour and several smudges later, Fiona still couldn't get Daniel Cann's face out of her mind. She reckoned him to be about her age, possibly a year or two older; not classically good looking but definitely masculine in spite of his prowess with needle and nylon.

"I shall have to ring Dodo," she told the walls, and forcing herself to finish the section she was working on, downed tools for the day and went downstairs to phone her friend.

Fiona couldn't believe it when, having punched out the first two numbers, another knock on the door disturbed her. She was dismayed to find her heart was racing, but when she opened the door, it was Corah.

"Hello Fiona. Ooh, I see you've been painting – well done!"

"Come in Corah, fancy a cup of tea or something stronger? I've just finished for the day."

"Cup of tea would be lovely, and I'm sorry to barge in, but I've left a bit early to fetch Sam from a school play rehearsal – he's one of the Three Kings and has to sing a solo verse – you know, *Myrrh is Mine* etcetera! He's terribly nervous about it."

"Can I come to the opening night?" asked Fiona, leading the way through to the kitchen.

"'Course. Would you really like to? Sam would love it."

"Yes, I would. I loved watching my two when they were small – they were so funny without meaning to be if you know what I mean, taking it all so seriously and doing their best. Neither of mine were born to be stars of stage or screen I'm afraid!"

"Neither is Sam,and he thinks dressing up is babyish but funnily enough, he's quite musical – can't imagine where he gets it from."

"I shall look forward to that, and I might need Sam as a guinea pig when I start writing my childrens' books."

"Oh! I didn't know you are going to do that."

"Well, that's the idea, once I've got this place sorted and my computer installed. I can't wait to start, actually."

"Great! It's all looking pretty good to me already, you've settled in really well."

Fiona put the tea on the table, politely this time with no slopping, noticing Corah's eyes taking in every detail of the room before coming to rest on the cat cage.

"How's your poor cat? Dan's a brilliant vet you know."

"He's getting on well thanks, and Mr Cann called in

earlier to see how he was. I was going to ring you to say thanks for helping but somehow I didn't!" Fiona finished lamely, secretly blessing Corah for mentioning Dan's name as all she wanted to talk about was him.

"Hmm yes, well I don't blame you for hesitating to ring. I'm afraid my family aren't very encouraging on the telephone. In fact, the real reason I called in was to apologise for Adam's behaviour on Sunday afternoon. He told me about it when he got home."

"Oh Corah!" Fiona saw the troubled eyes, the usual compassion sweeping over her as she beheld the poor woman."Don't give it a thought. Adam was quite within his rights I'm sure, and after all, he had no idea who I was, tramping across his farm. And maybe he's right about the footpath – I was just following the map."

"He's not right – it is a footpath, but he's freaky about privacy, and well..." She hesitated, "it would probably be better if you didn't go there. It's all a bit difficult you see."

"Look Corah, there are plenty of other places I can walk if I feel like it. It's not your fault and it doesn't worry me one jot so forget it. Tell me about Mr Cann – he seems to be a man on a mission."

"I think vets need to be dedicated to be any good and yes, he's certainly committed to the job. Folks like him round here, though he can be a bit short sometimes."

"I discovered that! But I expect his wife was waiting at home with a hot Sunday roast drying up in the oven. Still, it was good of him to call in and check on his patient."

"He hasn't got a wife, at least not one *in situ*." Corah finished her tea. "Any chance of a refill?"

"Sure."

"Your furniture looks lovely here – it's fitted in really well."

"I'm surprised he's not married. How long's he been here, or is he a native?"

"No, he came from Gloucestershire I think, though with a name like Cann I guess his family probably originated in

Devon. Dan's been around for about ten years I think, maybe longer, I can't remember exactly. When's your friend coming to stay?" Clearly Corah was not interested in Daniel Cann's private life.

"On Friday, and I hope she's staying for a few days. I'm going all out to get her room finished and nice for her arrival. My mother wants to come down soon too and she's rather fussy!"

"They must miss you being so far away – don't you miss them too?"

"Yes and no – useless answer!" Fiona laughed. "But I'm trying to stand on my own two feet for once, and sort out what I really want from life before it's too late, and I thought a clean break would give me that chance."

"You're very brave, I think – I can't see myself having the guts to do that."

"I would have thought the same when I was you age and anyway, you don't need to. None of us really knows how we might react until faced with something big, I don't think. I've even surprised myself, let alone my friends and family!"

"Suppose so." Corah frowned briefly. "I'd better go- don't want to keep Balthazar waiting!"

"See you soon Corah, and don't worry about Adam and the footpath."

"Thanks Fiona, and for the tea – 'bye for now." Corah scuttled out, the cares of her own little world heavy on her thin shoulders.

"Wowee Mactavish – did you hear that? He's not married!" Fiona forced the tiny syringe into his mouth and shot the antibiotic down his protesting throat before offering him a saucer of minced chicken.

'I'm going mad,' she thought. 'Not only talking to a cat but imagining for one moment that Dan Cann would be interested in me.'

Another hot flush surged upward as she poured herself a small whisky and sat down for a second attempt at phoning Dodo.

"Hi D – how's things?"

"Great to hear you, Fi- thought you were dead!"

"Sorry I haven't rung before but life seems to be all go."

"Poor excuse but I'll accept it as I think it's a good sign. Means you've cut the cord at last! I'm revving up for Friday though, so I hope you've killed the fatted calf or run over a pheasant or something – I'm expecting a slap-up banquet."

"You'll be lucky!" snorted Fiona. "More like casserole of mouse with boiled turnip I should think."

"I say Fi, we are blossoming. What did you ring for anyway?"

"To talk of course, you ass! I've had a very worrying time."

"Don't say you've grown a tail, or webbed feet?" Dodo gasped in mock horror.

"Not that I've noticed, but poor Mactavish got beaten up by a badger – or at least that's what the vet thinks. He's getting better but it was awful, I thought he was dead when I found him, all covered in blood."

"Oh Fi, I'm sorry to hear that, poor old boy. Is he going to be OK?"

"Yes, luckily. The vet came round today to check him over and said he was doing well. He's called Daniel Cann. I didn't like him to start with, but he was quite pleasant today."

Dodo pricked up her ears; it wasn't like Fiona to dwell on a strange man who happened to have treated her cat, and her voice sounded just a bit too casual.

"You seem rather interested in this Daniel Cann – is that why you rang?"

"Of course not!" Fiona blustered, "I hardly know the man. No, the main reason I rang apart from to have a gas, is to pick your brains. I've had a hot flush – well two actually." Fiona sounded worried.

"For goodness sake!" Dodo couldn't contain her laughter, "I thought I felt the earth shudder on it's axis – when did this momentous event take place? You must go in the *Guiness Book of Records* as the first middle-aged woman ever to have

147

a hot flush!"

"It's not funny." Fiona sounded cross,"It happened this afternoon when the vet left. I felt quite odd – all hot and tingly – really weird."

There was a long pause, then Fiona heard Dodo take a deep breath: "Fiona McLeod, some things are priceless, for everything else there's Mastercard!"

"What on Earth are you talking about?"

"Don't you ever watch telly? – Obviously not – *you are priceless!* Blow the jolly old change of life – if you ask me, *you've fallen in love!*" Dodo yelled down the line.

Now it was Fiona's turn to laugh. "Don't be ridiculous D – how could I have done? I mean, I told you, I hardly know him."

"Chemistry darling, your Bunsen burner has been ignited at last. Rather more successfully by the sound of it than it ever was at school!"

"But I don't understand, how could it happen after only two meetings?"

"I've just told you, if only you'd listen. Think back to when you met Hamish – how long did it take for you to fizz and tingle with him?"

"Well..." Fiona considered the question. "I don't remember ever fizzing or tingling, or flushing come to that."

"You must have felt something."

"Yes, I suppose so. A sort of um... wanting to give him a nice birthday present feeling."

"Oh God!" groaned Dodo. "No wonder he bunked off! That's not love, that's 'Mummy wants an excuse for a new hat and I'm on the shelf' crap. You never told me that at the time." Dodo sounded offended.

"Of course not, I thought it was normal. What am I to do?"

"What d'you think – get him of course, you clot!"

"But the last thing I want is a man, complicating my life. Anyway, why should he look at me?"

"*Gimme Gimme Gimme a Man after Midnight.*" sang

Dodo, "That way you have the best of both worlds, though you can start before midnight!"

"Oh Dodo," wailed Fiona, "please be serious. D'you think if I don't see him again I'll stop flushing?"

"Probably, yes. But I think it would do you the world of good to have a fling. Is he married by the way?"

"Corah says not but it sounds like he has been – he's about our age, possibly a bit older."

"Hmm, sounds a bit dodgy – the question they're all asking in Longbottom-in-the-Mire is 'Can Dan'?!" Dodo giggled at her pun but Fiona was not amused.

"I'm sure he's perfectly normal in that department – he wouldn't give off a current if he wasn't would he?" Doubt crept in. "Honestly Dodo, the vibes were terrific. But then," Fiona sighed hopelessly, "I expect they were only one way."

"Listen Fi, I've got to clear the line as I'm expecting an important client to ring about a wretched cherub she wants for her water garden, and I can see this conversation could go on for ever. But keep calm and we'll hatch a plot when I get down. This is terribly exciting news and I can't wait to see you. Well done Mactavish and the badger!"

"Oh D, roll on Friday – don't be late will you."

"No fear, I shall be down well before dark, and start creaming your face – I bet you look like the wrath of God!"

"Piss off!" The line went dead.

***

"Things are looking up!" Dodo addressed the half-finished cherub, "at last the old thing is beginning the grasp what life's all about!"

She adorned him with an outsize set of temporary wedding tackle, laughing as she imagined the horrified look on the prim client's face if she was to leave it in place.

***

Fiona's outlook was less sanguine, and for the first time since moving into Stone Lea, she slept badly. The prospect of continuing to feel as she did at the moment was daunting; a one-way ticket when it came to love was no good at all.

'Please let me go off him when I see him on Tuesday, please let me go off him,' spun round and round in her brain as she took refuge in the best antidote to distress – keeping busy.

That was not difficult as there was still a lot to be done before everything was ready to her satisfaction for Dodo's impending visit, but it was much harder to stop her mind dwelling on the consequences of her absurd infatuation. She was so happy in her new life, but now this unexpected complication had arrived to upset the applecart.

Whilst hanging the curtains in Dodo's bedroom, Fiona caught sight of herself in the dressing table mirror. Yes, D had been right, she did look like the wrath of God! Fat chance of attracting any man with a face and figure like that, and as for her clothes, even the non-fashion conscious Fiona realised that her wardrobe was appalling. She felt like the rope in a tug-of-war, pulled first one way and then the other – one team called 'I want the man' – the other, 'I don't want the complication'. Who would get their foot over the line first?

Radio Devon was playing *Wonderful World*, one of Fiona's favourites, and as Louis Armstrong's gravelly voice filled the room, she sat down on the bed and cried. She had been feeling slightly weepy all day, but had shrugged off the weakness and battled on with her jobs, determined to complete the task list she had made at breakfast. The spate of tears was short-lived, and by the time she had mopped up, Fiona felt much better.

Tomorrow she would bypass the village shop and visit Okehampton to stock up for the weekend. Menu planning was rather fun, and for Dodo's first night, Fiona decided to push the boat out and indulge in smoked salmon, fillet of beef *en croute* and the best selection of Devon cheese available. Her mother would be pleased to hear that her contribution had been well spent, and Dodo would have as near her fatted calf as possible.

While Fiona was ensconced at the kitchen table the next morning, making her enormous shopping list, a shadow passed the window, startling her. Glancing up at the back door, she was dismayed to see the tea-pot head of Adam Croaker peering in through the glass panes that formed the top half of the door. He was wearing exactly the same clothes as when they had confronted each other on Sunday, and he looked no less mad. As they made eye contact, he held up a brace of pheasants, joggling them at her so that their dangling dead feet danced a macabre tango in mid-air. There was no way she could ignore him.

"Corah thought you might like 'em." He thrust the birds at her, leering nastily when she hesitated to take the offering. "I'll hang 'em up in the shed, they'll do with a few days."

"Thank you Mr Croaker, I shall look forward to those." Fiona was determined not to give him the pleasure of her appearing the ignorant, squeamish townie.

"The name's Adam, by the way. Plucked and dressed pheasants before, have you?"

"Oh yes," Fiona lied, crossing fingers madly, "they do exist in Surrey too, you know."

"Wouldn't know, never been there." The eyes flickered over Fiona's shoulder and took in what they could see of the kitchen. "Nice place now, the Lea. Bit different to when you first saw it."

"Yes, Corah's done a great job and I'm very happy here, it's just what I was looking for."

"Hmm, lot of work and money for six months you know. Might you stay, d'you think?"

'Oh God, why doesn't he shut up and go – he gives me the creeps!'

"I don't know yet but I don't see why not. As I said, I love it here and even if I leave, you've now got a very lettable property as opposed to a virtual ruin."

"That's true. Ah well, glad you like it, and sorry about Sunday – didn't know who you were, you see."

"That's OK, and thank you for the pheasants."

"Right then, I'll be going – work to do. Father doesn't do much nowadays." Adam's attempt at affability was almost worse than his normal hostility, and it was a great relief when he clumped off, hanging the birds in the shed on his way out.

Fiona shuddered as she sat down again to finish her shopping list, whether at the thought of putting her hand up a dead pheasant's backside to remove the guts or Adam, she wasn't sure. She wondered, not for the first time, how Corah could ever have married him; maybe he wasn't really as scary as he seemed and was a loving husband. She shuddered again at the thought.

Finishing her list, Fiona decided to give Corah a ring to thank her for suggesting to Adam that she might like some pheasants – after all, he had said that it was her idea.

"Hi Corah, it's Fiona. I just wanted to thank you for the pheasants."

"What pheasants?" Corah sounded startled.

"Oh, Adam came round with some – I must have misunderstood," Fiona bluffed, "I thought he said something about you – silly me – anyway, it was kind of him to bring them, and he said 'Sorry about Sunday' too!" She laughed to lighten the tone before rushing on to change the subject. "How was the rehearsal by the way?"

"Fine thanks – Sam's getting quite keen now and as the other two kings are mates of his, he doesn't think it's sissy any more. Also, he likes the teacher who's in charge of the play which helps, as he can be a bit bolshy with some of the staff – her husband's our occasional relief milker and their boy's Sam's best friend, so he knows her out of school and she understands his occasional moods."

"That's a great help – my daughter Grania was a nightmare at that age! Always getting into trouble and difficult at home too, she grew out of it though I'm pleased to say. She's coming home for Christmas, plus a boyfriend, you'll meet her then I hope."

"I'd love to, and the rest of your family. New faces are at a premium round here!" Corah laughed.

"Better go Corah, I've got a huge shop to do and a ton of cooking – not my favourite thing! See you."

"'Bye for now."

'Aha' thought Fiona, 'so Corah had nothing to do with the pheasants. How strange that Adam had said it was her idea.'

Maybe it was some weird form of constraint that prevented him from appearing the author of a kindly gesture – or maybe not. She hoped there was no sinister ulterior motive involved. Impossible, after all, she was practically old enough to be his mother. Smiling to herself at the very idea, Fiona set out on her shopping trip, burying the little niggle of unease that had crept in as a result of her conversation with Corah.

Nestling in the shadow of Dartmoor, Okehampton exceeded Fiona's expectations and she made a mental note to bring her mother here when she came down. Angie would love the broad main street with its clock tower and enticing old pubs, and Fiona couldn't believe the quality of the stuff on sale in the supermarket.

As she stared at the contents of the fish counter, unable to choose between smoked salmon, smoked trout or massive great prawns, the jolly red-faced *chef de poisson* asked if he could help.

"Which would you recommend?" Fiona smiled at him. "Salmon, trout or the prawns? I want something really nice for a starter."

"Well me dearr," he burred. "I should suggest you try the trout. There's a little more flavour to 'ers than that salmon – verry tasty with a drop of the old 'orrse radish."

"I'll take your advice then and have enough for two big appetites, please."

"Excellent choice!" said a voice behind her and turning, she found herself face to face with Daniel Cann.

"Oh, oh hello!" she flustered, feeling her cheeks go pink as the dreaded flush mounted.

"I hope the two big appetites aren't you and that cat!" he smiled.

"No, no, certainly not." Fiona nearly dropped the package that the jolly vendor handed over the counter. "Me and a friend actually." She felt completely tongue-tied and thanking the nice man, made to push her trolley away. "I must get on." she said, not wishing to appear rude, but unable to cope with any more electric shocks in the middle of the supermarket.

"Me too." His interest appeared to wane, and she heard him order two dressed crabs as she sped off in the direction of fruit and veg.

Cross and unsettled, it took until she got home for her equilibrium to return to normal, and then it was only the workload that achieved it.

"By this time tomorrow Dodo will be here," she informed Mactavish, "and come hell and high water I'm going to be ready."

Hours later, the cooking was done, the trashed kitchen cleaned and the house dressed to kill. Flowers brightened up the sitting room and eating area, an array of new 'smellies' adorned the bathroom, and a pile of clean fluffy towels, including Mactavish's rescued shroud, hung over the radiator. Satisfied with her efforts, Fiona ate a scratch supper, bathed and flopped into bed, too whacked to bother to read, or even think about Daniel Cann.

***

Dodo had a clear run down to Devon without breaking too many speed limits, and arrived at Stone Lea in just over three hours, nicely in time for tea. Excited at the thought of seeing Fiona, she announced her arrival with several blasts on the horn as she swept into the drive.

Fiona rushed out to greet her, shouting "Welcome to Stone Lea!" as a long, jean-clad leg emerged from the car.

"Fi!" Dodo cried, jumping out, "Great to see you!" and they laughed together with happiness.

"Tea first or luggage?" asked Fiona.

"I haven't exactly bought a campaign chest with me so we might as well bring it in now!" Dodo pulled a sausage bag off the back seat and handed it to Fiona. "You take that and I'll bring the house-warming present." She took a large square box out of the back of the car.

"Ooh, that looks exciting!" Fiona led the way in.

"I've got a couple of other small offerings to help with the housekeeping but I'll get them in a minute." Dodo put the box down on the floor and gazed around in amazement. "Wow!" she exclaimed, "This is incredible – show me more, I can't believe the transformation – it's brilliant!" And they did a quick tour of the house, leaving Dodo's bag in her room on the way round. "Must have a pee, then let's have a cuppa – oh Fi," she declared, "this is fantastic!"

"Changed a bit, hasn't it?"

"I'll say!"

"Glad you like it – I'll go and put the kettle on."

Leaving Dodo in the bathroom, Fiona ran downstairs, delighted by her friend's reaction. Dodo was two minutes in the bathroom and then zipped back out to the car to bring in the mixed case of wine, box of truffles and ready-made moussaka that were her contribution to the housekeeping.

"Gosh, thanks D – that's really kind." Fiona acknowledged the gifts as they arrived in the kitchen.

"Don't mention it, I always like to ensure my needs are catered for! Tell you what, it's getting damn cold out there. It's been a beautiful day but I reckon we might be in for a frost."

"Let's light the fire – we'll have tea in style in the sitting room, I haven't done that for years. Stick a match to the fire and bring your house-warming present through – I can't wait to open it."

Dodo obeyed instructions, and wandered back to inspect the kitchen properly, her eye alighting for the first time on Mactavish. "Oh my God!" she giggled, "What a sight that poor cat is!" Mactavish looked extremely grumpy as she peered at him through the bars of his cage. "Can't he come out? He looks mega fed up to me."

"He doesn't like being laughed at," Fiona tried hard not to laugh herself, "and he's supposed to stay in there till the stitches come out on Tuesday."

"Aha!" smirked Dodo. "Of course! Mr Can Dan Casanova Veterinary – to hear is to obey! How are the flushes by the way?"

"Not now Dodo please, and Cann has two n's so your pun is off course. Tea's ready and I'm dying to open my present."

"It's not off course, it's a homophone, so there."

"I don't know what a homophone is and I don't want to know so stop trying to make me feel intellectually inferior and bring the crumpets."

Enjoying the familiar badinage, they made their way through to the sitting room where the fire was already blazing up the chimney, relishing the dry oak logs that Sam had stacked into the shed.

Kneeling down in front of its warmth, Fiona set about opening her present, unable to imagine what it could possibly be. Chewing up her crumpet, Dodo watched as Fiona broke open the box and waded through the bubble wrap, wherein nestled a beautifully sculptured life-size bronze cockerel. She lifted him out with great care, gazing in admiration. "He's wonderful Dodo – absolutely wonderful!"

"I'm glad you like him – he's a reminder of the first time you said the 'F' word and your life changed for ever. And incidentally, I didn't do what you suggested!"

"Glad to hear it!" Fiona laughed, "I shall always treasure him D, and I can't thank you enough."

"I have to admit he isn't real bronze, he's cold cast bronze resin – and he doesn't crow!"

"That's a relief!" Fiona placed the magnificent cockerel carefully on a mahogany D-end table that sat in an alcove that had once been a doorway. "I might find a better place for him eventually but I'll leave him there for now where he's safe and I can gloat over my new treasure. You'd better sculpt a hen to keep him company! How is work, by the way?"

"Very busy, actually. I can't imagine why, but commissions keep rolling in. My last exhibition went pretty well, and the county appears to be populated with females with more money than taste."

"But that's good, isn't it?" Fiona was confused by her friend's lack of enthusiasm.

"Hmm." Dodo took another crumpet. "Yes and no. Good for money but not so good for me."

"How d'you mean?" Fiona limited herself to one crumpet.

"Well, the thing is I'm OK financially, but only if I keep taking these boring commissions. I'm kind of stuck between the devil and the deep blue sea because I haven't got quite enough money to do my own thing and risk it not succeeding – and because I have to do these endless cherubs and little doggies, I haven't got time to do it anyway."

"You know what the answer is, don't you?"

"You tell me." Dodo ate the last crumpet.

"A husband!" Fiona giggled.

"Oh dear," sighed Dodo. "I think the Devon air has finally claimed your marbles! You of all people should know the drawbacks – piles of laundry, fussy appetites and 'I've lost my glasses' – bollocks to that!"

"Not at all, if you play your cards right. A husband could pay all the bills and then you can create bizarre monstrosities to your heart's content – a few more smelly socks in the wash isn't going to take up that much extra time."

"Fi, I do believe your metamorphosis is getting out of control, and what's more, I want to hear *all* about Can Dan."

"There's nothing to tell about him." Fiona sounded aggrieved.

"Now look Fi, we've never kept any secrets from each other, and I know that you fancy him, even if you haven't cottoned on yet. The trouble with you is you don't know what all this flushing and tingling means. I do and I'm telling you, so let's stop all this waffle and get to the nitty gritty!"

"*Yes yes yes!*" Fiona cried, falling back in the chair and kicking her legs in the air, "I'm absolutely potty, obsessed, ape-shit crazy about him and it's driving me nuts! But why should he look at me?" she wailed, feet flumping back onto the floor.

"No reason at all if you continue to go around looking like a thrice-mashed turnip. But fear not, help is at hand and I have great plans for your transformation into the Helen of Longbottom-in-the Mire."

"Abracadabra – hope you've bought your magic wand 'cos you'll need it!"

"Not at all. An Aunt Dorothy make-over should do the trick – plus a visit to your nearest civilised town, if such a thing exists!"

"Hey! That's not a bad idea." Fiona was enthusiastic, "Exeter must be OK and dear Uncle Greg sent me a cheque for £5k so I've got a few quid in hand."

"I say, that was decent of him – how is the old boy?"

"Sounded fine when we last spoke. His leg's mending well and the lovely Diana still seems to be in close attendance. He's getting very excited about some horse in this syndicate thing he's bought into – he only owns about one-hundredth of a hoof but that doesn't seem to matter!"

"What's its name? I must keep an eye out for it – might be worth a bet – you never know."

"I can't remember, but I'll find out sometime and let you know." Fiona got up to put a log on the fire and clear away the tea things. "Shall we go for a short walk before it gets dark? There should be a good sunset tonight – but we haven't got much time left."

"Good idea, I'll get a coat." And after a quick inspection of the small garden, they tramped off down the lane.

"This is marvellous Fi," enthused Dodo, drawing great breaths of the chill evening air into her lungs. "Not a sound of a car or a sight of a street light – I could get to like this. And who knows, we might get lucky and hear the chilling cackle of an early evening witch, echoing across from the glowering moor!" She made a silly quavering 'wweeerr' noise, clutching at Fiona's arm in mock fright.

"Don't spook me!" Fiona pleaded, quickening her pace. "Did I tell you about the shadow in the garden?"

"No?" Dodo's voice rose in query.

"I'm sure it was nothing really, but I thought I saw a man lurking in the garden and when I went to draw the curtains, he disappeared into the trees."

"Gosh, was he stunningly attractive and sexy?"

"It's not funny Dodo – it frightened the life out of me."

"Sorry Fi," Dodo couldn't quite keep the amusement out of her voice, "it must have been scary, you being alone and defenceless, but I'm sure you probably imagined it."

"Maybe," Fiona frowned, "but it *is* isolated and so quiet – a bit different to Wood End – and don't forget I've never lived alone before."

"Yes – I can see that, but you're OK with it really, aren't you?"

"Oh yes, I love it here, and as you say, it was probably my imagination. Come on, we'd better get back – it'll be dark soon."

As they marched along the lane on the last leg of the walk they saw a tall, gaunt figure coming towards them. He wore a flat cap, an ancient scruffy tweed jacket, and carried a stout stick that appeared to have been cut from a hedge. Below the knee, his long skinny shanks were encased in an enormous pair of gum boots that appeared almost too heavy for the legs to lift.

"Who on Earth's that?" whispered Dodo as they drew nearer.

"I don't know but at a guess I should say it's my landlord."

The old man made as if to trudge on by but emboldened by Dodo's presence, Fiona decided to force a meeting. "Good evening," she smiled, "lovely one for a walk."

He stopped reluctantly, staring at the two women. "Yerrs, 'ers be."

Fiona noticed that all bar one of the buttons were missing from his jacket and the old turkey neck stuck out of a collar so frayed that most of the material had disappeared. "Are you by any chance Mr Croaker?" Fiona tried again.

"Yerrs."

"I'm very pleased to meet you – I'm Fiona McLeod from Stone Lea and this is my friend Dodo who's staying for a few days." She held out her right hand in greeting.

After a pause, he laid his stick against the hedge, removed his cap and took her outstretched hand in a firm, desiccated grasp. Dodo stood back and kept her hands in her pockets.

"I love your house," Fiona battled on, "and Corah's done a terrific job on it, I'm so pleased."

"'Errs doos things well, yerrs." And to Fiona's surprise, his rheumy, porcine eyes twinkled and he smiled at her, his gums populated by the occasional yellowing tooth.

"You must come in one day and see it – have a cup of tea."

"Verry kind of e missus. Best be on now, day's done." He sniffed the air like an aged hound whose hunting days were long gone, before picking up his stick and nodding to his tenant.

"'Night Mr Croaker." Fiona called out as the figure disappeared up the lane and was swallowed up by the darkness.

"Crikey!" Dodo gasped. "He's unreal! God I'm freezing, let's run." She set off to jog the last couple of hundred yards back to the house.

"I think he's rather sweet." Fiona panted, as ever trying to keep up.

"You don't think he's the mystery peeping Tom, do you?"

"Don't be stupid!"

"Race you to the front door!" Dodo sprinted ahead, winning easily. Bolting the door, they both made a beeline for the fire, which was glowing quietly but in need of some more logs.

"Be a star and get some wood in could you D, while I feed Mactavish – it's in the shed."

"Hey Fi, like the road-kill!" said Dodo as she reappeared with an armful of wood. "When are we going to eat them?"

"I'd forgotten all about them – Corah's husband Adam

bought them round. I'm not sure I'm up to dealing with them to be honest, I thought I'd dump them in the wood and let some creature of the night enjoy them."

"No fear! I'll do them if you like, can't be much different to a chicken and I've done plenty of them in my time. I'll cook them too – they'll be delicious and I can't bear waste."

"Great if you don't mind, let's have them on Monday – he said they could do with hanging for a day or two."

"What's he like?" Dodo enquired, getting a bottle of wine out of the fridge.

"Horrible! He gives me the creeps and I think he's a bit bonkers. He's not too bad looking I suppose, if you scraped the cow muck off, but he's got those mad, staring pale blue eyes that psychopaths always have in books and movies. I told you about the incident of the foot path didn't I?"

"Hmm yes, you did. Still, you don't have to worry old thing, you'd be a bit on the antique side for him, I should imagine."

"Well that's one consolation for being over the hill I suppose, and he can't be that bad for Corah to have married him."

"Perhaps he ravished her in the silage clamp and then imprisoned her in a milk churn until she agreed to unholy wedlock."

"Yes indeed, that could well have been it!" Fiona played along with Dodo's daftness whilst getting the *boeuf en croute* out of the fridge to paint the pastry with beaten egg.

"Don't tell me!" Dodo eyed the dish. "A giant Devon pasty, how exquisite, lumps of turnip in *sauce au gristle* with a drizzle of *pomme de terre frappe* – oh heaven!"

"How did you guess – I presume you like your gristle rare?"

"Yerrrs!"

"Oh Dodo!" hooted Fiona, "I can't tell you how good it is to see you and have a real laugh again."

"I know," agreed Dodo, "I can't think of anyone else I ever really laugh with like I do with you. I am rather bothered about you though." she sounded serious.

"Oh! Why?"

"Tsch!" Dodo sucked her teeth thoughtfully, "I fear you might be over intellectually challenged living in Longbottom. I mean, d'you think you can keep up with the cerebral powers of your neighbouring Devonians? I don't want you getting an inferiority complex at your time of life."

Fiona threw her pig's head oven-glove at her friend, missing by miles and startling Mactavish as it landed on his cage. "Why don't you go and have a bath or something useful like that and leave me in peace to prepare the fatted pasty? For your information, Ms Smart Arse, my Devonian neighbours know a lot more about a lot of things than you do so boo snubs!"

Rescuing the glove and hurling it back, Dodo jumped up and, sniffing an armpit, curtsied elegantly before heading towards the door. "I take the hint Mistress McLeod, and go to scrub my odiferous body. But be warned, I have tidings to impart upon my return."

Dodo made the most of her bath, shaking liberal quantities of Fiona's 'smellies' into the steaming hot water, and it was only when she noticed that her fingers looked like white prunes that she realised how long she had been there. By the time she reappeared downstairs, Fiona had changed into a clean pair of trousers and supper was minutes away.

"That was one of the best baths I've had in years – the water's boiling."

"The Rayburn's incredibly efficient and now I've got the hang of the oven temperature, I'm completely hooked on cooking on it too – I wouldn't change it for anything." Fiona nibbled a pistachio nut and pushed the bowl towards Dodo. "Let's eat, it's all ready and I want to hear what these tidings are you have to tell me." Head on one side, she studied her gleaming clean friend. "If I was to hazard a guess, I would say by the look in your eyes it has to do with sex!"

"You rat!" laughed Dodo, "Now why ever should you think that? How d'you know I'm not thinking of taking the veil!"

"Pigs have got more chance of flying!" Fiona snorted, leading the way through to the table.

"I say, this looks good, I'll light the candles. You going to have the computer in here?"

"I thought so, yes. There's plenty of room in that corner and a convenient plug socket. It's coming this week and the man's going to get it all rigged up for me."

Dodo filled the glasses and they drank to Stone Lea and Fiona's career as an author before attacking the smoked trout.

"Out with it D, who is he?" Fiona refused to be kept in suspense any longer.

"You'll never believe it, but it's Puncture Man!"

A look of complete bemusement settled on Fiona's face as she took a forkful of trout.

"Get with it, dopey! Think back to our little boating sortie just after the lovely Hamish bolted."

Swallowing the fish in the nick of time, Fiona's mouth fell open as the penny dropped. "I don't believe it!" she practically shrieked. "I seem to recall your views on him being less than complimentary! Tell all, for heaven's sake – how on Earth did you meet him again?"

"He turned up at my exhibition and though he didn't buy anything, he commissioned an abstract sculpture he called 'Man and Fish' – just the sort of work I love – he set no parameters and went away a satisfied client."

"In more ways than one I've no doubt!" giggled Fiona.

"You can say that again," Dodo kissed her fingertips. "I tell you, he sure knows how to make a girl tick in the sack!"

"But does he live near you and what's his name and situ and all that, and what about the girl in the boat?" Fiona was fascinated.

"Help! Where do I start? His name's Philip Gaskill, he lives near Guildford, works in the City, divorced with two grown-up sons and... wait for it, *the bimbo's his niece!* I can't tell you Fi, he really is quite divine, in and out of bed."

"Hold on D, I don't want to ruin the Devon pasty – back

in a sec!" Reappearing with a flourish, Fiona deposited the full plates on the table. The fillet was cooked to perfection, the heart of the meat blood red graduating to brown on the outside and oozing juice that mingled with the chopped mushroom and herb filling and the crisp golden pastry.

"Oh yum!" Dodo sniffed ecstatically at the delicious smell wafting up from her plate. "This is as good as an orgasm- and much harder to come by!"

"Speak for yourself, I'm beginning to wonder if I've ever had one!"

"Just you wait till you hook Can Dan!"

"Will you shut up about the wretched man – go on with your love life and give me some red wine. How old is he and when did you first do it?" Fiona asked eagerly. " I mean was it terribly romantic, a candlelit dinner with soft music and all that?"

"Not at all, actually," Dodo giggled at the thought. "I kind of took the initiative, and we did it on the studio floor! He was inspecting Man with Fish but got a bit more than he bargained for."

"Gosh, how exciting – but must have been rather uncomfortable?"

"Small price to pay for a good shag and he was underneath – he got clay all over the back of his cashmere sweater!"

"Dodo!" gasped Fiona. "You really are the end."

"Well, you asked me! Anyway, it's time you learnt something about the job – you can't behave like a blushing virgin when Dan leaps on you – not at your age!"

"He's not going to leap on me, but I'm beginning to wish he would" (in *vino veritas*) "though I'd be terrified of being useless. I couldn't strip off – I mean, think of all the cellulite, horrible blobby thighs, lardy stomach, and my bush is getting a bit thin and straggly!" Fiona wailed in despair.

"Clip it then, and for God's sake stop fretting about a bit of blubber! Not all men like shagging a stick insect – he'll have you warts and all if he fancies you and I expect at his age he's got a few warts himself."

"But what about love?"

"What's love got to do with it you banana? It's lust you need! Get wild, unlock your inhibitions!" Dodo collapsed with laughter at the look on Fiona's face – "I bet you and Hamish never got beyond the missionary position – ever try *soixante-neuf*?"

"What d'you mean?" Fiona looked confused before adding, "VAT 69 was Hamish's favourite whisky."

"Aarrggg!" Dodo mock head-banged the table in despair. "Never mind Fi, let's concentrate on your make-over first and then move on to Sex Lessons for Beginners."

"What about the *Kama Sutra*?" Fiona asked innocently, having heard of, but never seen, the well-known text.

"Um no!" Dodo shook her head, trying to contain her hysterics."Too advanced, you'd probably get cramp or pull a muscle! Don't worry Fi, if he's any good he'll push you in the right direction – rather like ballroom dancing without the damage to your feet!"

"The whole thing sounds highly alarming but I'll probably never get him anyway – I'm not exactly a raving beauty." Fiona bit her lip thoughtfully, trying to remember if Hamish had ever paid her a compliment – and failing.

"There's nothing wrong with you kiddo that can't be put right and don't forget we're off to Exeter on Monday to burn a hole in Uncle Greg's handout. Top of the list, sexy underwear – there's nothing like a pair of faded baggy cotton drawers to produce an uncooked cocktail sausage at the *moment critique!* Oh no, it's *au revoir* thick gussets, *bienvenu* thongs!"

"Don't imagine you're going to get me into a thong! I wouldn't be seen dead in one – it would probably be gobbled up by my enormous buttocks anyway!" Fiona giggled at the idea.

"Hmm, one could almost feel sorry for it!"

"Bitch!"

"I've got to stop laughing Fi, my diaphragm's aching!"

"Me too!" Fiona wiped her eyes. "Want some coffee?"

"I don't think I do, thanks. That was a brilliant dinner – absolutely delicious and I know I shall sleep like a log. Why don't we sit by that lovely fire for a bit and then I think I'll head up to bed – all this country air has sapped my stamina."

"Sounds ideal" agreed Fiona, yawning, "and we'll leave the washing up till the morning."

ADAM

When daybreak woke the countryside the next morning, the only open eyes at Stone Lea belonged to Mactavish, who was getting increasingly fed up with his confinement. His plaintive 'miaows' fell on deaf ears as Fiona and Dodo slumbered on, impervious to anything but their dreams.

The cold, clear skies of the previous evening had given way in the early hours to low cloud and the inevitable misty drizzle that blotted out all but the nearest views of the surrounding country.

Full daylight had come by the time Fiona stumbled downstairs, hungover and in her dressing gown, and she shivered as she put the kettle on and gave Mactavish his breakfast. Waiting impatiently for the kettle to boil, it took her some time to realise that the much vaunted Rayburn had gone out. The kitchen was a tip and the water was stone cold.

"Damn and blast!" she cursed, irritated beyond belief as she fished the electric kettle out of the back of a jumbled cupboard. Tea was the first essential, but after that, the Rayburn.

'How the hell do I get the bloody thing going?' she wondered, visualizing a weekend without its vital comforts. 'Ring Corah – she must know.'

Corah was instantly helpful, and would be on her way in twenty minutes when Sam was back home and breakfasted after helping his father with the milking. It was sure to be something simple – she sounded confident.

Deciding not to wake Dodo, Fiona took her tea back upstairs to drink while getting dressed. The idea of being caught in her dressing gown by the up-with-the-lark type Corah did not appeal; the disdain reserved by the habitually early riser for the lie-a-bed would fall from on high onto hers and Dodo's tousled heads.

Hearing a noise from below, Fiona dragged a comb through her hair and ran back downstairs to find Sam in the kitchen talking to Mactavish.

"Hello Sam, that was quick. I hope you had your breakfast."

"Yes thanks." he smiled, still kneeling by the cage. "Can I take him out?"

"Well…" Fiona hesitated. "He's supposed to stay put till Tuesday when the stitches come out. But maybe it wouldn't matter if you took him into the sitting room – don't let him escape though, whatever you do. Where's your mother?"

"She's outside checking the oil or something." Sam stood up holding a delighted Mactavish who, purring loudly, rubbed his battered face against Sam's cheek in appreciation. "Dad says I can do your wood and grass if you like." he added hopefully.

"That would be marvellous for me, we must discuss the terms of your employment." Fiona smiled at the boy with his father's face but mother's eyes and slight frame.

"Dad said 'No' first but Mum got cross and they argued, then he said OK."

"Oh dear," Fiona felt guilty. "I'm sorry to have caused an argument between your parents."

"Don't worry," he shrugged, "they're always having them – grown-ups do you know."

Deciding not to mention Sam's remarks, Fiona went in search of Corah, desperately hoping she would be able to work the oracle and coax the reluctant stove back into life. Corah appeared out of the shed, with a satisfied expression on her face that promised good news.

"Morning Fiona. I think we're in business, you'll be pleased to hear."

"That's great news! What was the problem? You'd better show me in case it happens again."

"Looks like the valve that controls the oil flow got stuck – it happens sometimes. I've jiggled it about so fingers crossed it works when I light up. If it happens again I'll get onto the people who put it in, could be a faulty valve – it's a reconditioned one – they sometimes have little niggles."

Crossing several fingers, Fiona watched as Corah struck and stuck a match into the works, peering intently into the bowels of the cooker.

"We have lift off!" She shut the door and stood up, brushing off the knees of her trousers.

"Corah Croaker, you're a genius!" Fiona laughed with relief. "Thanks a million – and I'm sorry to have been a bore. Got time for a coffee?"

"That would be rather nice – Adam's busy till lunch, so why not? Where's Sam, by the way?"

"He's in the sitting room with Mactavish – and watching telly by the sound of it."

"He'll love that! Poor lad's seldom allowed to at home – his mates at school are always banging on about what they've been watching and he can't join in. He's not allowed to use Adam's computer either, it's in the farm office and that's out of bounds."

"That must put him at a big disadvantage in this IT-mad day and age." Fiona put the coffee on the table.

"Thanks, it does and it's not fair. He's very bright you know for a nine-year-old, and already determined to go to university. Oh well," Corah sighed, "I expect he'll end up following in his Dad's footsteps, though at the moment farming's a dirty word to him."

"My computer's arriving this week," Fiona suddenly had a brain-wave, "why not let him come down and use that? I shan't be writing morning, noon and night."

"That's sweet of you Fiona, and I'm sure he'd love to. He won't be any trouble, I can promise you that. I don't know what Adam would think though."

"Give it some thought Corah. After all, I'll be trying to write for children, so Sam can be my junior editor as well as doing his own thing." Fiona was enthusiastic about the idea.

"I'd love him to be able to come here – it would do him good – and he likes you because you don't talk down to him. Leave it with me and I'll catch Adam when he's in a good mood and have a word with him."

"I know it's none of my business Corah, but what's Adam's problem? I mean, why's he so difficult about Sam?"

"God, I wish I knew!" Corah sighed heavily, a pinched look spoiling her open face. "I'm no shrink, but I think it's a sort of jealousy thing that goes back to his childhood. It's a long story, but you see Adam had four older sisters – his mother had to keep going till she produced a son and heir, or rather a son and labourer. Of course by the time he arrived, his mother was quite old and absolutely doted on him, and he adored her. Then one day she went on a coach trip to see the sights in London, taking the eldest daughter with her. Father-in-law was dead against them going, but the trip was organised by the WI and for once she got her way. You can guess the rest – the coach had a blow-out and crashed, killing five people including Adam's mother and sister."

"God, how ghastly!" Fiona was gob-smacked.

"Poor Abraham was devastated, and he's never really got over it. He sort of disappeared inside himself and never came out again. From what I can gather, it all had a disastrous impact on Adam too."

"I'm not surprised. Dodo and I met him in the lane last night – he's not exactly chatty, is he?"

"Understatement of the year!" Corah smiled. "But believe me, underneath that morose exterior lies a good man. He and I rub along fine and Sam loves him – they get on like a house on fire, rather better than Sam does with his father, I'm afraid."

"That's often the way though, isn't it?" Fiona tried to smooth over an obviously tricky situation. "It's easier for grandparents somehow – they can have all the fun and none of the responsibility if you know what I mean. I can't wait!"

"I suppose you're right." Corah sounded gloomy but to Fiona's relief, changed the subject. "Your daughter's coming home for Christmas, isn't she?"

"Grania, yes. She's been abroad for over a year and she's bringing a boyfriend. Fingers crossed he's presentable – unlike her mother, she's what you might call zany! I'm hoping she's going to stay this time but who knows. My son Roddy's abroad too and I do miss not having them around, but that's children for you!"

Having woken up with a dry mouth that screamed for a cup of tea and hearing voices, Dodo dragged on some clothes and appeared in the kitchen.

"Morning Fi, kettle on?" Spotting Corah, she greeted her with a broad smile. "Aha, the magician herself!"

"Hello again."

"You remember Dodo, Corah?" said Fiona.

"Yes of course, but why am I 'the magician'?" Corah laughed.

"Well, Fi tells me you are responsible for the amazing transformation of Stone Lea from hovel to Hilton in a few weeks!"

"That's kind of you to say so, but it was really the builders who deserved the medal," Corah insisted. "I was merely the supervisor."

"False modesty!" Dodo beamed. "It's great and you've been clever with the design."

"We're going to finish the painting this weekend with any luck, are we not?" Fiona fixed Dodo with a steely stare, eyebrow raised.

"Of course boss," Dodo saluted, "my hands are just itching to get round a paint brush."

"I'll leave you to it then – wouldn't like to hold up the workforce!" Corah joked, before extracting Sam and Mactavish from the sitting room.

Goodbyes said all round and the cat safely back in his cage, Corah and Sam set off back to the farm, walking briskly and laughing together about something Sam said.

"Poor thing." Dodo turned away from the window and picked up her tea. "Now there's another candidate for the Dr Dorothy Make-Over Clinic."

"I thought she was in quite good form." Fiona started tidying up the debris from the night before. "I think she enjoys coming down and Sam certainly enjoyed a chance to watch telly – apparently he's hardly ever allowed to at home."

"Well.... I know she laughed a bit and seemed quite happy, but the eyes give it away. There's a sort of underlying desperation that never quite disappears. I reckon that Adam's some sort of a pig to her and the boy."

"Hmm." Fiona agreed, "I fear you're probably right but she married him, for better or for worse, and there's nothing I can do about it. I thought I might take them to the latest Harry Potter movie when it comes to Exeter, by way of saying 'Thank you' to Corah – and I know Sam seldom has a treat."

"What a brilliant idea!" Dodo was wholehearted in her approval. "Even the awful Adam couldn't object to that."

"Hope not." Fiona didn't sound convinced. "Let's get on with breakfast, then we can get going. I suppose you want to stuff your face with piles of bacon and eggs?"

"No, don't bother – couple of bits of toast will do fine – I'll take you to the pub for a slap-up hunger-assuaging lunch between coats. By the time you've got the painting gear ready I'll have gobbled up this toast and we can get slapping."

By soon after one o'clock, the first coat was finished and the pub beckoned. After a quick tidy up, Fiona and Dodo took off for Longbottom and the Black Dog Inn, well-pleased with the morning's work.

"'Allo 'allo what's this?" Dodo swished into the pub car park. "Drunk in charge of an 'oss – Longbottomers ride KO."

Drawing to a halt, Dodo looked with interest at the scene on the other side of the parking area where a sweating horse, held by a slim female dressed in Ratcatcher, appeared to be having a hind leg inspected by a helper. A pool of blood below the leg disclosed the reason.

"Oh dear, looks like an accident." Dodo observed, "I wonder if she's been hunting – should think so judging by her clothes."

"I've no idea." A disinterested Fiona was rummaging in her handbag. "Don't know anything about it – have you got a comb? Mine's disappeared."

172

"You should learn about the things that go on around you and don't bother with a comb till you've had a decent hair cut!"

"Cow! I thought hunting's been banned anyway – let's get in before the pub fills up." Fiona got out of the car, casting a glance at the object of Dodo's curiosity. The glance turned into a goggle as, with eyes popping, she grabbed Dodo's arm and dragged her back into the car. "My God – it's *him*!" she hissed.

"Who?" Dodo was nonplussed. "What are you on about?

"*Dan Cann* of course, idiot – the man bending down – the vet!"

"Great!" Dodo's eyes lit up, "Now I can view Romeo. Come on, let's go and say hello."

"Not on your life – cover me on the left, we're going straight into the pub." Dodo had no option but to obey.

Pushing through the Saturday lunchtime beer-drinking crowd, Fiona rushed to a little table hidden from the bar and sat down with a thump, colour spreading up to the roots of her hair.

"Bugger me, Fi, you've got it bad!" exclaimed Dodo laughing as she shifted her chair so she could see one end of the bar. "You're behaving like an idiotic teenager – I can't understand why you want to avoid him."

"Neither can I but I just know I do. I always look a sight when I bump into him and he somehow unnerves me – I don't know why."

"Well I do! Probably better if you don't see him till you've had your make-over, but there's no reason why I shouldn't. What d'you want to drink?"

"Um, lemonade shandy please."

Dodo left Fiona hidden in her corner, and joined the queue at the bar. When her turn came she tucked a menu under her arm, grabbed the drinks and battled back to their table.

"Here you are, I've chosen and I'm off to the loo."

"You've only just been before we left."

173

"Weak bladder you know – sign of old age." Winking theatrically, Dodo shot off before any further objections could be raised. Heading out into the car park, she saw that the horse was now bandaged up and the girl was speaking on her mobile, presumably arranging transport for the injured animal. Daniel Cann was packing his gear away in the back of the Subaru and slammed the door down as she wandered by.

"Is the horse going to be all right?" Dodo asked casually, as if in passing.

"What?" He hadn't noticed her. "Oh yes, yes fine. Nicked an artery which always looks worse than it is. A horse can loose a lot more blood than that before it's in trouble." A brief smile touched his eyes as he turned back to the girl.

"I'm off now, Anna – you shouldn't have any problems, you've got some Depomycin if it blows up?"

"'Spect so somewhere. Frankie's on his way with the lorry – and thanks for coming out Dan. He went so well this morning too." She gave the horse a pat.

"Well done – see you."

"'Byeee." she gave a coy little wave as Dan drove away.

"Would you like me to get you a drink while you're waiting?" Dodo decided there was some sleuthing to be done here.

"That's very kind of you." Anna smiled, her face open and friendly. "I could die for a brandy and soda – its been one hell of a morning!"

'Hmm,' Dodo thought, 'hard riding, hard drinking and hard what-elsing – please don't let her be after Dan, rather young for him but men being men, who knows.'

"You're a star, thanks a million." Anna downed half the drink in one swallow. "Ah, that's better! Look, it's a bit embarrassing really but I haven't any money on me. Are you local? I could drop it in sometime."

"Forget it – it's a token to Devon from Surrey. Is your horse OK? The vet seems to know what he's doing."

"He'll be fine, thank goodness. He's my best point-to-pointer, won three hot Opens last season, but he's really a spring horse so there's ages before he needs to be 100% fit. Old Dan's fine for things like this but he's not so good on legs and wind, Barry's the man for those."

Dodo nodded knowledgeably without having the faintest idea what Anna was talking about, and having got no further with her sleuthing, gingerly stroked the animal's nose and bid Anna good bye.

"Hang on a sec, I can hear Frankie coming." Anna finished her drink and handed Dodo the empty glass as the racket materialised in the shape of an ancient, diesel fume-belching cattle truck which roared past the pub and juddered to a halt in a gateway.

"My darling husband thinks he's Michael Schumacher!" Anna made a face and grinned before thanking Dodo again and leading the star point-to-pointer away to the lorry.

***

"Sorry Fi." Dodo rushed back to their table.

"Where on Earth have you been?" Fiona sounded aggrieved. "Don't tell me, there was a huge queue and then the door jammed!"

"Don't be sarcastic. As a matter of fact, risking life and limb, I was doing some snooping on your behalf – I even touched a horse!"

"Well I hope it bit you! For goodness sake let's order, and my glass is empty."

Doing as she was bid, Dodo ordered their food and returned with full glasses, able at last to settle down to lunch.

"You can stop looking like a hen with an egg jammed up its arse and listen. He's v-e-r-y sexy – wow! But don't worry," Dodo added hastily, noting Fiona's peevish expression. "I'm well-suited at the moment! And I *promise* I didn't say a word about you... but the good news is, I give him a big thumbs-up *and* nubile little Ms VPL tight bum with the wounded nag is happily married to Frankie with the crappy lorry! So no problem there and we can proceed as planned with the seduction of Cann Dan!"

"Dodo," sighed Fiona, "you do talk the most unutterable load of rubbish!" And humour restored, she joined Dodo's laughter as the plump, jolly waitress arrived with their food.

Tucking into a vast plateful of steak and ale pie, Dodo continued to recount her conversation with Anna. "The news is not all good though," she giggled through a mouthful of chips, "according to Anna, Dan's not too good on legs and wind, so don't expect an erotic calf massage and absolutely no farting!"

"Thanks for the info – I'll keep off the artichoke soup, if we ever get that far. What did she mean, for heaven's sake?"

"I presume she was referring to his veterinary skills – though I didn't realise horses suffered from wind. Apparently Barry's the man for that, along with the legs."

"Well, I've no intention of getting anywhere near a horse so Barry is unlikely to come my way, wind or no. But truthfully, what did you *really* think of Dan?" Fiona leant forward intensely, squashing her shirt cuff into a mound of heavily-dressed coleslaw.

"Truthfully?" Dodo paused, sucking in breath, eyes to the ceiling, as if in search of the answer to an impossible question. "Phoow!" she exhaled, shaking her head. "Absolute *smasher*!" She grinned at Fiona like the Cheshire Cat.

"Do you really mean that?"

"I *really* mean that Fi, no joking. As my old Dad would have said, I liked the cut of his jib. We only spoke about two words but I know men, and he's OK. So eat up your coleslaw like a good girl – by the way, most of it's on your sleeve – and let's get on. We'll get this wretched painting out of the way and concentrate on your make-over. No mean task," she couldn't resist adding, "and I don't want a balls-up on that front!"

"I can't eat any more, it's a bit sludgy. I hope you noticed my choice of food by the way – salad." Fiona's tone expressed her distaste.

"I did, I did." Dodo nodded in approval. "Those thighs of yours are high on my list, not to mention the lardy stomach!"

"You're so mean – I hope you get fat one day then you'll know what it's like."

"You're not fat, at least only your head, but you have got a bit flabby. Exercise is the key, so let's hightail it back to the ranch and go for a run. Well, a walk then." Dodo relented as she saw the look of horror cross Fiona's face.

"What about finishing the painting?"

"Bugger the painting, that's not going to catch Can Dan. Anyway, we'll easily finish that when we get back – we can paint on till supper if needs be."

Dodo paid the bill and they made their way back to Stone Lea. Booted and spurred, they set out on a fearsome route march that marked the official beginning of Fiona's Catch-Dan campaign.

"Goodness!" Fiona flopped down exhausted on a kitchen chair as they tramped back in two hours later, "I'd no idea I was so unfit."

"Don't you feel better for it though?" Dodo bounced about in a nauseatingly lively fashion.

"Hmm, suppose I might once the pain subsides."

"Do it every day and you won't believe how quickly you'll find that walk a push-over. I promise you, you'll feel so much more energetic and less constipated for some proper exercise."

"I'm not constipated thank you very much – never have been."

"Metaphorically not literally I meant, you idiot! Come on, I need a fix and the smell of the paint pot beckons."

"Oh no!" groaned Fiona. "Can't we stop for tea? Anyway, emulsion doesn't smell and I thought your particular fix was called 'Silk Cut'."

"Yes no yes no, whatever is applicable but I'm going painting. *A Fish Called Wanda*'s on telly later and I intend to relax in front of that after a slap-up dinner – I've seen it a thousand times but it's such a hysterical movie who cares. What's on the menu for tonight?"

"Avocado and prawn mousse followed by chicken à la

McLeod with baked potatoes and broccoli."

"Mmm yum!" sighed Dodo. "What perfection!" She looked at her flaked-out friend thoughtfully for a second. "I tell you what Fi, I'll knock off that painting in no time, so why don't you chill out with a cup of tea, get the fire going, put the finishing touches to supper and then go and have a nice long soak in the bath. After all, you've done all this amazing cooking and I've done nothing. That way, we'll get everything we planned done and both be able to relax."

"That's an offer that sounds too tempting to refuse – so I won't! I have to admit to being fed up to the back teeth with painting. I'll bring you up a cup in a minute – and thanks D."

"No sweat – I feel unusually vigorous actually, I think the Devon air must agree with me."

And Dodo skipped off upstairs to get on with the job. She was well over halfway when Fiona popped her head round the door to see how she was getting on, and announce her intention to take over the bathroom for the suggested soak.

"I should easily be finished by seven, then we can play at being ladies of leisure!"

"That's fantastic." Fiona was impressed. "And unlike me, you seem to have all the paint on the walls and none on yourself!"

"It's all to do with being an artist by trade. Talking of which, I hope we can hang the pictures tomorrow – that's something I love doing – and you've got one or two quite nice watercolours amongst the ghastly stereotype prints!"

"Don't be rude about my collection – actually most of them were Hamish's anyway."

"That explains it – at least you didn't swipe *Monarch of the Glen*, that would have been too much!"

"I didn't swipe any, Hamish said I could choose first, except for those gruesome dark oils of dead creatures and vegetables that came from his mother."

"Well that's something, I suppose. Trust that old faggot to have produced those. I'll find you some real paintings one day, when you've inherited all dear Uncle Greg's money."

"I'm going to have my bath."

"Good idea."

Dodo chuckled to herself, amused by the way Fiona never failed to rise to the bait. The expression reminded her of *Man and Fish*, which in turn reminded her of Philip Gaskell.

Being a mindless occupation, painting walls gave time for thought, and as Dodo skillfully manipulated her brush round the doorway, she came to the conclusion that she felt more for him than for any of the many other men who had passed through her life. It was more than his prowess in bed that appealed, and she was slightly alarmed to have to admit to herself that she found his company stimulating and tender; above all else, he made her laugh. What a nuisance it would be if she were to fall in love – that was not part of her life-plan at all.

Job finished, Dodo tidied up and went downstairs to wash out the brushes.

Fiona was still upstairs, so she went through to the sitting room to check the fire, and having piled on some more logs, decided to lay the table ready for supper. The eating area curtains were still open, and before drawing them, she gazed through the window at the night sky whilst listening to an owl hooting somewhere out in the dark, beyond the reach of mankind. The Devon weather seemed to have the capacity to change rapidly, and the overcast day had now given way again to a clear, chill night with few clouds scudding across the starry sky. Enjoying her quiet moment of contemplation, Dodo reached for the left hand curtain. Infinity was beyond her comprehension, and much as she loved gazing at the universe, it always left her feeling insignificant and perplexed.

"Lucky old owl!" she sighed aloud, pulling the curtain. "He hasn't got any problems beyond straightforward survival."

Then, as she reached for the other one, she saw the figure of a man dart away towards the lane.

There was no mistaking what she had seen.

"Bloody hell! So Fi wasn't imagining it after all."

Dodo's gut reaction was to chase after him, but realising that would be futile, she drew the curtain and went through to the kitchen to find her cigarettes and a glass of wine. Dodo sat for a minute or two, wondering whether or not to tell Fiona about her sighting. It would spoil the evening if she did, but on the other hand, not to say anything would be irresponsible. Besides which, she was really concerned about who he was and what his motives might be. The thought of her friend being stalked by some lunatic when she was all alone was too horrible to contemplate. Hearing Fiona's footsteps on the stairs, Dodo jumped up, and grabbing some knives and forks made towards the table. She had reached a decision, and that was to tell Fi in the morning; there was nothing to be gained by telling her now, but much to be lost if the evening was ruined by worry.

"Ooh, you've scrubbed up well!" Dodo greeted Fiona, noticing how much better her skin looked.

"I've heeded your words of wisdom and started on the wrinkles regime. Deep cleansing and a face pack I dug out of a still-unpacked box."

"I'm impressed!"

"Thanks for laying the table – there's plenty of hot water if you want a quick dunk."

"I'm fine thanks, last night's effort will see me through for a while, don't want to strip all the natural oils out of my skin you know, particularly with the approach of winter!"

"That was Mummy on the phone – she sent you some sort of a greeting – not exactly love but near enough!"

"How is the old thing?"

"Sounded fine, rather perky actually and dying to come down now she's heard you're here. I suspect she thinks she should have been my first guest but when I explained we were still flat out with a paint brush, her enthusiasm cooled slightly!"

"Give it another week and you'll be finished I should

think – my room's extremely warm and comfortable as it is, she'll be fine in there."

"She's made a 'provisional booking' for a couple of nights in the middle of November – needless to say her diary is chock-a-block! I said three nights would be more worthwhile but apparently she's turned up some old crony from the past who lives near Honiton so she's breaking the journey with her."

"Sounds ideal. Anything to be done in the kitchen?"

"No – I think we can retire to the fire. You got any good CDs on you? I wouldn't say no to a spot of background music and I can't find mine – not that they're much good anyway."

"As a matter of fact I have." Dodo sounded pleased at the idea. "Lots of our old favourites, *American Pie,* Bob Dylan and some real old '60s stuff to remind us of our long lost youth. They're in the car – I'll go and get them."

Returning a couple of minutes later, Dodo handed Fiona the CDs.

"You choose while I lock up."

"I don't always bother." Fiona was already sifting through the pile, searching out her favourite songs.

"What?" Dodo feigned shock. "A suburban little thing like yourself!"

"There are very few burglaries round here according to the locals – let's kick off with Bob Dylan – I haven't heard *Mr Tambourine Man* for years."

"Great choice – but I still think you should lock up at night whatever the locals say." Dodo was alarmed at the thought of the anonymous prowler gaining easy entry to the house. Fiona would think differently about it when she heard what Dodo had to tell her tomorrow.

***

She did, and her reaction confirmed that Dodo's decision to withhold the bad news until the morning had been the right one. Their evening had been perfect; untarnished by fear as they drowned out Bob Dylan and company with a sing-along of their own, before recalling with hilarity the many incidents of their youth that the music brought to mind.

"So I didn't imagine it after all!" Fiona shivered with horror next day at the bad news. "But are you *absolutely* certain it was a man?"

"One hundred and ten percent Fi, I promise you. The thing is though, what to do about it? I can just imagine what the police's reaction would be: 'So you say Madam, but were you wearing your spectacles at the time?' or 'And how many glasses of wine did you say you drank that evening?' Not to mention your 'age' – why is it a common misconception that menopausal females go a bit bonkers I wonder? I've never met any that have."

"Could be useful I suppose, if you've murdered your husband or somesuch, you might get away with manslaughter."

"Hmm – 'M'Lud, my client, under gross provocation, (Section 101 of the 1726 Act of Grievance) did assault the deceased with Exhibit A whilst the balance of her ovaries was disturbed.'"

"For heaven's sake, Dodo!" Fiona couldn't help giggling. "Please be serious. *What am I going to do*? I can tell you one thing, I'm not bloody well letting some nutter drive me out of Stone Lea. I agree about the police though, but I think I ought to tell them and you never know, there might be some harmless weirdo around who's a known Peeping Tom. Could you make out what he looked like or was wearing?"

"'Fraid not, no." Dodo shook her head after trying hard to recall the sighting. "It was all too quick and too dark."

"I cannot imagine what the point of it can be for whoever's doing it. I mean, what is he hoping to gain – if my car's here and the lights are on, it's obviously not an ideal burglary scenario and if he was going to break in regardless and bang me over the head, then he would have done it by now."

"He's probably hoping to catch a sight of you in the nude!"

"Well he must be loony then! Anyway, he'd have a ladder

wouldn't he?" Fiona was always practical.

"Could there be anyone who resents you being here?"

"I don't know anyone here yet except the Croakers, and I must be manna from heaven to them with all the rent I'm paying, and looking after the property. No, I can't understand it at all."

"Look Fi, you should tell the police tomorrow and beyond that there isn't much you can do at the moment. But you *must* lock up properly and I suggest you tell Corah about what's going on – at least she's within spitting distance, and keep your mobile to hand and a knobkerrie under the bed – better still, get that veterinary in there! Now I'd better go and pluck those wretched pheasants. Have you got a lock on your bedroom door, by the way?"

"No, not that I've noticed."

"Right. First thing on the shopping list for tomorrow is one large bolt. I'll fix it – I'm rather ace at DIY, and it's no good turning you into a raving sex pot for Can Dan if someone else gets there first!"

"Oh go and do the pheasants Dodo, and stop scaring the living daylights out of me! Meanwhile, I'll clear up last night's mess."

Dodo took a kitchen chair and the rubbish bin outside as Fiona had decreed 'Definitely no plucking in the house'. Inspecting the weather and finding it sunny and still, Dodo decided to perform her task in the open air in preference to the shed which was dark, ratty and redolent of rotten apples. Having finished plucking the hen, Dodo went to get a knife to hack off its head and feet before tackling the cock. Lost in thought, she nearly bumped into a man who had padded quietly round the corner of the house and was heading for the back door.

"Oh! Hello, you startled me – are you looking for Mrs. McLeod?"

"Could be – she in?"

"I think she's in the kitchen – I'm just going in to pick up a knife, so if she's not there I'll give her a call."

The man inspected Dodo's plucking site and as she in turn looked at him, the penny dropped: the tea-pot head, the mad eyes, the dirty boiler suit – yes, this was the Adam Croaker of Fiona's description.

"See you're doing the birds then, didn't think Fiona would want to."

"It's not a problem for her," Dodo bristled. "She's busy doing something else at the moment." And she brushed past him to get into the house first. She was surprised he referred to Fiona by her christian name, and wondered whether Fi had given him permission. She was even more surprised when he followed her into the kitchen.

"I'll go and find her. Who shall I say wants her?"

"Adam."

"Right."

Hearing footsteps on the stairs, Dodo rushed through to warn Fiona about her visitor. "Adam Croaker's here." she whispered.

"Oh no! What does he want?"

"I don't know but he knows you're in – I'm afraid I told him."

"OK, don't worry, I'll deal with him." As they returned to the kitchen, Fiona greeted him brusquely "Morning Adam, what can I do for you?"

"I'll go and finish the plucking." Dodo winked at her friend as she took the big Sabatier chopping knife off the magnetic rack and, waving it behind Adam's head, went back outside.

"Corah told me about the Rayburn. I came around to check it was going all right."

"It seems fine, thanks Adam. Corah said if it happens again we should call in the people who installed it."

'Why doesn't he eff off?' Fiona thought. 'I'm dying for a cup of coffee.' But suddenly remembering Corah, she relented; after all, he was her husband and Sam's father. "I was about to put the kettle on when you came in, would you like a mug of coffee?"

"White with no sugar is how I like it." Adam parked himself against the Rayburn.

'Do you by Jove?' Fiona thought. 'And what about a please or a thank you?'

"Cat looks better, then." Adam prodded the cage with a gum-booted foot, earning a hostile stare from Mactavish.

"Yes." Fiona had to stretch round him to reach the now boiling kettle. "The stitches come out on Tuesday, and then it's back to normal."

"Taking him to that vet then, are you? Waste of money, I'll have 'em out, no problem."

"I think I'll stick with Mr Cann, thanks. I'd rather he signed him off as he's been treating him." The thought of the brutish Adam ripping Mactavish's stitches out was too horrible to contemplate, let alone missing a chance to see Daniel Cann.

Conversation dried up as Fiona sat sipping her coffee, but she noticed that Adam was watching her slyly over the rim of his mug as he slurped the hot liquid. It made her feel very uncomfortable, and she was about to go and SOS Dodo when he spoke. "You've met the boy then?"

When Adam wasn't shouting abuse, his monotone speech left Fiona wondering whether he was asking a question or stating a fact. "Sam? Yes indeed. He came down with Corah when the Rayburn went out. I'm very pleased he can keep my log supply going, and I expect he likes a bit of extra pocket money – most children of his age do. You must be proud of him, he's a very nice boy."

"Could be worse. Bit skinny, like his mother." He might have been discussing a bull calf, not his son, for all the emotion that his voice held.

Glancing at her watch, Fiona finished her coffee and got up to put the mug in the sink. Somehow, and she didn't care how, she had to get rid of him.

"I'm afraid I've got to boot you out Adam. We're due to leave in five minutes and my chum's obviously forgotten the time." And before any further drab utterances could come forth, she zipped outside to grab Dodo.

"Come on," she hissed urgently, "we're going out *now* – get it?"

"Got it! Yuck, these birds' bottoms smell revolting – I shall need several jars before I stick my hand in there!" Catching Fiona's vibes, Dodo shovelled everything into the shed at top speed and dashed back into the kitchen – ignoring Adam, who remained fixed to the cooker.

"Hadn't you better hurry and change, Fi?" she said pointedly. "I'll be two minutes – we're late!"

"I'm coming – marching orders Adam, I must go!" At last taking the hint, Adam Croaker shambled out, his filthy boots leaving a trail of mud on the kitchen floor.

Slamming the back door, Fiona shouted to Dodo, "you can come out now – he's gone. But I think we'd better drive off somewhere anyway – I'll grab a coat to cover my clothes, then let's go."

After waiting a couple of minutes, they walked briskly out to Fiona's car and drove off, noticing that Adam had made little progress back up the lane towards the farm.

"Good thinking." Dodo remarked as she saw him turn and stare at the disappearing car as Fiona put her foot down and flew over the potholes to give an impression of urgency. "We might as well go and have a quick snort in the pub while we're at it. He can't lurk around for that long, then I'll be fortified to delve into those disgusting blue arses while you get lunch!"

"Brrr!" Fiona shivered. "Suits me – anything to wash the taste of him out of my mouth as it were. Why does he give me the creeps so badly, d'you think?"

"Because he *is* a creep of the first order that's why, and I tell you what Fi, I reckon he's your stalker."

"Oh God Dodo, that would be the end, but I have to say the thought had crossed my mind too!"

"I've got an idea. Think up some pretext for asking Corah round – she seems to like a chat – and we can bring it up in conversation, not mentioning Adam obviously, and just see how she reacts. You never know, he might have been at it before and they've hushed it up."

"Hmm..." Fiona pondered. "I wouldn't want her to think I was accusing him – the whole thing seems so unlikely."

"I don't agree. From what you've told me and from what I've seen of him, I really think he *is* a nutter – but let's hope I'm wrong." Dodo smiled brightly, trying to cheer Fiona up as they went into the pub.

Corah jumped at the invitation to come round on Monday evening at any time between five and seven. Sam was going to stay the night with a friend and Adam would be milking, so it would be perfect for her. Fiona had explained that they were off to Exeter on a shopping spree to revitalise her wardrobe, and that there was a small problem she would like to pick Corah's brains about over a drink rather than the telephone.

The next round of hunt-the-mystery-stalker organised; the pheasants relieved of their guts; Dodo resuscitated with several glasses of wine, and lunch eaten, the two women retreated to Fiona's bedroom to sort out her clothes. It took Dodo a minute.

"Hell's teeth Fi!" she snorted, "Get the bin liners – this lot is on its way to the nearest charity shop! On second thoughts, maybe the Council tip would be the answer. Wow!" she pulled out a drab paisley-patterned wool dress, "this could go to the prehistoric artefacts museum!"

"God you're rude!" Fiona squeaked indignantly. "Hamish gave me that for my 30th birthday."

"And boy, does it look like it!" Dodo snatched the offending dress away from Fiona's rescuing hands and leaping over to the window, bundled it up and threw it out.

"I have to admit it has got rather tight round the waist." Fiona pretended to sob as they peered out of the window to wave goodbye to the condemned garment, lying forsaken on the path below. Thereafter the process degenerated into a riot, clothes flying amidst argument and laughter, bin liners bursting and Fiona left with next-to-nothing to wear.

"That's better." Dodo surveyed the scene with satisfaction. "By this time tomorrow Phase One should be more or less complete. We'll stock up with new make-up, get you booked in for a decent hair do, facial and leg wax and you'll be away – *You Sexy Thi-i-n-n-g*" she sang, gyrating her hips.

"I'll never be a sexy thing!" wailed Fiona, "Not at my age, and anyway, who's to say it won't all be a waste of time and money? He's probably got his eye on someone else."

"Don't be so negative – you'll never get him with that defeatist attitude – make an effort to look half decent when you take Mactavish in, but play it cool and Bob's your Uncle – with any luck!" she added.

"Bob's not my Uncle – but thank goodness Greg is!"

"I'll drink to that – in fact I could do with a nice cup of tea right now!"

"Me too, let's go, and we can make a list while we're at it for tomorrow."

"You and your bloody lists!" laughed Dodo. "Four pairs of crotchless knickers, two black thongs, one easily removable topless dress – reminds me of school with a difference – I'm all in favour of impulse shopping."

"Well, you impulse and I'll list," Fiona wrote determinedly on a notepad, "and between us we might find something. I hope so, otherwise I shall have to unpack the bin liners or go naked."

"Over my dead body, on both counts!"

MAKE-OVER

A combination of list and impulse proved hugely successful, and elated but exhausted from tramping the streets of Exeter, Fiona and Dodo returned to Stone Lea, the car bulging with bags and boxes.

"Ahhh!" Fiona subsided into a chair and kicked her shoes off. "Stick the kettle on D, I feel as if I've run the London Marathon."

"But what a triumph," Dodo was thrilled, "I never thought we'd get anything like that amount of shopping done in one hit."

"Neither would we if you hadn't bullied and bossed me all day."

"Well, aren't you pleased that I did?" Dodo was beginning to get annoyed.

"Of course I am, I could never have done it without you and I think you deserve a medal for perseverance in the face of adversity! Actually, I'd forgotten how exciting new clothes can be, and what an incredible lift they give you – I may be temporarily clapped out, but I feel ten years younger already and can't wait to wear my fabulous collection. I just hope an opportunity to tart up comes along soon and for the right reason!"

"Don't worry Fi, it will, and then you'll wonder how you can get the clothes off quick!"

"Talking of quick, Corah'll be here in a minute – I'd no idea it was so late."

"God, I'd forgotten all about her! I'll take everything upstairs while you drink your tea and we can have a good old gloat when she's gone."

"Thanks Dodo – for everything – you know how much I appreciate it."

"You don't need to, fathead, that's what best friends are for. Us old beans have got to stick together you know – tell each other when we spot a whisker and all that sort of thing –

we might as well make the most of our crumbling bodies while we can – sex on a Zimmer might be a bit tricky!"

And laughing at the expression on Fiona's face, Dodo lugged all the shopping up to the spare bedroom and began unpacking while waiting for Corah. She didn't get very far before voices from below proclaimed Corah's arrival, and stopping only to hang up a stunning knee-length burgundy velvet jacket, Dodo joined the others in the sitting room.

"Hi there!" She smiled at Corah, noting that she looked slightly less lank and wispy than usual.

"I hear you've been busy, Dodo." Corah returned the smile. "Fiona's been telling me about your marathon day in Exeter."

"I was just saying how I badly needed one or two things to impress the new neighbours!" Fiona made a quick face at Dodo, feeling it would be tactless to reveal the true extent of her spending spree.

"I like that!" joked Corah. "You'll be doing well if you can find any worth impressing!"

"Come on," laughed Dodo, "they can't all be that bad."

"No, of course not. There's lots of nice people around really, it's just that we don't get out and about much."

"Well I don't want to get out and about too much either, at the moment." Fiona could see troubled waters ahead and changed the subject. "What would you like to drink, Corah? Dodo and I will have a glass of wine I expect, but there's whisky or gin if you prefer."

"Good gracious no!" Corah sounded horrified at the idea. "I never drink spirits – actually we hardly ever drink at all."

"Very wise." Dodo came back with a bottle of white and three glasses. "However, I'm sure a glass of wine would do you nothing but good – there's red if you'd rather."

"Thank you Dodo, a glass of white would be perfect – it's a bit of a treat but I don't see why not, do you?"

"Go for it girl, and here's to you!" Dodo raised her glass, "For all the work you've done on Stone Lea to make my old friend so comfortable."

"I'll second that!" And feeling in need of some Dutch courage to bring up the stalker question, Fiona followed suit with an extra large swallow.

"That's so kind of you both, I can't tell you how much your friendship means." Seeming pathetically grateful for little more than normal civility, Corah took a tiny sip of wine.

"Drink up, Corah!" ordered Dodo, topping up her own and Fiona's glasses. "No problem with the breathalyser between here and the farm!"

"Hmm, 'tis rather nice." To their astonishment, she downed the rest in one and held out her glass for more.

Fiona could hardly bring herself to mention the mystery intruder in case it should spoil Corah's brief moment of fun and relaxation. Her worry was short-lived, as to her relief, the ball was taken out of her court by Corah herself, followed up by Dodo.

"You said you wanted to pick my brains about something – you'd better do it quick before I have any more wine!" Like all non-drinkers, a little went a long way and Corah was already beginning to sound abnormally blithe.

"I'm sure it's nothing much," Dodo took the initiative, "but Fi and I have both seen a man lurking in the garden after dark. She told me about it when I came down and I assumed it was either wishful thinking or one too many!" Dodo kept her approach light-hearted. "But when I went to draw the curtains the other evening, there was no question about it – he was there."

"I know it sounds a bit alarmist," Fiona picked up the thread, "but we wondered if you knew whether there was a known Peeping Tom in the village or anything like that?"

There was an uncomfortable silence, and the carefree look that had come over Corah's face disintegrated like a squashed tomato. "Oh!" was all she said, but the gloomy inflection said it all. "I'm very much afraid..." She took a deep breath, "that it's Adam."

"Oh Corah!" Fiona could have wept for her. "I'm so sorry to be the cause of trouble for you – but how can you be so sure it's Adam? It could be somebody else that you don't know about."

"No, it isn't. It's happened before you see, and I know the symptoms. I've been suspicious lately but I prayed I was imagining it and I never dreamt in a million years that it was you – I'm the one who should be sorry." Corah ended sadly, the old care-worn expression back on her face.

"That's nonsense." Dodo insisted. "You can't be held responsible for your husband's behaviour, and neither of us would think of blaming you in any way. Tell us about it though – I'm not being nosy but it might help to get it off your chest and anyway, poor old Fi can't go on having her heart rate increased every time she draws the curtains!"

"And I've got no intention of leaving Stone Lea either." Fiona emphasised.

"Oh, Fiona, of course not. What an awful thought!" Corah's fingers raked through her hair in horror. "Look, if you really want to hear, I'll tell you the bones of what I know."

"Go on!" urged Dodo, slipping another drop of tongue-loosening plonk into Corah's glass.

"Well, apparently Adam's problems all go back to his mother's death when he was only a young lad."

"Ah yes," Dodo nodded, "Fi told me about that."

"He suffers from some syndrome or other," Corah continued, "but I can't remember the name – everything's a 'syndrome' nowadays as far as I can see – anyway, what it boils down to is that Adam has an unnatural obsession with older women – apologies, Fiona!" She managed a laugh.

"Don't worry," Fiona interjected, "I certainly fall into that category!"

"He's never been considered dangerous or anything like that – it's more a sort of stalking thing – kind of subconscious search for comfort I suppose. The trouble was, when the accident happened there were no kindly old aunts around to step into the breach, so the task of being mother fell on Sara, the second daughter who was about sixteen at the time and apparently quite bright. She had ideas of her own for expanding life beyond being a brood mare for the clodhopping farmer's son that Abraham had his eye on for her, and she deeply resented having to sacrifice her life to run the house and bring up her brother. I believe she was very jealous of him as well, him being the apple of his mother's eye. The result was obvious – she was pretty foul to him by all accounts – but Abraham had counteracted his devastation by immersing himself in the farm and more or less turned a blind eye to what went on in the home. As long as the housekeeping was OK and the children physically well, he didn't seem to care."

"How do you know all this, Corah?" asked Fiona, fascinated by the terrible tale.

"From Maggie and Tabs – the two other sisters. They're both married with kids and living in the Cornwall. They come up from time to time to see Abraham – they're nice people and we get on fine."

"What about Sara?" Fiona asked.

"Huh, Sara!" Corah made a face. "The only time I met her was at our wedding. She never married and lives in London doing some middle-powered job. Adam won't have her name mentioned, but she keeps in touch with her father and would like to come down more. She hasn't been for ages though because of the trouble it causes with Adam."

"That's a pity. But you said Adam has done this before?"

"Yes, there was some trouble a few years ago with a woman who lived in Longbottom. Personally I think she encouraged him and then got windy and told him to push off. There was a frightful row and she threatened legal action, but she was very unpopular in the village and the police said there wasn't a case to answer as she had taken Adam up of her own free will and there was no assault or anything like that. She sold up and left soon after and that was the last time Adam's been on the blink."

"Had he been in trouble before that?" Dodo was curious.

"Several times, apparently. It started during his last term

at school when he was expelled for pestering the science mistress. God, if it wasn't so awful it would be funny – could I have some more wine please?" Corah sounded as if she were about to burst into tears. "I've bottled all this up till I could scream – thanks Dodo – and do you know something, you two are the only non-family that I've ever told. The Croakers are ace at hushing things up and I only discovered about Adam's problem after I married him, when his psychiatrist insisted I attend the consultations with him – 'You are of vital importance to your husband's mental health, Mrs Croaker', I can hear him saying it now. Oh God, why did I ever marry him?" Tongue loosened by wine, verbal diarrhoea was setting in.

"Why did you?" Dodo never minced words.

"Why do you think?" Corah practically screamed.

"Ah, the wages of sin!" muttered Dodo.

"But at least it produced Sam." Fiona knew all about maternal love.

"That's the sick joke," Corah's laugh was ugly. "It didn't. I miscarried. You're right of course about Sam, Fiona. When he came along, everything changed for me – and Adam no longer seemed important. I'd do anything for my son, including hiding from him what his father really is – but he's foul to Sam half the time, and if you really want the truth, I wish the bastard would drop dead."

Nobody spoke for a minute, because neither Fiona or Dodo knew quite what to say. They saw the naked despair in Corah's face as she realised that her alcohol-induced outburst had revealed her true feelings, and that was something Croakers did not do.

"If things are that bad, why don't you leave him?" Dodo couldn't understand a woman tolerating such a situation.

"So many reasons, Dodo." Corah flicked back a wisp of dull blonde hair. "I've no money of my own, I've nowhere to go, there's poor Abraham who needs looking after, the old inhabitants of Longbottom would put me in the stocks if they still had them – and of course, there's Sam. It's a case of 'for better, for worse' I suppose."

Dodo shook her head in bewilderment, unable to comprehend Corah's dumb acceptance of her hopeless situation.

"My God!" Corah jumped up suddenly, "I'd no idea it's so late – Adam will be in from milking in a minute, I must go."

"We shall have to talk tomorrow, Corah." Fiona was adamant. "Obviously I'm terribly sorry this has happened, but something will have to be done about Adam – this can't go on, you know."

"Oh, don't tell me Fiona, don't tell me! I'll sort something out tomorrow, I promise. *Please* don't tell Vera or anyone in the village, that's all I ask – and I'll ring you or pop down the minute I can. I'll get onto Dr Anningsley first thing – he's the psychiatrist."

"OK, Corah, I'll wait till I hear from you. Did you walk down?"

"Yes – I'd better run." Corah sounded desperate.

"Come on," Dodo jumped into the breach. "I'll whizz you back."

And she pushed Corah out of the front door and into the the car.

"God!" Dodo blurted out, returning a few minutes later. "Is that some screwed-up woman? It's scary that anyone could even contemplate staying with that psycho – she's nearly as off her rocker as he is, if you ask me."

"You can't say that, the poor thing doesn't know which way to turn. It sounds as if Adam hasn't had a problem for ages and then I come along and it all starts up again. Did she say anything in the car?"

"No, nothing. Just 'Thanks' – then she jumped out like a rabbit and ran into the house. I think she was too flustered and terrified to speak."

"Dear oh dear," Fiona sighed, "it's so awful for her, I can't bear to think about it."

"To hell with that – get real!" Dodo fumed. "You're living here alone and there's a raving lunatic stalking you – bugger her problems, you're the one I'm worried about. I'm not leaving here tomorrow unless I get some assurance that something's been done about her bloody husband."

"I know D, and I am nervous about being alone but I still can't help feeling sorry for her – it must be so ghastly. I can't imagine how I would have felt if Hamish had turned out to be a nut case."

"Well that's a thought and a half, I must say! Still, better to be bored to death than beaten to death I suppose!"

"Don't say that, for heaven's sake! Adam's quite harmless, Corah said so – just a nuisance really. Let's forget it for tonight and go upstairs and admire my new designer wardrobe. I'll wait and see what happens tomorrow."

"That's the most sensible thing you've said all night – *and* – we all know what happens tomorrow don't we?"

Fiona looked blank for an instant and then gasping, clapped her hand to her mouth. "Mactavish!" she exclaimed. "The poor darling, I've forgotten to feed him."

"Go and give the brute a minced mouse meatball quick – if he dies of starvation, *no excuse to visit the veterinary*!" Dodo chanted, twirling off to get a screwdriver to fix the bolt she had bought in Exeter to secure Fiona's bedroom door.

Cat fed and bolt fixed, their orgy of gloating over the spoils of the shopping binge was interrupted by the telephone, and Fiona groaned with annoyance as she tore herself away from her new treasures to answer it. She returned with a smile on her face: "Guess what?"

"Wait, don't tell me!" Dodo gestured dramatically, "You've been voted Turnip Queen of Longbottom-in-the-Mire!"

"How did you know?" Fiona shrieked, grabbing a slinky black dress and pirouetting round the room with it held to her body.

"OK, I give up, who was it?"

"Uncle Greg. One of his syndicate horses is running at Exeter next week and he's asked me to go to the races there with him."

"Hey, that's great news – that'll be a bit of fun!"

"What on Earth d'you think I should wear? I've never been racing." Fiona sounded worried.

"Haven't a clue, neither have I. Tell you what, there's usually telly racing on Saturday afternoons so why not watch it and study the smart ladies of the turf." suggested Dodo.

"That's a brilliant idea – imagine Uncle Greg if I turned up in all the wrong gear!"

"What's the horse called? I might risk a small wager on it." Dodo liked the idea of a gamble.

"Loveatfirstsight – all one word."

"Gosh!" Dodo raised her eyebrows, "It could be an omen for you and Dan – if the nag gallops to victory he will declare undying love and ravish you on the spot!"

"And if it falls flat on its face or comes last," Fiona giggled, "what then?"

"Hmm, not so good! I wonder why they run the words together like that – I've noticed it before when I've been looking at the runners in the paper – it looks weird."

"I didn't know you followed racing." Fiona sounded surprised.

"I don't really, but occasionally I have a look in case some name jumps out and then I have a miniscule bet. I once won £5 on a horse called Dodo's Darling!"

"I know why they do that all one word thing, Uncle Greg told me. Apparently you're only allowed 18 letters and spaces count too, so Loveatfirstsight as four words would have been too many. You can't have any old name either – your choice can be vetoed if deemed unsuitable or rude."

"Oh, that's a pity! I was planning to name my first racehorse Yawanarsole – it means 'beautiful one' in Uzbec!"

"I think you should name it Miss Bullshit!"

"I think you should go and get my supper – we've 'dun gloatin'!"

"I think you should call your next house 'Dun Shaggin'!"

"No fear!" Dodo grabbed a pillow and threw it at Fiona who, fielding it deftly, mis-aimed her throw-in and knocked over the bedside light. Miraculously nothing was broken and laughing like a couple of idiots, they went downstairs to eat Dodo's pheasant casserole.

"Do you think other people of our age behave as stupidly as we do?" Fiona asked through a mouthful of pheasant breast.

"I've no idea – never thought about it. More fool them if they don't is what I say! Did you know that laughter is one of the best things for you – that and the adrenalin rush that comes when you crack a really difficult cryptic crossword clue."

"I can't do crosswords, you know that."

"You could if you tried." Dodo paused. "But I've had a better idea for improving your well-being and longevity."

"What's that? This is delicious, by the way."

"Orgasm – multiple preferably!"

"Well in that case, set the date for my funeral!"

"Just you wait till our Dan gets going – I can see you living to be a hundred. It's never too late to start enjoying oneself you know, and at our age it's positive thinking that counts – not giving in to the inevitable deterioration of the flesh."

"Hmm, easier said than done – but I take your point." Looking thoughtful for a moment, Fiona swirled her wine round in the glass. "I must say though," she continued, "I feel a completely different person since I got over the shock of Hamish's departure."

"I can tell that, just by looking at you, and it's great. I bet Hamish is rueing the day he left you for old crotchless Crutchley."

"I very much doubt it," Fiona snorted. "If he could see me now he'd probably have me sectioned!"

"How's the divorce going by the way – mind if I have some more casserole?"

"Help yourself – fine as far as I know. The Decree Nisi hasn't come through yet but that's only a matter of time – there are no problems that I've heard of, and I think Hamish is as keen to get on with it as I am. Once that's done, Uncle Greg's allowance starts rolling in." Fiona rubbed her hands together with glee.

"Good old Greg – you're very lucky – money may not be everything but it sure helps, and if you take a leaf out of his book on how to make the most of life, you'll do OK."

"He is rather wonderful." Fiona agreed, "I'm really looking forward to our day at the races."

"You'll have a ball, and I bet he's mugged up on all the racing jargon. I can just imagine him holding forth on fetlocks and furlongs and short-heads etcetera – let's hope Loveatfirstsight doesn't suffer from wind or you'll have to call in Barry!"

"Might make it go faster!" Fiona started giggling again and refilled her glass.

"Steady, " cautioned Dodo, following suit, "we don't want yellow eyeballs at evening surgery do we – might frighten Mactavish."

"Speak for yourself, Miss Teetotal of the Year."

"Ah, but I'm not seeing Philip till Wednesday – plenty of time for liver purification. I hope he's up on the bridle or whatever you racing people say, I could do with a good bang!"

"On that charming note, I suggest we retire to the fire and make ladylike conversation – it might help suppress your withdrawal symptoms." Leading the way, Fiona meandered through to the sitting room, thinking as she went how much she would miss Dodo's company when her friend left the next day.

***

Dodo made the most of her last lie-in, and Fiona had hardly finished clearing up the kitchen when Corah's frenzied face popped up at the window. Quickly letting her in, Fiona was relieved to notice no black eyes, and carrying on with the drying up, listened while Corah gabbled the news that Adam had agreed to go and see Dr. Anningsley later on that morning. Of course he hadn't admitted to anything, but she had managed to make him think that his psychiatrist wanted a routine chat and happened to have a cancellation in an otherwise busy schedule. Corah would, of course, let Fiona know the upshot of the consultation as soon as she could.

No sooner had Corah rushed off, than the telephone rang. It was the computer man, wondering whether he could come round this afternoon instead of Thursday because his wife's dentist appointment had been changed and he had to take her to Okehampton as she couldn't drive.

Racing the hoover round the sitting room floor to gobble up the debris of squashed crisps, flakes of bark and Dodo's occasional spilt fag ash, Fiona tripped over the lead and with a spark and a 'phut', the vacuum died, taking all the electricity with it.

"Blast!" she exclaimed, wanting to have everything done before Dodo appeared and having no idea how to deal with electrical emergencies. "Now what the hell do I do?" As if in answer, Mactavish chose that moment to set up a terrible catawauling.

"What on Earth's going on?" Dodo strolled into the mayhem. "Has that cat got toothache or something."

"Shut up Mactavish," Fiona shouted, dolloping some food onto a saucer and shoving it into the cage. "The wretched hoover's blown up the electricity."

"I expect it's only the trip switch – where's the fuse box? I'll have a look."

"Haven't a clue – I've never had to find it."

Shaking her head in amazement at Fiona's lack of basic household savvy, Dodo set off in search of the electrical nerve centre of Stone Lea. Having reset the trip switch and mended the hoover plug, Dodo showed Fiona what to do if such a thing should happen again, before settling down to her breakfast.

Fiona recounted the events of the morning so far, and Dodo was relieved to hear that Adam would soon be in the hands of his psychiatrist. Pushing her empty boiled egg shell aside, she sipped her coffee, brow furrowed in thought. "You must keep this place properly locked. Whatever Corah might report after the consultation, Adam is clearly very unstable. You've got to promise me, and if he turns up, on no account let him in. Will you promise?" she insisted.

"I promise, D – I promise I'll lock up and that I won't let him in. I don't like the idea of him creeping around any more than you do."

"Good. Now..." Dodo smiled, trying to lift the 'last day of the holidays' feeling that had settled over them. "There's only one thing I've got to say to you, and that's 'evening surgery'!"

"Oh my God Dodo, I'm so nervous I can't tell you!" Fiona abandoned her Rayburn cleaning and sat down with a plonk at the end of the table. "Wouldn't it be awful if he was ill and some other vet stood in."

"Most unlikely I should think unless he's been bitten by Cruella de Longbottom's pet vampire bat – you're sitting on my fags by the way."

"Oh! Sorry." Fiona fished out the squashed pack and lobbed it at Dodo. "I'll wear all my new casual country kit," she continued enthusiastically, bobbing up and down like a child, "and maybe paint my nails." She stretched out a hand for inspection. "Perhaps not, they look rather stubby."

"Why not wear a ball gown and tiara while you're about it? After all, this is Longbottom-in-the-Mire, not just any old vet's surgery!"

"Look – you're supposed to be calming my nerves, not winding me up."

"*F-i-o-n-a* – as I can see you've gone completely barmy, I must insist that you listen for two minutes. You are taking an ancient moggy to a very rural vet's practice where most of your fellow pet owners will have straw in their hair and shit on their boots – or the other way round. I'm not having my seduction plans ruined by you turning up dressed like a regurgitated dog's dinner!"

"What do you suggest then?" Fiona tried to sound hoity-toity and failed.

"Hang loose!" Dodo emphasised, "wear the new jeans, polka dot polo-neck to hide creasing skin, fawn cashmere sweater – understated chic and suits your colouring but don't let Mactavish near it – Barbour jacket and dockers – there you are! Tell you what, I don't need to go till two-ish so if you wash your hair, I'll blow dry it properly and do your make-up. I know what your idea of putting on a face looks like!"

"What d'you mean?" Fiona squeaked indignantly.

"Smears of foundation, blobs of powder and a ghastly slash of granny's lipstick!"

"Then why didn't you tell me years ago if it was that bad?"

"Pointless, that's why. Hamish wouldn't have noticed if you'd covered your face in boiled cowpat!"

"Hmm," Fiona sighed. "I suppose you're right. Anyway," she brightened, "I'll take you up on the offer then I might learn how to apply all that expensive stuff you made me buy – who knows, I might get to need it again."

"Good thinking kiddo. I'd better go and pack in a minute – my room looks like a bomb's hit it. I'll do the bed if you give me some sheets, then it'll be ready for your mother."

"Don't worry, I'll have loads of time and I'd rather spend what's left of your visit with you. It's only a bread and cheese and salad lunch I'm afraid, unless I pop down to the shop."

"No no, don't bother. A quick bite will do me fine and definitely no booze!"

***

A little later, Dodo stood back and admired her handiwork. A light touch of blusher over the tinted foundation and some discreet eye make-up had worked miracles. "There! What d'you think?"

"Brilliant!" Fiona stared back at her reflection in the mirror. "I don't look too bad, do I? I've been resigned to the ravages of time but my new look gives me some hope – you're a genius!"

"Elementary my dear Fiona, elementary!" Dodo laughed,

delighted at Fiona's reaction. "It's amazing what little it takes to improve the outlook."

"I shall hardly dare move till I get to the vet's, and I've got to deal with the computer man after lunch."

"Let's hope he doesn't take a fancy to you and ruin my efforts!"

"Don't be stupid, Dodo! We'd better go and have lunch or you'll be running late."

"Better had, I suppose. I wish I could stay longer, but I've an important client coming tomorrow morning and I must do some bread-and-butter work anyway – more boring cherubs!"

"I wish you could stay too – I shall miss you dreadfully."

"*Tant pis!*" Dodo tried to sound cheerful. "Anyway, by the time you've seduced Can Dan, you won't even remember my name!"

"Bollocks, to use one of your favourite words! And what about your Thursday 'bang'?"

"Yes!" Dodo clapped her hands. "Always find something to look forward to, that's the secret for killing the blues."

Bread and cheese hastily swallowed, lemon squash drunk and the heavy-hearted goodbyes kept to a minimum, Dodo revved up and drove away.

Fiona waved until the car disappeared out of sight, before walking disconsolately back into the house. Stone Lea seemed very quiet and dull without Dodo – but before Fiona had time to dwell on her visit any further, a loud rapping on the front door knocker announced the arrival of the computer man.

By the time he had installed the machine, run through the basics and drunk several cups of tea, time was getting on and Fiona's brain felt as if it had spent 24 hours on an Urdu version of *Mastermind*. The man, whose name was Andy, presented no danger to Fiona's hair-do or make-up; the computer was the object of his passion, and as he caressed its unresponsive skin and extolled its many and varied virtues, whilst frantically clicking away on the mouse, Fiona thought she would go mad. At last she managed to get it into his head that she was only interested in its most basic talents, but she would call him if there were any problems. Graciously presenting her with a free mouse mat covered in red hearts and the slogan 'I love my computer!' Andy scooped up his paraphernalia and left.

Quickly freshening up the litter in Mactavish's cage, Fiona rushed upstairs to change and check her face and hair. Not bad, she decided, pulling a face in the mirror and spotting a fragment of watercress wedged in a front tooth.

'Thank God I noticed!' she thought. 'Things on teeth are only slightly less awful than a bogey!'

Sounding the all-clear on both counts, she shrugged into her stiff new Barbour, grabbed a startled Mactavish and set off for the Longbottom vets' surgery.

When she arrived, there were several other cars already parked up, and as it was a first come, first served system, Fiona realised that her agony would be prolonged by a considerable wait.

"I know what, Mactavish," she addressed the cat, "I'll book us in and we'll wait in the car for a while. That way I won't get all hot and red in the face."

Mactavish stared silently back at his mistress, his expression one of stern disapproval as she got out of the car and disappeared into the surgery.

"I understand that your cat might be uneasy waiting with all these dogs around him, Mrs McLeod, but if you want to keep your slot, I should prefer you to be back in with him in ten minutes." The knowledgeable Sandra assessed the assembled canines, "None of this lot will be long and Mr Cann runs to a tight schedule."

How could ten minutes seem such an eternity when normally it was hardly time to iron a couple of shirts or sweep the kitchen floor? Returning to the car, Fiona sagged in her seat as her Waterloo drew near, the waiting game doing nothing for her *sangfroid*. After eight minutes had passed, she gave up the unequal struggle and lugged the cage into the waiting room.

The three remaining dogs leapt up, strings of saliva dropping from their slavering jaws as they panted with anxiety and heat. Three owners grabbed at leads as their pets strained towards the new arrival, scenting a possible kill. Poor Mactavish scowled at them through his bars, arching his back and hissing ferociously while Fiona smiled weakly and squeezed onto the end of a small bench, most of which was taken up by an obese woman holding an equally obese pug. The likeness of owner to dog was remarkable and as they snuffled and wheezed away together through their squashed snouts, Fiona stifled a rising urge to giggle by concentrating on a unpleasant poster showing photographs of the numerous types of worms your pet would get if you didn't dose him several times a year with Slayworm Extra.

The other two occupants sitting opposite Fiona were deep in conversation and appeared unaware that their respective dogs, having given up on Mactavish as a source of entertainment, were taking an unseemly interest in each other's rear ends. Fiona prayed that their consultations would be as short as their upstanding quivering tails, and bored with the worms, moved onto the Lost & Found section.

Homes were required for several 'enchanting' mutts, and the thought had crossed her mind that a dog might be rather a nice companion, and would also provide a stimulus for the daunting exercise that Dodo was so insistent she take as part of her anti-flab campaign. But judging by the surgery posters, worms were the least of a dog's worries and by the time she had digested ticks, fleas, Leptospirosis, Distemper and diarrhoea, she decided to give dog-owning a miss.

The titanic duo waddled and snorted their way into the holy of holies, and as the door shut on the murmur of Dan's voice, Fiona had an insane desire to turn and run. Her prayer that she would go off him had remained unanswered and as her skin prickled and the heat rose, she accepted that she was sunk. Why oh why had Mactavish had to have a dust up with a badger? Perhaps she should have had him put down as her mother had suggested, then none of this would have happened. Her heart was about to be broken and all she would get in return would be a huge bill and a cantankerous old cat!

"Mactavish Mcleod?" A voice broke into her dismal thoughts and springing to her feet, Fiona looked into the smiling face of the cause of her woe.

"Oh hello, Mr Cann!" Fiona returned the smile nervously, reaching briskly down for the cage, mindful of his 'tight schedule' and of bossy Sandra watching from her cubbyhole office.

"I'll take that fat cat." He beat her to it, whisking Mactavish into the consulting room and dumping him on the table. "Go off when you like Sandra, I doubt anyone else will come in now," Dan shouted, "I'll lock up."

"Righto Dan – see you tomorrow."

'At least she's not seeing him tonight then' thought Fiona as she listened to Sandra's reply before the door shut between them and she was alone with Daniel Cann.

"Well now, old chap." He took Mactavish out of his cage. "Let's have a look at you." Mactavish purred and smiled with gratitude as Dan stroked his head and blew gently in his ear. Fiona wished it could have been her. "Hmm…" he looked up at Fiona, "I should have been a seamstress! He's done very well, I'm delighted. Could you hold him while I nip these stitches out? Won't take a second."

Fiona grabbed hold of Mactavish, who seemed reluctant to relinquish his coveted position in Dan's arms, and tried to look competent whilst keeping the cat from clawing her cashmere sweater.

"Relax, Mrs Mcleod." The vet turned to get some scissors and a pair of tweezers, "He won't feel any more than a tiny tweak, but it would be a help if you could keep him still."

'I'm doing really badly – Dodo will kill me.' Fiona turned beetroot red and silently begged Mactavish to behave. For once he did, and in no time at all, the best mono-filament nylon that had saved the cat's face lay in a chipped enamel kidney dish.

"There!" announced Dan. "He can now return to normal life and once the hair's grown back, he'll hardly look any different."

"Thank you very much, Mr Cann – I really thought he'd had it when I found him."

"I know you did – I've never seen a fraughter-looking cat owner!" He smiled. "And by the way, everyone calls me Dan around here, we don't stand on ceremony. Do you have a Christian name, I wonder?"

"Fiona."

"My sister's called Fiona so I might remember! Did he like the smoked trout by the way?"

"Who? I don't know what you mean." Fiona looked blank, then searching her mind quickly, the penny dropped – the fish counter in the supermarket. "I didn't give it to Mactavish!" She sounded incredulous.

"I meant your friend who was coming to dinner."

"Oh! It wasn't a man, it was my best friend Dodo. She came for a long weekend." Fiona decided not to mention the pub car park meeting.

"Ah!" He looked thoughtful. "Corah said you live alone at Stone Lea – it must have been nice for you to have had some company."

"It was – she only left today but I've been too busy to miss her yet." What about the famous 'tight schedule' Fiona asked herself – could this incidental chatter indicate an interest in her? A slight dizziness spun in at the thought. Make sure he knows you're footloose and fancy- free' Dodo had stressed. But how can I without sounding too obvious. The dizziness vanished.

"Yes," he agreed. "Keeping occupied is a cure for most ills."

Heart thumping, Fiona took the plunge. "I've certainly been flat out with changing my life since my husband left in August." Noticing Mactavish's tail twitching crossly, she rushed on before Dan had time to speak. "Look, I must go – Mactavish wants his dinner – it's OK for him to go out and about now, isn't it?"

"Absolutely – you can forget it ever happened." Dan smiled.

'Like hell!' she thought.

"I must get on too – I'll carry him out for you – your super-smart cage is pretty heavy with him inside."

"Please don't worry, I can easily manage." Fiona gabbled, snatching up the cage and heading out, banging it against the doorjamb as she went.

"'Bye then, Fiona."

"Goodbye..." she hesitated. "Dan. And thank you."

Fiona scuttled off to the car as quick as she could go, resisting the temptation to look back. Had she done so, she would have seen the vet's tall frame silhouetted against the surgery lights as he watched her leave.

When Fiona arrived home, Stone Lea was cold and dark. The heat of her nervous arousal cooled rapidly as she hurried about the business of rendering the house hospitable once more, checking locks, drawing curtains and lighting the fire. With great relief, she stowed Mactavish's cage away in the shed before finally bolting the back door and feeding him the special 'liberation' dinner of cod steak and chicken she had prepared for him.

Pouring herself a small whisky, Fiona sat down by the Rayburn and watched as Mactavish ate it up with relish before winding himself round her legs, tail up and purring loudly, thrilled with his new-found freedom. Absent mindedly stroking his plump orange back, her thoughts turned to her encounter with Dan, and having enjoyed his bit of attention, Mactavish left his mistress and stalked off to re-explore his home territory.

Putting down her glass, Fiona noticed a previously unseen envelope with her name on it lying on top of the jumble of papers that cluttered the dresser top, her efforts to confine her desk life to the designated corner of the eating area off the kitchen having so far failed. Ripping it open, she found a short message from Corah.

*'Called in but you were out and phoning is difficult –
hope you don't mind my letting myself in. Visit to Dr.
Anningsley went well so don't worry. Adam is facing
up to the problem (more than half the battle) and is
booked for regular sessions with Rosabelle
(Anningsley's sidekick) who's helped a lot in the
past. Poor Abraham is v. upset. Speak soon. Love
Corah. PS Sam dying to take up your computer offer
but think it should wait till this has blown over.'*

'And to think I left Surrey for some peace and quiet to re-establish my life!' Fiona smiled wryly at the whisky bottle and resisted the temptation to lower its level. Nevertheless, Corah's note sounded good news, and the next item on the agenda was a phone call to Dodo to report on the surgery visit and make sure she had reached home safely.

Twenty minutes later, when Fiona had repeated verbatim every word that had passed between her and Dan and to her excitement, had got the thumbs up from Dodo, she stuck a ready-made fish pie in the oven, boiled up some frozen peas and crashed out with supper in front of the television.

Mactavish slept, curled up on the sofa, and suddenly things began to take an upward turn. Adam seemed to be under control, and Dodo's reaction to the Dan saga was definitely positive; on both counts Fiona would have to wait and see, but for the moment things could be worse. Clearly a trouble-free life belonged in the realms of fantasy, wherever you lived. For every up there had to be a down, and perhaps if that wasn't the case, the adrenalin would dry up and boredom set in – exactly what had happened before Hamish's defection, Fiona admitted to herself. Musing peacefully away with only half an eye on the improbable detective drama unfolding on the screen, Fiona finished her supper and dozed off.

PROGRESS

Arising early next morning, Fiona dug 'Basic Computer Skills for Middle Aged Ladies' out of her attaché case and sat down to play with her new toy. The lovely Stella's computer classes seemed a lifetime away as she pressed the start button on her own PC for the first time, and watched it flicker into life.

Ideas for stories and characters had been forming in Fiona's mind ever since her move to Stone Lea, but this was her first chance to settle down and put them on paper in a properly structured and readable way. She liked the concept of writing for the very young, for it reminded her of happy days when Roddy and Grania were little and she used to read them bedtime stories – which she often enjoyed as much as they did.

Proudly typing *Chapter One* at the top of the page, Fiona began her career as a wannabe author: 'Mr and Mrs Turvy and their daughter Topsy lived in a tiny little house that was always dreadfully untidy. Even the chimney had a habit of turning himself upside down when the cold wind blew from the north and he wanted to warm his hands. Then the trouble was that his feet got cold instead. The Turvys liked animals and they had many different breeds, but queen of the small farmyard was an enormous old sow called Higgledy Piggledy who had given birth to more baby Piggledys than even Mr Turvy could count...'

An hour later, Fiona had pressed the Delete key more times than any other on the keyboard, and staring at a blown up photo that hung on the wall in front of her of the children in Mull, her brain-to-finger co-ordination dried up. Why had writing seemed so easy when she wasn't actually trying to do it? Determined to beat her first bout of writer's block, Fiona made a cup of coffee and, returning to the computer, tapped on.

Another hour later, Fiona had managed two pages that

pleased her. A rumbling stomach declared lunchtime, so she decided to shut down and start up again after tea when her flab-reducing walk was accomplished, and the inevitable boring household chores done. As she watched the screen go black after telling her that Windows was shutting down, her optimism was restored and her mind focused on the future adventures of Topsy Turvy. At least for a period of time, young Topsy acted as an antidote to 'Dan-itis' – a serious disease to which Fiona had now become acutely susceptible.

With the approach of November, darkness was closing in early, and Fiona loved the evening ritual of cosying up Stone Lea for the long nights. When the wind blew and the rain rattled on the windows, she thought of her father who, in spite of never having been a sailor, enjoyed using nautical expressions such as 'batten down the hatches'. The domestic evening routine filled her with a comforting sensation of peace and security, and now that the Adam situation was deemed 'under control', she no longer worried about shadows in the garden.

"I shall quickly become very selfish," Fiona informed a disinterested Mactavish, who was busy performing his ablutions on the hearth rug.

Being sole mistress of her destiny was an entirely new experience, which she was beginning to find very agreeable. Imposed timetables had become a thing of the past, and flexibility was proving to be an attractive alternative. For the first time Fiona understood why Dodo had chosen independence over marriage.

"I've spent over three decades living someone else's life, and now I'm damned well going to live my own," she prattled on. "The children don't need me any more – it won't be long before they regard me as a duty and spoof for 'Who's to look after Mum in her dotage?'"

Grimacing at the thought of old age, she chucked a log on the fire before heading back to the computer. Determined to establish a regular and disciplined routine for writing, she cursed inwardly when two seconds after pressing the start up button, the telephone rang.

"Hello," she snapped curtly.

"Oh dear," answered a male voice. "Sounds as if I've rung at a bad moment. Is that you Fiona? It's Dan, Dan Cann the vet."

"Oh, oh!" she stuttered. "Yes, hello, sorry – no it's fine." Spontaneous combustion jittered her finger, which inadvertently double-clicked on Recycle Bin.

"You sound rather harassed. If the house is on fire, I'll ring back later."

"Oh no, please don't – there's nothing in Recycle Bin anyway..."

'Oh God, shut up you fool!' Fiona's brain was whirling.

"Well, at least I'm not in there."

"Where?" Fiona had completely lost her wits.

"In Recycle Bin of course!"

"God I'm sorry – it's my new computer!" Fiona pulled herself together. "Mactavish is fine, never better actually – I presume that's why you rang," she blundered on.

"Certainly not! I know that wretched old cat's fine – it's his owner I'm more interested in. I was hoping you might like to have a tooth-testing steak and a bottle of gut-rot in the pub with me tomorrow night."

"Oh!" Fiona could hardly breathe. "Um, why not – I mean I'd love to – thank you, that sounds great. What time?"

"Eight-ish, if that suits you?"

"Perfect. I'll see you there then."

"I shall look forward to it. Don't be late and good luck with your binning!" The phone went dead.

Any idea of furthering the adventures of Topsy Turvy flew straight out of the window, and Fiona feared the sound of her thumping heart must have reached Longbottom-in-the-Mire.

Only that morning she had read an article in the local paper about a woman in her mid-fifties, who had unaccountably upped and died of a heart attack whilst inspecting a fossil collection on show in Oldworthy

Brampton village hall. Efforts to revive her had failed. If a petrified snail could bring on heart failure, a date with Dan must mean certain death!

Breathing deeply to stay her panic and ignoring the rheumatic twinge that thoughtlessly chose that moment to shoot down her left arm, Fiona rang Dodo.

"He's asked me out tomorrow!" she shrilled down the line without bothering to say 'Hello'.

"*Fantastico!*" replied Dodo in kind. "I knew he would – brilliant – what's the score?"

"Supper in the Black Dog."

"Wow – big deal! Not exactly soft lights and violins. Still, it's a start I suppose."

"Dodo, get real, this is Mid-Devon for heaven's sake. Anyway, if he'd asked me to a hot dog under a hedge I'd be over the moon."

"Forget the bread!"

"Don't be daft!" Fiona giggled. "You know perfectly well I'm not into first date shags, to use your charming lingo."

"No comment. But now listen – about your preparation and get-up..." Dodo proceeded to give Fiona advice on all aspects of her appearance and behaviour on the great night.

Eventually signing off and thoroughly confused by Dodo's instructions, Fiona shut down the computer and went upstairs to select her attire for tomorrow night. Anything that had to do with her forthcoming date with Dan filled her with a gut-tingling exhilaration, and she wanted to think about nothing else.

"Early night, Mactavish!" Fiona threw him a morsel of unwanted lamb chop before turfing him out of the sitting room. "No bags under the eyes tomorrow!" And speeding one grumpy cat on his way, she shut up shop and went to bed.

Fiona slept badly and awoke to the sound of rain beating on the windows.

'Bother it,' was her first thought of the day. 'I shall have to keep my hair dry or it might go frizzy!'

The omens continued bad when she discovered Mactavish eating the hind end of a half-dead rabbit outside the back door. Gritting her teeth, she administered the *coup de grace* with the knob end of the poker, which silenced the horrid squealing, but covered her carefully deep-cleansed and creamed hands in soot.

Corah blew in on her way to Okehampton to reassure Fiona that Adam was back on the straight and narrow. He had even encouraged Sam to come down and use Fiona's computer, provided he 'behaved himself and wasn't a nuisance to Mrs McLeod'. The inevitable cup of tea later, Corah sped on her way, Fiona having decided not to tell her about her forthcoming rendezvous with Dan. Sufficient unto the day, and no doubt that day would not be long in the coming once they had been spotted dining together in the Black Dog Inn.

Dodo had instructed Fiona to undertake her major facial and bath at tea-time. Leaving it till later might result in overly pink cheeks and a shiny nose. Sipping her mug of detoxing green China tea, Fiona was contemplating a cucumber eye-pack now or later, when a rap on the front door interrupted her important meditation.

Irritated before she had even opened the door, her humour was not improved to find a dumpy little woman she had never set eyes on before standing on the threshold.

"Good afternoon – Mrs McLeod I presume?" she chirruped gaily, "Urania Clotworthy, Chairperson of the Longbottom Ladies' Circle at your service."

Fiona's heart sank.

"Oh, hello." She made little effort to sound enthusiastic.

"Vera At The Shop told me you had settled in amongst us and of course I felt it my duty to introduce myself." Urania Clothworthy's weatherbeaten face poked out of an enveloping macintosh hood, beaming with self-importance and bossy enthusiasm.

"Well," Fiona demurred. "I am rather busy at the moment..." The rain pattered down on Urania's hideous hood.

"But you'd better come in." Upbringing got the better of inclination.

"Oh! So kind." The little woman bolted in, eyes instantly flickering nosily round Stone Lea. "Do call me Urania by the way, everybody does." She bustled forward, shaking like a plump elderly Labrador and showering second-hand rain drops all over the newly-painted cross passage walls. "It *is* such an unusual name, I *do* know – I was conceived in Greece you see, where my parents were studying mythology. Daddy was a Muse man and darling Mummy lived for the stars."

'Oh God!' Fiona groaned inwardly. *'Why did I let her in?'*

"I'm afraid I can't offer you a cup of tea as the Rayburn's gone out and I don't have an electric kettle." Fiona blushed at her lie.

"Oh, you poor dear!" exclaimed Urania. "If only I'd know I would have brought a Thermos flask!"

'Thank God you didn't...' Fiona very nearly said it aloud.

"That's a kind thought, but never mind. Like I said, I am rather busy at the moment and then I have to go out, so I'm afraid I haven't much time right now." – *'Why can't the woman take the hint and shove off – no chance.'*

Desperate to keep Urania out of the kitchen, where she would instantly rumble Fiona's subterfuge, and no doubt inform the entire population of Longbottom that 'The new woman at Stone Lea is either mad or hiding something dark', Fiona offered her a seat in the sitting room.

"My goodness! You have made this lovely. Such an interesting old property." She gazed around, calculating the number of people the room would accommodate. "And if I'm not much mistaken, that charming little domed alcove was once the creamery – the fire would have been underneath but blocked off now of course. Oh, my dear," she rolled her piggy eyes upwards and fluttered a stubby hand. "The Ladies would absolutely die for a gathering here – several of our members are very knowledgeable about old houses, you know."

"Well, I'm very sorry..." the time had come to stamp on Urania Clotworthy for once and all, "but I've come down to Devon for six months' uninterrupted peace to write a book..."- *'more lies but who cares?'*- "And I'm afraid I am going to be extremely anti-social in the process so regrettably, the Longbottom Ladies Circle will not be part of my itinerary." Fiona risked a wrinkle by smiling sweetly to soften the blow. Too late, she realised her catastrophic mistake.

"A writer in our midst!" shrieked Urania, both stubby hands fluttering this time, and trotter-like feet kicking up in ecstasy. Fiona's denial of the Circle was completely ignored. "This is too thrilling for words! My dear Fiona," trotters back on the carpet, she leant forward conspiratorially, eyes gleaming. "You *must* meet Eileen Truebody – Eileen has been published!"

"Really?" Fiona's tone screamed indifference.

"Yes indeed – *Myths of Moor & Mire* – love the alliteration! Of course Eileen is frightfully clever you know – definitely a blue stocking, as we used to refer to the brainy gels in my day."

"Good on Eileen!" Fiona stood up, hopeful that bluntness might pierce Urania's seemingly impenetrable hide. "Now I must ask you to leave as I am running late already." She went and opened the front door, leaving Urania no option but to go.

Casting an accusatory glance at Fiona, she finally crossed the threshold out into the rain. "Goodbye then Mrs McLeod, I shall tell the Ladies of the Circle all about you."

'I'll bet you will.'

And poking her face up at Fiona, who noticed two long white whiskers sprouting out of the jutting chin, Urania fired her parting shot. "Had your attitude been a teeny bit more sororial, I would have invited you to join the cast of the Christmas pantomime – Jack and the Beanstalk!" With that, she turned immediately and stomped off down the path.

Fiona stared after the retreating figure, mouth open in

astonishment. Could such women really exist or had she done an Alice, only in a chair instead of on a bank? No, she seemed to be wide awake and, laughter bubbling up and overtaking her, Fiona skipped into the kitchen to brew a fresh cuppa and slice the cucumber. Poor Daddy and darling Mummy, anything less heavenly or celestial than their daughter would be hard to perceive, let alone conceive – certainly no 'immaculate' conception where Urania was concerned.

Time was slipping by and after ten minutes of cucumber eye restoration, Fiona considered the moment had arrived to have her bath. Staring into the fast-fugging mirror, she was disappointed to notice little improvement in the eye area. Att least her teeth looked good after a recent visit to the hygienist – a zealous young woman who had scaled and polished every tooth in Fiona's jaw until they gleamed and sparkled and Fiona cried 'mercy'.

Sinking into a froth of herbal bubbles which quickly went cold and expired with the arrival of the soap, Fiona dwelt thoughtfully on Dodo's latest axiom: *Man rates woman by shagworthyness; woman rates man by 'will he look after me?' Apparently men can't help being prick-driven, it's all part of the caveman syndrome.*

'I'm not quite sure where that gets me with Dan though.' Fiona ran some more hot water. 'I'm perfectly capable of looking after myself now, and sex doesn't matter to me one way or the other. Dirty underpants, smelly socks and 'I don't like haddock'? No thanks, been there done that.'

Play it cool, Dodo had decreed. Fat chance, when the churning in Fiona's stomach could have driven the Titanic.

"My God!" Fiona leapt out of the bath and rushed to the mirror. Yes, she had stayed in too long and too hot, her face was like a beetroot. Drying quickly, she quit the steamy bathroom and whipping off her shower cap, padded through to her bedroom to cool down and start in earnest the formidable task of preparing for her first date in over thirty years.

***

Later, pushing open the door of the Black Dog Inn, Fiona prayed Dan would be there to greet her. A terrible fear that he might have been called out to resuscitate some stricken animal overwhelmed her as she glanced round the chattering groups assembled in the bar. Wisps of smoke curled up above grinning, unfamiliar faces, and mentally screaming help, Fiona blanked out and couldn't remember what Dan looked like.

"I do like a woman who doesn't keep me waiting!"

Suddenly Dan was by her side, looking just as he had looked the day they first met.

"Come on." He took her arm. "I've bagged a nice quiet spot in the corner by the fire."

He drew her towards their table, courteously pulling out her chair for her to sit down. A brindle greyhound lay by the fire, the loop end of its lead secured under Dan's chair leg. It raised its elegant nose briefly in greeting before subsiding back into sleep.

"That's Lakeview Holly." Dan introduced the dog. "Failed track dog turned lap dog! Now what would you like to drink, Fiona? Judging by the expression on your face, you could do with a stiffener – I'm only Dan Cann the local vet, not Bluebeard you know!"

"I'm sorry," Fiona pulled herself together. "I was just a bit nervous in case you didn't turn up, I mean, in case you'd had an emergency or something. A glass of wine would be lovely, thank you."

Dan went off to the bar and reappeared with a bottle, glasses, a half of bitter and two menus tucked under his arm. "Take the menus before I drop this lot, can you?" Fiona pulled them out and rescued the beer so Dan was able to sit down without spillage, and pour her the wine.

"Here's to you Fiona McLeod," he raised his tankard. "And may I say how very fetching you look this evening?"

"Thank you." Fiona downed a large swallow of Dutch courage, furious to find herself blushing foolishly and burying her head in the menu, hoped he wouldn't notice.

Silence fell as Dan too set about choosing his food. Unable to read the small print properly without her glasses but determined not to put them on, Fiona selected avocado salad followed by steak and chips. Closing the menu and looking up, her eyes met Dan's green killers, and she realised he had been studying her instead of his menu.

"I was going to offer you my glasses but I see you've managed without them!" His smile turned her to jelly. "I'm glad we've got the choosing business over – I hate people who can't make up their minds and waste good talking time bothering about what they're going to eat. I always have the same thing when I come in here – garlic mushrooms and steak pie."

"Why did you bring two menus then?" Fiona was puzzled.

"So you would think I was busy choosing when in fact I was busy watching you – a far more agreeable pastime!"

"Oh!" Fiona frowned, not quite sure yet about his leg-pulling.

"Come on, drink up." He topped up her glass. "It'll be closing time before you relax at this rate."

"Oh dear, I'm being terribly boring aren't I?" Fiona agonised, unable to loosen up. "I am sorry, really I am and I know it sounds utterly pathetic but... well... I'm not used to going out with men and I'm a bit nervous."

Dan threw back his head and laughed out loud before leaning over and taking her hand in his and squeezing it. "You are adorably funny – you don't need to tell me what you're feeling, your face is an open book and a very enjoyable one too. To find so artless a woman of your age is nothing short of a miracle – and all because of a horrid old cat!"

"Mactavish is not horrid." Annoyed at her own naïvety and ruffled by his words, Fiona crisply defended her furry friend.

"That's better." Dan let go of her hand. "Now we can

settle down to some serious conversation. I want to know all about you, and maybe you shall hear a bit about me whether you like it or not. But first, I'm hungry so let's whistle up the food."

Fiona's nerves began to slip away, and the warm glow from the fire that bathed her outside spread inwards, as the sense of pure happiness at being with Dan triumphed over apprehension.

Eating, drinking, talking and laughing, Fiona couldn't believe it when the landlord called 'Time!'

How could the time have passed so quickly? Dan disappeared to pay the bill as Fiona sat staring into the dying embers of the fire, wondering what on Earth had hit her. She had certainly never felt like this with Hamish.

Dan reappeared. "Right, that's done. On your feet, you females!"

He picked up the dog's lead before helping Fiona on with her new and amazingly expensive tweed jacket. Described as a 'must for every county lady for every occasion', she had blanched at the price but Dodo had insisted she buy it.

'It's fab darling!' she had giggled, as the poncing purveyor tweaked at the stiff cloth and breathed 'heaven'.

"Hmm," murmured Dan. "This smells new – needs a few cat hairs and a bit of mud on it if you ask me."

"I didn't ask you!"

"Come on, time to go – and your jacket is the most up-market garment seen in the Black Dog for 100 years so don't go getting all hoity-toity about it!"

Smiling, he took her arm with his dog-free hand and they walked out into the car park.

"The Opening Meet's on Saturday," Dan announced as they arrived at Fiona's car. "It's a Lawn Meet at Grimblesby Hall and I always like to go, emergencies permitting. I could pick you up at 10.30 if you've nothing on – I mean engagement-wise! After all, now hunting's been banned, support is even more important."

"Do they really have all the horses on the lawn? It must

be ruined." Fiona tried to sound interested.

"Oh my God!" Dan doubled up. "D'you know you looked just like Celia Johnson when you said that – I'm an old movie buff and I adore Celia Johnson, by the way. *No you numpty!* A Lawn Meet is when the host provides cheap port and a luke-warm bite-size sausage roll in a muddy field near the house!"

"Oh, is that fun?" Fiona was nonplussed.

"That's a matter of opinion of course but to most who live round here, the answer is a big yes. Not only is it fun, but a complete way of life and if you wish to integrate with your new-found fellow men, it's time you learnt what makes them tick."

"Hmm, well..." – now Fiona was enjoying winding Dan up – "I'll give it a try, it sounds marginally better than the Longbottom Ladies Circle!"

"Ah – you've met Urania!"

"Indeed I have."

"Bad luck! There's only one worse creature in Longbottom and that's Pookin, her hypochondriac Shih Tzu."

"What on Earth's a 'shitzoo'?"

"It's a particularly unattractive breed of dog – one of those where you don't know which end's which."

"And another thing, how can people still go hunting if it's banned?"

"The hounds follow a false scent that's been laid in advance – that's perfectly legal."

"Well – I'm learning something new every day."

"And getting cold into the bargain – I shall look forward to seeing you on Saturday. And come here." He put his hands on her shoulders. "My mother always believed in saying good night with a kiss and she was a very wise woman." Drawing Fiona close, he bent his head and kissed her on the cheek.

"Thank you for a lovely evening." Knees buckling, Fiona sank into the car and drove slowly home, savouring every minute of the the past three and a quarter hours.

***

"Dodo – it's me! I know it's late but you said to ring whatever the time."

"Hi, how was it? Tell all!" Dodo put down her book and grabbing a cigarette, settled back to hear Fiona's eagerly awaited report. She crossed her fingers that the news would be good.

"Oohh..." Fiona sighed. "It was fantastic – he really is completely swoonworthy!"

"*Great*! Did you do it?" Dodo was enthralled.

"Of course not you clot, I've only just got home from the pub – he did kiss me in the car park though."

"Tongue sandwich?"

"Well no actually – just on the cheek but I think he's sussed I don't want to be hurried."

"Bollocks! I told you I thought there must be something wrong with him – you'll be dead before he gets to the nitty-gritty at this rate. Time is not on your side, my dear!"

"Dodo, there is more to life than bonking you know and anyway, he told me why he is as he is, as it were."

"What on Earth do you mean?"

"Not married when he's so attractive, of course. Apparently he was married but his wife was desperate for children and it turned out he fired blanks from having mumps as a child – can you believe it! He was keen to adopt, but she was adamant about wanting the real thing. Anyway, she went all funny about it and left him."

"Gosh!" For once Dodo was momentarily lost for words. "I say, that's a bit rough."

"I know – she couldn't have loved him very much. Reading between the lines, it sort of blighted his faith in true love I think, but there's no doubt that they bonked themselves nearly to death in the effort to produce, so there's no problem there – should I wish to go that far of course" Fiona added primly.

"That's the main thing, that Can Dan is henceforth to be known as Dan Can, and I don't imagine baby Canns were in your game-plan anyway!" giggled Dodo.

"It's not funny – the poor man was terribly hurt and all these intimate revelations were dreadfully embarrassing, though I must say he has such a funny way of saying things it didn't really matter at the time – and for your information, an Italian woman of over sixty had a baby not long ago, so look out!" Fiona drew breath.

"I hope he's not still hankering after the ex – d'you know if she's still around?"

"No – definitely not. It all happened years ago. She remarried and produced and lives in Kent."

"That's all fine but surely he must have had some affairs since then?"

"I'm sure he has, but they weren't mentioned and I was hardly likely to ask."

"Did he ask about your thrilling love-life?"

"Yes he did. It was rather like the Spanish Inquisition without the thumb screws – I told him all about Hamish and the dreaded Crutchley."

"That must have taken up a *Nouvelle Cuisine* nibble! What did he say?"

"He said Hamish must be a complete lunatic or blind in both eyes. Can you imagine anything more romantic?"

"Aaahhh!" Dodo failed to stifle her laughter. "I think it's time you went to bed!"

"Seriously D," Fiona sounded intense. "Do you think it's going OK? I mean I'm really keen on him, you know."

"How could I ever have guessed?!"

"I played it cool like you said – well, as cool as I could!"

"You're doing fine kiddo, it all sounds pretty encouraging to me so keep me posted. When are you seeing him again?"

"On Saturday. He's taking me to the Opening Lawn Meet – though in fact it's in a field, fox hunting you know." Fiona tried to sound knowledgeable.

"God, you are an ass!" Dodo laughed. "It's called the Opening Meet, drop the Lawn bit. It's taken as read it'll be a lawn meet or at a pub – it's an important occasion you know.

Wear clean knickers – all those tightly britched bums and big steaming horses send a man's testosterone surging – you could well end up being shagged under a double-oxer!"

"I've no idea what that is and I don't like the sound of it anyway – that's it for now, I want to go to bed and re-live every moment of my dinner at the Black Dog Inn Longbottom-in-the-Mire Devon England Great Britain the World and Universe!"

"Oh God!" Dodo groaned. "You've got it bad – I can't stand any more yuck and I've finished my fag so... goodbye!"

***

Chortling happily to herself, Fiona put down the phone and danced up the stairs, warm waves of ecstasy breaking over her body like surf on the seashore.

Halfway up, she suddenly remembered Mactavish – the unwitting catalyst of her new-found euphoria. He hadn't turned up to greet her in his normal fashion, but in her rush to ring Dodo, she had forgotten all about him. Hoping he wasn't out and about on another trouble-making spree, she nipped back downstairs to look for him. He was curled up fast asleep on the mat in front of the Rayburn, and although Fiona hadn't been into the kitchen, she was surprised the cat had not come through when she was talking to Dodo in the sitting room. It was very unlike him not to bother to say hello, but his food bowl was empty and when she stroked him, he opened a lazy eye and purred quietly before going back to sleep.

"I know the feeling, old chap," she smiled, giving his cheek a last rub before switching out the light and going up to bed.

'Blow Dodo's skin care routine, I'm too knackered,' Fiona thought, feeling guilty. But the thought of all that cleansing, toning, creaming and brushing was too much, when all she wanted to do was fall into bed and dream of Dan. The most zealous pre-sleep thinking that had ever been thought failed to entice Dan into Fiona's dreams, her subconscious chucking up a pastiche of nonsense that bore no relation to her daily actions and hopes.

***

But as all days do in the end, Saturday morning arrived and dreams were no longer necessary. Sitting beside Dan in his scruffy Subaru, Fiona gazed in astonishment at the quantity of assorted transport that crawled up the narrow lane leading to Grimblesby Hall. Predominantly Land Rovers, interspersed with every four-wheel drive vehicle under the sun, ATVs, cattle trucks, horse trailers, scooters and even one horse-drawn gig – the hairy occupant of the shafts prancing excitedly as smartly turned out hunters weaved their way past him and trotted on eagerly towards the Meet. Eventually they turned into a field, the car park for the occasion, before walking a couple of hundred yards to join the throng that was gathering in front of the magnificent old house.

Picturesquely situated by a ha-ha with the house as a back-drop, stood the huntsman and his hounds; the whipper-in stood on the right flank with the two joint-masters together close by, chatting to the many foot followers who approached them to wish them well and celebrate the opening of another season. Fiona was aghast at the magnitude of it all. The scarlet coats of the hunt staff and masters were immaculate, and the obliging early November sun glinted on their highly polished brass buttons. The patient horses were polished and plaited like animals from a fairy tale, and the hounds stood quietly by, sure in the knowledge that soon they would be up and away to do the business for which they had been bred.

"Oh look Dan, there are the Croakers." Fiona was pleased to spot a familiar face.

"Come on then, we'll go and say hello – more chance of getting a drink over there too!"

Many people greeted Dan as they walked over to where the family stood. Even Abraham had come and he raised his battered cloth cap as Fiona smiled and said good morning. Corah grinned and winked at Fiona when she saw Dan in close attendance, but Sam was too busy fixing up a ride on the back of a friend's ATV to take much notice, and only a sharp prompt from his mother elicited a quick 'Hi'.

Adam alone remained glum as he stared first at Fiona and then at Dan.

"You two come together then?" he said eventually as Fiona chatted to Corah and a tray of drinks appeared.

"That's right, Adam," Dan replied. "I picked Fiona up and I must say, Stone Lea's looking in grand shape nowadays. Cows all right? Here, like a drink?" – he went to pass Adam a glass.

"Don't touch the stuff." Adam muttered ungraciously and without another word, he turned away scowling and walked off.

"Boy bit crabbid z'morning." Abraham had overheard his son's rudeness.

"Not to worry Abraham," Dan smiled at the old man. "We all get out of bed the wrong side from time to time."

Abraham nodded his silent thanks for Dan's understanding as he watched his son disappear in the direction of the car park, before wandering off himself to join a little knot of old cronies standing close by.

Cheeks pink with the effects of unaccustomed mid-morning alcohol and the excitement of being with Dan again, Fiona left Corah to rejoin the object of her rapture.

"You're looking very pleased with yourself," he said as she bounced up. "I hope I'm not going to have an inebriated woman on my hands!"

"What happens next?" Fiona asked, ignoring his quip.

"Well, *feminanus ignoramus*, at any minute the Huntsman will toot on his horn, doff his cap to the assembled company and trot away to do his job. That's when we go and find a nice pub for a spot of lunch."

"Can't we watch for a bit? I've never been on a hunt before – though I've read a bit about it in the papers with all the hoo-ha about the ban going on."

"You must get the jargon right, Fiona." Dan affected a pompous tone. "One doesn't 'go on a hunt' or 'watch for a bit' – you go hunting or follow, but you can 'watch' hounds work."

"Don't be so horrid." Fiona turned even pinker. "How am I supposed to know? After all, I'm only a suburban goldfish owner!"

Hooting with laughter, Dan grabbed Fiona in a bear hug, too quick for her to resist. "I'm only pulling your leg, you delightful idiot!" She tried and failed to break away. "I don't care what rubbish you talk and if you want to follow, then follow we shall – but I am terribly hungry."

Fiona was spared an answer and gained release as at that moment, the senior joint-master called for silence and made a short speech, thanking Sir Torquil and Lady Grimblesby for their hospitality and reminding people that they would be 'hunting within the law'. He then nodded to the huntsman, called 'Hounds please', and with a short 'toot' on the horn, the huntsman led the pack forward through the parting crowd and away across the field.

"What a marvellous sight!" breathed Fiona, watching the mounted field fall in behind the Masters, laughing and chattering and greeting friends amongst the foot followers. Steady old cobs mingled with hairy ponies, and fiery thoroughbreds fizzed and sidled with impatience for a gallop.

Fiona recognised Anna-of-the-tight-breeches dashing past on a plunging dappled grey with a red ribbon on its tail.

"Sorry Toby!" she shouted, giggling, as the grey let rip with an enormous buck and a fart, causing the unfortunate Toby's mount to join in the fun and dump him unceremoniously on the ancient turf.

Anna sat unmoved and cantered on, relaxed and at one with her crazy steed.

"Hang on to yer eyeballs Anna!" Toby laughed, clambering back on board as a red-faced mother jogged past, towed along by an excited Shetland pony with tiny child bobbing about on the end of a leading rein.

"Heavens!" gasped Fiona, who had never seen anything like it in her life. "She's brave."

"Anna's all right." Dan sounded admiring. "She can ride

anything. That's a 4-year-old she's hoping to run next season – nice type, well-bred too."

'Oh dear,' thought Fiona. *'I've never even ridden a beach donkey!'*

"Why's it got a red ribbon on its tail?"

"Because being a youngster and a bit flighty, it might kick. Also, in this crowd it helps stop people ramming her up the bum."

'My God, why did I ask?' Fiona nearly died, having no idea what Dan meant, and making a mental note to tell Dodo to wear a red ribbon when in Devon unless she wanted her bum rammed!

Obviously hunting was a dangerous pastime, riddled with pitfalls of every kind which Dan seemed to consider quite unremarkable. Bearing in mind Dodo's warning about steaming horses and double-oxers, Fiona decided that perhaps after all lunch in a pub was the sensible option to the thrills of the chase.

"I think you're right Dan, about not following. There are so many cars and people and I'm hungry too, now I think about it."

"Sensible woman!" Dan smiled and took her arm. "Come on, it'll take us a while to get out of here anyway." And he marched her off towards the car.

"Look Dan, there's Urania – oh! and that must be the awful Pookin. She's carrying a placard – good heavens, it says 'OBEY THE BAN'!"

Fiona had noticed numerous badges on lapels, most saying 'Bollocks to Blair', and was rather awed by Urania's courage at entering the dragon's lair. Perhaps with any luck she might be bum-rammed to death, and the Longbottom Ladies Circle die with her; but no, Pookin sported a red ribbon round what Fiona presumed to be his neck – though as Dan had observed, it was difficult to tell which end was which.

"Good old Urania!" he laughed. "She always turns up at the Opening Meet. Everyone treats her as a friendly joke and hopes the hounds will eat Pookin, but..." his tone turned serious, " Urania and her kind have won, though in reality, it was more about toff-hating than cruelty."

"But most of these people didn't look like toffs."

"They're not, but it all became political – though silly old Urania is probably one of the few who genuinely thought hunting was cruel." Dan looked tight-lipped. "Hurry up, if we get at the back of the queue, we'll never get lunch."

They sprinted back to the Subaru and joined the line of vehicles pushing towards the gate. An ATV roared past and cut in, a small boy riding on the back.

"There's Sam!" Fiona waved out of the window, and was rewarded by a huge smile and returned wave as Sam recognised her, before the ATV shot past the cars and disappeared into the lane.

"Nice kid, that." Dan said, narrowly avoiding the bumper of the Land Rover in front. "Thank God for Corah, though. That Adam's a queer fish and pretty sour today for some reason."

"Hmm, I noticed that." Fiona agreed.

"Oh well, that's his problem." Dan dismissed the subject. "Ours is to find a good pub and I know of just the one." He smiled at Fiona and gave her right knee a quick rat bite.

"Ouch!" she squeaked. "You brute!"

But he just smiled and drove on.

Lunch was a dream, and by the time they arrived back at Stone Lea, Fiona would have rushed under the first available oxer, double or no. But Dan clearly had other ideas, and announced that he had to get on as his sister and family were coming to lunch tomorrow and he had done nothing about preparing for their visit.

"Not even time for a coffee?" Fiona tried not to plead.

"Better not – I wouldn't like the old sister to think I'm the hopeless housekeeper that I am!" he joked. "But would you come to the Hunt Ball with me? It's next Saturday – short notice I know but now I've got my hooks into you I don't want to let you go."

"Oh Dan, I would love to but my mother's coming down for her first visit and I can't abandon her." Fiona could have wept.

"That's a pity – I shall have to seek out some other Longbottom lovely for the night then, won't I." He put his arm round her and kissed her on the mouth. "Off you go."

Fiona dragged her shaky legs out of the car and watched as he reversed into the lane, raising his hand to her before disappearing out of sight.

Her thoughts in turmoil, Fiona wandered into the kitchen and made herself a cup of coffee. A phone call to Dodo was definitely a must this evening, and in the meantime, she had better pull herself together and do some writing. She was surprised to notice that Mactavish was still asleep by the Rayburn and had left some of his food, but he seemed contented so she left him in peace and went to the computer.

Darkness fell as she struggled with her story, and she was amazed to find she had been working on the computer for over two hours when the telephone interrupted her.

"Fiona dear, it's your mother."

"I do know your voice, Mummy! How are you? I was going to ring you this evening for a chat. I'm really looking forward to your visit."

"That's why I'm ringing." Angie sounded harassed. "Bad news I'm afraid. Old Pinker died suddenly this morning, Mrs P just rang and the poor old thing's in a terrible state. The awful Pearl's away, and son Eric's wife's having her innards out – I ask you! Mrs P doesn't seem to have a clue what to do so I really feel I shall have to postpone my visit till the old boy's safely under the sod – it's the least we owe her."

"Goodness Mummy, I would have thought Mrs P would have been delighted!"

"Don't be ridiculous Fiona – and you ought to come up for the funeral."

Fiona's heart sank. "What did he die of?"

"Heart attack." Angie sounded short. "The point is, I shall have to change my plans, but the following week is fine for me so I hope it is for you."

"Yes, of course – let's go ahead as planned but a week later, no problem."

"Good, I shall look forward to it, and I'll let you know when the funeral is as soon as I hear."

"OK, but it's a long way and maybe you could represent me – I'll write to dear Mrs P straightaway."

"We'll see about that – and of course you must write. I consider her to be a member of the family – without her my grandchildren would probably be gypsies by now!"

"Thanks Mummy. Of course I would come if it was Mrs. P's funeral, but I hardly knew him and he was a bit of an old misery."

"That's not the point – one attends funerals to support the living, the dead don't care."

"I know that, but..." Fiona floundered before quickly changing the subject, "How's everything with *you*?"

"Could be worse, could be worse. I had a nice letter from Roddy last week and an extraordinary post card of a naked man's bottom from Grania – I think she must have sent it to me by mistake."

"I'm glad they're both keeping in touch." Fiona giggled at the idea of the postcard, and felt a twinge of guilt about her own recent lack of communication with her children.

"Well Fiona, I must hurry on now," her mother continued. "Off to bridge with the P-B's – speak soon – and don't forget Mrs P's letter."

"I won't, Mummy – and lots of love. 'Bye for now."

"Thank you, God!" Fiona cried, leaping up to find Dan's home number. "Why you want old Pinker up in heaven beats me, but now I can go to the ball!"

CONSUMMATION

Sunday came in vile, with torrential rain beating down as if it wanted to wash Devon off the face of the earth. Dartmoor was blotted out, and Fiona felt restless and flat as the day stared her in the face, last night's high evaporating with the downpour. Such a day presented the perfect opportunity for hours of creative writing, but somehow Fiona's inspiration had vanished. Sitting at the computer, she failed to write anything pleasing, and after struggling for over an hour, gave up.

It was times like these that she missed not having Dodo within easy reach. The telephone was fine, but even a lengthy gossip like they'd had the previous evening was no substitute for the real thing.

Next Saturday and the Hunt Ball seemed a year away and she ached to see Dan again. Also, Fiona was beginning to worry about Mactavish.

Her feline friend was definitely not himself, but his acceptance of some warm milk and a short stroll in the garden went some way towards allaying her fears. Ringing Dan was out of the question as he would be busy with his sister's visit, and there was no real evidence to suggest a *crise de chat*.

'I must be using Mactavish as an excuse to hear his voice' Fiona decided. 'I expect the old boy's just feeling pissed off like me.'

Leaving the cat asleep on the sofa, she decided to cheer herself up by planning her preparations for Saturday night, before forcing herself out for a walk. Booking a hair appointment was the first priority on Monday morning. Frightening grey hairs were creeping in, and Fiona had never been any good at DIY hair-do's. Expert re-styling and highlights were an essential need.

Somehow she would need to find out the dress code; never having been to such an event, she had no idea at all and shuddered at the thought of turning up in the wrong rig. Who to ask was the problem, as she didn't want to appear ignorant in front of Dan who obviously thought her ignorant enough about country sports and pastimes as it was. Maybe Corah would know, and Fiona made a mental note to give her a ring that evening.

In the event, all thoughts of ringing anyone but Dan went clean out of Fiona's head. On returning from her walk, she shed her wet clothes and went straight through to check on Mactavish. To her horror, she found him flopped over on his side and barely breathing.

"Dan, it's me." Her voice was urgent. "I know you're busy with family but it's Mactavish, I think he's dying."

"Don't panic Fiona, I'll come over right now."

"God Dan, I'm sorry to be such a bore but I don't know what to do."

"My sister's gone and you could never be a bore anyway. Don't touch him – I'm on my way."

Fiona sat miserably watching and waiting – how could ten minutes seem like ten hours? At last the Subaru swished in and she ran to open the door as Dan jumped out, carrying a battered brown leather bag, his professional mantle overcoming his personal one as he strode into the house and brusquely greeted Fiona.

"Where is he?"

"In here."

Fiona led the way into the sitting room and watched in silence as Dan examined the sad prone body, until so recently such a vibrant and valued part of Fiona's life.

"I'm sorry Fiona," Dan stood up. "You were right, he is dying. His heart's failing and there's nothing I can do but help him on his way."

"Isn't there anything you can give him?" Fiona stared at him, white-faced and numb.

"No, nothing. Luckily for him he's not a human being to be kept alive for the sake of it when his time has come." He whipped a small syringe and bottle out of the brown bag.

While he filled it, Fiona knelt down, and giving her old pal's faithful furry head one last kiss, bade him farewell and went out into the kitchen, tears running down her cheeks.

A pair of arms went round her as she sat weeping at the table, and a chin rested on the top of her head.

"I'm so sorry, my darling girl," said Dan, all professionalism gone. "But he didn't suffer, I can promise you that – and he'd had a good innings."

"Kitchen roll, please," Fiona squeaked, head down, horror at the thought of what she must look like almost overcoming her grief.

A large red spotted handkerchief appeared on the end of a hand in front of her face, and she blew and wiped furiously before stuffing the now sodden article into her pocket, and finally turning to face Dan.

"Thank you Dan." She snuffled, trying to pull herself together. "Sorry to be so wet but... well... he'd been around for so long you see, a sort of relic of another life and my only companion."

"I would have thought you a hard and unfeeling woman if you had reacted any differently," Dan replied, leaning on the Rayburn.

"God, I must look a sight!" Fiona knew it was a silly thing to say but couldn't stop herself.

"I shall ignore that particularly stupid remark and enquire if there is any whisky in this house, because if so, I wouldn't say no to a small tot."

"Oh!" Fiona jumped up. "Of course, I'll get you one."

"Have one yourself, it'll do you good."

"Why not..." She fetched the bottle and glasses and let Dan pour the drinks.

"What shall I do...? With Mactavish, I mean?" she asked sadly, tears still not far away, as Dan handed her a small glass of whisky.

"What would you like done with him? I can take him away or we could give him an honourable burial in the garden."

Fiona swallowed a mouthful of whisky and thought for a moment while Dan watched her in silence. "I think I'd prefer for you to take him. After all, Stone Lea wasn't his home for long and supposing some other animal dug him up – that would be too awful."

"Sensible choice." Dan agreed. "Now look Fiona, I've had an idea and I don't want any argument." He finished his drink and put the glass down on the table. "I shall be back home in about half an hour to an empty house full of food left over from lunch and I would like you to come and share it with me."

"Well if you're sure Dan, I'd love to – the thought of sitting here all alone isn't very appealing, I must say."

"Good. Do you know where I live?"

"Yes, no, I think so, I'm not sure."

"Make up your mind, silly! It's the scruffy white thatched house on the right up the hill out of Longbottom on the Moor road. OK?"

"Yes, I know where you mean."

"I'm off now, but half an hour and don't be late!"

He squeezed her shoulder and disappeared into the sitting room to collect the poignant bundle that had been the instrument of their meeting.

The front door banged shut and Fiona was left to contemplate the unwanted food bowl and half-used tin of cat food that sat on top of the fridge. Crying again, she threw both into the dustbin before pouring herself a splash more whisky and forcing herself into the sitting room to put the guard in front of the fire. She would inform all interested parties of Mactavish's demise tomorrow, when she felt less emotional.

The prospect of supper with Dan spelt danger. Somehow Fiona knew that tonight would be crunch time, when she would have to decide – 'to do it or not to do it' – that would be the question. Realising that she looked a complete wreck, Fiona went upstairs to tackle a lightning transformation. Quick bath, definitely clean knickers and slap on some makeup; already running late, there was no time to attempt hair resuscitation. Then the phone rang.

'Blast and damn – I'll leave it' she thought, coming downstairs two at a time. 'On second thoughts, better not.'

"You bin running or something, darling niece?" Uncle Greg's voice boomed down the line.

"Oh hello Uncle Greg, yes, I'm just on the way out."

"Not literally I hope!" he chuckled. "Won't keep you then but just to say looking forward to seeing you Tuesday."

"Tuesday?" Fiona went completely blank.

"Yes, Tuesday – Exeter races – have you forgotten? Loveatfirstsight's big day!"

Fiona had indeed forgotten all about it.

"Oh yes, of course I remember." She tried to sound convincing. "Can't wait to see you – what's the form?"

"Meet me in the Owners & Trainers Bar at noon for a curly sandwich and a jar or two. I'll leave a ticket for you at the gate – just say your name – jolly nice gel in the ticket place. Let you go now – got a beau have you? Good show, hope he's better than the last one, ha-ha! *A bientot,* as they say."

He put the phone down, leaving Fiona in a total whirl.

But Tuesday was Tuesday; now was the present, and Dan. Fiona was running even later, and there was plenty of time to find out about a day at the races tomorrow.

***

"Sorry I'm late."

Dan had opened the front door before Fiona had time to knock.

"Stop apologising!" He took her hand and drew her into the hall before kicking the door shut. "I've never met anyone who says 'sorry' so much!"

And he led her through into a long low-beamed sitting room where an enormous fire blazed at one end, Holly the greyhound sprawled in front of it on a bean bag.

Sitting her down in a deliciously comfortable chair whose floral pattern cover had seen better days, Dan disappeared for a minute or two before returning armed with wine and a plate of anchovies on toast.

"It's only a cold supper, unless you know how to make bubble & squeak with the leftovers, so I thought we'd kick off with these. Hope you like them."

"I love them." Fiona munched up several, impressed by Dan's offering. Hamish wouldn't have had a clue about such things. "What a fascinating house." she observed, gazing around her at the extraordinary mixture of elegance and shambles.

Lovely antique pieces did battle with piles of junk and tatty furnishings, and the massive beams that crossed low above their heads sagged alarmingly in their ancient splendour.

"It suits me." Dan replied, easing his tall body into the chair opposite. "It's a Devon long house, frightfully inconvenient in some ways, but I love the feeling of age and history it gives me. It's stood for hundreds of years and seen more than I shall ever see – births, deaths, joy, despair, who knows what – I'm merely a passing drop in its ocean, a very small part of its ongoing existence. Buildings like this make me feel so insignificant yet at the same time, I'm part of their story – quite an awe-inspiring thought. D'you like it?"

"What I've seen I think's lovely, and it's got a sort of..." Fiona paused, "spirit of its own that sees and hears."

"Hmm, I'm glad you think that. I felt it the first time I looked at the house. That's really what made me buy it – although there are no stories of ghosts as far as I know." He laughed. "All sounds a bit fanciful but it's home to us and we love it, don't we?" He gave the sleeping dog a nudge with his toe, the brief opening of an eye being the only response. "Would you like to see the rest of the house? I could bore you to death with a guided tour complete with lecture on bygone rural living and ancient architecture!"

Fiona knew Dan was trying to cheer her up but the effects of the heat, wine and a traumatic day were catching up with her and she wanted nothing more than to stay by the fire. "Do you mind terribly if I save that treat for another time? I'm so comfortable here I don't think I shall ever move again!"

"Oh yes you will, I don't want you turning into dust in my best chair!" Dan got up and taking both Fiona's hands, pulled her to her feet. "We'll save the guided tour for another day but I shall drag you to the kitchen, where you can sample the delights of my amazing cooking."

Had everything in the kitchen been new and sparkling and featured in a glossy magazine, it could have been described as 'retro'; in fact it was genuinely antiquated and distinctly grubby. A thickly-grimed original cream-coloured Aga was set in the old inglenook fireplace, another muddy beanbag on the slate floor in front of it. A large scrubbed pine table heaped with papers took up most of the other end and somewhere in between, an enormous blackened dresser dominated the low ceilinged room. The deep china sink with wooded draining boards that rested in front of the window had probably once been some good woman's pride and joy. Now it was chipped and stained, and the worn draining boards piled with dishes and saucepans, reminding Fiona that Dan's sister and family had been to lunch.

"How was your sister?" she enquired, as Dan reappeared through a narrow drop-latch door carrying a large platter of cold beef.

"Old Fiona? Funny that, why do you women all have to be called Fiona? So confusing!" He went back for a plate of cold vegetables. "She's fine thanks, very impressed with my cooking, and my niece and nephew are pretty good sorts too."

"Has she got a husband?"

"No, sadly Derek died of cancer about three years ago."

"Poor thing, how awful for her."

"Yes. It was very rough, he was a good man – but she's pulled through and the children are getting on with their various lives. Daughter Rachael's still unmarried, which upsets her but there we are – these modern girls seem to leave it a lot later than our generation."

"I can understand how she feels, neither of my children are married either."

"You women!" Dan laughed. "All you can think about is marriage and babies." His hand glanced gently over the top of her head as he passed her chair on the way to find the carving knife.

Holly the dog arrived, and Dan threw her a chunk of beef which she caught deftly and swallowed in one gulp before scraping the beanbag into an acceptable mound and settling down to sleep.

"Not too much for me please Dan, I'm not very hungry." Fiona watched apprehensively as he sliced away at the joint.

"Two slices OK? Got to keep your strength up, you know."

"That's fine thanks, and only a spoonful of veggies."

The cold concoction of roast potatoes, leeks, carrots and peas that he had mixed up together on the same plate looked rather unappetising.

'Oh dear' she thought, 'I should have rushed eagerly to the Aga and made bubble & squeak. Too bad.'

Fiona felt knackered and far from buoying her up, the wine was fast making her sleepy. Here she sat, in the stronghold of her heart's desire, and all she could do was stifle a yawn. They ate mostly in companionable silence, Dan consuming an enormous plateful in the time it took Fiona to finish her modest helping.

"Coffee?" he asked, scooping up the plates and putting them in the dishwasher.

"No thanks Dan – I think really I'd better go, I'm afraid I feel awfully tired."

"Not the proverbial headache I hope!" he quipped.

Getting his meaning, she laughed. "No, certainly not – more like old age, I fear!"

"Nonsense! You've had a bad day, that's all that's wrong with you. Come and sit by the fire with me while I have my Sunday glass of port – I'd like that very much. Anything for you?"

"I'm fine, thanks."

They returned to the sitting room where this time, Dan sat on the sofa and pulling her down beside him, put his arm round her shoulder.

"D'you know something Fiona McLeod – I fell in love with you at the fish counter in Okehampton. There you were, so wonderfully spiky and flustered, turning as pink as the lobsters when you saw me. 'I wonder why she blushes when she sees me?' I asked myself during the drive home – 'Could it indicate a reciprocal passion or does she suffer from an obscure complaint?!'"

"Oh Dan!" Fiona laughed. "Can't you tell?"

And after a mouth-watering tongue sandwich, he broke away.

"Yes, I definitely think I can! Nevertheless," he continued, idly stroking her hair as she lay against him, "I sometimes feel I'm battling through a jungle, and just when I see a gap in the undergrowth, some enormous Triffid springs up and blocks my path before I can get through."

"Oh dear, perhaps your machete needs sharpening!" Fiona giggled.

"I rather thought perhaps my machete might be the cause of the problem. To use a corny phrase, I am a man and I do love you."

"I know Dan and I'm sorry about the Triffid – whoops, mustn't say 'sorry'! – and it's not your machete, but I don't want commitment. You see I've only recently become a person in my own right and I'm rather enjoying it."

"Darling, you're talking complete rubbish as usual! Commitment doesn't automatically mean the destruction of a personality – in fact it can often mean completely the opposite. The greatest boost your fragile confidence could have would be to discover that fact for yourself."

"Shall we go and put your philosophy to the test then?" Fiona couldn't believe it but there – she'd said it – too late to duck out now.

"Madam, I should be delighted!" And kissing the top of

Fiona's head, he pushed her off and got up to put the guard in front of the fire. "But first, I must put the dog to bed. Bedtime, Holly," he addressed the sleeping animal, "on your feet, you lazy hound!"

Holly got up reluctantly and after a long stretch, followed her master out towards the back door.

"Come with me," Dan called to Fiona. "She won't be long – a quick pee and back into the kitchen – greyhounds are very lazy you know."

So the three of them sauntered out under the clearing night sky. Holly sniffed around on the grass, choosing an acceptable peeing spot, but before anything happened she suddenly snapped her head up and ears pricked, paused for a second before woofing and racing off into the dark.

"I don't believe this." Dan sounded annoyed. "She never normally disappears."

"Dan!" Fiona grabbed his arm. "There's someone moving in those rhododendrons – that's what she's seen."

"You're right – stay here." And he raced off across the grass behind the dog.

Fiona's heart sank as she waited shivering in the doorway. She knew instinctively that her stalker was back, and that the figure in the garden was Adam.

What seemed like an age later, Dan and Holly reappeared, both out of breath.

"Whoever it was had too much of a start on us." Dan led the way back into the house and locked the door. "Oh well, more than likely some lads from the village larking about. Get on your bed, Holly!"

As the dog settled down, he gave her a biscuit and turned out the lights.

"Not lost your nerve I hope?" he smiled, taking Fiona's hand and giving it a squeeze as they headed upstairs.

"Of course not." Fiona replied, over-adamant.

She had decided not to mention the Adam scenario and spoil this momentous moment in her life, she could deal with that problem tomorrow. It was the thought of Dan seeing her naked that filled her with trepidation. Orange peel thighs, thinning bush and droopy bosoms all combined together along with numerous small age-inflicted blemishes to destroy her new-found confidence. And it didn't end there. Hamish was the only man she had ever slept with, and even that was some time ago. The gospel according to Dodo implied that Fiona knew nothing about sex apart from the basic requirement for procreation.

'Help!' Fiona's nerve was failing fast, along with the effect of the wine, as they arrived in Dan's bedroom.

What lurid acts would she be expected to perform, or endure; what contorted positions force her on-the-plump-side, unathletic body into? Standing helplessly in the middle of the room watching Dan draw the curtains and switch on the bedside light, Fiona was on the verge of funking when two long strides brought him face to face with her.

"Don't forget I'm past my prime and a bit out of practice too, you know." He smiled, as if reading her mind. "And I'm not going to ravish you – at least not yet!"

"Could we have the light out?" Fiona murmured as he started undoing her shirt buttons, a casual stroke here and there sending tingles whizzing through her in a most appetising way.

"Only the overhead." He made a long arm for the switch while blowing gently in her ear. "I like to see what I'm getting! And anyway, to me you're beautiful – nothing you're hiding under these tiresome clothes could change my mind so let's hurry up and get them off!"

***

Fiona woke up in the early hours of the morning and staring into the darkness, wondered if she really was the same woman who had stood dry-mouthed and fearful in the middle of the room not many hours ago. The sleeping body beside her confirmed that it had not all been a dream. Dan may not be able to make bubble & squeak, but when it came to making love, he was top of the class and she exhaled a great breath of ecstasy at the delicious memory.

To think she had wasted all those years, enduring Hamish's laborious and unimaginative thrusts as he clambered on board, pumping away before collapsing with a grunt, in the belief that that was all there was to sex between normal couples.

Now at last Fiona could understand Dodo's enthusiasm for the male member. Dropping a kiss on the naked shoulder beside her, Fiona turned over, and with the afterglow of sex still permeating through her being, drifted off back to sleep.

At 6.30 am, the alarm shrilled out, waking Dan with a start. Grabbing the still sleeping body beside him, he shook it into life, cursing under his breath. Fiona's first vision of Monday morning was a pair of green eyes, a blue-shadowed chin and a dishevelled head of thick dark hair.

"Why the hell didn't you wake me earlier so I could have my wicked way with you all over again?"

"What on Earth's the time then?" Fiona came awake properly, excited by the thought of another bonking session.

"Get up time, bugger it – and I'm off for a cold shower!" Jumping out of bed, Dan disappeared into the bathroom, his enormous hard-on speaking for itself.

"What a waste!" sighed Fiona, wondering why on Earth he had to get up so early. 'A vet's life I suppose' she thought, as she reluctantly followed suit.

Sitting at the kitchen table with a cup of tea, watching a shaved and brushed Dan munching up a bowl of cornflakes, Fiona couldn't imagine anything more wonderful than being with the man who had made her feel as she had felt last night. This really must be love, she decided, hardly able to refrain from grabbing him as he slurped down a glass of orange juice before heaping sugar into a mug of Nescafé.

"I must see you again tonight, darling," Dan spluttered as the scalding coffee burnt his mouth. "Can you come over?"

"Why don't you come to me?" Breaking through Fiona's haze of passion shone a little chink of new-found independence. Besides, the thought of having someone so fantastically special to cook for mysteriously turned the chore of housekeeping into a joy.

"Darling Fiona, I don't care where we meet, so long as you open your arms – and your legs – to me like you did last night."

"There's a strong possibility I might oblige," Fiona tried to sound pompous, "but on the other hand, I might not."

"I'll risk it – just so long as I don't have to share you with anyone."

"Oh, I was thinking of asking Urania over!" Fiona teased.

"Great stuff – I've always fancied trying a spot of troilism!"

"What's that?"

"Sexual activity involving three persons simultaneously."

"Honestly Dan, it sounds revolting."

"Come here, you silly woman!" Dan laughed, getting up. "I must go – 90% of the animal population of Longbottom-in-the-Mire seems to be off colour at the moment."

And giving her a kiss that set her fanny on fire, he grabbed a jacket and calling the dog, hustled her out.

When Fiona got back to Stone Lea, she thanked God for Dan. The house was cold and empty with no Mactavish to greet her, and she knew how easily she could have felt depressed and lonely. And there was the problem of Adam to be faced. Of course she had no proof that last night's intruder had been he, but somehow she knew in her bones that it was.

Suddenly there was so much to be tackled, Fiona hardly knew where to start. Everything must be perfect for Dan when he arrived, including herself, and she ought to speak to Corah to find out where Adam had been last night. Also, there was her day out at Exeter Races to be planned for; but first things first – a mug of tea and a phone call to Dodo were top priorities.

"Hi," Dodo answered straightaway. "I picked up your message last night but too late to ring. I'm so sorry about dear Mactavish, I really am – poor old you."

"Thanks D, I must say I was very upset. I mean the old thing's been around for so long I can hardly remember life without him."

"Did you blub a lot, and was the veterinary surgeon on hand to enfold you in his comforting arms or did he tell you to brace up and stop being so suburban?" It was impossible for Dodo to remain serious for long.

"Yes and no." Fiona sounded irritatingly coy. "As a matter of fact..."

"*You didn't?*" Dodo screeched, interrupting, knowing her friend far too well to be bluffed.

"*We did!*" Fiona collapsed with laughter.

"*And...?*" Dodo waited with bated breath.

"It was *fan-bloody-tastic* – I'd no idea such bliss could exist. I must have come about six times – can you imagine – and this morning my legs were so stiff I could hardly walk!"

"Making up for lost time no doubt!" Dodo couldn't resist a dig before continuing. "Welcome at last to the wonders of the world of sex. Better late than never old fruit, and I'm thrilled for you, truly thrilled. When are you seeing him again? If you're anything like me with a new man, you won't be able to keep your hands out of his trousers for a week or two."

"I bet you it lasts longer than that," Fiona snorted indignantly. "You've sacked Philip already, I suppose?"

"Actually no, he's proving to be quite a sticker and I'm rather happy with that at the moment – excellent technique in the sack and no suffocating attempts to interfere with my life as yet."

"Sounds serious by your standards."

"Hmm," Dodo sounded dubious. "I doubt that but I'll keep you posted. And you didn't answer my question about when you're seeing Dan again?"

"He's coming round for supper tonight – in fact I'd better go, I've tons to do and I want everything spot on."

"Oh dear, oh dear," chanted Dodo. "First true love at fifty-four, my chum's become a dreadful bore!"

"Beast! Think of all the shag talk I've endured from you over the years!"

"At least it was more exciting than anything you had to tell me. Now you run along and prepare for lover boy – nice clean sheets and subtle lighting to help the wrinkles! And don't try and break my record, you might have a seizure!"

"Goodbye."

Smiling to herself, Fiona took her Delia standby cookbook off the shelf and sat down to plan the menu. She wanted something that could be made in advance, not liking the idea of slaving over the hot stove, red faced and flustered while Dan was there. Fiona's cooking had always been rather basic, as the combination of Hamish's housekeeping allowance and attitude that food was for nourishment rather than pleasure, had squashed flat her culinary enthusiasm early in their marriage. Getting nowhere and bearing in mind the lack of time available – and her mother's belief that men preferred 'un-mushed quality fare' – Fiona slapped the book shut and decided to dash to Okehampton and buy smoked trout, steak and some nice cheese. Vegetables were easy, and if she got it right, grilling the steak could be turned into a chic little TV drama style cameo. Thanks to dear Uncle Greg, Fiona's budget was now able to support such occasional luxury, her own everyday spending being modest.

Grabbing her handbag and coat, Fiona was on the way out when, to her dismay, Corah's head came bobbing past the kitchen window, closely followed by Sam. "Shit!" she muttered under her breath, but there was no escape.

"Oh sorry, Fiona," Corah twittered, "trust me to arrive just when you're going out."

"No matter, come on in. I mustn't be too long though – I'm off to Okehampton to shop. Hello Sam, no school today?"

"No, brilliant – school's shut cos the bogs are blocked!"

"Sam!" Corah remonstrated. "Don't speak to Mrs McLeod like that. What you mean is that the drains are giving trouble."

"Aw Mum, that's the same thing, ain it?"

"And don't say that – say 'isn't it'. Anyway, I'm stuck with you for the day, bogs or no." And she pulled Sam's ear as he grinned at Fiona, sensing an ally. "We were wondering whether Sam might use your computer; not for too long but he's got some projects to do that it would really help with."

"Of course," Fiona agreed with alacrity. "As long as you don't go into My Documents and bin Topsy Turvy, help yourself. Stay as long as you like Sam, I shall only be away about an hour."

"Wicked! Thanks a lot, Mrs McLeod." The boy was genuinely delighted. "Now I shan't be the only one in my class not to have a PC!"

Laughing with him in his enthusiasm, Fiona took him through to her desk and settled him down at the dreaded machine. In spite of not having one at home, his operational skills obviously so exceeded Fiona's that she left him too it without further ado.

"He's so sweet," she smiled at Corah, "he reminds me of Roddy at that age, though rather better looking."

"You're very kind Fiona and thank you, but don't let him catch you calling him 'sweet'!"

"Don't worry, I haven't forgotten everything about small boys – quick cuppa?"

"No thanks, I know you want to get on." Corah hesitated, frowning, unsaid words obviously hanging on her pale lips.

"Actually, I wanted to speak to you, Corah." Sensing her reticence, Fiona decided to take the bull by the horns.

"Ah, yes." A look of apprehension flashed across Corah's face. "It's Adam, isn't it?" She spoke in an undertone, obviously anxious that Sam should not hear.

"I don't know for sure, but that's what I wanted to talk about."

Then Fiona told Corah about the mystery intruder on last night's visit to Dan. Poor Corah's face collapsed miserably as she listened to the story that Fiona had to tell, confirming her worst fears. "I'm afraid he did disappear last night and by the time he came back, I'd gone to bed. I didn't dare question him because I could tell he was angry – I'm so frightened for

Sam, you see."

'And yourself,' thought Fiona. *'The bastard.'*

"Look, I must go now," Fiona gave Corah's hand a quick pat. "But I'll be back in about an hour so come down later – Sam'll be fine and if he wants a Coke tell him to help himself from the fridge."

Overwhelmed with thanks, Fiona sped away to Okehampton, Corah's pathetic gratitude making her see red as she roared along the narrow lanes. Why didn't Corah get real and accept that her husband was a nutter and do something about it? The man was a menace, and reading between the lines, clearly not averse to physical violence. The softly-softly shrink policy had obviously failed; surely the time had now come for more drastic action.

Narrowly avoiding a smashed wing mirror, Fiona steadied up and mentally sacked the Adam problem that was spoiling her excitement about Dan's first dinner at Stone Lea.

'Blast and damn him!' She pushed her pound coin into a trolly and trundled off towards the fish counter.

***

Home again an hour later, Fiona was unloading the car when Sam popped out and offered to help.

"That's very kind Sam – if you take this bag I can manage the rest. Be careful, it's some rather special wine."

"Are you having a party, Mrs McLeod?" he asked, as they arrived together in the kitchen.

"Not exactly a party Sam, just a friend for supper. You know him I think – Mr Cann, the vet."

"Cool! I really like him. I 'spect he was nice about poor Mr Mactavish – Mum told me about that, jolly sad for you. Our teacher said pets are good for lonely old ladies." The wide hazel eyes were full of concern as they stared up at a laughter-smothering Fiona.

"Yes Sam," Fiona controlled herself. "I was very sad when he died, but he'd had a good life and I didn't want him to suffer. And by the way, I may be old but luckily I'm not lonely."

"Hmm." Sam sounded thoughtful for a moment. "Still," he brightened, "you can always get another cat, there's loads of kittens nobody wants, you know."

"I'll think about it. How did you get on with your project?"

"Oh, brilliant! When's Mr Cann coming?"

"Not till this evening – have you had a Coke?"

"No, Mum said I shouldn't 'imp'- something on your hospitality."

"Impose, I expect. Would you like one?"

"Pleeeze!"

"Help yourself – here's a glass and there's a can in the fridge."

"Thank you. Dad doesn't like Mr Cann."

Fiona paused in mid-unpack, startled by Sam's remark. "Well, everybody can't like everybody in this world you know, Sam. I like him, but then I don't expect you like every boy in your class at school, and maybe there are some boys who don't like you. It doesn't mean the not-liked person is bad."

Sam sipped his Coke thoughtfully for a moment before replying. "That's the sort of thing grown-ups say, but you see I know Mr Cann's nice and Mum thinks so too, so I don't understand why Dad doesn't. My friend Jack said my Dad's a 'sandwich short of a picnic' but I don't know what that means."

"And I don't suppose your friend Jack does either, so don't worry about it." Fiona put the last of the shopping away and decided it was definitely time to change the subject.

Sam didn't agree. "But you see Mrs McLeod," he persisted, "I don't think I really love my Dad like Jack does his. He's always cross and once he twisted my arm so it nearly snapped and he shouts at Mum. Jack's Mum and Dad aren't like that nor are Joshua Luxton's." He looked at Fiona over the top of the Coke glass, awaiting an answer.

"I don't know, Sam." Fiona thought hard before replying. "I expect your father has a lot to worry about with the farm and gets tired and that makes him cross. I'm sure he loves you just the same but maybe finds it difficult to show it – some people do, you know."

"Yeah…" Sam shrugged, putting down the empty glass. "Could be. I'll bring some more logs soon, bet you'll be wanting a fire most nights now it's winter."

"Ooh, yes please Sam, and don't let me forget to pay you."

"No fear!" He grinned, the problem of his father forgotten. "Here's Mum."

"Successful shopping trip?" Corah asked Fiona, a hint of inquisitiveness in her tone.

"Mr Cann's coming to supper," piped up Sam, just as Fiona had decided not to tell Corah.

"I say!" Corah raised her eyebrows and winked at Fiona.

"Why d'ya say that Mum?" Sam frowned.

"Never you mind, you go on home Sam and clean out the chicken coop – no dawdling mind – and get it done before your father comes in. Then you can go and be with Grandad."

"Goodee!" Sam set off up the lane, swiping at imaginary foes with a stick he had found in the hedge.

"Sam and Abraham are great friends," Corah smiled at Fiona, "and thank you so much for letting him use your computer."

"I'm very happy to have him here," Fiona replied truthfully, "and it's good for children to be able to be with their grandparents I think – I used to adore staying with mine – all the fun without any of the discipline!"

"That's true, and Abraham loves taking Sam round the farm and teaching him all about nature – he's terribly good with him and Sam loves it. I wish he was able to feel the same way about his father."

There was a moment's silence before Fiona, anxious to get on with her preparations, picked up the thread.

"Hmm yes, Adam. What are you going to do about him? He's still stalking me and it can't go on." Her voice was loaded with determination.

"I know," Corah sighed. "I'm going to see Mr. Anningsley again tomorrow morning to discuss the way forward. But I have to say I'm at my wit's end. Of course when I asked Adam this morning, he refused to tell me where he was last night. In fact..." she hesitated, the memory obviously painful, "he got rather abusive. Then he said he's got a lot of farm paperwork to do and would be home all evening so I could stop asking questions and mind my own business. I can't tell you how sorry I am about all this, Fion," she ended dismally.

"Oh my God, Corah," Fiona sighed. "So am I! It almost makes me wish I had never come here."

"Don't say that, Fiona. If it hadn't been you it would have been someone else. No," Corah pulled herself together and jumped up, "it's time I faced up to it. Adam will never be completely cured, but I've lived in hope and tried to shield Sam and poor old Abraham – for myself I don't care, I stopped loving Adam long ago but living in cloud-cuckoo land is never the answer to life. I'll leave you to get on – and have a great evening with Dan. I'm so thrilled about you two – he's just the nicest man imaginable."

"Thanks for that, Corah. Let me know how things go tomorrow and if there's anything I can do to help you."

"I will." Corah managed a wan smile before turning and walking out of the door, her thin shoulders sagging with the cares of her world.

Time was flying, and determined to be completely ready and up together when Dan arrived, Fiona steamed on with her preparations. As, for the best reason in the world, she had had very little sleep the night before, these included an early bath and feet-up with face mask and eye-pack. She missed Mactavish's company and the daily ritual of making his dinner, and the Adam situation was alarming to say the least, but the excitement of seeing Dan again overrode all these emotions and worries.

For now, she was completely focused on the forthcoming evening and never contemplated the possibility that being a vet, some animal emergency might cause him to cancel. It didn't, and when the knock on the door announced his arrival, Fiona was ready and waiting.

"Mrs McLeod I presume!" Dan stood on the doorstep looking divine, a bottle of wine in his hand.

"Do come in!" Fiona giggled as he dumped the bottle on the floor and grabbed her in a passionate embrace.

"Grrr!" he growled, coming up for air. "If I wasn't so hungry I'd take you to bed here and now!"

"Well, if you'd stop trying to suffocate me, you might get something to eat and then both your appetites can be satisfied!"

"What a wonderful woman you are. Mind you, I don't know yet whether you can cook – I'm quite happy with the satisfaction of my other appetite, but you know what they say, don't you?"

"No I don't and who's 'they' anyway?"

"The way to a man's heart is through his stomach."

"Sounds like a recipe for indigestion to me." Fiona laughed as they walked through to the kitchen. "Are we allowed to sit by the fire with a drink first?" she asked. "Supper won't take long – it's nettle broth followed by fricassee of sheep's ear!"

"I think it essential I should prime myself with a very large whisky before facing such a hideous-sounding gastronomic ordeal."

"Help yourself – and I'll have a glass of wine." Fiona indicated where she had set the drinks tray, and put the vegetables on while Dan poured out.

"Where's Holly, by the way?" Fiona asked.

"In the car – I wasn't sure whether or not you'd invited her as well."

"Of course, bring her in. Now dear Mactavish isn't here she's very welcome."

"Love me, love my dog." Dan quipped as he went to get her.

"I never said anything about loving you," Fiona retorted,

"but I do like your dog!"

Holly rushed in, madly wagging her long whippy tail, feet scrabbling on the slippery slate floor as she tore round the kitchen before leaping up at Fiona to express her thanks.

"Calm down, you crazy dog." Dan barked, and ever obedient, the dog followed them quietly through into the sitting room and lay down in front of the fire.

Fiona thought she had never felt so happy in her life as they relaxed together for the first time. All her fears about sex and cellulite had evaporated with the passionate hours of the previous night, and her only remaining nag was the need to tell Dan about Adam Croaker.

'Get it over, done with and out of the way.'

She pinched herself, unwilling to tarnish the evening of her dreams. Noticing the sudden frown and expression of tension that flashed across Fiona's face, Dan put down his glass and leaned forward in his chair.

"What's up, my love?" His antennae quickly picked up Fiona's anguish, and she told him all about the problem of Adam.

"Bloody man," Dan commented angrily as Fiona finished her tale. "I've always thought him an oddball but never imagined anything like that. I'm sorry for Corah, who's a good bird, but if you ever have another hint of him stalking you, I shall insist that you go to the police."

"Let's hope it doesn't arise." Having got it off her chest, Fiona wanted to forget the problem and recapture her acute sense of happiness at being with Dan. "Come on, I think it's time to satisfy one of your appetites."

And she led the way through to the eating area where the smoked trout was waiting on the candlelit table. The steak was perfect, the vegetables *a point*, and the Camembert running nicely away over the edge of the cheese board in the direction of the Bath Oliver biscuits.

"Hmm!" Dan sat back, patting his stomach appreciatively. "I could live with you, that was the best sheep's ears I've ever eaten! Coffee's my speciality – shall I make some? Women are useless coffee makers."

"Carry on!" Fiona was delighted to be relieved of the tedious task. "It's all set up ready to go – boiling the kettle shouldn't be too taxing."

Silently congratulating herself on the success of the dinner, Fiona sat sipping her wine while Dan fiddled about in the kitchen, waiting for the kettle to boil.

'Poor old Hamish,' she smiled to herself. 'He never managed to ignite my enthusiasm for cooking, even in the early days – what a silly, naïve person I must have been to think I was ever in love with him.'

"Penny for them?" Dan watched her as he reappeared with the coffee.

"Oh, nothing." Fiona came back to the present. "I was just thinking of something of no account."

"One of the many things I love about you, is that you could never deceive me. Your thoughts are written all over your gorgeous face, and at times I suspect they're rather idiotic ones!"

And he kissed the top of her head before pouring out their coffee.

"Thanks for that – and I don't mean the coffee," she replied, longing for the moment when they could leap into bed.

"Drink up," he commanded, as if reading her thoughts. "Appetite number two beckons! Better chuck Holly out for a pee then she can sleep in the car – she's happier on her own territory and I don't want to be disturbed at a vital moment by her howling!"

Hardly able to keep their hands off each other, Fiona blew out the candles and started the dishwasher while Dan put the guard in front of the fire and set about dealing with his dog.

Fiona was about to join him in the garden when suddenly, the explosion of a shotgun rent the silent night air, followed by a cry.

As she dashed out, Dan stumbled out of the dark, his

hands over his face, blood seeping through his fingers and dripping onto the cobbles.

"Oh my God!" Fiona gasped, her heart thudding with terror as she ran towards him.

SHOCK

"Bloody hell!" groaned Dan, blundering into the rubbish bin as Fiona tried to guide him back into the kitchen, closely followed by an excited Holly who licked eagerly at the fresh blood. "Lock that door and ring the police – Shit!" He swore in agony. "It's that mad bastard Croaker for sure."

"Bugger the police!" Fiona cried. "You need an ambulance and quick." Hot waves of panic washed over her as she tried to steady her racing heart and think straight to cope with the crisis.

"I don't need an ambulance – *fuck off Holly* – it's only a few pellets in the face and luckily not my eyes. Old Doc Springrice'll do for that – get me a large whisky and the phone." Dan took his hands away from his face.

Fiona shuddered at the sight, and felt the blood drain into her shoes as she stared, white-faced with shock. Dan looked even worse than Mactavish after his attack.

To her amazement, he started laughing, wincing with pain as he did so.

"Fiona darling, if only you could see your face! I'm not going to die you know, I've only been peppered and I do hope you're not going to pass out on me before you've got the whisky bottle!"

"Oh Dan!" she wailed, "I've never been so terrified in my life."

"Well now at least I know you care, but for God's sake stop standing there like a dying duck and do something useful!"

Flooding with relief, Fiona sped into action. Whipping a clean drying-up cloth out of the dresser drawer, she gave it to Dan to hold on his face to mop the blood, before fixing him a drink and passing him the phone. Deciding she could do with a stiffener too, she poured a modest shot and listened, as he rang first the police and then the doctor – who appeared from the way Dan spoke, to be a good friend. That done, he sat back in the chair and exhaled an enormous breath.

"That's put the tin hat good and proper on appetite number two – sorry about your cloth! The bleeding's nearly stopped though, so I'll just sit quiet for a bit. Get me a wet rag can you, I'll clean my hands."

"Of course." Fiona kicked herself for being so hopeless. "What's happening?" she asked, carefully wiping his hands herself but not daring to touch his face.

"PC Plod and the Doc are on their way, so we wait and hope. What a state of affairs, and just when I was..."

The shrill ring of the telephone cut off his words.

"Hello," Fiona snatched it up.

"I say, you sound jolly brusque – anything the matter?"

"Oh Uncle Greg, sorry, yes, no, I mean..."

"Are you tight Fiona? You sound most peculiar!"

"And you sound just like your sister!" Fiona managed to laugh.

"Just checking you are on course for tomorrow – much looking forward to seeing you m'dear."

"Me too and don't worry, I won't be late and I'm really looking forward to it."

"Jolly good show – Loveatfirstsight's in cracking form they tell me and the going's perfect so we'll have a little wager and a jar or two and a capital day out – *á demain*." He rang off.

"That was my Uncle." Fiona began to tell Dan about her day at Exeter races tomorrow, but she hadn't got beyond the horse's name before the telephone rang again.

"Fiona – it's me, Corah," she sounded breathless with worry. "Adam's gone missing and I've no idea where he is – I'm sorry to butt in on your evening with Dan but I'm terrified he's lurking round Stone Lea."

Fiona took a deep breath but as she started to speak she heard a car draw up in the drive.

"You'd better come down *now*, Corah," she tried to sound calm. "I'm afraid there's been an incident and Dan's been shot."

"Oh my God!" Corah shrieked down the line, "Is he…?"

"He'll be OK – but we've rung the police and I think I hear them now. Dan's sure it was Adam, and so am I."

"I'm on my way." As she put down the phone, a loud banging on the door announced the arrival of PC Plod and his underling. Fiona let them in and put on the kettle. The only ploddish aspect of the policeman, whose name was Clive, turned out to be his feet – which were enormous. As Fiona brewed the statutory mugs of sweet tea, a no-longer-bleeding Dan filled him in on the events of the night.

Clive had hardly begun to digest the full saga of Adam, some of which he apparently knew already as they had been at school together, when a frantic Corah rushed in. Whey-faced and demented, she froze at the sight of the tableau that met her eyes. Fiona was the first to make a move and taking Corah's hand, dragged the rigid body into a chair and pushed her down.

"Get a grip, Corah," she commanded, sensing hysterics on the horizon. "Dan'll be OK – but you falling to bits won't help anybody."

Fiona looked pointedly at Clive, silently inviting the policeman to pick up the reins.

"I'm ever so sorry, Corah 'bout all this," Clive responded to Fiona's silent suggestion, "but you tell me if you think 'tis Adam like these folks reckon."

"Oh Clive," Corah raised a tearful face. "Yes yes yes – for sure it's Adam! I've checked the gun cupboard and his gun's gone – whatever can I do?"

"Best thing you can do, Corah luv, is get on home case Adam turns up. If he do, you ring me 'eres on this number straightway." Clive gave her a card and added. "But else you look after old Abrum and young Sam and don't you be forgettin ye'sel."

"Clive's right, Corah," Dan backed up the policeman. "Adam's got to be found as soon as possible and eventually home is the natural place for him to go. After all, it can't be much more than about half an hour since it happened."

"Well, if you're sure, I'll go back to the farm. And Dan," poor Corah hardly knew what to say, "I'm so terribly sorry."

Whatever Dan's reply was going to be, it was cut short by the arrival of a short stout red-faced little man carrying a black bag – obviously Dr Springrice.

"'Evening all," he grinned, "where's the patient? Ah! there you are Dan – trust you to get a face full of lead and ruin my evening! Put your head back." He inspected Dan's bloody face. "Hmm – won't make you any uglier than you are already! And this I take it is the lovely lady of Stone Lea?" Turning to Fiona, he took her hand and kissed it, smiling reassuringly into her eyes as he did so. "Madam, if you would be so kind as to allow this revolting specimen of manhood into your bathroom where I presume you have hot running water, I shall endeavour to return his countenance to something resembling its normal ill-favoured mien."

"Of course." Fiona couldn't help smiling at the funny little man to whom she had taken an instant liking: "Up the stairs and first on the right. There are plenty of clean towels in the cupboard if needed."

"Thank you my dear and don't worry, a few digs with the forceps and a blob of iodine and he'll be as right as rain. Tell you what, I'll save the shot for you – it's the ideal thing for cleaning the port decanter!"

Dr Springrice hustled Dan off up the stairs.

"I'd best be off home then," Corah cast a desperate glance at Fiona and Clive. "I wish there was something I could do or say to help, but there isn't."

"You go and do as Clive says," Fiona gave Corah a quick hug. "It's for the best – and ring me if there's anything I can do to help you and Sam. It's not your fault." She finished, hopelessly trying to bolster up the crushed woman as she walked, bent and beaten, out of the back door.

"I be on my way too, Mrs McLeod – and thank you for the tea." Clive put his empty mug on the table. "Detailed statements can wait till tomorrow. I'm to the car to get onto County HQ – this be too big for local, we've a mad man with a shotgun to find. Lock up and stay inside and soon as can there'll be a patrol car outside and up at the farm for protection. This be a bad business."

Not looking entirely sorry, he strode out, followed by the silent sidekick, leaving Fiona alone in the kitchen.

Ruminating on the events of the night so far, Fiona decided it was probably the most exciting event that had ever happened in Clive's entire life as a policeman; certainly it was the most dramatic that had ever happened to her.

Wondering whether to go upstairs and see how the pellet extraction was going, Fiona felt a long wet nose push into her hand.

"Poor Holly – we've all forgotten about you." Fiona stroked the dog's head. "Don't worry, your master will be here again soon and we'll find you somewhere nice to sleep."

She was rewarded by an appreciative whiffle and vigorous wag of the long tail, which swished Dan's empty glass off the chair where he'd left it. Smiling to herself at the unimportance of one broken glass but worried about the dog's feet, Fiona pushed Holly away and sped for a dustpan and brush. Hamish would have been furious, and once upon a time she too would have considered it a grave matter.

'How can I have changed so much so quickly and at my age?' she pondered, chucking the broken fragments into the bin.

But now was not the moment to analyse her metamorphosis, for footsteps on the stairs announced the arrival of Doc Springrice and her pellet-free lover.

"Mrs McLeod – may I call you Fiona – I humbly present a small handful of shot and the best-I-can-do-for-his-ugly-mug Dan Cann!" Peering theatrically round the kitchen, he tapped his nose and winked before continuing. "And if that young Clive's gone on his way, I wouldn't say no to a wee dram."

"Of course," smiled Fiona, fetching a glass. "We're very grateful to you for coming out. If we'd had to go to A&E we'd have probably been there all night."

She stifled a giggle as she looked at Dan's face, which was now a nasty pock-marked yellowy-brown, patterned with little dots of dark crusted blood where the shot had penetrated the skin.

"Shut up woman and don't make me laugh – it hurts!" Dan sat down with the Doc, constraining Holly's ecstatic welcome.

"Don't let the dog lick your face, Dan," the Doc advised, "it might catch some pernicious disease!"

And downing his not so wee dram in one swig, he hoisted himself up on his short legs and bade them goodnight.

"Her Majesty awaits, and no doubt you two have better things to do than sit talking to an old fool! And, my dear," he took Fiona's hand, "the same applies to you as to the dog. But there are plenty of parts of the human body to provide pleasure other than the face!"

Chortling away merrily to himself, Dr Springrice picked up his bag and bounced out, waving aside their mutual exclamations of thanks.

"What a night!" Dan sighed. "And according to the good doctor, there's no reason for it to end now. The spirit is definitely very willing but I fear the flesh may be a little weak."

"Oh Dan," Fiona put her arms round him. "I think all I want to do is flop into a warm bed with you beside me. Is your poor face very painful?"

"Not at the moment – I can't feel a thing but that's the problem," he replied, yawning. "Doc gave me a shot to dull the pain but I fear it's dulled everything else as well – I feel a bit floaty."

"Come on, let's go to bed before you crash out, I don't fancy carrying you up the stairs! Holly might be cold in the car – will she be happy on the sofa?"

"She'll be delighted – give her a bit of bread and shut the door and she'll think she's in paradise – and make absolutely certain the house is properly bolted and barred."

Dan staggered upstairs, and in spite of the drama, Fiona's

hormones sparked into life as she helped him undress. But the uncooked chipolata that greeted her as she whipped down his striped boxers said it all. Within two minutes of sinking into the warm clean-sheeted bed, he was asleep. She kissed him carefully on the mouth and while opening the window, was relieved to see a police car sitting outside the house. At least she could sleep peacefully, secure in the knowledge that they were protected from any further attack from Adam.

***

The effects of the Doc's dope having worn off, Dan woke early feeling sore and randy. The chipolata had turned into a mega-wurst, and Fiona's muddled dream was interrupted by a rude awakening of a blissful kind. Freed now from all her previous inhibitions and lack of confidence, Fiona responded eagerly to Dan's desires, and as she lay sated in his arms after a blistering climax, she silently thanked La Crutchley for having removed Hamish from her life forever.

"Not bad eh, for a couple of oldies!" Dan expertly massaged her head.

"I'll say. Hmm! That's nice – now I know why cats like head-rubbing. How's your face feeling?"

"A lot better than it was ten minutes ago. Seriously though, it's fine – rather stiff and sore but nothing a few days won't put right. I'd better get up in a minute and get moving."

"Me too, though I wish we could stay here all day doing what we've just done!"

"Really Fiona, you quite shock me – and I thought you such a sweet, moral little woman! Besides, whatever would your uncle think if you stood him up at the races."

"If he knew the reason, knowing him he'd probably think I was being very sensible!" Fiona laughed, dragging herself reluctantly out of bed and throwing on some clothes. "I'll get some breakfast on the go and see if our guards have any news of Adam."

"I'll be down in a minute – no point in worrying about shaving. Come here and give me a kiss – and I like my egg boiled for precisely three minutes fifty-four and a half seconds!"

Fiona put the kettle on before releasing Holly from the sitting room and going outside to speak to the police. Adam had not been found, and they were expecting to be relieved shortly. A cup of tea would be most welcome – it had been a long night.

By the time Fiona went back into the house, Dan was down and pottering about in an attempt to find the necessary requirements for breakfast. Obviously suffering from a bout of insecurity during the night, Holly had ripped up one of the sitting room cushions, and having cleared up most of the remnants, Dan was profuse in his apologies.

"Don't worry, Dan." Fiona couldn't give a hoot. "It was a horrid old thing anyway. Adam's still missing though, which *is* bad news."

"Yes," he replied thoughtfully. "We'll have to make a plan with the police before you go to the races. You mustn't be alone here until he's been found."

"These two are expecting to be relieved soon, and I want to leave at about 11.30, but they said they thought the big chief would be in touch before then."

"I would imagine so, they'll want statements and evidence and God knows what, and no doubt the local press will soon be onto it. Look, I ought to go. Ring me on my mobile when you leave Exeter, and forget about Adam for a few hours and have fun – it'll do you good."

Dan hugged Fiona tight, reluctant to let her go.

"Beggin' your pardon zirr." Policeman No.2 shuffled his feet and coughed as he stood in the doorway with the empty mugs.

Fiona sprang back, pink in the face as Dan pinched her bottom before walking out to his car.

"Don't peer at the goldfish," Fiona called after him. "They might die of fright!" Waving at her, Dan loaded Holly and himself into the car and drove off.

Fiona had hardly had time to clear the breakfast when another police car rolled up and an important-looking uniformed officer got out, followed by two plain-clothed detectives.

'County' had arrived. Gone was the homely camaraderie of Clive and friend, for the head man was no kindly DCI Barnaby. Polite but insistent, he declined refreshment and grilled Fiona for over an hour. How she wished Dan had been with her for support during the questioning, and as her honest answers seemed to be twisted and thrown back at her, she began to wonder who he considered the guilty party to be.

Meanwhile, the two jaded night-watchmen were yanked out of their car to search the garden and nearby surrounds under the watchful eye of the uniformed officer. Longbottom-in-the-Mire would soon be all agog, for nothing so exciting had happened for over a hundred years, when old Ephraim Cobbledick had forced his unwanted attentions on the Widow Rugglesaw in order to secure her lands and livestock.

At last the DCI concluded the interview and rose to his feet. With a smile that reached no further than the base of his nose, he thanked Fiona for her co-operation, jerked his head at aspirant DCI, and swished regally out of Stone Lea.

"Bastard!" Fiona muttered, glancing at her watch and wondering what the next move might be. Her question was quickly answered by the arrival of another car which, to her great relief contained, amongst others, Clive.

"Mornin' Mrs McLeod." In he clumped, a smile that included his eyes lighting up his plain face.

Fiona could have kissed him.

"Oh Clive, I'm so pleased to see you – I'm due to leave for Exeter races quite soon to meet my Uncle and I don't want to be late, but I'm not sure what's happening – tea?"

"That'd be grand – Dan all right this mornin' then?"

"He's fine thanks. A bit sore and looks a sight, but a few days'll see him OK."

"Good man, Dan. Put me Ma's ol' dog away last year in exchange for a pot of marmalade. Good job." Fiona made a mental note to ask Dan whether he would have preferred a pot of marmalade to her body in payment for administering Mactavish's terminal injection.

"Still no news of Adam then?" she asked.

"Nope, 'fraid not." Clive looked worried. "That family be cursed if you ask me – we was lads together you see and mind you, he was always a queer one since his Ma died – hit him real bad."

"Yes, Corah told me about it – rotten thing to happen and now this, poor things."

"Hmm." Clive shook his head. "Now you get off to the races Mrs McLeod – they'll be keeping a watch here till Adam's found, so you'll be all right."

"Oh good, that's a relief." Fiona glanced at her watch. "I must get a move on. Thank you Clive, and I'll see you again I expect."

She left him drinking his tea and rushed upstairs to change.

***

It took Fiona less time than she had allowed to get to the racecourse, so rather than wait about in alien territory, she sat in the car park until it was time to meet Uncle Greg. A variously attired assortment of eager-looking people hurried past on their way to the enclosures. She needn't have worried about what to wear, as it appeared that more or less anything was acceptable. Nevertheless, she was pleased with her choice of tweed skirt, warm jacket and fake fur hat, which struck a nice balance between the jeans and trainers brigade, and the party frocks and high-heeled shoes that went tripping by.

Time to go, and Fiona followed the herd towards the ticket booth where she was given her badge and a racecard, and directions to the Owners & Trainers Bar.

As she pushed open the door she was practically flattened by a smartly-dressed man rushing out.

"Terribly sorry," he apologised, puffing frantically on the last centimetre of a cigarette. "Got a runner in the first to saddle and I'm late. Tell you what," he threw the butt away, "have a few bob on, he's well in at the weights."

And grinning at Fiona, he strode quickly away, leaving her too bemused to think to ask the horse's name.

The bar was hot and crowded, and loud, knowledgeable voices rose with wisps of smoke towards the ceiling. Fiona was just beginning to worry about ever finding Uncle Greg in the mob when she saw him weaving his way through, moving towards her.

Evidently he had taken up his new-found passion with a vengeance, for he was wearing the uniform of the well-dressed male racegoer, complete with binoculars and brown Trilby. Even his silk tie was decorated with tiny jockeys wearing different racing colours.

"Darling niece," he boomed over the hubbub, "lovely to see you!" They kissed warmly, Fiona experiencing a surge of love for her funny old uncle. "Just time for a quick snort before the first – bit of a crush today – all come to see Humdinger of course, his first outing of the season."

"Why's Humdinger so special?" Fiona shouted over the noise.

"By Jove, old girl, keep your voice down! He's only won two Cheltenham Gold Cups and a King George!" Uncle Greg harrumphed.

"Sorry!" Fiona giggled, noticing the raised eyebrows of a smart horse-faced woman standing behind Uncle Greg.

"Don't you worry dear!" A chirpy north country voice belonging to a small female sounded in her ear. "There's more to life than a horse and nowt so daft as a man!"

Fiona smiled her thanks as the little woman joined the exodus from the bar.

"Drink up," ordered Uncle Greg. "Jockeys are up and the stand'll be packed in a minute. Follow me."

They sped out of the fast-emptying bar towards the action, Fiona fervently hoping that the whole day would not take place at such a breakneck pace; seemingly it wasn't only the horses who had to gallop. As they squeezed into the stand, she wondered how on Earth anyone could see more than a small part of the race. Each end of the long oval circuit seemed miles away, and most of the back straight completely obscured by bushes and trees. Suddenly, the incomprehensible list of figures on a giant screen in front of the stands turned into live horses, and Fiona's wondering was over as the tape sprung back and the runners for the Makebelieve.com Handicap Hurdle raced towards the first flight.

Uncle Greg muttered and gnashed his teeth as his fancy pulled up before three out, but as the leading horses jumped the last, the roar from the stands reached a crescendo and the winner flashed past the post a bare half-length in front of his rivals. "Photograph, photograph!" boomed the judge over the tannoy.

"Jin Shin Do got it." Uncle Greg announced, and was proved right.

As the horse came back into the winners' enclosure, Fiona recognised her earlier contact as he greeted the sweating animal with a grateful pat.

"Oh look!" she said, excited at having something useful to say at last. "That man bumped into me on the way into the bar and told me to put some money on his horse."

"Well why the Dickens didn't you tell me, silly girl? It went off at 7-1!"

"You didn't give me much chance!"

"Hmph – never mind – make it up on the next." And Uncle Greg started off down the steps, Fiona trailing in his wake.

"What happens now?" She darted up beside him. "When's Loveatfirstsight's race?"

"She's in the fourth, so plenty of time yet."

"Could we have something to eat then, and a chance to talk, or do we just rush about all day?"

"What!" Uncle Greg sounded startled, as if Fiona had made the most extraordinary suggestion.

"It would be nice, I haven't seen you for ages and I am rather hungry."

"Well... um," he wavered. "Hmm, don't see why not – have to hurry though."

And off they sped again.

Settled at last at a small table with a sandwich, sticky bun and cup of coffee, Fiona enquired after her uncle's health and well-being.

"Capital capital, never better – the old pin mended a treat." He bit into a beef sandwich.

"And is this all due to Diana or Loveatfirstsight or both?"

"The four footed filly m'dear!" he guffawed. "Her beautiful Titian locks knock spots off poor old Diana's blue mop – between you and me the old gel's fading a bit, got rather starchy about my new hobby." His false teeth clattered slightly in indignation as he chewed on the beef. "Come to think of it, never seen you look better either." He sat back, scrutinising Fiona, one eyebrow raised.

"I never have been."

"Must be a man." Uncle Greg pronounced accurately, wiping his chin with a large yellow spotted handkerchief. "Nothing like love to revitalise the middle-aged female."

"As it turns out, you're quite right." Fiona laughed. "But I do love Devon too."

"Who is this chap then? Right type I hope." Uncle Greg became avuncular. "Can't have you marrying some weirdo fortune hunter, by Gad!"

"Uncle Greg, I haven't got a fortune and I'm not intending to marry him."

"Phoof! Why ever not if you love him? And you will have a fortune when I go – at least a small one."

"I'm rather enjoying my independence actually – it seems I can have the best of both worlds. Isn't that what you've always done?"

"I'm a man – quite different – come on, jockeys are up. Tell you what, we'll go down to the last – give you a close-up of what it's all about."

And once more they were on the move, nipping in the bud Fiona's desire to recount the dramatic events of the previous night.

Arriving at the last fence, Uncle Greg led the way up onto a small wooden platform where they took second place to a group of photographers. Having forgotten her glasses, Fiona could only just read the racecard which told her that the coming race was a two mile novice chase; according to Uncle Greg, the shortest distance raced over by National Hunt horses, and the most spectacular.

As the eight runners thundered down towards the first fence on the first circuit, Fiona couldn't believe the speed they were going and as they sailed over in a blur of colour, birch flying and jockeys shouting, she suddenly knew why Uncle Greg was hooked. Next time round it would be the last fence and the chips would be down. She couldn't wait. Then she saw them; heard the smack of whips on muscle, the snorting breath, the roar from the stands as three in line with two close up behind, the leaders took off.

With a terrific crash, the horse nearest the rails rooted the fence and turned a somersault, bringing down the one behind it. Fiona gasped in horror as man and beast hit the turf in a melée of flailing, steel-shod hooves. The lucky ones galloped on up the run-in, flat to the boards to reach the coveted winning post first; receding back views, heading for glory and another world.

The brought-down horse jumped up quickly and galloped off in pursuit, its jockey limping away cursing, but the other horse lay prone on the ground, its flanks heaving. Miraculously, its jockey too seemed unhurt, and quickly undid the girths and surcingle to release the tiny saddle, the reins looped over his arm. Within minutes, the casualty squad arrived on the scene and a large green screen was swiftly erected round the fallen horse. Fiona's heart sank.

"Come on, Fiona." Uncle Greg took her arm. "No point gawping."

"That's so awful – will they have to shoot it?" She was upset.

"Let's hope he's only winded – afraid accidents do happen

in this game though."

As they walked back up the course towards the stands, a distraught-faced little female carrying a leather lead rein ran past them towards the scene of disaster.

"Is she the horse's groom, d'you think?" asked Fiona, turning back to watch her progress.

"'Lass', Fiona. You don't have grooms in racing – lads and nowadays lasses."

"It must be awful for them when the horses get hurt. After all, they're the ones who look after them all the time – the owners hardly ever see them I imagine."

"True m'dear, but don't dwell on it – owners do care too you know, but some more than others."

Fiona's reply was cut short by a cheer from those who had remained in the stands, binoculars fixed on the last fence.

"Excellent." Uncle Greg looked back down the track. "He was just winded after all."

Fiona felt a surge of relief as she saw the screens being removed and the horse being led back up the course by his diminutive handler.

"Can we wait and see him come back?" she asked, feeling much more involved now in the day's events.

"Don't see why not – it's Humdinger next so we can get a good slot by the paddock if we stay down here, like to see the great horse close to, but so will everyone else."

The expression on the little lass's face said it all, and as she led her still blowing but unhurt charge past them en route to the racecourse stables, Fiona couldn't resist calling out to her.

"I'm so pleased he's all right."

The girl pulled the horse up, patting him for the hundredth time and smiling broadly. "Thank you," she said from the bottom of her heart. "He's such a sweetheart, I don't care what he does as long as he comes home safe."

"What's his name?"

"Barton Jack," she replied, "but I call him Squiffy!"

And the impatient Squiffy towed his lass onwards before

Fiona could do more than call out: "Good luck!"

Uncle Greg was 'grumphing' in the background, anxious to get to the nearby paddock and not too approving of Fiona's hobnobbing with lasses.

'Blow that' she thought, 'I'm just beginning to realise where the grass roots of this game lie. Who cares about money when these beautiful brave animals are what it's all about?'

As predicted, a huge crowd was gathering round the paddock, but Humdinger and most of his ever-hopeful rivals were still in the pre-parade ring close to where she and Uncle Greg stood, the horses walking quietly round before being saddled.

"Why don't we watch from here?" Fiona suggested.

"Supposed to be behind the rails you know." Uncle Greg sounded huffy, and bowing to superior knowledge, Fiona followed him back into the public area.

They still had a good view of the proceedings, and watched in awe as the famous Humdinger made his entrance. Even Fiona could see that he was something special, and as Uncle Greg muttered about 'look of eagles' and 'could be another Arkle', she gazed in admiration as he strode majestically round the paddock, acknowledging his admiring public as he went. From the tip of his gleaming aristocratic head to his shiny oiled feet, he oozed class and superiority, and Fiona felt quite sorry for his pedestrian rivals, unbeknown to her, but top class horses in their own right.

"No point backing against the favourite in this." Uncle Greg sniffed knowingly.

"Why don't you back Humdinger then?" Fiona inquired innocently.

"At long odds on? Certainly not. Save my fire power for our little flyer!"

Though his trainer had apparently 'left a bit to work on', Humdinger duly obliged and demolished his toiling opponents as if swatting flies. Content with their hero, a small section of the crowd began to drift away towards the car park, affording a little more space for the remaining devotees.

Now it was the turn of Loveatfirstsight. The little chestnut filly danced into the paddock, chewing anxiously on the bit, her ears flicking backwards and forwards as she took in the scene around her. Uncle Greg practically burst with pride as he and Fiona stood in the middle of the ring, with some other members of the syndicate and the trainer, a weatherbeaten little man called Victor who had once been a successful jump jockey.

"She's rather small compared to some of the others," Fiona whispered, not daring to comment out loud.

"Tough though, and a real athlete," Uncle Greg assured her. "She's flat bred of course, and a late foal – today's an outing, it's March we've got our eyes on."

"Oh, what happens then?"

"Cheltenham Festival of course, and the Triumph Hurdle," Uncle Greg hissed, before turning to listen to Victor.

"She's schooled well at home and been much more settled in her work recently," Victor told them, "but she'll need the run today. I'd rather leave her a bit short first time out than have her boil over."

Fiona thought of a kettle and wondered what happened to a horse when it boiled over. Certainly the racing jargon took some learning.

Suddenly a troop of skinny, brightly-coloured men marched into the paddock, and one wearing blue and white stripes made his way over to Loveatfirstsight's entourage, where he touched his cap to the owners before talking, arms crossed, to Victor.

"You know her well enough, Dickie," Victor gave his instructions. "I imagine that thing of Darleys'll make it."

"Tony's going on too so there'll be plenty of pace," Dickie replied.

"Good. Drop her in, get her settled and don't knock her about – educational today. How's the ground riding?"

"Bit dead but she won't mind that." Dickie whacked his boot with the end of his whip.

A bell rang and the connections walked briskly over to where the travelling head lad was stripping the paddock sheet off the filly's , as she spun around the lad who was leading her up.

"Keep her on the move, Jo," Victor instructed, and he legged Dickie expertly up into the saddle as Loveatfirstsight strode keenly on round the paddock.

Landing as light as a feather, he stroked her neck and spoke softly to her as the sweat began to run under the saddle. Shaking her head as if to say 'Let's get on with it', she swung out onto the course where, in perfect harmony, she and Dickie made their way to the two-mile start.

"Good luck to us!" Victor bared his teeth in a nervous grin, and puffing on a quickly lit cigarette, shot off into the stands.

"I'm off to the bookies – you up for a wager?" Uncle Greg asked, nerves kicking in as Fiona hesitated. "Make up your mind, they'll be off in a minute," he snapped.

"Put a pound on for me, I'll stay here." Not having ever had a bet in her life, Fiona wasn't sure what to do and didn't want to risk another gaffe.

Uncle Greg hurried away, returning rather out of breath as the runners came up into line, tension etched all over his face.

"They're off!" the commentator announced – and the field of three-year-olds set off towards the first flight of hurdles.

Dead ground or no, the pace was hot and the blue and white colours were nowhere near the leaders. By the time the runners rounded the final bend, several tail-enders had pulled up and two riderless horses galloped madly alongside the rest.

Then, when all hope seemed lost, Fiona saw little Loveatfirstsight steadily making up ground on the inside. Uncle Greg grabbed her arm so hard it hurt and she feared he might have a heart attack as, red in the face with excitement, his roars of encouragement raised the roof of the stand, causing the people in front of them to mock-block their ears in amusement. Darley's front runner had slipped the field, and held on to win by two lengths from the fast-finishing Loveatfirstsight – the rest some lengths adrift of the two principals.

Leaping down the deep concrete steps at a perilous pace for a man of his age, Uncle Greg practically knocked poor Victor over as he beat him on the back in congratulations, while they waited by the second slot for the filly to return.

"Great run, Guv." Dickie jumped off the heavily-blowing horse. "She'll come on a ton for that, and Cheltenham'll suit her down to the ground – she'll stay on up the hill no trouble – I never even got serious with her today."

"Well done, Dickie," Victor's eyes gleamed with hope. "She's useful."

And he said no more, for between two experts, there was no need.

Dickie hurried off with the saddle to weigh in and get ready for the next race, and having no other runners, Victor accepted Uncle Greg's invitation to a 'refresher'. 'Horses away' came over the tannoy, and Loveatfirstsight was led away by a grinning Jo, to be washed down and cooled out before the long journey home.

Only three other syndicate members had turned up to see the race, and having watched the re-run on the television screen in the bar, the little group chattered happily away, discussing the exciting prospect of having a potentially decent horse. Fiona stood on the edge listening, trying to absorb the technical lingo. Several people greeted Victor in passing, and thumbs-up and 'Nice one Vic' confirmed that the cognoscenti were equally impressed.

What a day it had been. Exhilarated but exhausted, Fiona was not sorry when Uncle Greg said that he ought to leave before the last race.

He had booked a taxi to take him back to Exeter station to catch the late afternoon train for London, but Fiona suggested he cancel the taxi and she would drive him. It would give her an opportunity to tell him about Dan and the events of last night, and she wasn't in any particular hurry to return to Stone Lea and the police. She would ring Dan when she left the station to let him know what was happening.

Uncle Greg was predictably astounded by all that had happened and insisted that she stay with Dan until Adam was found. Her glowing description of her lover had sufficiently impressed him into agreeing that he sounded 'an okay sort of a chap', though the name Daniel elicited a 'Hmph – bit Biblical!'

Laughing and sad to part, they embraced fondly and Fiona waved farewell as her uncle disappeared into the station.

Having rung Dan as promised and arranged to go over to his house for the evening, Fiona pushed a CD of soothing Classical Favourites into the player and drove peacefully back home. It seemed that was to be the last interlude of peace she would experience for the foreseeable future.

Pulling into the drive at Stone Lea, Fiona was surprised and alarmed to find no police presence. Letting herself in, she locked the door behind her and after putting on the kettle, went to check the flashing answer machine. The first call was from her mother, informing her about Pinker's funeral.

'Oh dear, that will have to be dealt with this evening.' Fiona thought, having no intention of going.

The second caller left no message, but the third was Dodo. Fiona had left a brief message on her phone after the drama the night before, but had forgotten all about it in the excitement of the day.

"Bugger me Fi!" shrilled Dodo's voice. "It's better than a trashy book. Am coming down tomorrow – can't wait to hear all. Ring *ce soir.*"

As the beeps marked the end of the message, a flashing blue light outside caught Fiona's eye. The police were back.

Opening the front door, she found a grave-faced Clive on the threshold. "Come in Clive, I'm just brewing. Any news?"

"'Fraid so Mrs McLeod." And adopting a formal manner, he gave her the stunning news. "The body of a man was found washed up on the rocks below Leapers Point earlier today. It has now been positively identified as that of Adam Croaker."

Fiona gasped as he continued.

"It seems he took his own life while the balance of his mind was disturbed – 'fraid the ole blue Land Rover went over too – pity about that."

Clive reverted incongruously to his normal self before, sighing deeply and putting his hat on the table, he sat down with a bump.

"Oh, Clive!" Fiona was horrified. "God, how terrible – in a way I feel responsible. I mean, if I'd never come here it wouldn't have happened."

"No missus, no no." Clive shook his head slowly. "You must never think that. T'was comin' sooner n' later, poor mazed Adam."

"What about Corah and Sam and old Abraham? It's too dreadful."

"Corah and Sam be gone to her folks and ole Abrum's daughter Sara's comin to see t'him, poor soul."

Both shocked at the news, they drank their tea in silence before Clive went on his way, huge feet heavy with sorrow at the harrowing turn of events.

Fiona sat on, trying to sort out her mixed emotions, and looking herself squarely in the face, she admitted the truth – she had hated Adam and was glad he was dead. Surely in the long run it would be better for Corah and Sam, and maybe even for the blighted Adam himself.

The house felt cold, and a shiver shook right through her. The only place she wanted to be was with Dan.

'I'll ring Dodo and Mummy from there,' she decided, unable to stop shivering as she threw a few essentials into a bag before locking up and leaving without further ado.

Dan had already heard the news and instinctively understanding how she must be feeling, he said little but just held her tight in his arms until he felt the tension drain out of her and the shivering stop. Then he sat her down in front of the fire and handed her a small brandy.

"Get this down you, darling. It's pork chops for supper – I'll go and put them under the grill."

The brandy burnt down Fiona's throat, making her feel queasy. Disliking it as she did, she persevered and it had the desired effect. Her blood flowed again and feeling much better, she made her phone calls while Dan busied about in the kitchen.

Angie was crisp, and difficult about her daughter's non-attendance at Pinker's funeral, but Fiona managed to sidetrack her with news of the day at the races. Recounting the Adam drama could wait.

Dodo was in flying form and Fiona's spirits soared at the thought of seeing her the next day. Though agog for an update on the saga, when Fiona told her she was with Dan, Dodo giggled something incomprehensible about 'bonkability' and rang off.

"Won't be long." Dan returned from the kitchen and sat down on the sofa next to Fiona. His face looked much better already and soreness or no, he clamped his mouth onto hers, and as his hand found its way up under her shirt, her response was instant. Watched by a bemused Holly, they slipped down onto the floor ready for action when the strident beeps of a smoke alarm sounded.

"Don't worry darling – it's only the chops!" Dan mumbled in her ear. "The house isn't on fire but I am!" He made his point.

BOMBSHELL NO.2

Driving back through the autumnal November lanes to Stone Lea after a typically snatched Dan-style breakfast, Fiona's spirits rose high above the low grey clouds that threatened to dump their rainy burden at any minute. Dan didn't care about her spare tyre and age spots – he loved her for who she was, not what she was. The sex they shared was still a sensational novelty – and narrowly missing a tractor as her mind wandered, Fiona wondered how long such an intense level of excitement could last. She had no yard-stick by which to judge, as with Hamish, it had never existed at all.

The sorry affair of Adam's death had shocked Fiona deeply, but she had to admit that the dismay she felt for the remaining Croakers was overridden by the relief that she and Dan were now safe from his mad intentions. Devon had not turned out to be the haven of tranquility she had imagined – far from it – but the 'downs' were more than submerged by the 'up' of Dan. Tingling inside with happiness, Fiona picked a stubborn piece of burnt crackling out of a tooth and smiled to herself at the memory of last night.

Both Dan and Clive had told her that there was no need for her to talk to the press unless she wanted to, because all they would reasonably require for the local papers would be contained in the official police press release. Fiona had no desire to talk to the press at all and as far as she was concerned, the sooner the unpleasant affair was closed, the better; so she was extremely annoyed to find a journalist sitting on the doorstep when she arrived back at Stone Lea.

"Fiona McLeod?" A pushy young man in a drab grey anorak leapt out of a equally drab grey car. "I'm from *The Courier* – could you spare a few minutes?"

"I'm sorry, but I've no comment to make." Fiona tried to sound politely off-putting.

"You must have something to say," he pressed on, undaunted. "It's not everyday we get a stalker in these parts –

and a suicide. Some background about your previous life, Surrey wasn't it?" he almost sneered. "Perhaps you got stalked there too!"

"I can only repeat what I said – *no comment.*"

"I'm only trying to earn a living for the wife and kids you know," he tried wheedling. "And people round here like to know what gives – livens up their lives."

"Well, I'm afraid their lives will have to be livened up some other way. Try reporting the fat-stock show and maybe your wife and children will get a bit of free beef!"

Feeling rather pleased with her riposte, Fiona dashed in through the back door and nipped into the sitting room, where she hid behind the curtain to spy on his next move. To her intense relief, his perseverance level was less than his desire to feed his wife and children, and awarding Stone Lea a V-sign, he climbed into his car and drove away.

Having said she hoped to arrive in time for lunch, Dodo would already be Devon-bound, so Fiona's first job was to get her room ready, before organising food and shopping. Knowing her friend's penchant for spur-of-the-moment decisions and early rising, Fiona got a move on.

Shaking a cloud of sleepy flies out of the curtains and grabbing the hoover to suck them up, she broke one of the carefully nurtured nails she had been planning to paint for the Hunt Ball on Saturday.

"Blast and damn!" Fiona rushed to the bathroom for scissors and emery board before the temptation to rip off the hanging victim overcame her.

"P-a-a-a-r-p," sounded a car horn below, and before Fiona had cut off the broken nail and crossed the landing, the front door banged and a shout echoed up the stairwell – Dodo had arrived.

"Hi!" shouted Fiona, taking the stairs two steps at a time. "Great to see you but what on Earth are you doing here already? You should only be at Wincanton by now."

Dodo stood at the bottom of the stairs surrounded by supermarket carrier bags.

"Well I must say! That's a fine welcome – here am I, laden with provisions, just driven flat out to Outer Mongolia to succour my friend in her hour of need and all I get is 'You should be in Wincanton' – I suppose you haven't even made my bed!"

"Not only have I made your beastly bed, but I've even cleaned the dead flies out of your room, so there!"

And laughing with the joy of seeing each other again, they embraced briefly before unloading the rest of Dodo's luggage and carrying her provisions into the kitchen. Fiona's worries about shopping were swiftly eradicated as a vast quantity of luxurious ready-made meals spilled out of Dodo's plastic bags.

"Wow!" she exclaimed, packing things into the fridge. "We shan't starve by the looks of it – you're a star Dodo, I have to admit I hadn't quite got round to food."

"Too busy shagging that Dan man I wouldn't wonder!" Dodo replied, giggling. "Not to mention THE drama – God, I can't wait to hear all about it. You poor old thing though, must have been a bit of trauma, but fancy anyone wanting to stalk you – should have given the old ego a boost!"

"My ego is no longer in need of any sort of boost, thank you very much – I'm a beautiful, mature and independent woman with a burgeoning career as a writer and an irresistible talent for sex!"

"Oh my God, Fi!" Dodo spluttered. "You really are a scream – for heaven's sake put the kettle on, I'm dying for a cup of coffee and we'll have to go to the shop after lunch – I'm running out of fags and we must get the local paper. I was expecting to find you besieged by journalists and photographers – in fact I was rather hoping for an interview myself – you know the sort of thing, 'Oldest friend arrives in hour of need'."

"I'm sorry to disappoint you." Fiona made coffee. "But I just sent a seedy young man from *The Courier* away – strictly no comment."

"You are a spoil-sport, I mean you could become quite a

celebrity."

"Honestly, Dodo. It's an incident in my hitherto dull life that I would rather forget – and would you mind not using the sugar bowl as an ashtray!"

"Whoops sorry, didn't notice. Hmm, this coffee tastes good – where's that nice onyx ashtray you nicked from Hamish?"

"I'll get it – and it's mine anyway – at least, it was a wedding present from a distant cousin of Mummy's, so I consider I've more claim to it than Hamish."

"Quite right, and anyway I seem to remember him promising to endow you with all his worldly goods, not to mention worshipping you with his body and keeping only unto you etcetera – what a load of mumbo-jumbo!"

"Not really, I intended to stick to my vows when I made them and I expect he did too." Fiona couldn't resist a giggle. "Gosh! When it comes to 'body worship', poor old Hamish didn't know where to begin!"

"I must say, Fi," Dodo sat back, scrutinising her friend, "I've never seen you look better. There's a sort of bloom about you and a glint in your eye that was never there before – and I don't think it's all a result of my beauty regime."

"You could be right!" Fiona smirked, tossing her head. "Seriously though, I do feel a different person. Odd don't you think, to change so much at my age?"

"It's certainly unusual," Dodo scratched her head. "But then you were a bit of a drip before!"

"What d'you mean?" Fiona bridled, "You used to call Susan Weatherspoon a drip, and I was nothing like her."

"Of course not. She was a swot and had BO – you were angelically clean and definitely not academic!"

"Well then," Fiona overlooked the implied criticism of her brain power, "why was I a drip?"

"Because you always accepted without question what life threw at you, be it the foul Miss Ogle of the science lab or the repressive Hamish of the marital home."

"Oh!" Fiona was rather taken aback by Dodo's home

281

truths. "Why didn't you tell me at the time?"

"Character formation doesn't work like that – it's not a tangible thing like one of your shopping lists, it's the influence of events and a slice of self-analysis. In your case, it would seem that two males are entirely responsible – one for going and one for coming as it were! Talking of which, when am I going to meet this man properly?"

"I haven't made any plans at all yet, everything's rather rushed at me in the last few days. How long can you stay?"

"Till Friday, but I must be on the road really early in the morning. The local art school's 'mature' student group is due in after lunch to reap the benefits of my wisdom, poor things."

"You are a glutton for punishment!" Fiona laughed. "Do you get paid?"

"No, unfortunately – community spirit and all that. Actually I don't mind, they're terribly enthusiastic and grateful, though completely devoid of talent. Come on, let's go to the shop – then after lunch, I'd like to go on a tour, have a good look round and maybe a walk if the weather improves."

"Fine by me." Fiona was happy to agree to almost anything. "But what d'you want to look round for in particular?"

"Oh, this and that," Dodo replied vaguely.

Then collecting up coats and bags, she drove them down to the Longbottom Village Stores.

***

"You go in, Dodo," Fiona suggested, "I don't want to find a whole crowd of village gossips all yacking about me and Dan and Adam."

"Oh come on, don't be feeble – you've got to go in sometime and anyway, it looks empty to me."

Dodo peered into the shop through the car window before getting out and, going round to the passenger door, opened it and dragged Fiona out too. The shop was empty, and the splendid Vera greeted them warmly from atop a groaning milk crate from where she was hanging a selection of lurid coloured socks on an overhead hook.

"Gude mornin' my luvs," she sang out, dropping a bunch at Dodo's feet before climbing ponderously down from her perch and taking Fiona's hand in her work-worn sausage fingers. "Lor massy," she continued, squeezing hard, "now thit be a purty rucksel an' all, yu pawer dear – aul Perce an' me, us wuz tellin' bout Adam on'y t'other day, a praaper tawud 'ee bin awiz an' no gude 'ee come to."

Heartily relieved to find that the local verdict had gone in her favour, Fiona extricated her hand from Vera's grasp and smiling into her champion's concerned and kindly face, picked up the errant socks and put them on the counter.

"Bloomin' things!" Vera chuckled, double chins wobbling. "But yu be alrighty yerzel? Us 'uv worrit 'bout 'ee."

"I'm fine thank you Vera, and so's Dan. It's Abraham and Corah and Sam I feel sorry for."

"They's better off way out'n – tidden rate for lill tacker t'live thit away." Having pronounced judgement, Vera turned to the business in hand.

"I'll have those socks, please." Dodo astounded Fiona, and by the look on her face, Vera too. "And four packets of Silk Cut. Oh, and the *South-Western Daily Press*."

"Zummin else?" Vera looked hopefully at Fiona.

"Oh, yes." Fiona couldn't bear to say no. "Half a dozen hundred-watt light bulbs and a strip of wooden clothes pegs please, Vera."

"What on Earth do you want those for when it rains all the time?" Dodo whispered, as Vera disappeared into the nether regions to search for Fiona's requests.

"To put on your nose. At least I've got the thumbs-up, and won't be put in the stocks and pelted with mangle wurzels as the scarlet woman from 'Zurrry' who led Adam on – that's a relief," she finished quickly as Vera reappeared, puffing mildly as she dumped the required articles on the counter.

Paying up, they said their goodbyes and carried their purchases out to the car.

"What *are* you doing now?" Dodo demanded as Fiona suddenly dived onto the back seat and hid amongst the packages, squashing two light bulbs in the process.

"Get in and drive," Fiona hissed urgently. "Urania's coming!"

Completely nonplussed but getting the gist, Dodo obeyed orders, and waving at the startled dumpy figure complete with Pookin, roared out of Longbottom.

"Phew!" Fiona emerged from her hideout. "That was close – she is the most dreadful woman!"

"Weird name – Urania." Dodo slowed the pace.

"Oh she's frightfully proud of it, and her surname's Clotworthy – I ask you!" Fiona giggled.

"She looked rather put out when I waved." Dodo sounded pleased.

"Serve her right, the nosy old bag! I'll bet she's just itching to know all about the Adam situation. In fact," Fiona couldn't stop laughing, "I'm expecting an invitation at any minute to lecture the Longbottom Ladies' Circle on 'Hints and Hopes for Stalkees'!"

"Do pull yourself together – I don't want one of those terrible hysterics fits like we used to have at school – it makes me cough!"

"Serves you right for smoking!" Fiona started coughing herself as some spit went down the wrong way.

Snapping a clothes peg by Dodo's nose, they giggled and coughed their way out of Longbottom, somehow managing to arrive back at Stone Lea without ending up in the ditch.

"I say, Fi!" Dodo grabbed the newspaper while Fiona stored away the remaining light bulbs."You're not headlines – can you beat it, second fiddle to old Charlie boy, that's a bit much!"

"What old Charlie boy?" Fiona demanded, "Wait, let me find my specs."

"HRH Prince of course – who d'you think? He's been

visiting an ailing cheese factory to boost the morale of the soon-to-be-curdled work force! Ha-ha, get the pun? *Look*, there's a picture of the Cann Dan Man," Dodo babbled on. "Croaker family history, bla-bla, and you're mentioned too – wow, celebrity status at last!"

"God Bless the Prince of Wales!" Fiona found her glasses. "Shove over and let me see." And she snatched the paper away, fearing what might be written there.

'Vet Shot by Suicidal Local Farmer' headed the report on the events of the previous two days. A small and blurred picture of Dan and another similar one of Adam decorated the text, which to Fiona's relief was largely factual and devoid of the sensationalism that she had so dreaded. She was referred to as 'Mrs Fiona McLeod, a divorcee from Surrey', who had been the 'unhappy object of Adam Croaker's attentions. Mrs McLeod and Mr Cann were known to be seeing each other, but which of them had been the intended victim would remain forever a mystery.'

"Thank heaven for that." Fiona exhaled a deep sigh. "Now let's hope that's the end of it."

"I'll drink to that – except I haven't got a glass! Joking apart though, it must have been a hell of a shock, you poor old thing – you certainly sounded a bit crazy on the phone."

"You can say that again, I was bloody terrified." Fiona whirled the lettuce dryer at double speed. "I really thought Dan was going to die and I would be next. Let's change the subject and have lunch, then we can set sail on your mysterious tour of Mid-Devon."

"Ah yes." Dodo got up. "Shall we have the duck paté and some salami? I bought some proper bread too, that needs eating fresh."

"Sounds great – that and salad do you?"

"Wedge of cheese perhaps and I shall be well satisfied."

Lunch over, they loaded boots and macs into Fiona's car, and armed with a selection of maps, set out on an exploratory drive around the Devon countryside. Precisely what they were looking for was not, as yet, clear to Fiona. It soon would be.

Coasting through a small village on the western fringes of Dartmoor, an unusually silent Dodo suddenly decided she wanted to stop.

"Pull in here, Fi." She pointed to the forecourt of a ramshackle building which might once have been a village shop. "Now..." she announced, turning with a smug grin to her compliant chauffeur. "Have I got news for you!"

"What are you up to, what is this earth-shattering news?"

"Hold onto your eyebrows – I'm shacking up with Puncture Man and we're planning to move down here!"

There was a moments stunned silence, then Fiona let out a whoop of astounded delight.

"Hey, that's fantastic news! You being miles away's the only thing wrong with Devon. But I don't believe it – *you* giving up your independence and settling for one man; what about all that getting bored of bonking the same bloke stuff? I'm absolutely stunned!"

"Hmm, well," Dodo sucked her teeth and made a face, "I'm not exactly giving up my independence and he knows I'm not into marriage, but I suppose the time comes to us all when the thrill of the chase looses its excitement and we settle for the final kill. Also, I'm getting a bit pissed off with having to churn out cherubs to balance the books, and spending half my life in a traffic jam. Philip's quite rich you know – he's retired early with a huge pension and his house is worth a bomb compared to prices down here. And my rent's going up and my darling little house is falling down. I've awarded a points system to the pros and cons, written them all down and lo and behold, the pros come out top!"

"Oh, Dodo!" Fiona couldn't get over the news. "That is brilliant, but do you really think you'll be faithful to the poor man?"

"Only time will tell. But I do like him – the man, as well as his prick – and he's got the message about not expecting me to change. So... here's hoping! The thing is, we need to find a 'des res' with room for my studio – that's what my magical mystery tour is all about."

"You're surely not thinking about buying an old shack like this though?" – Fiona indicated the building that they were sitting outside.

"Good God no! It was just a convenient place to pull up and tell you the glad tidings. I like the village though, and the area." Dodo gazed around speculatively.

"We must get onto all the estate agents and buy the local papers, and try the internet." Fiona was enthusiastic. "Have you done anything like that yet?"

"Heavens no! I only decided to go ahead with the scheme about 48 hours ago and anyway, Philip wants to wait till the spring to sell his house – it's a crap time of year now. But when the time does come, maybe you could do some reconnaissance for us. That's of course, on the assumption that you haven't decided to move back to sunny Surrey when your six months are up."

"*No way!* Apart from loving the country, I have, as you're so keen on pointing out, got a lot of catching up to do on the orgasm front – mind you, at the rate we're going I shall soon overtake you!"

"You'll need to live to about 150!" Dodo snorted.

"Don't you be so sure! You've probably worn Philip out prematurely whereas Dan is only just reaching his prime." Fiona was determined to get her own back.

"We'll see about that! Come on, let's get on. Can you believe it but some of my ancestors came from these parts and I want to have a look in the churchyard where they might be buried – bet they were a dull lot!"

And following Dodo's navigational instructions, Fiona drove off out of the village.

The ancestors proved elusive, but the two friends enjoyed a bracing walk over Dartmoor and returned to Stone Lea as darkness fell, feeling physically tired and mentally refreshed.

Fiona lit the fire and collapsed into a chair.

"That was great. Not so keen on the walking but love the after-effect; a kind of sensation of energised tiredness and well-being. It's a bit the same as sex really."

"Very much so," Dodo agreed. "That's why sex is a vital part of healthy living. Kettle's on – d'you want a crumpet?"

"Yes please – loads of butter, and a scrape of Marmite."

"Naughty naughty!" Dodo shook her head. "Think of your spare tyre!"

"I don't give a stuff about my spare tyre! Dan likes a cosy body and anyway, it might come in handy if we have a puncture!"

Tea over, Fiona closed her eyes and thought of Dan. Dodo was reading the paper, and the combination of the walk over Dartmoor and the heat from the fire made Fiona drowsy; within minutes she nodded off.

She and Dan were revving up to make love under an outsized gravestone, but Dan turned into old Pinker who was complaining about the lawn mower at Wood End Cottage except it wasn't Wood End, it was the village shop in Longbottom and her mother was behind the counter selling broken light bulbs and burnt pork chops...

***

"Phone, Fi." Dodo's voice broke into the dream, waking Fiona with a start. "I took the liberty of answering it as you were dead to the world – and snoring!"

"Who is it?"Fiona yawned, shaking her head in an effort to come back to reality.

"Who do you think?! And don't forget I want to meet him."

But it seemed Dodo's ambition was to be thwarted. Fiona reappeared about ten minutes later with the news that Dan had been called away to help out an old friend from veterinary college whose ancient mother had gone potty and needed moving into a home immediately, her resident carer having walked out under the strain.

"That *is* a blow," Fiona grumbled. "I was hoping he could have come over tomorrow evening – how annoying of the old mother! Apparently her son and Dan have been best mates since college and help each other out in emergencies and he didn't want to let him down."

"Couldn't the friend have got a locum?" Dodo too was disappointed.

"Evidently not. Dan said something about the usual one being on holiday and his friend's a one-man band."

"Where's Dan got to go?"

"Wild west Cornwall – he's on the road now. Still, he'll be back on Friday night in time for the Hunt Ball on Saturday."

"Yoicks tally-ho!" cried Dodo, making a strange noise that was supposed to be a hunting horn but sounded more like a cockerel with its beak tied shut. "Oh God, Fi," she laughed, "I cannot imagine you at a Hunt Ball!"

"I'm getting into all that sort of stuff now you know." Fiona adopted a superior tone of voice and stuck her nose in the air. "And just think, next year we'll all be able to go together!"

"Darling, the thought thrills me! But now it's time to open the bar – the great meeting of the two Ds will have to wait till my next visit."

Feeding the fire while Dodo played barmaid, Fiona tried to analyse her feelings about Dan's temporary defection to Cornwall. Certainly the news had come as a disappointment, but on the other hand, it was rather nice to have her time with Dodo to herself. If and when she and Philip moved to Devon, things would be very different, and Fiona was not entirely sure she liked the idea of sharing an attached Dodo.

"How's your old mother by the way, isn't she coming down soon?" Dodo reappeared with the drinks and crisps.

"Yes, next week. She's fine as far as I know but miffed with me for not going to old Pinker's funeral."

"You told me. I wonder if Mrs P wore her ping-pong balls for the great occasion!" Dodo giggled.

"Probably! Maybe she dropped them into the grave instead of earth so Pinker would feel at home in his eternal sleep – that would be the ultimate sacrifice. Poor Mrs P," Fiona added, feeling guilty at her levity. "Mummy said she was very cut up and got quite cross when I suggested it must have been a relief."

"You told me that too – repetition is the first sign of mental decay so watch out, you could end up with an enormous telephone bill, telling everyone the same thing twenty times. Seriously though, old age really is ghastly isn't it? I mean, what are you going to do with your mother if she gets beyond it? You can't spend your life tearing up and down the A303 but you're her only offspring as far as we know, and therefore responsible."

"Sufficient unto the day," replied Fiona, through a mouthful of smokey bacon crisps. "Who knows what the future holds – maybe you and I should book a slot in one of those old folks' homes where you can have your own little suite but communal eating and recreation, whatever that might be when you're half-dead!"

"Brilliant idea, that would be a hoot wouldn't it – we could make our own 'recreation' seducing a dashing nonagenarian or two!"

"What on Earth's a nonagenarian when it's at home?" Fiona washed the remaining crisps down with a swig of wine.

"Someone in their nineties, *ignoramus*."

"How horrible – I can't imagine anything worse!"

"Nonsense, don't forget we'll all be looking like an elephant's arse by then – probably be blind as well – and there's Viagra for the old boys who can't get it up! Hmm," Dodo enthused, her imagination running wild. "I can see us now, zooming on our zimmers, remaining strands of blue hair streaming out behind along with our marbles as we race round the quad – there's always a quad in those sort of places – first prize, a night with the least dead man, second prize, two nights!"

"Of all the rot you've ever talked Dodo, that's the rottiest!" Fiona doubled up with laughter, clutching her aching diaphragm as a bout of hysteria took hold.

Undaunted, and somehow managing to control her own

hysterics with the skill of a professional comedian, Dodo began the continuation of her vision of life in an old people's home, when the telephone rang.

"Ooh!" Fiona jumped up. "Bet it's Dan."

She cleared her throat and tried to sound normal as she answered the insistent ring.

"Mum? Hi, it's me." Grania's voice shrilled down the line. "You do sound odd – not having a fit or anything are you?"

"Darling! Wonderful to hear you, how are you? Telephones are amazing aren't they? You sound as if you're just up the road."

"Well actually Mum, I kind of am."

"What do you mean?" Fiona's heart missed a beat. "You're not back in England are you – in London?" Her voice rose in hope.

"Yes and no." There was a pause. "Actually, we're at Exeter St. David's station. Any chance you could come and fetch us?"

Fiona clamped her hand over the phone and shouted at Dodo. "Bring wine, I think I'm going to faint!"

"Are you there, Mum?" Grania sounded anxious.

"Yes darling, yes of course – just a bit startled, that's all. Stay put and I'll be along as fast as I can. Dodo's here at the moment, staying for a couple of nights."

"Brilliant – do hurry won't you – I've forgotten how cold England is and we're freezing."

"Um…" Fiona waved the proffered wine away mouthing 'Better not'. "Who's 'we' by the way?"

"Jumbo of course, do get with it Mum!"

"Ah yes, of course, silly me. I can't wait to see you – I'll get moving now."

"Great, thanks Mum and 'bye."

Dodo was hovering on tenterhooks, waiting to hear what drastic event had occurred to cause Fiona to call for the now rejected alcohol. Sharing her delight and amazement at the news of Grania's arrival, Dodo immediately sprung into action to organise the practicalities of the return of her erratic god-daughter.

"You get off now, Fi, I'll zip round and make beds and get supper on the go – have you got enough petrol?"

"Yes, luckily I filled up yesterday. And I know the way as I took Uncle Greg back to the station after the races. I just can't believe Grania's here! Sheets are in the bathroom cupboard – oh, and there's a wonky leg on the bed, um..." Fiona's agitation made her dithery.

"Stop fretting and get going, I'll manage."

"Thanks D – see you whenever and don't forget the fire." Fiona rushed out, hardly able to believe that she would soon be with her daughter again, after nearly eighteen months.

***

As she pulled into Exeter St. Davids, an air of desertion hung over the railway station. Seeing no necessity to park in the car park, she drew up directly outside the main entrance and hooted the horn before getting out and heading towards the lights of the waiting room. As she came within sight of the door, it burst open and a strange, scruffy tanned body topped by a dreadlocked head hurtled out.

"You've made it, Mum!" shouted a familiar voice, and the apparition rushed into her arms, hugging and kissing her. Laughing together as they inspected each other after the excitement of the initial embrace had died down, Fiona saw a towering black figure emerge from the waiting room and advance hesitantly towards them.

Turning at the sound of the closing door, Grania dashed to his side and smiling encouragingly up at him, drew him to where Fiona was standing.

"Mum, meet Jumbo. Jumbo, meet my Mum."

Fiona's heart missed a beat, and she cursed Grania for not having told her that her boyfriend was black. Pulling herself together, she took the proffered hand and shaking it firmly, smiled up into the serious, good-looking face that broke into a beaming smile of its own as she greeted him.

"Welcome to England Jumbo, and to Devon in particular."

"Thank you Mrs McLeod, it's very kind of you and I hope our unexpected arrival hasn't put you to too much trouble."

"You don't need to welcome Jumbo to England, Mum, he was at Oxford," Grania chipped in, her face showing relief at her mother's apparent acceptance of her man.

"Goodness, how very clever!" Fiona replied, unable to think of anything else to say. "Let's get on home now and talk in comfort, I'm sure you two must be hungry. Where's the rest of your luggage?"

She looked at the two rucksacks that sat on the ground at their feet.

"That's it Mum, we travel light!"

"Gracious me, I should say so – come on then!" She led the way to the car.

"You get in the front, Jumbo" Fiona instructed. "You'll die of cramp in the back – I'm afraid this car isn't designed for long legs!"

Once everybody was squashed in, they set off back to Stone Lea.

Poor Jumbo hardly got a word in edgeways, and the situation did not improve as Dodo greeted the travellers. Three females all talking and shrieking at once proved too much for him, and he loped quietly into the sitting room and collapsed in front of the fire.

Grania raced enthusiastically around the house, exclaiming with delight at what she found.

"Wow Mum, it's really cool!" The ghastly dreadlocks bounced up and down as she sprang down the stairs, having finally inspected every corner of Stone Lea. "I can't wait to see it all in daylight! Can I raid your room for a sweater? The only one I've got's a bit thin."

"Help yourself darling, but not the fawn cashmere please." Fiona cringed at the thought of her incredibly expensive jersey in the hands of her mad daughter. "I'm exhausted Dodo!" she gasped happily as Grania disappeared on her sweater-foraging mission. "*But what do you think of that*?" she whispered frantically.

"What?" Dodo replied with annoying *sangfroid*.

"Jumbo of course, you idiot!"

"I think he's absolutely divine, frightfully good looking and I suspect alarmingly intelligent – and for God's sake stop whispering," Dodo hissed back. "Where is the poor man by the way?"

"Must be in the sitting room." Fiona hurried through to track down the silent Jumbo. "Ah, here you are!" He got up as she entered the room. "Would you like a drink, we're having one and Grania won't be long – she's upstairs on a quest for a jersey, probably wrecking my tidy drawers!"

"I wouldn't say no Mrs McLeod; a glass of wine if that's possible, thank you."

"Red or white? And do call me Fiona, we don't stand on ceremony here."

"Whatever's open, with a preference for red." His engaging smile revealed a row of brilliant white teeth.

"Red wine for Jumbo, barmaid!" Fiona shouted out, sitting down in the chair opposite him.

"All right if I have a bath?" Grania's voice floated down the stairs.

"Make it quick, supper's nearly ready," shouted back Dodo, on her way into the sitting room with open bottle and glasses.

"Thanks D – anything I can do to help?"

"No fear, this is a gourmet dinner, not stewed trotters and turnips! You and Jumbo relax, it'll be ready in about ten minutes." Dodo returned to the kitchen, tactfully leaving Fiona and Jumbo together.

"I'm sorry Mrs Mc... Fiona, dumping ourselves on you like this. Grania seemed determined to surprise you for some reason," he said, obviously embarrassed.

"Don't worry, Jumbo, I've known my daughter for 27½ years and although it's certainly a surprise, it's a very pleasant one. Where've you come from though – you must be exhausted if you've been battling with airports for days."

"We are a bit travel-weary but in fact, we've been in

France for a couple of days, staying with my parents. Dad's a middle-wig in the diplomatic service and they've been in Paris for the last nine months."

"Oh, really?" Fiona's vision of mud huts and grass skirts faded rapidly. "What do they think about you and Grania?"

"Well, after the initial shock, they liked her very much." His smile was ironic. "They're quite broad-minded you know – and not racist!"

Suddenly seeing the relationship from his parents' point of view, Fiona laughed at her own blinkered vision. Jumbo was charming, and anyway, there was no indication as yet that the two of them had long-term plans for a future together.

As Dodo announced that dinner was served and would they all hurry up, Grania clattered down the stairs dressed almost entirely in Fiona's clothes. The threadbare jeans and skimpy T-shirt had been discarded, and apart from the dreadlocks, Grania looked nearly normal. Luckily she had resisted the temptation to purloin the fawn cashmere.

Dodo had excelled herself in the kitchen, but progress was slow as neither Grania, Dodo nor Fiona drew breath throughout the entire meal. By the time they had finally finished and cleared away, yawns all round indicated that it was time for bed.

Sitting on her bed in her dressing gown, Fiona waited at the back of the queue to get into the bathroom to clean her teeth. Suddenly remembering that Dan hadn't rung, she glanced at her bedside clock to check the time – 12.45 – too late. The bathroom door opened and footsteps padded across the small landing in the direction of Fiona's room. Grania arrived in the doorway.

"Hi Mum, can I come in?"

"Of course, darling." Fiona smiled, remembering the days when a very small Grania used to appear in the middle of the night and jump into her side of the marital bed during a thunderstorm. "It's wonderful to have you back, come and sit on the bed."

"It's great to be back – and you do like Jumbo don't you?"

"Very much, but I hardly know him and obviously he was a bit of a shock – you could have told me, you know."

"Yes, sorry – but I kind of just didn't. I thought you might freak." Grania's normally smooth and carefree brow furrowed, and casting an apprehensive glance at her mother, she took a deep breath. "Thing is you see, Mum, you're going to be a grandmother!"

UPS AND DOWNS

Aurora reared her head over Stone Lea, no sign of human life evident to welcome her. Fiona was the first to stir and having slept fitfully, woke feeling heavy and unrefreshed. Grania's bombshell of the night before had left her emotions in turmoil once again, and waved goodbye to the chance of the much-needed battery recharge of a good night's sleep.

She dressed quickly, and crept downstairs and out into the garden to breathe in some fresh air, and try to unravel her tangled feelings. A tap on the kitchen window revealed Dodo, pulling a silly face and waving at her through the glass, unaware of the latest news. Coming back in, Fiona told Dodo straightaway, and they sat together over a pot of tea discussing the implications of her impending grannyhood.

"No wonder you look rough." Dodo raised her eyebrows. "What are they planning to do?"

"Well, I must say they seem to have it all worked out." Uncaring of her diet, Fiona heaped sugar into her tea. "Apparently Jumbo's already got a good job lined up as head geologist on an oil field somewhere in Hampshire – and they want to get married, which is something I suppose in this day and age."

"Oh, well," Dodo cheered up. "Things could be a lot worse! Little coffee babies are rather sweet you know, much nicer than pink ones – and at least it won't be a bastard."

"God!" Fiona groaned. "I shudder to think what Hamish will say."

"That's not your worry now" Dodo replied.

"I know, but Grania asked me to break the news. For once I refused her, and I've told her they must both go and see Hamish as soon as they leave here – he is her father after all. I suppose I'd better tell Mummy." Fiona sighed at the thought.

"Talking of your mother, whatever did she think of the Adam and Dan tale?"

"I haven't told her yet," Fiona bit her lip. "I thought I'd wait till she comes to stay, then I can play it down – make it sound less dramatic. Now my news will pale into insignificance compared to the antics of her grand-daughter."

"Oh, I don't know," Dodo pondered. "She's more broad-minded than you might think. I shall be surprised if she has the vapours over any of it. Give her a stiff gin and hope for the best! How are the Topsy Turvys by the way?"

"Getting nowhere fast at the moment, I'm afraid. I never seem to have time to get down to writing and get my mind into gear. I try to think about the story when I'm driving or doing boring chores but it just doesn't seem to work."

"Hmm," Dodo shook her head. "Lack of mental discipline I fear – you won't succeed without that, you know. Still," she relented, "I must admit your own life has been rather topsy-turvy recently, which doesn't help."

"Ha ha!" Fiona's mood lightened. "Let's have some breakfast and make a plan for the day, or what's left of it by the time those two lie-a-beds appear."

"Good thinking – boiled egg do you?" Dodo was already on the move.

"Please – I think I'll try Dan's mobile while you're boiling." Fiona went through to the sitting room to find his number.

An impersonal voice informed her that she had reached the voicemail of Daniel Cann and to leave a message. This she declined to do and feeling let-down and grumpy, she returned to the kitchen.

"No go?" Dodo fished the eggs out of the pan.

"No, damn it – he might have rung me, bastard!"

"Eat your egg before it gets hard. He's probably up to his eyes in constipated hamsters and tortoises with toothache!"

"Anyone can find time for a two minute phone call if they really want to." Fiona grouched, giving the top of her egg a whack that nearly squashed it.

"*Are* you in love with him, or is it just the novelty value of having an ace bonker on the doorstep for the first time in your life?" Dodo asked thoughtfully.

"I honestly don't know. I love being with him and he makes me laugh, and his attentions certainly are flattering – it's difficult to say and I don't know how you can tell really."

"Put it another way, if he asked you to marry him, would you say yes?"

"Hmm, not sure about that," Fiona frowned. "I'm not sure I want to marry anybody again. Anyway, he hasn't asked."

"Bet he will!" Dodo grinned knowingly. "Good Lord, I hear the clump of feet above our heads – your grandchild must be on the move!"

"Shut up, don't make me feel any older than I do already this morning – and it's not due for seven months so I can stay young for a bit longer."

"It's not obligatory to turn into a grey haired old frump sitting in the corner with a crochet hook nowadays just because you're a granny," Dodo lectured. "You'll be mumbling and dribbling in a rocking chair by the time it's crawling, with your attitude!"

"Probably long before then, at this rate."

Hearing the postman arrive, Dodo got up and went to fetch the letters. "There's a nice handwritten one, the rest looks like junk as usual." She handed the mail to Fiona.

"I recognise that writing, but can't think whose it is." Fiona ripped the letter open and scanned the A4 sheet. "Oh no, I don't believe it!" she muttered, reading on.

"Who's it from?" Dodo was itching to know.

"It's from Corah." Fiona finished reading the letter. "Abraham's decided to sell the farm lock, stock and barrel except for Stone Lea and enough acres to keep a few of his precious Devon Ruby cattle, and he and the spinster daughter want to come and live here. That means I'll have to be out by the end of March – I can't bear it." Fiona stared at Dodo in dismay.

"Shit Fi, I *am* sorry, and just when you were getting together again – that's a real whammy. What else does she say?"

299

"Oh nothing much – she and Sam are fine and he likes his new school. They're living with her parents near Ivybridge while she looks for somewhere to rent. Apparently when the farm's sold Abraham's going to buy them a house and set up a trust for Sam so they'll be OK financially. She plans to bring Sam up here quite often when the dust's settled a little, so he can be with his grandfather and see his friends again."

Heavy-hearted, Fiona binned the junk mail and put Corah's letter away in her desk. "Let's forget it for the moment – I don't want to spoil Grania's day with bad news and me being gloomy. I think I hear them coming."

Well-refreshed and bursting with energy and enthusiasm, Grania and Jumbo were ready to fall in with any plans that were on offer. In the end, the stand-by formula of a pub lunch followed by motorised exploration and a walk was voted Number One choice. Much to Dodo's delight, Jumbo turned out to be a fellow Sherlock Holmes devotee with a burning desire to tramp over Dartmoor in search of the fictitious Great Grimpen Mire; an ambition that brought forth groans of horror from Fiona and her daughter.

"You two can stay in the car and yack!" Dodo suggested. "Jumbo and I will stride undaunted o'er tor and bog and when you hear a spine-chilling howling, you can come and rescue us – though I doubt that even the *Hound of the Baskervilles* in full cry could penetrate your chatter!"

"You never know," Fiona laughed, "we might even see some real hounds."

And deciding that the first stop had better be Okehampton to equip the light-travellers with suitable outdoor clothing, the party set out.

The weather was kind and the day went well. Fiona sacked her worries and never thought about Grania's scenario, Dan's lack of communication or her impending eviction at all. Her liking for Jumbo increased with every hour that passed, and to see her complex and wayward daughter so obviously happy filled her with joy and relief.

The Great Grimpen Mire remained elusive, in spite of

Fiona and Grania finally deciding to join the search party, and they all returned home in the highest of spirits. Jumbo offered to cook supper, firmly declining Grania's offer to help; clearly he had little faith in his future wife's abilities in the kitchen.

"Good heavens, Dodo!" Fiona sat with her friend while Grania fiddled about upstairs. "Things have changed since my day – can you imagine Hamish cooking supper – poor old Jumbo, I can see he'll be changing the nappies as well."

"Probably breast-feeding it too!" Dodo laughed. "A truly modern man – and here's to them both." She raised her glass.

"Hear, hear!" Fiona wholeheartedly joined the toast as Grania walked into the room with a can of Coke. "Have you told your brother?" she asked.

"No, not yet." Grania sounded hesitant. "Roddy's seriously un-cool Mum, and I didn't fancy a lecture."

"He'll have to know sometime – why don't we ring him now?"

"No Mum, pleeeze – not yet. You see Jumbo and I've got a plan, but it rather depends on you."

"Well spit it out then, I'm not a mind reader you know." Fiona wondered what was coming.

"We've decided we don't want a trad wedding – you know, church and all that stuff. We're going to nip into a registry office so it'll all be legal and no bother, but we would like a small party," Grania smiled hopefully at her mother, "and we'd like to have it here."

"What a brilliant idea!" chipped in Dodo, "And I've got an even better one – why not have it on your old mother's birthday in December? Two celebrations for the price of one and much more fun than Christmas!"

"Coool!" cried Grania, "Good old Godmum – let's get planning."

"Look hang on a minute you two – and Grania, if you say 'cool' once more I won't agree to anything. You're an expectant mother now, not some idiotic teenager." Fiona felt her grasp on the situation slipping away.

"Oh come on Fi, it's a great idea you must admit." Dodo was enthusiastic. "We could call it a marriage and coming-out party!"

"What rubbish are you talking now, Dodo? I hope you're not suggesting the baby's going to appear in December." Fiona was lost.

"Aw Mum – you're off the planet!" Grania and Dodo fell about laughing.

"*No!*" Dodo spluttered, "It's *your* coming-out party – out of your shell and domestic slavery at last."

Hearing all the laughter and shouting, Jumbo appeared in the doorway carrying a plate of nuts and olives.

"That *is* kind, Jumbo," Fiona smiled up at him. "Come and sit down if you can stand being in a mad house."

"Seems like I'd better get used to it! Have some nuts."

"We were discussing your wedding arrangements – I hope you've been consulted and that Grania's 'We' is not the royal one?"

"Don't worry Fiona, I'm happy to go along with whatever she wants as long as we have a weekend in Paris sometime to celebrate with my family. I'm afraid a proper honeymoon won't be possible as I'll only just have started my new job."

"Won't your parents be able to come over if we have a party for you? Obviously I'd very much like to meet them."

"Maybe they could." Jumbo sounded pleased and surprised at Fiona's suggestion. "After all, it's dead easy from Paris to Exeter."

"Good. We shall certainly send them an invitation and you must encourage them – have you any brothers and sisters?"

"Three sisters." Jumbo pulled a face. "Sucha's married and in Africa, Bella's in London qualifying as a lawyer, and Rosa's still at school – I think she was the unexpected result of Mum and Dad's terminal fling!"

"Funny how you young people always think us wrinklies incapable of anything!" Dodo, who was subconsciously eavesdropping, interrupted her *sotto voce* party planning with

Grania. "Just you wait thirty years, Jumbo boy!"

"Bet you haven't given up sex!" Grania whispered to her godmother.

"Will you pull yourself together Grania – I'm not deaf yet." Fiona glared at the chair opposite where Dodo sat with Grania perched on the arm. "And stop egging her on Dodo – you two have always been a bad influence on each other."

"Sorry ma'am!" They both gave a little bow whilst trying but failing to keep a straight face.

"Get Mum a drink, Jum." Grania got up and kissed him. "Chill her out a bit!"

"I'm quite chilled out thank you Grania, but I *am* hungry, and I'm sure Jumbo doesn't want his culinary efforts spoilt by any further delay. Let us continue to discuss the party in a civilized manner after supper."

It was decided that the only possible venue for the party was the Longbottom-in-the-Mire Victory Hall. Hotels would be too expensive and too far away, and it would be impossible to fit everyone into Stone Lea. Fiona would mastermind the food, and she felt sure Vera would be able to supply a couple of girls or boys to help on the night.

All that remained was to fix a date and book the hall, and once that was confirmed, the invitations could be sent out and rooms reserved in the pub and nearby B&Bs if necessary. Fiona's birthday was on the 17th December which, as luck would have it, fell on a Saturday. Provided the hall was free, it would be the perfect date to celebrate marriage, birthday and Christmas all in one hit. Party fever ran high, and the minute supper was over, Grania grabbed pen and paper to begin compiling the guest list.

"How many d'you think Mum?"

"No more than 30 – the hall's not very big and neither is my pocket."

"But Jum and I have got loads of friends in London," Grania wailed, having imagined a rave of at least a hundred.

"I'm sorry darling, but that's the limit." Fiona stood firm.

"That's fine," cut in Jumbo. "I'd rather have a small

family party with our real best friends, and we'll see the others when we're in London and after all, it is your birthday party too."

"Hope I'm going to be invited!" Dodo lit a cigarette.

"Not if you keep puffing smoke all over me," Grania fanned the air. "Look, it says on that pack that smoke could damage my baby."

"Move over the other side of the table then," Dodo fired a riposte.

"Shut up you two," Fiona was tired and hurt.

Yet again Dan had failed to ring, and the news about the cottage had cast a shadow.

"Why don't you make your list first, Fiona?" Jumbo suggested. "Then we can fill the quota that's left."

"That's the best idea I've heard so far," she smiled her thanks. "But as you two haven't got to leave till after lunch tomorrow, why don't we do it in the morning? Don't worry Dodo," she added, "you and Philip will be top of the list."

"Who's Philip?" Grania demanded.

"My current lover of course, silly girl."

"Cool — whoops, sorry Mum!"

"Right, that's it." Fiona got up. "I'm off to bed, see you all in the morning."

"Me too," Dodo added, "I've got to leave early so I'll say goodbye to you two — I don't imagine you'll be up at sparrow fart o'clock." And kissing her goddaughter and Jumbo, Dodo joined Fiona on the climb up to their beds.

***

Dodo left as planned just before seven the next morning, having drunk a quick cup of tea with Fiona, who had got up to see her off. Returning to the kitchen after waving her friend away, Fiona fought a short mental battle between clearing up the chaotic house and writing; writing won hands down, and armed with coffee, she settled in front of the computer.

Two uninterrupted hours later, footsteps overhead alerted Fiona to the impending arrival of Grania and Jumbo, and remembering in the nick of time to click on 'save', she shut down. Feeling fresh and inspired, she was pleased with her progress – obviously early morning writing was the only way forward if she was ever going to succeed.

"'Morning Mum." Grania slopped into the kitchen, dreadlocks sticking out in all directions. "OK if I fry up for Jumbo?"

"'Course darling – there's bacon and eggs in the fridge. What about you?"

"Yuck, no thanks, piece of toast will do me. Have you found out about the hall yet?"

"No, but I'll try now. It gives the number of the person to ring in the village newsletter, but I'm not sure where it is." Fiona went off to find it.

Their luck was in, the hall was free on the 17th from 5pm onwards, when the primary school children would have finished rehearsing for their Christmas concert.

"That doesn't give us much time to decorate and set up," Grania moaned on hearing the news. "Why can't the little brats clear out sooner? The racket they'll make will probably turn everyone deaf anyway!"

"I'm not deaf," Fiona replied, alarmed at her expectant daughter's attitude to small children.

"That's irrelevant – you're not going to the concert."

"No, but I've listened to enough of your 'rackets' over the years."

"Oh, point taken!" Grania flopped Jumbo's rubbery egg onto a plate. "*Ready Jum!*" she bellowed up the stairs before continuing. "We'll just have to be really up to speed with the preparations – Dodo's brilliant at that sort of thing."

Fiona's intended retort about her own capabilities was cut short by Jumbo's arrival in the kitchen. In contrast to his future wife, he looked washed, brushed and on the ball.

"I hope you slept well," Fiona smiled at him. "The party's on for the 17th so do ask your family as soon as possible, won't you? I would so like to meet them."

"I sure will," he replied with feeling, "and I know they

feel the same way."

"You must let me know as soon as you hear from them so I can arrange somewhere nice for them to stay – they might find the local pub a bit rough if they're used to embassy life."

"Don't worry, Mum," Grania dropped a lump of marmalade on the table en route to her toast. "Jum's folk are chilled out – his grandma was born in a mud hut!"

"Grania!" Fiona fixed her daughter with a steely eye, horrified at her rudeness.

"Don't worry," Jumbo laughed. "It's quite true and we're very proud of what Dad's achieved. And, I may add," he hacked into his burnt bacon, "she was a much better cook than your daughter!"

"Jumbo," Fiona sighed, leaning back in her chair, "I can't tell you how relieved I am that my grandchild will at least have a civilized father!"

Breakfast finished and the eating area table cleared away and wiped clean of Grania's sticky debris, Fiona suggested they sit down together and compile the guest list for the party.

"Would you mind if I left you two to it and went for a walk?" Jumbo asked. "I could do with some exercise."

"Carry on Jumbo, there's a footpath just off the lane. It's well marked so you won't get lost." Fiona wondered if he was giving her a chance to be alone with Grania or whether he really wanted exercise.

Grania blew him a kiss before turning to her mother. "He's a fitness freak and mad on sport – you should see his six-pack – brilliant at tennis and not bad at cricket either. Poor old Jum," she laughed, "he can't wait to get life going in Hampshire so he can get into all that stuff."

"Hmm, I don't know about six-packs, but I'm afraid you take after me in one respect – useless at sports and rather lazy!"

"That's me!" Grania gave her mother a quick hug. "Dad wasn't much good either."

"Talking of your father, I wonder if we should invite him

and The Doberman to the party – what d'you think?"

"*No way!*" Grania practically screamed. "If he wants to celebrate his only daughter's marriage, he can do something himself in London but I bet he won't – miserable old b..."

"Be quiet Grania and listen to me, or there'll be no party," Fiona snapped. "Pull yourself together and stop behaving like a child. In seven months' time, you are going to be a mother and it's high time you grew up. You look like nothing on Earth, you appear to have no idea of responsibility or how to run a house and home. When I was your age... " she got no further.

"Aw Mum, not that old lecture pleeeze! I promise I'll be brilliant – I'm just too excited by it all at the moment to be grown-up but once I'm a wife and mother you won't know me, I'll be so serious and dull!"

"I suggest you start by getting rid of that dreadful hair-style before you see your father and grandmother, and buy yourself some decent clothes."

"We haven't got any spare cash till Jum starts his job, but when we're up and running I'll look round for something too – I don't plan to be a stay-at-home mum for ever." Grania looked hopefully at her mother.

"I see," Fiona raised her eyebrows while reaching for her cheque book.

"Thanks Mum – you're a star. You won't recognise me when we come down for the party!"

"I didn't recognise you at Exeter station." Grania missed Fiona's irony. "Now shall we get on with the guest list?"

That didn't take long. Fiona had already written down her invitees, which with themselves came to a possible seventeen, leaving Grania and Jumbo with the rest of the allocation plus a B list to allow for refusals.

"Why don't I design the invite on the computer now?" suggested Grania. "Then if we leave for Exeter in good time we can find a shop to copy it onto card and take ours with us."

"That's a good idea," Fiona agreed. "You'd better get a

move on though. I don't know Exeter that well, and Jumbo said he didn't want to be late getting into London."

"I'm putting your address and phone for RSVPs – OK?"

"Of course, I'm the caterer after all – and if your friends are anything like as scatty as you, you'd better underline RSVP several times." With Grania's 'raspberry' blowing in her ears, Fiona went upstairs to start stripping the beds.

***

Exeter came up trumps, and with no difficulty at all they found a shop selling office equipment and stationery, where the invitations were produced in the time it took them to have a cup of tea. Being well before rush hour, the traffic was light and they arrived at the station with time to spare.

"Don't wait, Mum." Grania remembered her mother's dislike of prolonged goodbyes. "The train won't be in for ten minutes and knowing good old England, it'll probably be late."

"I think I'll slip on then – get on with things at home."

"Thank you for everything, Fiona," Jumbo held out his hand, "but most of all for Grania."

Smiling, Fiona took the hand in both of hers and held it. "I hope you never have cause to regret that remark – and as your future mother-in-law, don't I get a kiss?"

"Yahoo!" cried Grania, causing a few heads to turn as Jumbo obliged.

"'Bye Mum, I'll ring Sunday to let you know how the Dad scene goes if we get to see him – maybe he and The Doberman live in a kennel and eat raw bones!" She gave her mother a quick hug and a kiss.

"'Bye darling – look after yourself, and you *must* contact your father."

Returning their wave as they walked away, Fiona watched until they disappeared from view.

'Funny' she thought a little sadly as she started the car. 'Grania's no longer mine after all these years. Still, it had to happen sooner or later; that's how the world goes on – generations rolling by, the old departing, the new arriving.

Where's life gone?'

But by the time she walked back into Stone Lea, there was only one thought in Fiona's head. Where the hell was Dan and why hadn't he rung? Tomorrow was the Hunt Ball, but if he was going to treat her like a convenient old shoe and chuck her in the back of the cupboard when not needed, then he'd better think again. Angry now, Fiona rang his home number and getting the answer-phone, left a curt message expressing her displeasure.

Feeling a lot better for her verbal discharge, she set about clearing up the house. There was plenty to do in that department, but time too for some writing before an early night to catch up on lost sleep. The last few days had been hectic, and she had to admit that now all the excitement was over, her energy levels were dropping fast.

Determined to get back to the computer, Fiona forced herself on with the housework. The hoover jammed half way through Dodo's bedroom floor and belched out a cloud of filthy dust all over the cleaned room.

"Shit – that's it!" Abandoning the offending machine, she ran downstairs, made herself a cup of coffee and switched on the computer.

'Topsy's best friend, Kay Otical, had won a luxury weekend for two on the moon, and Kay had invited Topsy to go with her. Thrilled with the invitation, Topsy texted her acceptance back immediately and became so excited she very nearly went over the moon a week too soon. But what should she wear, that was the problem? 'I know' she thought, 'I'll go to Clone Rangers, they'll have something suitable.' And running to find her mother, Topsy...'

An insistent knocking on the front door dragged Fiona back to reality, and wondering who on Earth it could be at this time of night, she went to see.

'If it's Urania and her crappy Ladies Circle, I shall be really rude' Fiona thought, storming towards the door.

It wasn't Urania, it was Dan.

"Oh, hello. It's you." She stood firm.

"Of course it's me! I got your message. Can I come in?"

"I suppose you'd better."

"What's the matter Fiona, what have I done?" Dan stepped inside and shut the door.

"Just failed to make any contact at all since you disappeared to Cornwall."

"God woman, it wasn't through lack of trying – your mobile was switched off the whole time!"

"I have got a land line too, you know."

"Well I don't know the bloody number, do I? I've always used the mobile, and you're not in the phone book."

"Of course not, I've only just got it."

"That's it then, is it? I'm out. Well if that's the way you feel, I might as well bugger off now – back to my Cornish tart!"

"She's welcome to you!" Enraged, Fiona stepped back to slam the door and tripped over the doorstop, whacking her funny bone on the wall as she fell. "Ow!" she exclaimed, furious with herself for loosing her dignity.

Too late. Dan's gorgeous green eyes began to crinkle and pulling her to her feet, he rolled up her sleeve and covered the injured elbow with kisses.

"Go you away, you beast!" She beat at him with her free arm.

"Not till I've kissed it better. I'm not taking a flawed partner to the Hunt Ball tomorrow night."

"I'm not coming."

"You jolly well are, and several times in the next few hours!"

"Pig!"

"Shut up, woman!" His mouth changed direction and stifled further speech.

***

Later...

"It's no good, Dan." Fiona shook him awake. "We'll have to have a midnight feast, I'm starving."

"Hmm," he murmured, wafting his hand vaguely over her

naked body, "you've just about eaten me alive, isn't enough?"

"You're no substitute for scrambled eggs on toast with smear of Marmite followed by cold apple pie."

"How romantic! No *petite mort* for you then, my darling."

"What's that?" Fiona rolled over and got out of bed.

"The feeling that's supposed to overcome you after a particularly good bonk – literally 'little death' – French you know."

"How ridiculous," Fiona laughed. "Typical French!"

"They would say typical unromantic English to think about food – but now you mention it, it does sound rather tempting."

Later again...

"That was delicious." Dan pushed his scraped clean plate away. "They say sex is better after a row, more fire and passion – we must try it more often! Laura and I never had rows you know, never had sex either once she discovered I couldn't give her the children she wanted."

"Hamish and I didn't row much either – I would never have dreamt of contradicting him. When I look at myself in the mirror now, I don't see the same person, the old me is sort of blurred – funny that. Sex to him was like washing the car on a Sunday, only rather more effort for less satisfaction! Anyway, don't let's talk about them and don't let's take up rowing either, I'm quite happy as we are."

She took his hand and squeezed it.

"God I'm tired" Dan yawned. "And to think that this time tomorrow we'll be grooving the night away at Grimblesby Hall!"

"Come on then." Fiona pulled him to his feet. "Up to bed and this time, to sleep."

"I'll second that!"

***

Grimblesby Hall stood four-square and timeless on its medieval foundations; a staunch bastion of the vanishing al English country life. Valiantly ignoring the strands of coloured light bulbs that , the old house graciously welcomed the l that flooded through its ancient portals.

lid, Dan? Just stop a minute and look."

‌‌‌‌‌uuig onto his arm as she tottered across the car park, trying not to lose a shoe in the rain-softened ground. "Doesn't it make you feel insignificant, to think those old stones have seen so much more than we will ever see and will still be there when we're long gone and forgotten – it's almost creepy and well, sort of bewildering in a way."

"The only thing I find bewildering is that you wouldn't let me drop you at the door."

"I told you, I don't want to be left alone with a lot of tally-hoing strangers!"

"You'll be the belle of the ball, my sweet, and if any other man so much as looks at you, I'll break his jaw!"

They joined the queue of chattering partygoers lining up to show their tickets to the doormen, who were dressed in full hunting rig, right down to their boots.

Fiona had never seen anything like it: ranging from 18 to 80, around two hundred people gathered together for the social event of the hunting year. Whiskery old chaps with complexions that matched their moth-eaten red tail coats and starched wing collars strained tight round fleshy necks, rubbed shoulders with noisy young men in baggy dinner jackets and garish waistcoats; there was even a kilt or two.

For the women, it seemed anything went. Blue-haired powdery dowagers resplendent in old taffeta curtains and lugging a king's ransom in diamonds chatted animatedly to pretty, skimpily dressed young girls; chic designer mingled with horsey frump, and Fiona laughed at herself for ever having worried about what to wear. Long, short, flouncy, classic, Silicon Valley – they were all there.

Nevertheless, she was pleased with her choice of black silk with chiffon sleeves – understated but chic. Carefully applied makeup and newly-styled highlighted hair set the seal, and for the first time, Fiona felt glamorous.

"Why have the men got different coloured collars and lapels?" she asked Dan as they made their way through the mob to find their table.

"They're called 'facings'. Each hunt has its own livery for evening dress, and if you look at the buttons on the coats, you'll see they're engraved with different letters, depending on which pack they come from."

"Why haven't you got a coat like that? They do look rather dashing."

"Because I'm not a member of a hunt and I would still have to be invited to wear the Hunt Button by the Masters even if I were."

"Goodness!" Fiona had no idea of the intricacies of hunting etiquette.

Ban or no ban, it seemed the show would go on.

Dan was warmly greeted by the rest of his party when they finally found their table, and introductions all round left Fiona completely bemused.

'I shall never remember anyone's names' she thought in despair as she shook the fourteenth hand.

Dan was obviously considered a good fellow and much back-slapping and kissing went on, including 'Anna of the wounded horse,' who was the only face amongst their party that Fiona recognised.

Dinner was a splendid buffet – and joining the queue for curry, coronation chicken, cold salmon, beef or the whole lot – Fiona inspected it all with interest to get ideas for her own little celebration next month. Everything looked delicious, and bearing their laden plates back towards the table, she begged Dan not to abandon her to the mercies of strangers when they sat down to eat.

"Nonsense silly, they're all dying to check you out and it's high time you broke into local society – you've been holed up in Stone Lea for quite long enough."

"Oh, Dan!" Fiona wailed. "You are a cad. I suppose they all know about Adam."

"Of course they do, you're something of a *cause celebre* actually!"

Arriving at their table, Fiona could say no more. Smiling at her already-eating neighbours, she sat down where Dan indicated she should sit.

"Hi there, Fiona isn't it?" spoken through a mouthful of curry. "I'm Frankie, other and worser half of Anna over there. That's George on your left but don't bother about him, if he's not stuffing his face he's asleep!"

"Watch your mouth, Frankie, or I won't let you use my sheep shed next spring! And I reserve first dance with the beautiful lady."

Fiona turned to her other neighbour. About Dan's age but three times the size round the girth, George had a charming smile and a wicked sense of humour, and Fiona liked him on sight. Her fear of being spurned as a suburban in-comer evaporated in an instant. One thing was certain about these people, they were all out to enjoy themselves and 'side' was not a word in their vocabulary.

"Madam, may I get you some pudding?" George offered as Fiona put down her knife and fork, unable to eat quite all she had taken.

"Thank you, but not too much though, just a spoonful of fruit salad or something light would be lovely."

He battled off towards the buffet.

"How are Anna's horses?" Fiona turned to Frankie, pleased that she had thought of something halfway interesting to say.

"Bloody things!" he laughed. "How d'you know about them?"

She recounted the tale of Dodo's meeting with Anna in the pub car park.

"Ah yes, I was bloody annoyed about that – I was about to move some cattle when she rang through." Fiona remembered Dodo's description of the Schumacher lorry driver. "Have to say for the old girl though, she does pretty well with the brutes and she's got a strong hand for this season's point-to-points. Trouble is they cost a lot of money and the farm struggles to pay – keeps her happy though." His rough-hewn, genial face broke into a proud grin at the thought of his wife's future triumphs.

"I'm ashamed to say I've never been to a point-to-point." Fiona awaited his reaction, nervously fingering her empty glass.

"Nothing to be ashamed about – here, let me fill you up."

"Only a drop, please, I've a feeling I shall be chauffeur tonight." Dan was clearly well-away up the other end of the table.

"He's in good form, isn't he?" Frankie's eyes followed her gaze. "And none the worse for the shoot-out by the looks of things. Bad job that – talking of being ashamed, that wasn't much of a welcome for you to Devon – we're all pretty ashamed about that."

"That's kind of you to say so, but it's in the past now and best forgotten. I love Devon," Fiona added with feeling.

"Glad to hear it. You're good for Dan you know – loosened him up a bit."

George reappeared, expertly balancing three plates of pudding: two enormous portions for himself and Frankie, and a mercifully small one for Fiona.

"D'you know George, we have a sensible woman in our midst at last – she's never been to a point-to-point."

"Jolly good show!" George wiped a dribble of chocolate mousse off his chin. "Nothing to be gained except pneumonia and bankruptcy."

"I'd like to go though," Fiona laughed.

"Don't worry, you won't be allowed not to – Dan's always one of our duty vets anyway – not that he knows much about horses!" Frankie joked. "Talk of the devil!" And Fiona looked up to see Dan heading their way.

"These two turnip-heads looking after you properly?" Dan put his hands on Fiona's shoulders. "I hear the dreaded sound of Ronnie Riphay and the Rusty Buckets, thought we might try a dance."

"I say Cann, I booked first dance with the fair lady." George tried and failed to sound aggressive.

"Tough luck old boy – you shouldn't be so greedy. If your stomach gets any bigger you won't be able to find what lurks beneath!"

"Wouldn't do me much good if I could," George grumbled. "Moira seems to prefer thrillers to being thrilled!" And leaving them all laughing, Dan led Fiona away towards the sound of the music.

The magnificent ballroom with its sprung floor and minstrel's gallery was packed to bursting as Ronnie Riphay thumped out a medley of Glenn Miller favourites. Jigging round in Dan's arms to *In the Mood*, Fiona basked in the delight of being loved.

"Back to the table, my beautiful woman." He kissed her as the tune ended. "I can't monopolise you all evening."

And they left the ballroom to re-join their party, stopping to get a soft drink for Fiona on the way. She never had time to drink it as from then on, the evening spiralled into a whirl of activity as she was pushed, guided or spun round the dance floor, depending on the age and enthusiasm of her partner. From *My Old Man's a Dustman* to *Moon River*, the band played on, sweat running and eyes glazed.

Returning from a frantic Charleston with Frankie that left her feeling as if she had been trampled by a herd of elephants, Fiona was relieved to find Dan sitting at the table talking to Anna. Instantly taking in the meaning of her pleading eye contact, he patted the empty chair beside him and held her hand possessively when she sat down, exhausted.

People were beginning to drift away, the obligation of remaining with their own party over. The young headed to the disco, the old to their beds and the hungry to the breakfast bar. A friend of Anna's arrived and collapsed into the chair beside her.

Like many, she was beginning to fray at the edges, and Fiona was relieved when the two began discussing horses, freeing Dan for her alone.

"One last dance?" He stroked her thigh.

She smiled into his eyes, nodding her assent.

"We'll try the disco, I think I've done the Rusty Buckets!"

The strobe lighting flickered over the gyrating mass of bodies smooching round the dungeon-like cavern that was the disco. Conversation was a no-no but Fiona and Dan had no need of words. Appropriate to the late hour, the music was slow and to their joy, featured many old sixties favourites – the songs of their youth.

As The Shirelles sang out *'Will you still love me tomorrow?'* Dan murmured "and the next day and forever," into Fiona's ear before plunging his tongue into her mouth, his trouser-shackled hard-on prodding into her thigh.

Coming up for air, Fiona mouthed: "Let's go, I think we're shocking the young!"

"Bollocks to them," he mouthed back, but led her out into the passage and away back to the car park. The party was over.

***

Thank goodness it was Sunday, and Dan not on call. They slept late, and after an amusing postmortem of the night before, decided on a short walk for Holly's benefit before a pint in the local and a lazy afternoon.

Fiona had not yet had a chance to tell Dan properly about Grania's visit, Corah's letter or the plans for the party on 17th, and as they lounged in front of the fire, he listened with all ears as she recounted the events in her life which had taken place during his absence.

"Good heavens," he commented, a wry smile on his face, "you certainly haven't let the grass grow under your feet!"

"It's grown rather too fast for my liking," Fiona blew out her cheeks, "and my mother's coming down this week too, on Tuesday."

"Oh, really? I'd like to meet her. I presume she knows about me?"

"Well no actually, I haven't told her yet."

"Why ever not? I thought mothers and daughters yacked the whole time."

"We don't – at least not about that sort of thing. I don't know." Fiona searched for the right words. "I just wanted to keep you to myself for a bit longer, I can't quite explain why. To avoid endless questions and unwanted advice I suppose."

"I would like to meet her, though," Dan insisted. "You can't keep me under wraps for ever and anyway, they always say check out the mother to see what you might end up with in old age!"

Letting his last remark pass, Fiona agreed that the time had come to reveal his existence and that he should join them for supper on Wednesday.

"And now Dan, I'm going to love you and leave you," she went over to his chair and sat on his knee. "I need to do some catching up at home, and press on with my writing."

"I wish you wouldn't go, Fiona." Dan pulled her down into his shoulder. "I'm lonely without you and life seems rather pointless, sticking around here by myself."

"Nonsense," she kissed away his frown. "You'll be up with the lark, rushing about killing and curing all those little furry creatures and you won't have time to think about me!" She stood up, determined not to weaken. "'Bye Holly, look after your master."

The dog raised its long nose half an inch off the floor in acknowledgement, and went back to sleep.

Dan came out with her to the car and held her tight for an instant before she broke away and got in.

"Drive carefully, it's foggy," he said, and she waved as he stood staring through the murk at the retreating car.

<u>VISITORS VARIOUS</u>

Fiona wrote like a creature possessed; hour after hour she battered away at the keyboard, her fingers quickening with practice, her brain fertile as the story took hold and carried her on.

Something told her that Dan was on the verge of asking her to marry him when she was free. Living together would not be an option in his book.

Suffering a temporary block, she abandoned Topsy for a cup of coffee, and enticed by a shaft of rare November sunshine, put on a coat and took the mug out into the garden.

The prospect of having to leave Stone Lea by the end of March had badly undermined her plans for the future, but she was determined that this should not influence her answer if her senses proved correct, and Dan popped the question – after all, there must be other properties to rent or even buy. The latter was not a favoured option though. It would stretch her budget and having some 'spenders' for the first time in her life was proving to be an attractive experience, along with the independence that went with it.

"Independence," she said aloud to the unresponsive garden birds busily attacking the peanut feeder Sam had fixed up. "Why am I so hung up about it?"

The birds had no answer, but suddenly Fiona realised that the problem wasn't only independence, it was self-respect too – a necessity to achieve something in her life for the first time that was hers, and hers alone. Only the publication of her book could attain that goal, and then if Dan asked, maybe she would say 'Yes'.

'What an idiotic idea!' she laughed at herself, but fired up with determination she tipped the now cold remnants of the coffee onto the ground and walked briskly back to the waiting computer.

By Tuesday lunchtime, Fiona had written over 15,000 words; lost to the world, she was living with her characters and their adventures, and the *denouement* was now clear in her mind.

Suddenly feeling hungry, she checked the time and was horrified to find it was after two o'clock, and her mother would be here in less than two hours. Shutting the computer down, she grabbed some bread and cheese and set about putting the final touches to the house, before dashing into her bedroom to buff up her own appearance. In the nick of time. Two sharp beeps on a horn proclaimed the arrival of her mother, only minutes after Fiona finished making up her face and running a comb through her hair.

"Welcome to Stone Lea, Mummy," she cried, flinging open the front door as Angie prepared to get out of the car.

"Helloee!" A smartly-shod foot arrived on the gravel, followed by the rest of her mother, smiling and patting her hair as the wind whipped it out of place.

"How lovely to see you, Mummy! You found the way all right?" Fiona pecked her mother's immaculately made-up cheek.

"No problems at all dear – your directions were perfect. Shall we get my luggage in before it gets dark? Then I could die for a cup of tea."

Obeying orders, Fiona heaved the two heavy suitcases out of the boot, wondering why on Earth her mother needed so much luggage for a two-night stay.

"What a charming little cottage!" Angie gave Stone Lea the seal of approval, having inspected all the rooms whilst Fiona lugged the cases upstairs, lit the fire and put the kettle on.

"I'm so glad you like it, I'm very happy here."

"Hmm, I can see that, Fiona dear." She studied her daughter intently for a moment, head cocked on one side. "You look different somehow, better. Yes, definitely better."

"You mean I looked awful before?"

"Nooo – not awful but... well, you were rather a mousy little thing, always scuttling around looking nervous and drab!"

"Oh dear," Fiona laughed, "how dreadful for you having a daughter like that!"

"Don't be silly – you took after your father, it couldn't be helped."

"Poor Daddy!"

"Not at all Fiona, he was a wonderful man and I loved him till the day he died and, I may say, I miss him still." Angie gave a little sniff. "Hmm, if you ask me, I should say there's a man in your life. I've yet to come across any other reason for a woman of your age to change so."

"You don't miss much Mummy, do you?" Fiona smiled, and pouring out their tea, she bit the bullet and settled down to tell her all the hitherto untold dramas and events that had happened in her life since leaving Surrey, finishing with the plan for the party.

"*Fiona*! Get me a G&T before I swoon." Angie lay back in her chair, fanning her face with the November issue of the *Longbottom Listener*.

"It's only ten past six, Mummy." Fiona made no move.

"Foolish daughter," Angie's voice rose dramatically, "what matter the hour when trauma strikes the heart!"

"Mummy, this is Stone Lea, not The Old Vic – but if you insist, I shall get myself hither and fettle thee a drench."

The fizzing liquid restorative worked the oracle, and within minutes of the initial shock subsiding, Angie was preening herself at the prospect of becoming a great-grandmother.

"And just imagine," Fiona sighed, relaxed at last, "Uncle Greg will be a great-great-uncle."

"What an extraordinary thought! And let us hope my silly brother's ridiculous infatuation with horse-racing doesn't lead to his downfall." Angie snorted, disapproval etched all over her face.

"I don't see why it should," Fiona stuck up for him. "It's a very good thing to have an interest later in life. I hope he can come to the party."

"I'm sure wild horses wouldn't keep him away!" Angie

tittered at the equine reference. "We shall all be there, don't worry. I shall bring Mrs P down on the Friday and we can all pitch in and help with the food."

Fiona's heart sank as visions of mayhem and bickering in the small kitchen swam before her eyes.

"And I can't wait to inspect this man of yours tomorrow. Sex, that's what's woken you up – obviously poor Hamish was lacking in that department!"

"Really Mummy!" Fiona exclaimed, making a mental note to cut back on the gin tomorrow night.

"Don't worry dear, I'm not about to get all mumsy and confidential." Angie shuddered at the thought.

"Thank God for that. I'm going to start cooking in a minute, but there's no rush and the water's hot whenever you want to bath."

"You go on," Angie waved a red-nailed hand airily. "I shall sit here a little longer by this nice fire – I hope the bathroom's warm."

"Tell me when you come down!"

Angie's visit sped by and to Fiona's surprise, Longbottom-in-the Mire got the thumbs-up. The zenith was Dan. Fiona had never seen two people with so little in common click like her mother and her lover, and as the evening flowed on she began to feel superfluous to requirements as they chattered and joked together. When he came to leave, Angie even insisted on kissing him goodnight in the hall before tactfully disappearing up to bed.

"Your mother's a cracker – no worries there about what you might turn into!" Dan grabbed her.

"Apparently I take after my father – bad luck – ouch don't!" He pinched her bottom.

"Shall we do it on the sofa?" he suggested, nibbling her ear.

"Oh Dan, I don't know. Mummy might come down."

"Suppose you're right," he groaned. "God, it's like being a teenager again, caught *in flagrante* by the parents!"

"Mummy did say sex was good for the appearance."

Fiona murmured, closing her eyes in ecstasy as he kneaded her left breast, his spare hand in her trousers.

"Come on, quick!" Dan pulled her urgently into the sitting room where they made love standing up, under the beady eye of Dodo's cockerel.

***

Brisk and undemonstrative as always, Angie sped away the next morning, back to her own world of bridge, hair-do's and charity lunches. She left with assurances of her approval of Fiona's new way of life, and eager anticipation for the forthcoming party.

Relieved and happy, Fiona stuck a load of laundry in the machine before opening the computer and re-immersing herself in her literary task. Tapping merrily away, she nearly jumped out of her skin when a loud rat-a-tat-tat sounded on the window near her chair. Looking up, she was astonished to see Sam's grinning face pressed against the pane.

"Sam, what on Earth are you doing here? Come round to the back door." Fiona went through to let him in. "What a nice surprise!"

"You writing your story?" he asked eagerly, gazing up at her.

"Yes I am, and at last it's going well. You shall read it when it's finished though you might find it a bit babyish I think – it's really for younger children."

"I'd like to – it's an adventure isn't it? I like adventures." he replied seriously.

"Anyway Sam, tell me what you're up to – and where's your mother? Shouldn't you be at school?"

"Dentist!" He made a face. "Mum's coming in a minute, she's at the Barton with Grandad and Auntie Sara talking boring stuff. She said it was OK to come 'cos if you didn't like us any more you wouldn't have asked us to your party."

"Of course I like you," Fiona laughed. "Why ever shouldn't I?"

"Um, you know, Dad and that and having to leave the Lea." Sam's bright eyes peered anxiously through his mop of hair.

"What a silly thing to think. Coke?"

"Aw please." Sam's smile returned. "Mum's awfully silly sometimes but so are other peoples' mums."

He made a funny snort as the Coke bubbles fizzed up his nose.

"I hope you can come to the party, it's to celebrate my daughter Grania's marriage and my birthday."

"Yeah, Mum said we can, and we'll stay with Grandad."

"I'm afraid it'll be rather boring for you though Sam, all the guests are either old or terribly old!"

"I don't mind, I can be a waiter – or a barman." His eyes lit up.

"Tell you what, Sam," Fiona suddenly had an idea. "Why don't you see if your friend Jack would like to come too; I could do with another pair of hands."

"Cool!" Sam breathed. "You will get Mum to ask Jack's Mum won't you?"

"On one condition."

"What?" Sam's face fell.

"That you tell my daughter she's too old to say 'cool'!"

They were laughing together when Corah walked in.

"This sounds more fun than up at the Barton! How are you, Fiona? It's great to see you again."

"Ask Mum, ask Mum, ask Mum!" Sam chanted over Fiona's greeting.

"Be quiet Sam, don't interrupt," Corah admonished him, "but what is Fiona to ask me, anyway?"

"I thought it would be nice for Sam if Jack came to the party with you – the boys could be very helpful."

"That's very kind, Fiona, I'll ring his mother this evening." Corah sounded pleased. "Now buzz off Sam, I want to talk to Fiona."

"Can I use the computer?"

"Provided you don't lose Topsy Turvy and her new friend Crum Bumbeldy."

"You always say that, Mrs McLeod. I won't go into

Documents, I only want to do pictures."

Sam happily employed, Fiona and Corah sat down to tea and talk. The first thing that struck Fiona was how much better Corah looked. Gone was the pinched, care-worn face and the blue-black shadows under her eyes; her cheeks were almost pink and the lank rats' tails now a glossy collar length bob.

"You do look well Corah," Fiona commented. "I think you've put on a bit of weight – it suits you."

"Oh Fiona, I know I shouldn't say it, but the relief of not having poor Adam is something I can't explain. All I know is I feel a new woman and when I look in the mirror, I see one too! I'd forgotten what it was like to live without the constant fear of anger and bitterness."

"I think I do understand how you feel, only divided by about a thousand! When Hamish left, I panicked and wondered how on Earth I would cope alone, but gradually a strange new person began to emerge and here I am – still Fiona McLeod but feeling better – looking better so I'm told, and very happy. You'll get married again Corah, you're young and pretty with a whole new life ahead of you – and you've got a smashing son."

"That's the miracle, Sam seems fine." Corah shook her head in wonder. "I was just so freaked out about his reaction to it all, I didn't know what to do for the best. I even went to a child psychiatrist for help, and she advised me to tell him the truth in the softest possible way. She said young children have amazing powers of acceptance and re-adjustment, but if you tell them lies and they discover the truth later on, it can lead to all sorts of problems. My parents have been marvellous and Sam adores them, but they spoil him rigid and I feel cramped and beholden – I must find somewhere to rent soon or I shall go mad, not having my own home."

"Talking of renting, I'm soon to be in the same boat by the sounds of it."

"I'm *so* sorry about that Fiona, I really am, but I can see Abraham's point of view."

"So can I," Fiona agreed. "Don't worry about it, I can't pretend to be pleased but it's just one of those things. I'm surprised he wants to sell up though, after all the generations of Croakers that have lived here."

"I know, but now that Adam's gone I think he's given up hope – not that they ever really got on you know – usual old thing, son thinks father's out-of-date and father thinks son doesn't know what he's doing. But there's little more than a bare living to be made in the farm now and he's tired of struggling. Mind you, I suspect Sara's behind it – she's a bossy old fuss-pot who wants her cut of the loot if you ask me."

"Well, there ought to be plenty of that when the place is sold up."

"I don't know, small dairy farms struggle and the house is going to rack and ruin. The herd will fetch a bit but the tackle's pretty antiquated. It's sad really, but I expect some pop star will buy it and never live there."

"Why do you say the house is going to rack and ruin?" Fiona was curious.

"Because the thatch has had it, half the window frames are rotten, there's no heating and the wiring is a nightmare. I can't imagine what a surveyor would make of it!"

"Hmm, I see what you mean."

"But changing the subject, I gather you might not need to find a new house!" Corah looked saucy.

"You've lost me." Fiona replied, genuinely puzzled by her remark.

"One Daniel Cann – veterinary of this parish!" A neatly plucked eyebrow shot up – "A little bird told me you were seen in the disco at the Hunt Ball!"

"Ah-ha! And what a chatty little bird it must have been!"

"I think it's great Fiona, he's such a nice guy."

"Not bad, I'll agree with you there and I suppose we are what you might call an item, but I'm not going to live with him. Apart from anything else, my divorce hasn't come through yet, neither has he asked me to marry him."

"We'll see!" Corah looked knowing. "I'd better go I suppose. It's been great seeing you and I'm looking forward to 17th. You've put 'casual' on the invite but I'm not sure what to wear."

"Oh anything – anything eveningy you feel happy in, it really doesn't matter. Perhaps one up from jeans and trainers for my waiters though!" Fiona added.

"Of course – come on Sam," Corah called, "hurry up – we must go."

And goodbyes said, mother and son left Stone Lea for the drive back to South Devon.

'Now there's a changed woman if ever I saw one.' Fiona thought, washing up their tea mugs and Sam's glass.

She was glad Corah had called in and cleared the air of any silly thoughts that their friendship might be impaired by what had happened. It also saved her having to answer Corah's letter.

The Croakers' unexpected arrival had broken her train of thought and temporarily banished the Muse. Feeling the need for fresh air, Fiona put on her boots and Barbour and set out to walk the home circuit that took her round Stone Barton and back across the famous field where she first met Adam Croaker. A few gallons of water had flowed under the bridge since that day.

Puffing slightly as she topped the rise, Fiona paused to look down on the old house, resting quietly in its hollow. Apart from a wisp of smoke curling upwards from a tall chimney, there was no sign of life. There was mud everywhere and the proximity of the ramshackle farm buildings overshadowed the house, ruining its simple beauty. Corah was right, the roof was in terrible condition, with the ridge almost disintegrated; rick-thatch patches outnumbered the original, which was peppered with bird-holes and thick with moss. Maybe it was time for the Croakers to give way to new blood after all. Sam was the future now, and he would never settle for the life of his ancestors. His life would lead him away from Stone Barton, from the struggle of farming and the memories of his ill-fated father. Shivering with a combination of mental and physical chill, Fiona hiked on back to her cosy, happy little dwelling.

By 7.30 the phone had rung five times and she gave up the unequal struggle of trying to concentrate on her writing. For some reason best known to itself, the computer went blank during her chat with her mother, who was ringing in with unusually ardent thanks and news of her safe return. Pressing every possible key, Fiona failed to bring it back into life and had no option but to switch off at the mains.

"Oh shit!" She realised too late, she had forgotten to click on Save when the phone rang.

Uncle Greg was wildly enthusiastic about the party but would arrange his own accommodation.

"I like my comfort these days you know." And no, he would not be bringing Diana – she had been binned; but Loveatfirstsight was now anti-post third favourite for the Triumph Hurdle, the French hotshot having split a pastern on the gallops.

Dan reported that Moira and George had invited them to supper next week and he had accepted on her behalf, presuming she would be able to come.

'How dare he presume,' Fiona thought, but of course, her answer was 'yes.'

He then went on to extol the virtues of upright sex for the mature man until Fiona told him to get a grip and put the phone down.

Dodo had had a brainwave. "I thought I felt a mini-earthquake!" Fiona joked, but Dodo was serious. Whilst surfing the net on Fiona's behalf, she had found a small, recently-launched publishing company in Plymouth called Armada Publishing, who specialised in promoting West Country authors.

"It's a combination of vanity publishing and the real thing, but you'll have to find out the details yourself."

Fiona scribbled down the number, excited by the thought of a possible outlet for her work. Philip had got flu so sex was out, otherwise all was well.

And then there was Grania.

"Mum!" A crazed voice shouted down the line.

"Hello darling, what's up? You sound frantic."

"It's Dad," Grania wailed, "we've just got back from seeing him."

"And...?" Fiona held her breath.

"*Yikes!* He went absolutely ape-shit and can you beat it, the vile Doberman was there too snapping and snarling, the old bitch! How dare they? Poor darling Jum was splattered – I'll kill Dad!" she babbled on.

"Calm down Grania, and pull yourself together," Fiona shouted over her daughter's hysterical screeching. "I'm not surprised your father was less than thrilled with your news but I'm sure he'll come round eventually, and no doubt you didn't help matters by being rude."

"I wasn't Mum, I promise – he's just a horrid old fart and I never want to see him again!"

Secretly agreeing with her daughter, Fiona stifled a giggle before trying to do her duty.

"You are not, and I repeat *not*, to speak about your father like that. If you take my advice, you'll let the dust settle for a week or so and then ring him up and try behaving like an affectionate daughter. Ask to meet him for lunch somewhere, just the two of you, and show some respect and love for him. You'll regret it if you don't."

"But I don't love him or respect him," Grania whined. "And look what he did to you!"

"That's got nothing to do with it, he's your father and a quarter of his genes may come out in your child."

"*Yuck*, that's gross! My child is destined for perfection."

"Well I'm glad to hear that and I'm sure it will be – but will you do what I say for once, please?" Fiona's patience was running out.

"Yeah OK, I guess so Mum, I'll give it a whirl if you insist. Anyway," her tone brightened, "good news on the party front – so far all our mates can come and so can Jum's parents and Bella the London sister. Luckily Rosa's away on a school trip getting some culture – getting laid more like, knowing the little brat!"

"Oh good," Fiona ignored the last remark. "I'm so glad Jumbo's parents can come. I'll book them into the pub, they'd prefer that to B&B I think. Keep me posted on numbers, won't you?"

"Sure – I've got a brilliant dress lined up – hope I won't be too big to get into it."

"I don't think three and a bit weeks will make too much difference at this stage." Fiona laughed, her mind boggling at the possibilities of Grania's dress.

"By the way, Jum and I are going to get legal next Thursday and we're having a party in Bella's flat afterwards."

"Oh, darling, I'm so pleased. I shall buy half a bottle of champagne and drink your health."

"Brill! And thanks for everything, I'll let you know how the Dad scene goes. 'Bye for now."

Fiona put the phone down, metaphorically mopping her brow, before retiring to the kitchen to grill a lemon sole for her supper.

***

At one minute past nine precisely the next morning, Fiona rang Armada Publishing and spoke to one Crispin Wentworth.

Yes indeed, he assured her, they would be delighted to read her manuscript provided it was properly presented and included return postage if she wanted it back. Enquiring about the criteria for proper presentation, she was told to go and buy a copy of the *Writers' & Artists' Yearbook.* On second thoughts, Crispin relented. To save her the expense he would 'scribble' a few notes himself and email them through.

'He obviously thinks I'm some mad old crone starving in a garret,' Fiona decided. Nevertheless, at least it was a start.

The rain set in with a vengeance, and day after day the lowering skies chucked down their cats and dogs, blotting out the countryside. It was perfect weather for writing and by the end of the weekend, Fiona had finished the first draft. Mentally exhausted and liverish through lack of exercise, she flopped into bed.

Dan had been away all weekend, staying with his sister to celebrate his nephew's 21st birthday. He had asked her to go with him but she had declined – she was not yet ready to be completely 'itemised', neither did she want to lose so much writing time.

Crispin's email had arrived on Saturday, and Fiona could see immediately that in order to conform to his instructions, she would have to re-type the entire manuscript. And the 17th was drawing near with alarming rapidity.

Getting up early on Monday, Fiona had re-read and corrected the manuscript to her satisfaction by midday. Awash with coffee and feeling the beginnings of a headache lurking behind her eyes, she downed tools and went to inspect the larder. It was empty, and so was the fridge – a trip to the shop was a necessity.

Glancing at herself in the mirror, Fiona realised that it was not only her housekeeping that had been sacrificed to the Turvys, but her appearance as well. She looked like the wrath of God and was due to go over to Dan's for supper that evening. Writing or no, a major make-over would have to be undertaken before seven o'clock. But now for the village shop.

"Mornin' Mrs Mac." Vera's bright eyes gleamed through the gloom, her wiry grey hair standing out like a giant teasel.

"Hello Vera, how are you today, what's news in Longbottom?"

"Aw, could be wisser – funny you should cummin jis now cuz a genlemun bin asking for yerzel earlier."

"Really!" Fiona was startled. "Who could that be, I wonder?"

"Dunnaw mi dear, ee dedn't zay but I tull'ee zackly where yu be to."

"How strange – let's hope he's not the debt collector!" Fiona laughed, joined by Vera's cackle, which ended in a rattling cough.

Gathering up her purchases, Fiona bade Vera farewell and set off back to Stone Lea, still puzzling over who the mysterious stranger could be. Oh well, she shrugged, opening a tin of baked beans, time will tell. But for now, a quick bite before setting up the computer in accordance with Crispin's desired format.

Time did tell. Fiona had re-typed three pages when the sound of a car drawing up caught her attention. Getting up to peer out of the window, she caught her breath and sat down again with a bump.

"Oh God!" she groaned aloud, "I don't believe it!" as out of the car climbed Hamish.

Stretching and easing his back, he looked around, examining Stone Lea before plodding towards the house.

Pulling herself together, Fiona shot into the hall and flung open the door.

'However could I have fancied him?' she wondered, fixing a smile on her face in her determination to try and be civilised.

"This is a surprise!" she greeted him.

"Um hello Fiona – yes, I suppose it is." Hamish stood looking at her like some ancient bulldog, luckily without the drooling slobber.

"You'd better come in." She led him through into the sitting room and offered him a cup of tea, which he accepted.

"Now," she sat down opposite him, "what are you doing in the West Country?"

"Margaret and I are having a short break in Torquay."

"That must be exciting in November."

Hamish missed the irony. "Yes, we've found a very nice little hotel near the seafront – Margaret loves the sea you know, and of course the shops."

"Of course," Fiona shuddered inwardly. "But to what do I owe the pleasure of your visit? I can see you haven't come equipped to remove half the furniture!"

"Please don't be silly. You must know perfectly well that

we need to discuss your daughter, who appears to have gone completely off the rails."

"*My* daughter?" Fiona's voice rose, "Since when has she ceased to be your daughter too?"

"Sorry, our daughter Grania who, as I believe you know, came to see me with her er... boyfriend."

"Jumbo is not her boyfriend, Hamish, he's her about-to-be husband and father of her child – and the sooner you come to terms with that fact the better."

"I cannot understand how you can condone such behaviour. I find the whole situation most distressing – and poor Margaret is horrified."

Fiona's hackles rose, and her temper with them.

"I don't give a damn for Margaret's feelings – Grania is nothing whatever to do with her and as for 'condoning' our daughter's behaviour, that doesn't come into it. Of course I'm not over the moon, but it's happened. So get real Hamish, go with the flow or lose your only daughter."

"I don't understand your language Fiona, indeed I don't understand what's happened to you – you've changed so much."

"We are not discussing me – we are discussing Grania's future, which is far more important." Fiona tried to stem her rage. "Jumbo is a very intelligent, decent young man with a good job and a loving, humorous disposition. You don't like him because you can't see beneath the colour of his skin. I don't suppose his parents are too thrilled about their only son marrying a white girl with few aspirations beyond having a good time. Perhaps you'd rather Grania had turned up with some spliff-rolling lay-about Etonian!"

"Well I'm sorry Fiona, I think Grania's behaviour is disgraceful but as I can see I'm not going to get any support from you, I might as well go."

"Oh, hang on a minute, Hamish," Fiona tried to calm down and moderate her tone. "It's Grania we have to think about, and she's very upset about your attitude. Look at it this way, we can't change what's happened and I honestly think they will be very happy together, and Jumbo's very good for her. Try and see things from their point of view and look beyond the end of your own nose – it's her life not yours, and it would be so sad if you two didn't heal this silly rift. Please Hamish, just try for her sake, if not for yours."

There was silence as Hamish digested Fiona's impassioned speech.

"I suppose you're right," he sighed. "I shall think about what you have said and talk to Margaret when I get back to Torquay."

Gritting her teeth, Fiona managed to bite back a very rude retort, but deciding the time had come to wind up the meeting, she stood up.

"Thank you Hamish, I know you won't regret extending the olive branch even if you can't quite run to giving them your blessing!"

"Well, good bye then Fiona." He moved towards the door and making a super-human effort, turned up the corners of his mouth in an attempt at a smile. "You've been most helpful."

"See you at the christening!" Fiona couldn't resist a last crack, before slamming the door and breaking into laughter.

Later, bathed and changed, Fiona arrived at Dan's in good time, the relief of seeing him after Hamish causing her to give him an especially effusive greeting.

"You're looking very lovely tonight, my darling," he commented as they strolled towards the sitting room, passing the dining room on the way.

The door was open and Fiona caught sight of the table laid for two, complete with candles and napkins.

"Goodness!" she remarked, "We're very posh tonight – what's wrong with the kitchen?"

"Nothing," Dan sounded casual. "I just thought it would be nice for a change to dine in style – make sure you know how to handle it before we go to Moira's!"

"You rude so-and-so!" Fiona pinched him playfully. "How was your weekend?"

"Apart from missing you, it was fine. My sister was in great form and I think appreciated my coming up to do my avuncular bit and help keep an eye on the young. It's tough for her being a widow at her age. How about you?"

Fiona told him all about Hamish's visit.

"I think that's why I'm particularly pleased to see you – you've come out of the comparison rather well."

"It would be a poor state of affairs if I hadn't!" he laughed. "How's the party planning going?"

"I haven't done a thing about it apart from book the hall and send out the invites. I shall do it all in a rush at the last minute and it'll be fine, don't worry."

"Haven't you even thought about the menu? Most women start twittering weeks in advance."

"Nope," Fiona shook her head. "But I'll still be the hostess with the mostest when the time comes."

"Certainly some parts of your anatomy could fall into that category but I'm not so sure about your cooking! Talking of which, I'm going to leave Holly to entertain you while I go to the kitchen – and don't drink any more, I've got some decent wine for a change."

Holly's entertainment consisted of rhythmic snoring punctuated by the occasional 'yip' when her tail slapped the floor and her long, sprawling legs twitched as she chased her dream hares.

'How very comfortable this all is,' Fiona thought, as she gazed into the fire and let the memories of the day drain out of her.

Hamish and The Doberman belonged to her former life, a life she had no desire to even think about.

"Dinner is served, Madam." Dan stood in the doorway brandishing a wooden spoon.

The candles were burning, lighting up the *coquilles St Jacques* and bottle of *premier cru* Chablis that were waiting ready on the table as they sat down together, Dan still wearing his striped apron.

"Gosh!" Fiona exclaimed. "This is fantastic – but what's

it all about – it's not your birthday is it?" A sudden terrible thought hit her.

"No," he laughed, "that's in June – but it *is* our eighth anniversary."

"What d'you mean?"

"Oh unromantic one, we first met eight weeks and one day ago to be exact, when you brought Mactavish into the surgery and I fell in love with you."

"Aah, I see!" Fiona smiled. "I thought you fell in love with me at the fish counter in Okehampton."

"That chance meeting just confirmed my worst fears – what about you?"

"I certainly didn't fall in love with you in the surgery – in fact I thought you the rudest most arrogant man I'd ever met!"

"And dare I ask when your opinion of me changed?"

"It never has really! But… these peculiar flushes kept happening every time I saw you which, according to Dodo, meant I must be in love."

Laughing together, they attacked their scallops. *Tournedos Perigord* washed down by a scented, silky Fleurie followed, and overcome with awe at Dan's culinary prowess, Fiona was lost for words as she nibbled a small chunk of Cambozola. Topping up their glasses, Dan finished his cheese and sat back in his chair.

"I know you were very fond of Mactavish." he said in an unusually diffident way.

"Yes, of course I was, he'd been a friend for years." Fiona couldn't imagine why he'd brought up the subject of the old cat.

"Do you think Holly and I could replace him in your affections?"

"What on Earth are you talking about, Dan?"

"I'm asking you to marry me Fiona, that's what I'm talking about. I think us old retreads are a bit past the 'down on one knee bit' don't you?"

Fiona's heart lurched & her stomach turned a somersault.

"Oh Dan, I don't know what to say."

"Could you think about it and let me know?"

"I can't marry you anyway, until my divorce comes through." Fiona clutched at the obvious straw to buy time.

"I know that darling, but when it does?"

"I still don't know what to say – it's so quick and well..." she stuttered, seeing the disappointment in his eyes, "I do love you and I promise there's nobody else, but the problem's Fiona McLeod, she hasn't quite had time to work out who she is."

Dan got up, and standing behind her chair, put his arms round her shoulders.

"I do understand, I really do and I'm not going to press you. But just let me say that I shall never love anybody else like I love you and I will wait forever if that's what it takes."

"Darling Dan," Fiona leant her head back against the blue and white striped apron, "what an exquisite thing to say. I only wish I could be as sure as you – but I have to be sure, 110% for both our sakes and right now, I'm not."

"I know darling, I know. But be warned, I don't give up easily on something I want more than anything and that I know to be right."

"I realise what I'm saying must be very hard for you to understand." Fiona stroked the back of his hand. "I can't explain it properly but it's all to do with my stupid self-esteem, nothing to do with you."

"Self-esteem is seldom stupid, and I don't want nine-tenths of the package anyway. Come on, old thing." he stood up, yawning. "Let's go to bed and to hell with the washing up."

Happy to fall in with his suggestion, Fiona blew out the candles and went on up to bed, while Dan carried out his nightly dog, fire and lights routine.

She was ready and waiting when he appeared about five minutes later, but his normal ardour was missing, and to his chagrin, Dan failed to perform.

"Sorry darling." He gave up the unequal struggle. "Must

have drunk a bit too much."

"It doesn't matter," Fiona kissed him and held him tight. "I'm sleepy too and the wine was worth it!"

But she knew that the real reason for Dan's failure had nothing to do with the wine.

FINALE

'Oh God, more emotional turmoil – only this time I seem to be going backwards on a non-stop rollercoaster.'

Back at Stone Lea, Fiona sat staring at the wall above the computer. Why could she not have accepted Dan's proposal unconditionally – why must she make this wretched book the lynchpin for her future, knowing how difficult literary success would be?

Here she was, undeniably middle-aged, and her life was more of a mess than when she was married to Hamish. Realising how much she had hurt the man she loved made her feel guilty and miserable, and for the first time in weeks, she woke each morning feeling flat and pessimistic.

But that tiresome little worm of determination would not go away, and sacking all else from her mind, she struggled on towards the stars. Total rejection from Armada Publishing and the scribbling Crispin could not be contemplated. No, she was Drake, and if her powder ran low, she would beat the drum till it broke.

Thursday was D-Day. She had done it. Kissing the corrected manuscript good luck, she handed it into the post office in Okehampton before buying a half bottle of Moet at the supermarket. Today would see a double celebration, for in the afternoon, Grania and Jumbo would tie the knot.

The marriage of her only daughter had not turned out quite as she had visualised over the years. There would be no new hat for her, nor rustling tissue paper as the virginal white folds of a beautiful wedding dress were reverently unpacked. No pricking behind the eyes when the fidgeting, chattering congregation fell silent as the organ blasted out the opening chords of the *Wedding March*.

Never mind. As Fiona knew only too well, the splendour of the day was no guarantee of happiness in the future, and Grania's happiness was all that mattered. Fiona's obligation now was to ensure the success of her little party on 17th –

only two weeks and a day away. On Monday she would start the preparations in earnest.

Suffering a mild hangover from the unaccustomed midday drinking of champagne, Fiona was well off the ball when Dodo rang at tea time.

"You sound blotto! What's up?"

Fiona filled her in on recent events.

"Great stuff, and good for you for letting rip for once. Now Fi, I've been thinking, have you done anything about this party yet?"

"No, not really, but now the Turvys are out of my hair, I'm going to steam on."

"If it's a help, I could come down on Thursday and give you a hand – we want to decorate the place, I mean it is Christmas and all that, and you'll have heaps to do with bedmaking, food etc. In fact knowing you, I think I'd better make it Wednesday."

"That would be absolutely brilliant. Grania and Jumbo are coming on Friday but I'd like to be fairly organised before then. But what about Philip?"

"Oh he's OK, he can get a train down on Saturday morning and I'll pick him up. Have you thought about music? You can't drag all these kids down from London and expect them to go to bed at 9.30 with *Winnie the Pooh!* – You'll have to have a disco."

"Oh! Do you think so?"

"Christ, you idiot – wake up! You don't want them shagging with boredom all over the Longbottom Victory Hall, do you?"

"I must say I hadn't thought of it."

"Well get thinking and quick! You'll be damn lucky to get anyone now at this late stage. Got to go – but I shall keep bullying you, so pull your finger out."

Panicked by Dodo's autocratic instructions, Fiona sat down with *Yellow Pages* and thumbed through to 'Discos – Mobile'. Recognising the name of the one that had played at the Hunt Ball, she tried them first.

"Lady! You sure have left it a bit late." A fake trans-Atlantic drawl almost covered the Devon burr. "Hang in there – I'll zap the cheese-nibbler!"

Fiona listened to the obvious rustle of diary pages being turned over.

"Get that!" the voice returned. "It's your lucky day lady, we can squeeze in your gig – cooool!"

Fiona was too relieved to be irritated, and promising to post the deposit cheque off first thing in the morning, she put down the phone. Now all the essentials were tied up and she would put her mind to the details as planned first thing on Monday morning. Before then she could use a spot of relaxation, and there was dinner with George and Moira to be taken in on Saturday.

Dan rang to suggest she pick him up rather than the other way round.

"Then I can enjoy a glass of old George's vintage port." he said.

They had not seen each other since the night of the proposal, and Fiona experienced a twinge of nerves as she drove up to his house. But he kept his word not to press her and made no mention of Monday night.

George and Moira Prouse lived in comfortable shambles in a rather plain house surrounded, like Stone Barton, by farm buildings. A miscellaneous collection of dogs hogged the fire until booted out of the room by George, and a faint whiff of slurry hung in the air.

Fiona had already met two of the three other couples at the Hunt Ball, and when the ten of them sat down to dinner, she felt easy and relaxed in their company. Although most of them seemed to be involved in some way with farming, about which Fiona knew nothing, conversation flowed and she had no difficulty keeping her end up.

When eventually the food arrived, Fiona assumed that Moira had cooked with the idea of feeding her and George on cold beef and left-over vegetables for several days. Roast potatoes, mashed potatoes, parsnips, carrots, cabbage and sprouts vied for space on the table and Fiona had to request a smaller helping of meat and Yorkshire pudding when her plate appeared in front of her.

"Fiddlesticks! That wouldn't keep a flea alive." George scoffed when she finally got what she wanted.

Fiona watched in disbelief at the vast quantity of food that they chomped their way through. Clearly farming was an appetite-stimulating business, and Moira knew her onions when it came to entertaining their friends. Beaten by the bread-and-butter pudding and apple crumble, Fiona managed a ramekin of chocolate mousse and called it a day.

It was a riotous evening, culminating in several rounds of 'Prouse Charades' – a game which required each person to stand up and act the character whispered to them by their right-hand neighbour. If you failed to be guessed, your whisperer lost a point, but there was far too much shrieking and laughing for anybody to bother to keep score.

Dan was given Marilyn Monroe and was quite hopeless, but Fiona's *Hunchback of Notre Dame* was much applauded, earning her right thigh a riskily near-the-top squeeze from her neighbour.

The evening drew to a close, and with goodbyes ringing in their ears and slurry in their noses, Fiona drove Dan carefully home.

Finally falling into bed together as the clock approached 1.30 a.m, Dan proved Fiona's Monday night theory that the wine had not been responsible for his flop was correct. In spite of George's generous hospitality, it was definitely 'all systems go' and Dan performed like a champion stud. By the time Fiona had jerked and gasped her way through four orgasms, he could hold on no longer, and coming together with a simultaneous explosion, they collapsed in a breathless heap and fell asleep.

Having slept like a log on Sunday night, Fiona woke early on Monday morning feeling fighting fit and keen to attack the party. She had twelve days in which to organise what she hoped would be the best party she had ever organised in her life.

To her astonishment, virtually everybody had accepted, and pleading phone calls from Grania had caused her to weaken and allow a small extension of numbers. Grania and Jumbo's friends must arrange their own accommodation, but she still had her own small guest list to think about. Corah and Sam were no problem, they would stay at the Barton; Jumbo's parents and sister were booked into the pub; Dodo, Philip, Grania and Jumbo would stay at Stone Lea; but where could she put her mother and Mrs P? Angie had already indicated that she would prefer a more tranquil billet than the inevitably chaotic and noisy Stone Lea.

"Silly me!" She banged her head with a fist – of course, Uncle Greg could arrange rooms for them all in the same hotel – that would be perfect.

She rang him up then and there to ask him to fix it up. Having got his assurance that it would be done, she put a large tick by 'Accommodation' and moved on to the next item on the list – 'Hire of plates etc.'

The Longbottom-in-the-Mire Victory Hall could only provide a few thick, white and often chipped cups and saucers which were no use at all. Seizing the *Yellow Pages* once again, Fiona tracked down a firm in Okehampton who would be delighted to provide everything required including salts, peppers, and table napkins. For a modest surcharge, the equipment could be returned dirty and they would deliver on Friday and collect on Monday.

'Bugger the cost' thought Fiona and put another tick against Item Two on the list.

Item Three was 'Food', and that was where the major problem arose. What on Earth to have, and how could she ever manage to cook it all? Determined not to appear feeble by ringing Dodo to pick her brains, Fiona got out her limited library of recipe books and began the task of selecting a menu. Keep it simple was her culinary mantra. After much pencil-chewing and head-scratching, she decided on beef goulash – which could be pre-cooked and frozen – followed by trifle, the only pudding she liked making, and Grania's childhood favourite.

As threatened, Dodo rang the following evening for a progress report and Fiona was able to inform her in smug tones that everything was under control.

"There's only one vital ingredient you seem to have left out, Fi."

"What's that?"

"Booze!"

"Oh!"

"But… I've had yet another brainwave! Philip and I are planning a booze cruise next week – we fancy a decent lunch in France and I want to stock up on cheap fags. So, I'm proposing to make my wedding present to my god-daughter the drink for the party."

"Oh Dodo!" Fiona was overwhelmed by her generosity. "You are a star, that would be absolutely brilliant and thanks a million."

"Well, I don't want to be poisoned, knowing the sort of muck you'd go and buy! I'll get the beer too, it's so much cheaper over there. But you get the soft stuff – Coke and orange juice'll do, I should think."

"Will do, and can't wait to see you next week – I'm getting really excited about it now I feel vaguely under control."

"It'll be great! See you Wednesday."

Dan too was swinging in with the festive mood, and volunteered his two spare bedrooms should they be needed. The bedding might be damp but it would be better than the back of a car. More importantly, he offered Fiona the services of his cleaning lady, the stalwart but inappropriately named Mrs Quick, whose husband Nathan was the local chimney sweep. Not only would the good woman take charge of cooking the vegetables and heating the goulash on the limited facilities available in the hall's tiny kitchen, but she would also produce a clutch of offspring, nephews and nieces who would do all the work. Mrs Quick's vocabulary did not extend to the word 'hurry', but she knew a thing or two about catering. Remuneration was definitely cash only, so Dan warned Fiona to come suitably armed.

By Tuesday evening, Fiona was in a state of almost childish excitement. She had selected her dress for the party and had bought Christmas presents for all the family who were coming. Putting on a CD of carols from King's College, she wrapped them up, singing along to all the old favourites. Being born within eight days of Christmas was a swizz and her big day – presents, parties and being number one – had always been overshadowed by the greater event of the annual festival.

This year she was pleased. The holiday spirit, that by Saturday would be beginning to infiltrate the psyche of her guests, could only add to the celebration of her daughter's marriage and her own birthday. Fiona's only sorrow was that Roddy had rung to say he would be unable to make it due to pressure of work. If only he could have been there too, it would all be perfect.

As the last verse of *Oh Come All Ye Faithful* died away, Fiona finished the wrapping and put the presents in a corner of the sitting room. Scooping up all the paper and sellotape debris that littered the floor, she decided there was time to start a seating plan for Saturday night.

Easier said than done.

'How can I do that when I don't know the names of most of the guests?' she thought, and to her horror, she realised that she didn't even know Jumbo's surname.

The shock of Grania's unexpected arrival and the news of her pregnancy had completely blown out of her mind such things as what her daughter was now called – how could she have been so stupid?

Punching out Grania's mobile number, Fiona heaved a sigh of relief when her voice answered: "Mum, hi. How's everything going for Saturday?"

"Fine darling. Everything's organised but I want to discuss the seating plan with you and I'm ashamed to say, I don't even know your new name!"

"What a useless mother you are!" Grania laughed. "I'm now Mrs Lelongwe – I think it's fantastic and a million times better than McLeod!"

"Do you know Jumbo's parents' names?"

"'Course, they're Solomon and Elizabeth and Jum's real name is Njogu – isn't that wicked? It means 'elephant' in Kikuyu, that's why I call him Jumbo."

"Yes Grania, very good – even I can see that." Fiona suddenly felt tired.

"You're not in a strop are you Mum? You sound a bit stressed out."

"No darling, I'm fine and really looking forward to seeing you on Friday. Don't be late will you, there's a lot to do and you'll have to work out the seating plan for your friends as I don't know who they are."

"Sure, no prob. I'll do that when we get down. Can't wait – gotta go now, byeee!"

***

Putting the finishing touches to the guest bedrooms after lunch on Wednesday, Fiona was annoyed to see a strange car pull into Stone Lea.

It was a smart BMW Estate and she decided to lie doggo till its occupant was revealed. Travelling salesmen never came and Jehovah's Witnesses always walked – perhaps it was an agent looking for the Barton.

To her surprise and delight, it was Dodo. Flinging open the window, Fiona shouted out her greeting as Dodo stood on the drive below.

"Wow! Have you won the lottery?!"

"Hi Fi! No, it's dear old Puncture Man's little toy. He thought the mobile crap heap might not make it, weighed down with all this booze!"

"Hang on, I'll come and give you a hand." And abandoning her duster, Fiona ran downstairs.

"Gosh, champagne!" She heaved out a case with Lanson stamped on the side.

"Might as well to the job properly. After all, it *is* your birthday as well as the wedding and Christmas. We'd better put it all in the shed for the time being – keep the white and the beer cool, and we can bring the red into the kitchen on Friday."

"I'm dying to meet Philip properly – I still can't get over you two getting together, it's weird."

"Weird maybe but it's sure A-OK, I can tell you! When we've dumped this lot, I could use a bite and a coffee, then I'd like to take a stroll up the lane."

"You and your exercise!" grumbled Fiona, struggling under a weight of beer.

"There's a reason for it, I'll tell you when we're sitting down. Phew, that's better!" Dodo sipped her coffee and lit up. "Now, wait for it – the big news is that Philip and I are seriously considering buying Stone Barton when it comes on the market in the spring. That's why I want to have another look at it."

"I don't believe you!" Fiona exclaimed. "That would be marvellous, but what about all the land? Surely you don't want a farm?"

"No of course not, neither of us knows the first thing about farming. But if they sell it as a whole, we could flog off the land we don't want and just keep a few acres round the house – chances are they might sell it in lots anyway."

"Corah told me it's in a terrible state and needs tons spending on it."

"Doesn't matter Fi, it'll be reflected in the price and I rather like the idea of restoring an old wreck. Believe it or not, Philip's rather handy with the old screwdriver – and I don't only mean the one attached to his body!"

"Honestly D, you never grow up."

"Certainly not, it's the quickest way into the grave."

"Come on then, let's go and spy!" Fiona was all enthusiasm. "I know just the place to view from and don't forget it'll be dark by about four-thirty."

And bolting down a ham sandwich, Dodo got her outdoor

gear from the car and they set off up the lane on their reconnaissance mission.

***

Sitting in front of the fire on their return, Dodo exclaimed. "That could be one fantastic house. I'll march the old boy up there on Sunday morning – he can't fail to love it. I could make the perfect studio out of that stone barn in the yard, and with all those junky farm buildings demolished, there could be a lovely garden at the back."

"Oh Dodo!" sighed Fiona. "It would be so brilliant if it came off – I shall keep everything crossed for you."

"Not quite everything I hope! But it would be very useful if you could keep me posted on any info you can glean about the sale – Corah ought to know what's going on and we want to be ahead of the game if possible."

"Of course I will, and you can talk to her yourself as well if you want – she's coming to the party. I may have to come and camp in one of the barns!"

"Why not? You could become my farm manager!" Dodo laughed. "But now I think we'd better start thinking about Saturday – we've only got one clear day before the mob starts arriving."

So they put their heads together to make the final list of things to buy and tasks to do before the big night.

Dodo was a talented calligraphist, and had come armed with the tools of her trade and a pile of blank place-name cards. Seated at the eating area table, she carefully wrote all the names known so far, while Fiona cooked supper – the rest would have to wait till Grania arrived on Friday.

"It's such a bore we can't get into the hall till so late on Saturday. " Fiona moaned, as they returned from a massive shopping trip in Exeter on Thursday afternoon.

"Never mind," Dodo piled bags of purchases onto the table. "I'll make some table decorations tomorrow morning, then all we've got to do is lay the tables and sling a bit of holly around – no sweat. Where's the nearest tree to here?"

"There's one in the first hedgerow beyond the garden, and

it did have some berries on it but I expect the birds will have had them by now."

"Doesn't matter, I'll tart it up with some gold spray and red ribbon if need be. Ooof!" Dodo yawned. "I'm knackered. Early night tonight I think – the calm before the storm!"

"I'll go along with that" Fiona agreed, and Stone Lea was in darkness by 10.30.

***

Lunch over on Friday, they were congratulating themselves on achieving a remarkable level of organisation, when Grania phoned.

"We're running a bit late Mum, and the traffic's terrible but we should be down by six with luck."

"Oh, Grania!" Fiona was annoyed. "You told me you'd be here soon after lunch to help."

"Chill out, Mum!" The line started to crackle and hiss as Fiona began her sharp reply. "Can't hear you," shouted Grania, "signal's going." And that was that.

"Gives us more breathing space," Dodo commented. "I suggest we light the fire and crash out with the newspapers."

Fiona dropped off to sleep after three pages of trite news items and boring political opinions. When Dodo shook her awake, she couldn't believe it was nearly 5.30, and feeling grotty and stuffy, she went out to the shed for more logs.

Thinking she heard noises from the front of the house, she hurried back in, hoping to find that Grania and Jumbo had arrived. Dodo was coming back in through the front door, which she slammed shut.

"Oh!" Fiona looked disappointed. "I thought I heard the children arrive."

"Sorry no, only me – just checking I'd locked Philip's precious wheels. At least now if it's nicked he can't blame me."

"Nothing gets nicked round here – this isn't suburbia you know."

"Better safe than sorry. I want you upstairs, I can't decide on my gear for tomorrow."

"That's not like you."

"Don't argue, Fi." Dodo sounded strangely urgent.

"OK, OK, you bossy old bag, I'm coming."

They went up to Dodo's room where she banged about, talking unnecessarily loudly while pulling clothes out of a suitcase.

"Hi everybody – we've made it!" Grania's voice screamed from below and before Fiona could get to the door, Dodo had zipped past her and rushed to the head of the staircase, where Grania gave a thumbs-up.

"Hands over your eyes Mum, and promise not to cheat. We've got a surprise for you!" Grania was dancing around the hall, laughing with Jumbo and Dodo as Fiona felt her way downstairs.

"Goodness, whatever can it be I wonder?" Fiona prayed her daughter hadn't dreamt up some terrible scheme to shock her.

"Wait and see, wait and see!" Grania chanted, pulling her mother backwards into the sitting room. "And don't dare look till I say so."

"*De da!*" Grania cried, yanking Fiona's hands from her face – and there in the chair by the fire sat Roddy.

"*Darling*, I don't believe it!" Fiona stood rooted to the spot as her son jumped up and embraced her, to the applause and cheers of the other three.

"I wouldn't have missed it for the world Mum!" Roddy broke out of her clutches, his tanned face beaming.

"You're the most wonderful birthday present I've ever had in my life and quite the best surprise your sister has ever produced!"

"Hey Mum, that's gross!" Grania chipped in. "Roddy only wanted to come to make sure your zimmer frame was working!"

"In the words of your godmother – *bollocks!*" Fiona replied over the noise of their laughter.

"This calls for a celebration," cried Dodo, "and surprise surprise, there's a spare bottle of bubbly in the fridge!"

Helped by Jumbo, Dodo produced five glasses and a plate of exotic nuts, and when the cork popped and hit the ceiling and the wine fizzed, another cheer went up.

"Here's to Mum!" Roddy raised his glass.

"To my children, my new son-in-law and my old mate!" Fiona proposed.

"To the party!" Grania refused to be left out.

"To my new family!" Jumbo's turn next.

And finally from Dodo: "To us all."

By the time the excitement had calmed down, the bottle was empty.

"I vote we go to the pub for supper," Dodo proposed. "You can add that greasy concoction you knocked up this morning to the goulash tomorrow night, Fi."

Amid further laughter, the proposal was unanimously agreed, and Fiona rang the Black Dog Inn to ensure they had a free table. No problem, they could come any time.

When everybody had unpacked and changed, and Fiona had dug out some bedding for Roddy, who would have to sleep on the sofa, it was time to leave for the pub.

Roddy had flown in the day before, he and Grania having hatched the plan to surprise Fiona when his sister had rung to tell him about the party, and pleaded with him to come to England for the joint celebration. His flight had been a nightmare of delays and schedule changes, resulting in a heavy dose of jetlag and a light dose of sleep.

By 10.30 his eyelids were drooping and Dodo drove them home, the BMW being the only car big enough to fit everybody into.

"That was great, Mum," Roddy thanked his mother. "I'd forgotten the delights of good old English pub food and the climate to go with it. I get a bit fed up with the heat in Singapore."

"It's your Scottish blood, darling," Fiona smiled.

"Lunacy more like!" Grania enjoyed winding her brother up. "Anyone who prefers the English climate to the heat must be nuts!"

"Anyone who thinks they look attractive with a bunch of elongated millipedes on their head must be completely nutty, dysfunctional, brain dead, the lot!" Roddy fired back, swinging into the verbal sparring he and his sister had always enjoyed.

"Sorry about this, Jumbo," Fiona turned to her new son-in-law. "I'm afraid they can be awfully silly when they get together."

"Don't worry," he laughed. "I'm used to it. You should hear my family when we all get going – but for your sake, I hope you never do!"

"Come to that, Mum," Grania chipped in, "you and Dodo can be pretty infantile on occasions."

"Right god-daughter, that's you out of my Will!" Dodo threw a cushion at Grania, which narrowly missed the fire.

"Children, children!" Fiona's voice rose over the babble. "I can see Roddy's dropping, and as three of you are sitting on his bed I suggest we call it a day and go to our own more comfortable versions. And," she directed her gaze at Grania, "no lounging around in bed till lunchtime. There's still plenty to be done tomorrow – parties don't run themselves you know."

"OK Mum, don't nag," Grania made a face. "I get the message."

"Come on kids," Dodo got up. "Go with the flow!"

Goodnights said, she and Fiona went upstairs to grab the bathroom first.

"Isn't it wonderful, having Roddy back – when were you let in on the secret?" Fiona chatted to Dodo as she cleaned her teeth.

"Last week," Dodo rinsed and spat. "Grania rang me as soon as Roddy confirmed his flight. I'm just amazed it all worked out so well – if only you could have seen your face!"

"I was stunned. I couldn't think what Grania was up to, but to find Roddy sitting there was – well – I'm lost for words, but it was wonderful."

"I knew you'd be over the moon," Dodo dried her hands.

"All yours. Sleep well Fi – that was a very happy evening."

"You sleep well too, and thanks Dodo, you've been a brick. D'you realise we've known each other for 45 years?"

"That is a truly terrifying thought!" Dodo disappeared into her bedroom.

***

The first thing Fiona was aware of the next morning was the sound of the postman's van driving away down the lane. Pulling on her dressing gown, she went downstairs to see who had sent birthday cards. There were disappointingly few, but as she was going to see most of the faithful card-senders that day, it wasn't surprising. Amongst the other mail was a £5.00 birthday voucher from Somerfield, cashable on 'Confectionery only'; a handwritten bill for the use of the memorial hall, and a cream coloured A4 envelope with 'Armada Publishing' stamped on the front.

Fiona's heart jumped. Could this be the birthday present she wanted more than anything else – wouldn't Crispin have returned the manuscript if his response was total rejection? Taking the unopened envelope back to bed, Fiona shut her eyes, crossed fingers and ripped it open. Heart now pounding, her eyes raced over the two short paragraphs, ending with Crispin's flowery signature.

Skipping across the landing to Dodo's room, Fiona burst in, shaking the letter in her friend's startled face.

"Look D, look!" She tried to keep her excited voice down. "They've accepted it – they've accepted my book – well sort of."

"Christ Fi, you frightened the life out of me." Dodo sat up, shaking herself awake. "Give me my specs and let me see. Hey, that's *great*! It's a start anyway."

"It's not exactly a 100% acceptance, I suppose," Fiona was beginning to calm down. "I mean, they want lots of changes and I don't get paid an advance. Also I'll have to stump up if it's a complete flop, but I don't care, he sounds quite bullish and I like the bit about signing a contract to write a sequel, don't you?"

357

~ LUCINDA ROBERTS ~

"Sounds hopeful," Dodo agreed. "I shall be able to boast about 'my friend the author' – make a change from 'my friend the er... can't think what'!" Dodo couldn't resist a leg pull.

"Bitch!" giggled Fiona, knowing how genuinely pleased Dodo was for her. "I'll ring first thing Monday and fix an appointment to go and sort out the paperwork. Sounds as if it'll take ages to get published – I wonder what he means by 'further editing'?"

"Probably correcting your dodgy grammar! Seriously though, read the small print carefully and don't sign anything till you're absolutely sure it's OK, and if you're not certain, get hold of a specialist lawyer to help."

"I will, don't worry. It's taken me this unmentionable number of years minus six hours to realise I can achieve anything at all – I'm not going to blow it now!"

"Your poor old mother hadn't popped you out then yet?"

"No, she was probably labouring away while Daddy got pissed at the golf club. I didn't actually appear till after lunch."

"Bet you looked revolting – all red and crinkled and slimy!"

"Thanks mate! Actually, everyone agreed I was the most beautiful baby ever seen!"

"Bollocks!" Dodo sprung out of bed laughing. "It's time we got up, but before you go – *a very happy birthday authoress McLeod!*"

"Why do you two make so much noise at this hour of the night?" A frowsy Grania appeared in the doorway, wrapped in a bath towel.

"It's morning, and time to get up, that's why." Fiona replied.

"Show her the letter, Fi." urged Dodo.

"What letter?" Grania grumbled, but as she read it, her mouth dropped open in disbelief before turning up into a beaming smile as she looked at her mother in amazement. "Awesome! I'd no idea you could write, Mum."

And before Fiona could think of a suitable retort, Grania

354

flung her arms round her and the precariously secured bath towel fell to the floor.

"Oh my God!" Dodo screeched. "Look at the grandchild!"

"You can't even see it yet Dodo, so don't be silly!" Breaking away from her mother, Grania rescued the fallen towel and disappeared back to her room.

Poor Roddy had no chance of sleeping through the noise, and appearing at the top of the stairs, wished his mother a happy birthday before heading for the bathroom.

Reserving her place in the queue after Roddy, Fiona returned to her room where, sitting quietly in front of the dressing table mirror, she reflected on her life. The unremarkable face that stared back was nothing more or less than the one she had always seen, but something had changed inside. Fiona's identity had been defined by first her parents, and then by Hamish, with whom she had played the supporting role. But now, experiencing the thrill of achievement for the first time, she had become a complete person – 100% Fiona McLeod and nobody else.

"Bathroom's free, Mum." Roddy's voice floated through the door.

"Thanks darling, be down in a minute to cook breakfast."

Breakfast over, Fiona's presents opened and everyone assembled round the table, she ran through the task list. Grania's first job was to help Dodo finish the name cards and structure a seating plan for her's and Jumbo's friends. Roddy and Jumbo were to split up logs and fill the basket before fetching a quantity of ice from Okehampton to help keep the white wine and champagne cool. Then there was holly and ivy to be cut for the decorations; cars to be loaded ready to take off the minute the hall was free; the house to be clean and tidy ready for Dan, Uncle Greg, Angie, Mrs P and the Lelongwes, who would be arriving for a pre-party drink around 6.30 – and seemingly a million other jobs.

"We can't wait to meet Dan, Mum." Roddy said as Fiona finished her run-through of tasks.

"Hope he's not bling!" Grania giggled, "Imagine having a bling step-father – how gross!"

"I've no idea what you mean, Grania," Fiona was beginning to get hassled. "And he's a very good friend, but I never said anything about marrying him."

"Get real, Mum!" Grania kept on. "We can tell you're at it, you look kind of different – don't you think so, Roddy?"

"I think Mum looks great and if Dan's the cause, he must be a good bloke."

"Thank you, Roddy." Fiona smiled at her son. "Now could you all get on with your jobs and would you please beat your wife Jumbo, if she gives any more trouble!"

"Yes m'am!" Jumbo saluted. "With pleasure!"

And at last, the final preparations for the party were under way.

Dan rang to see if he could help with anything, but Fiona assured him that all was progressing as planned, and that she couldn't wait to see him that evening. Corah popped in with some giant, old fashioned pans from the Barton that she had offered to lend Fiona for the food, plus a large black rubber stock feeder which would act as the perfect wine cooler when scrubbed out and filled with ice.

Sam was at a loose end, as Abraham had been dragged off for the weekend by Sara to visit his last remaining cousin in Cornwall, so Fiona detailed off Roddy and Jumbo to keep him with them for the morning. Sam was highly delighted at the prospect, and Fiona also invited them to join the family at 6.30 for the pre-party drinks. Dodo disappeared to Exeter station to meet Philip's train, and by the time the working party returned from setting up the hall, they were back and having a late cup of tea.

Fiona greeted Philip warmly, and they laughed together about the puncture incident as the others gathered round to inspect Dodo's latest conquest. He certainly was good looking and suave.

'I can see why Dodo fancies him,' Fiona thought, watching him shake hands with the young, unperturbed by

Grania's blatant curiosity. 'But I wonder what he'll think of life in Devon.'

"Now listen everybody," Fiona banged the table, "there's hot water for three small baths and not much time left before blast off!"

"You go first Fi," Dodo suggested, "you're the hostess."

"Right. I'll only be two minutes – and get a move on, you children."

Wishing she could lie longer in the bath, Fiona was about to get out when Dodo stuck her head round the door. "OK to come in?"

"'Course, you've seen it all before!"

"I've bought you a tiny restorative – you look in need of one."

"Thanks D, I must admit I feel knackered already!"

"Get this down you – you'll soon get a second wind once everyone arrives."

"I hope Philip's all right, he must think he's come to a madhouse."

"Do him good." Dodo replied. "Don't worry, he's fine – he and the boys are getting the booze and glasses ready and looking after the fire. Give me a shout when you're out."

Changing at top speed, Fiona arrived downstairs with ten minutes to spare. The rest of the clan were still upstairs and she stood in front of the fire, pleased with her appearance and glad of the short breathing space.

Hearing a car she moved towards the front door, hoping it wouldn't be Jumbo's parents, with him not down to greet them. It was Dan.

"A very happy birthday, my darling." He put a small parcel on the hall table, before enfolding her in his arms and silencing her reply with a tongue sandwich. "You look stunning." He let her go.

"Dan," she stuttered. "I, er, I..."

"What is it woman? Spit it out!"

"I want to say 'Yes'."

'That's it! I've done it now,' she thought.

For a split second Dan looked blank, then as the penny dropped, his smile disappeared and he gazed intently into her eyes.

"Are you saying what I think you're saying, and are you absolutely sure?"

"I've never been surer – Mrs Cann, here I come! But don't say anything yet – I can't cope with all the kerfuffle. Later maybe if you want."

"What made you change your mind?"

"Oh, I don't know – got rather bored of the name McLeod I think!" Fiona kept a straight face.

"God I love you, you wicked woman!" And this time she was nearly suffocated.

"*Mu-um!*" Grania stood in shock at the top of the stairs, ogling the entwined couple.

"Ah, here you are, darling." Fiona and Dan parted. "Come and meet Dan. Dan, this is my daughter Grania."

"*Wow!* Hi Dan." Grania looked him up and down as they shook hands.

"Love your hair." Dan grinned, knowing how much Fiona hated the 'elongated millipedes'.

"Mum hates it."

"Really? I can't think why!"

But before Fiona could kick him, car doors banged and Angie, Uncle Greg and Mrs P swept into the hall. Angie elegant, Uncle Greg debonair and Mrs P resplendent. She hadn't let them down, and the ping-pong balls bounced and swung as her freshly crimped little head bobbed with excitement.

At the same moment, the remainder of the house party clattered downstairs and joined the clamour and confusion in the hall. Fiona tried to push the kissing, hand shaking, babbling horde into the sitting room, praying that Solomon and Elizabeth would be late and the hubbub died down before their arrival.

"Get the drink moving, Roddy." Fiona was getting frantic.

"I'll help." Dodo disengaged herself from Mrs P's embrace, rubbing her cheek, which had taken a direct hit from a ping-pong ball.

Corah arrived next, looking astonishingly pretty. Sam was staying with Jack, whose mother would drop the boys at the hall in good time for them to get their instructions. Apparently they were taking their role as waiters seriously and had both insisted on wearing white shirts and black trousers; Corah had bought them each a red clip-on bow tie.

Once Corah had been introduced and everyone given a drink, the decibels began to drop. Nevertheless, it took the Lelongwes two bangs on the door knocker before Fiona heard it, and calling Jumbo, she went through to let them in.

As she suspected, they were entirely charming and obviously devoted to their son. Being well-used to embassy parties and having a large family themselves, they were completely unfazed by the circle of strange faces that awaited them. Warmly welcomed by all, a hoot of laughter went up when Mrs P told them in no uncertain terms that Jumbo was to be a good husband to 'her baby' or 'Lord luv us', she'd have something to say about it.

Anxious to be at the hall in good time to welcome any early arrivals from London, Grania, Roddy and Jumbo left soon after, their departure leaving the oldies with more space and less noise in the cramped sitting room.

Uncle Greg had taken an instant shine to Elizabeth Lelongwe and they were laughing together over his Parisien reminiscences, while Solomon and Angie discussed the merits of the modern golf club. The others chattered away in a group around Mrs P who, determined not to miss out on a word, stretched her vertically challenged body to its full height and gave them the benefit of her unusual philosophy in no uncertain terms.

Hovering on the fringe, Fiona watched with amusement and pleasure, secure in the knowledge that she would be only too happy to share a grandchild with Elizabeth and Solomon Lelongwe. Catching her mother's eye, she earned a wink and a smile – Angie had also given the thumbs-up.

"Time you left I think, Fiona," she announced. "Hadn't you better make sure the staff are properly drilled?"

"It's not the Trooping of the Colour, Mummy! But it's probably time Dan and I went on."

And she left to get her coat, slipping Dan's present into the pocket to open on the way.

"Come and give your old uncle a kiss, m'dear," Uncle Greg demanded. "Must say, you look a gel in a million tonight – a filly to be proud of!"

"I fear at my age I should be described as a mare, but thank you anyway!"

"Fetlocks to rival Loveatfirstsight's," he muttered, planting a firm dry kiss on her cheek. "She's all yours, old man." He handed Fiona over to Dan.

"See you lot later." Fiona called back, leading her future husband out of the front door. "Don't rush Dan, I want to open your present before we get there."

And as they left the bumpy lane for the road to Longbottom, she tore the paper off the small parcel and opened the scuffed blue leather box. Nestling on a bed of age-browned silk lay an exquisitely wrought antique silver-mounted lapis lazuli brooch.

Glancing at her face as she opened it, Dan was rewarded by a smile of delight and a kiss that nearly caused him to swerve into the bank.

"I hope you like it, it belonged to my mother. My father gave it to her when I was born, and it was her favourite piece."

"Oh Dan, it's beautiful!" Fiona gasped. "Stop the car, I want you to put it on for me."

"I'll do it in the car park – if we don't get on the others will be up behind us."

He put his foot down on the accelerator.

"Perfect," he said when he finally pinned the brooch on, delighted with Fiona's reaction. "It's the ideal colour for your lovely eyes, and I know my mother could not have wished for a better home for her precious brooch."

The party went like clockwork, and even Fiona's goulash got the seal of approval. Her mother sparkled, Uncle Greg couldn't keep his eyes off the scantily dressed young females, and Solomon and Elizabeth never stopped smiling and talking. Roddy wheeled Mrs P round the dance floor until she complained the noise of the disco was making her head spin, though they all knew the champagne was the culprit.

Suddenly the disco stopped and a groan went up. As the disgruntled dancers returned to their seats, Sam and Jack raced round topping up all the glasses and Dan stood up, banging the table.

"Ladies and gentlemen!" he shouted – and the room fell silent. "Tonight we are celebrating two very special occasions – the marriage of Grania and Jumbo and the..." he paused pointedly, "I won't say what birthday of Fiona." There was a ripple of laughter as someone gallant shouted out "35th!" before Dan continued. "I would like to thank Fiona, and all who helped her for giving us such a splendid evening."

"Hear hear!"

"And to propose a joint toast to Grania and Jumbo. And to Fiona, who for some extraordinary reason has kindly consented to be my wife."

The room erupted in a cheering, table-banging ovation as glasses were raised and the toasts drunk. Fiona was practically crushed in the congratulatory embraces of her friends and family, and as an announcement came over the microphone that Fiona and Dan would lead off the dancing, the lights dimmed and *All You Need is Love* filled the hall.

Beckoning Grania and Jumbo to join them after their first circuit, the two couples rotated round the floor until the music died away, when another round of applause broke out. Then the strobes flickered, the disco revved up, and the floor once more became a heaving, jerking mass.

Angie, Uncle Greg and Mrs P were the first to leave, followed by the Lelongwes, who had to return to Paris early the next morning.

Sam and Jack were removed in disgrace, having been discovered with a near-empty bottle of wine in the men's loo. Tight and dishevelled, they were dragged out giggling, and to Corah's fury, Sam was sick in the car park.

"We're going to slide away soon, Fi," Dodo came and sat down by her friend. "Brilliant party!"

"I'm dying to go too – d'you think we can?"

"Why not – us oldies have done our bit."

"Grania's out with the fairies as usual – I'd better have a word with Roddy. Thank God he keeps his feet on the ground, bless him – I couldn't cope with two barmy children!"

"See you back at the ranch then – and if you're up for it, there sure are some things to talk about!" Dodo disappeared to find her coat.

"Come on darling, time to go home." Fiona took Dan's arm. "Roddy's in command now and I'm flagging – too much excitement for one day at my age!"

And they wandered out into the cold December night.

"Wish we could have a white Christmas." Fiona leant on Dan's shoulder as they drove back to Stone Lea.

"I don't." He massaged her thigh. "It always means more work and less play, and I've got plenty of that in mind for this Christmas!"

"Do you know something, Dan?" Fiona encouraged his wandering hand. "I'm so happy, I could even be nice to Urania!"

"Well I can assure you, Mrs Cann-to-be, that if Urania Clotworthy ever breaches my portals by so much as a millimetre, I shall sue for instant divorce."

"Hmm, she might even become my best friend!"

"And pigs might fly!"

Removing his hand to change gear, Dan turned into Stone Lane. Drawing up outside the house, he switched off the engine but made no move to get out.

"Aren't you coming in?" Fiona asked.

"No darling. I think on this occasion discretion might be the better part of lust. After all, we've got the rest of our lives together now." He stroked her hair. "*But...* I wouldn't say no to a good old fashioned snog – I haven't had one for about forty years!"

By the time Fiona had waved Dan away, Philip had gone to bed, but Dodo was still up, washing glasses and clearing the debris from earlier in the evening.

"You're a star, D!" Fiona yawned, flopping into a chair. "I'm whacked. Leave all that now and let's just take ten minutes together in peace and quiet, in front of what's left of the fire."

"Fancy a nightcap?" Dodo didn't need much persuading to down tools.

"Why not. Just the tiniest dram would be perfect."

Fiona kicked up the dying embers while Dodo brought glasses and bottles, and at last they were able to relax.

"Were you amazed by Dan's announcement?" Fiona asked, feeling that perhaps she should have told her old friend that she was going to accept his proposal.

"No way! As soon as I read Crispin's letter, I guessed you'd go for it – and you'd have been a fool not to. Dan's the right bloke for you – at last!" she couldn't resist adding. "I have no doubt whatsoever that you two will genuinely live happy ever after and I couldn't imagine anyone better to take care of my old mate for the rest of her life."

"Oh D, I'm so happy to hear you say that, and I think right now I must be the happiest person alive! But what about you and Philip?"

"Hmmm – well!" Dodo swallowed a large gulp of wine. "I have to say I'm having second thoughts – and I've done a lot of thinking. One thing I know for sure is that I shall never get married. I can't explain it really, but I suppose I'm just not the monogamous type. Philip's great in so many ways – I mean he's good looking, rich, hot stuff in bed and all that, but at the end of the day he's actually rather boring! I think it took tonight to make me realise that hooking up with him permanently would be a mistake."

"But what about your plans for the Barton?" Fiona was distressed.

"Too bad I'm afraid. It's all much too big an undertaking by myself, but…" she paused to top up their glasses, "I'm not saying I shan't look around for something smaller down in this neck of the woods – I can ply my trade just as well here as anywhere so watch out, I may well still end up on your doorstep!"

"Well, that's all that matters, so make sure you do, otherwise I shall miss you and may well turn back into a house-frau of the mid-Devon variety!"

"I doubt that – but for now, I think it's bedtime. But before we go, one last toast – *To the Doberman!*"

"What on Earth d'you mean?"

"Well, if The Doberman hadn't lured Hamish away, you'd still be stuck in your crummy little rut, withering away into a boring old age."

"Gosh, that all seems an age ago," Fiona sighed. "I can hardly even remember what Hamish looks like."

"Just as well," Dodo replied. "You've come a long way since then – and you and I've come a long way together."

"We sure have D, we sure have. And I couldn't have done it without you."

"Bollocks!" said Dodo, and they drained their glasses and went to bed.